A LIFE-CHANGIN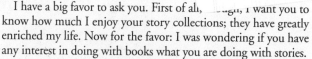

Several years ago I received a letter that c... remember who wrote it, only what she said. I...

Dear Dr. Wheeler,

I have a big favor to ask you. First of all, ...ugh, I want you to know how much I enjoy your story collections; they have greatly enriched my life. Now for the favor: I was wondering if you have any interest in doing with books what you are doing with stories.

You see, while I love to read, I haven't the slightest idea of where to start. There are millions of books out there, and most of them—authors too—are just one big blur to me. I want to use my time wisely, to choose books which will not only take me somewhere but also make me a better and kinder person.

I envy you because you know which books are worth reading and which are not. Do you possibly have a list of worthy books that you wouldn't mind sending to me?

I responded to this letter, but most inadequately, for at that time I had no such list. I tried to put the plea behind me, but it dug in its heels and kept me awake at night. Eventually, I concluded that a Higher Power was at work here and that I needed to do something about it. I put together a proposal for a broad reading plan based on books I knew and loved—books that had powerfully affected me, that had opened other worlds and cultures to me, and that had made me a kinder, more empathetic person.

But that letter writer had asked for more than just a list of titles. She wanted me to introduce her to the authors of these books, to their lives and their times. To that end, I've included in the introduction to each story in this series a biographical sketch of the author to help the reader appreciate the historical, geographical, and cultural contexts in which a story was written. Also, as a long-time teacher, I've always found study-guide questions to be indispensable in helping readers to understand more fully the material they're reading, hence my decision to incorporate discussion questions for each chapter in an afterword at the end of the book. Finally, since I love turn-of-the-century woodcut illustrations, I've tried to incorporate as many of these into the text as possible.

There is another reason for this series—perhaps the most important. Our hope is that it will encourage thousands of people to fall in love with reading, as well as help them to discover that a life devoid of emotional, spiritual, and intellectual growth is not worth living.

Welcome to our expanding family of wordsmiths, of people of all ages who wish to grow daily, to develop to the fullest the talents God lends to each of us—people who believe as does Robert Browning's persona in *Andrea del Sarto:*

Ah, but a man's reach should exceed his grasp,
Or what's a heaven for?

Joe Wheeler

Note: The books in this series have been selected because they are among the finest literary works in history. However, you should be aware that some content might not be suitable for all ages, so we recommend you review the material before sharing it with your family.

FOCUS ON THE FAMILY®
Great Stories

the farther adventures of robinson crusoe

by
Daniel Defoe

Introduction and Afterword by
Joe Wheeler, Ph.D.

TYNDALE

Tyndale House Publishers, Wheaton, Illinois

THE FARTHER ADVENTURES OF ROBINSON CRUSOE

Copyright © 1999 by Joseph L. Wheeler and Focus on the Family

Library of Congress Cataloging-in-Publication Data
Defoe, Daniel, 1661?–1731.
  The farther adventures of Robinson Crusoe / Daniel Defoe; with an introduc-
tion and afterword by Joe Wheeler.
    p.   cm. — (Focus on the Family great stories)
    Includes bibliographical references.
    ISBN 1-56179-764-2
    I. Wheeler, Joe L., 1936– .   II. Title.   III. Series.
PR3404.F37   1999
823'.5—dc21   99-10190
                                                                          CIP

A Focus on the Family book published by Tyndale House Publishers, Wheaton,
Illinois.

Illustrations by Walter Paget. Taken from Daniel Defoe, *The Life and Surprising
Adventures of Robinson Crusoe, of York, Mariner, as Related by Himself* (New York:
McLoughlin Brothers, 1890). All illustrations are from the library of Joe Wheeler.

Joe Wheeler is represented by the literary agency of Alive Communications, 1465
Kelly Johnson Blvd., Suite 320, Colorado Springs, CO 80920.

Editor: Michele A. Kendall
Cover Photographs: PhotoDisc, Inc.
Cover Design: Bradley Lind

Printed in the United States of America

99 00 01 02 03 04 05/10 9 8 7 6 5 4 3 2 1

TABLE OF CONTENTS

LIST OF ILLUSTRATIONS

Introduction

DANIEL DEFOE AND *THE FARTHER ADVENTURES OF ROBINSON CRUSOE*

The saga of Robinson Crusoe didn't end when he left his island and returned to England. On the contrary, after marrying and raising a family of his own, our hero returns to the island to see how the people he left behind fared. After satisfying himself that a true community had been established there, Crusoe and his man Friday accept passage on a merchant ship going to the Far East. Soon they're embroiled in one heart-pounding adventure after another.

Defoe, at the relentless urging of his readers, rushed to get the second part of Robinson Crusoe's saga, *The Farther Adventures,* into print—in the same year that the first part had been published! Clearly, readers were curious to know the results of the explosive forces Crusoe had so cavalierly released on his poor island. Nordhoff and Hall released similar forces in their *Mutiny on the Bounty* many years later; two books were required—*Men Against the Sea* and *Pitcairn's Island*—to tell the rest of the story. Defoe accomplished it in one book: *The Farther Adventures of Robinson Crusoe.*

But Defoe knew that just having Crusoe return to his island wouldn't have been enough to satisfy his readers; consequently, he launched Crusoe and Friday on additional adventures into a world virtually unknown to Defoe's contemporaries. Because Defoe lived on the cutting edge of geographical and travel knowledge, he was able to take his readers on a journey equivalent to the ones conducted by science fiction writers today. Hence the magic of this book.

I was lucky, as a child, to read the full saga of Crusoe rather than the truncated one featured in so many modern editions. And I speak not just of

Farther Adventures itself but in terms of the complete rather than abridged texts of both parts. Editors and publishers have often corralled all of Defoe's action sequences and rejected the rest, especially the philosophical and spiritual sections. Consequently, many readers who thought they knew Robinson Crusoe's full story are going to be surprised when they read the full text here for the first time.

It is, admittedly, a rather unvarnished, sometimes brutal story, complete with all the sociological baggage writers of Defoe's time often brought to their work, such as prejudice against other cultures and acts of violence against helpless victims. Lest we be unduly smug, in America, just a few years before Defoe wrote this book, the good citizens of Salem, Massachusetts, were executing innocent women as witches. Truly, each age has its own forms of barbarity.

It is this honesty, though, that I love about the Crusoe story. There is no Monday morning quarterbacking here, no revisionistic rewriting of the past: just the world as it appeared to scholars and novelists of the eighteenth century.

Let's join Crusoe on his adventures beyond the island. I guarantee that it's a journey well worth taking.

About the Introduction

For decades, one of the few absolutes in my literature classes has been this: *Never read the introduction before reading the book!* Those who ignored my thundering admonition lived to regret their disobedience. Downcast, they would come to me and say, "Dr. Wheeler, I confess that I read the introduction first, and it wrecked the book for me. I couldn't enjoy the story, because all the way through I saw it through someone *else's* eyes. I don't agree with the editor on certain points, but those conclusions are in my head, and now I don't know *what* I think!"

Given that God never created a human clone, no two of us will ever perceive reality in exactly the same way—and no two of us *ever should!* Therefore, no matter how educated, polished, brilliant, insightful, or eloquent the teacher might be, don't ever permit that person to tell you how to think or respond, for that is a violation of the most sacred thing God gives us—our individuality.

My solution to the introduction problem was to split it in two: an introduction, to whet the appetite for, and enrich the reading of, the book; and an afterword, to generate discussion and debate *after* the reader has arrived at his or her own conclusions about the book and is ready to challenge my (the teacher's) perceptions.

About This Edition

It has been a formidable task to update, and make more readable, this three centuries' old icon. I do not think it has ever been done before. Let me explain:

First, the language was generally archaic. What was most confusing was not the words themselves, but their current usage and connotations. Frequently, after reading a section, I would shake my head and think, *What is Defoe saying?* Individually, the words made sense, but the way in which they were grouped was sometimes unclear. I decided to resort to my unabridged dictionary and dig backward in time. Once I discovered what the word meant to Defoe, I could understand what he was saying, and to help the reader I either footnoted the term or phrase (by far the easiest option) or found substitute words that were used during the eighteenth century. In other words, I did not use modern synonyms.

Second, the book is filled with sentence-paragraph monstrosities that seem to go on forever (Defoe's trademark, by the way). For the most part, they are brilliantly constructed. So much so, in fact, that I found them hard to restructure without appearing heavy handed. In most cases, I left the paragraphs as they were, only breaking them up where I found significant topic shifts or a change of speaker.

Third, and even more of a problem, there were no chapter divisions or subheadings to break up the text. Not many of us today relish tackling a book that has absolutely no breaks in it. To remedy this situation, I reread the text carefully to see if, by chance, I could find built-in chapter breaks. Fortunately, Defoe's text has a rhythm to it that made these breaks fairly easy to determine. As for chapter titles, I tried whenever possible to use Defoe's own words (often borrowed from running heads in the original text).

Fourth, I wanted to bring back what has been virtually lost during the last century: marvelous woodcut illustrations. These were true works of art that not only captured wonderfully the essence of the scenes being depicted but also give us faithful depictions of objects, people, cities, landmarks, and so on, at the time.

If I have been successful in doing what I set out to do, you will read a very old text in words that will make sense to you, in paragraphs of humane length, with subheads that will propel the story along, with chapters that will give you places in which to break off, and with illustrations that will enable you to visualize the world about which you are reading. In short, you will read an old book that seems contemporary but that still retains the charm and integrity of the original.

Movie History

Strangely enough, I have not found any movie versions of *The Farther Adventures of Robinson Crusoe*. Of course, it would be a difficult book to capture in celluloid—especially, aspects such as the cannibalism and ever-present violence and bloodshed of the time. However, if done correctly, it would make a wonderful miniseries.

About the Author
Daniel Defoe (1660–1731)

The following sources were used as the backbone of this minibiography of Daniel Defoe: Paula R. Backscheider's monumental *Daniel Defoe: His Life* (Baltimore and London: Johns Hopkins Press, 1989); Brian FitzGerald's eminently readable *Daniel Defoe: A Study in Conflict* (Chicago: Henry Regnery Company, 1955); Peter Earle's *The World of Defoe* (New York: Athenaeum, 1977); Michael Shinagel's Robinson Crusoe: *Norton Critical Edition* (New York: W. W. Norton, 1975); Frank H. Ellis's *Twentieth-Century Interpretation of* Robinson Crusoe (Englewood Cliffs, N.J.: Prentice-Hall, Inc., 1969); and the 1946 edition of *The Encyclopedia Britannica*.

— — —

Daniel Defoe was born in London in the year of our Lord 1660. In the eleven years before his birth, a great deal had happened in Britain. On January 30, 1649, the faithless Charles I had been beheaded in front of the Banqueting House in Whitehall; the Puritans had taken control of the government and, under Oliver Cromwell as Lord Protector, effectively abolished feudalism and divine right government. But Cromwell died on September 3, 1658, and his son Richard's feet would prove too small for his father's shoes. Thus it came to pass that Charles II had arrived only weeks before the birth of baby Daniel, the third child born to Alice and James Foe, staunch Puritan Presbyterians.

Charles II's arrival promised a new beginning for England and blessed relief from the bloodshed of the previous eleven years. FitzGerald tells us why: ". . . once more Christmas would be celebrated. No longer would mince-pies be sinful or plum-pudding banned. To visit the theatre would stop being a crime. Sports and pastimes would no longer be frowned on and ruthlessly regulated. And once more the ancient English festival of May Day would be celebrated—there would be music and laughter when villagers and townsmen too danced round the maypole" (FitzGerald, 10).

No torch of rejoicing burned in the window of the Foe house in Cripplegate, however. Now that the monarchy had been restored, what would happen to them? The Puritans had been oppressed for many years before they governed supreme under Cromwell. Now they were at the mercy of a new king. Would he respect their rights? It didn't take long to find out.

Charles II and his ministers were determined to pulverize those who refused to conform. The sledgehammer blows were consecutive and devastating: The Corporation Act of 1661 stripped Puritans of their citizenship rights and ruined many financially; the Uniformity Act of 1662 expelled Puritan ministers from the Anglican Church; the Conventicle Act of 1664 banned Puritans from gathering in groups of five or more; and the Five Mile Act of 1665 further restricted the movement of dissenting ministers.

Those who refused to comply with these acts were, in effect, expelled from society. They were excluded from municipal corporations, barred from civil or military service, forbidden to teach or be taught in the university, and for good measure, subjected to discriminatory fines and laws.

The Foe family life centered around their Nonconformist (or Dissenter) pastor, Dr. Samuel Annesley, a towering figure who would have a great impact on the life of little Daniel. On August 24, the day the Act of Uniformity went into effect, a sober congregation filed into Annesley's church. Annesley stood tall and uncowed behind the pulpit: He was determined to stand true to his convictions. How would his parishioners respond? Were they willing to pay the price?

The Foes were among the 15,000 Nonconformist families and clergymen who did pay the price. All in all, some 60,000 took their stand. Annesley would lead the way, being arrested again and again for his refusal to quit preaching—which he continued to do daily. He preferred to stay in prison rather than pay the fine that would set him free.

It was quite a fall for this eminent man, who was educated at Oxford, was chaplain to the Earl of Warwick, was awarded the honorary doctor of civil law degree at Oxford by recommendation of the Earl of Pembroke, had preached before the House of Commons, had been confirmed in his St. Giles pastorate by King Charles II, and was himself the nephew of the Earl of Anglesey. How could he conscientiously be reordained when his 1644 ordination had taken place in the presence of Warwick, Lord High Admiral of England's navy, been presided over by seven Presbyterian ministers, and been confirmed by the laying-on of hands? To accept reordination would be to render null and void all the marriages, baptisms, and commissions he had performed through the years (Backscheider, 8–9).

Young Daniel would never be able to forget the strength of this man's convictions. Again and again, "the vilest of men" would disrupt Annesley's Sunday services; and the minister and his congregation would be fined, each time at a higher rate. The doors of parishioners' homes would be broken down, and children pilloried and then hauled off to Bridewell Prison to do hard labor; boys were publicly scourged. Samuel Wesley, father to Charles and John, remembered how his minister father died from an illness contracted during one of these imprisonments. The worst periods of Dissenter persecution occurred in 1662–1664, 1670, and 1681–1685. So fearful were parents that they had their children copying down the Bible in longhand just in case their Bibles were taken from them. Annesley's own home was broken into, and his household goods and library seized—leaving his family with nothing.

Then, in swift succession, came two terrible natural disasters: The plague of 1665 and the Great Fire of London in February 1666.

During the Middle Ages, one word struck terror in people's hearts: *plague.* The plague was also called the Black Death, because the skin of its victims often turned blackish in their mortal agonies. The first recorded outbreak in Europe occurred during the sixth and seventh centuries. Seven hundred years later, it returned with a vengeance, starting in seacoast villages and inexorably spreading inland, killing wherever it went. Not for fifty long years did it recede. In the fourteenth century, it came again. In some areas of Europe, up to 75 percent of the population died. It is estimated that this one occurrence of the epidemic killed 25 million people, one-quarter of the population of Europe. In England, over 75 percent of the population died.

By the sixteenth century, incidences of the plague had decreased drastically. In England, there was hope that it had finally run its course. Not so. Isolated cases were reported late in 1664 before a bitterly cold winter stopped its progress. Then, in the spring of 1665, it sprang up again and slowly marched its deadly way across London. Those who could flee did so—about two-thirds of the population. Of the one-third unable to leave, about half died (close to 100,000 of London's total population of 460,000). The Foes were among those who stayed in the city. Daniel was five years old.

FitzGerald vividly re-creates the experience:

> . . . everyone who possibly could hastened away from the City, and from the window of the upstairs room over the little shop Daniel could see nothing but wagons and carts, with goods, women, servants, and children; and coaches filled with the well-to-do, and horsemen attending them, all hurrying away . . . "a very terrible and melancholy thing to see."
>
> This hurrying away of the people lasted from morning to night and continued for some weeks. . . .Then followed terrible days. The death-rate rose with frightening rapidity. The parish of St. Giles, Cripplegate, was thickly populated and the plague raged with particular virulence there. One by one the houses in the neighbourhood of old Foe's shop were closed, some by order of the magistrates, others being voluntarily evacuated. The door of each silent house was marked with a large red cross and the inscription "Lord have mercy upon us!" scrawled across it. Trade and business were brought almost to a standstill. Grass grew among the cobble-stones of what were normally busy thoroughfares, and those few persons who ventured along them walked rapidly down the middle of the street to avoid the smells which issued from the infected houses. But few persons did so venture: even at midday the City streets were all but deserted. . . . (FitzGerald, 22–23)

As the epidemic approached its peak in August, Foe sent his family to the top floor of the house, where he had stockpiled provisions to last a long time. Then, after locking the shop, he joined them. There the Foe family lived for the next few weeks, subsisting on bread, butter, cheese, and beer. They would not have touched any meat for fear of infection. Their only means of communication with the outside world was a watchman standing on the street below.

Occasionally, James Foe ventured outside, only to come back with tales of the horrible scenes. One day, while he was running some errands, a casement window flew open above him and a woman leaned out and shrieked three times before uttering in a tone that chilled his blood: "Oh, death, death,

death!" James was the only one on the whole street; no doors or windows opened at the woman's cries—only silence. After a moment, James continued on his way.

The nights contained their own special horrors: Out of the quiet darkness "would come the ringing of the bell and the ghastly cry of the burial men, 'Bring out your dead! Bring out your dead!' The grinding axles of the deadcarts creaked and groaned under their heavy loads as the wagons made their way down the narrow streets, bound for the great pits which were dug to receive the bodies" (FitzGerald, 24).

At fifty-seven years old, Defoe could still vividly recall the horror, the gruesome sights, sounds, and smells, of that summer. In his *Journal of the Plague Year,* he wrote:

> [A] young woman, her mother, and the maid, had been abroad on some occasion . . . ; but, about two hours after they came home, the young lady complained she was not well, in a quarter of an hour more she vomited, and had a violent pain in her head. . . . While the bed was airing, the mother undressed the young woman, and just as she was laid down in the bed, she, looking upon her body with a candle, immediately discovered the fatal tokens on the inside of her thighs. Her mother . . . threw down her candle and shrieked out in such a frightful manner that it was enough to place horror upon the stoutest heart in the world; nor was it one scream, or one cry, but the fright having seized her spirits she fainted first, then recovered, then ran all over the house, up the stairs and down the stairs, like one distracted, . . . and continued screeching, and crying out for several hours, void of all sense, . . . and, as I was told, never came thoroughly to herself again. As to the young maiden she was a dead corpse from that moment. (FitzGerald, 25)

After three weeks, the outbreak suddenly ceased. Soon the streets were filled again with people, laughing, shaking hands, calling to each other, praising God. "One by one the houses which had been shut were opened up; the rich emerged from their seclusion in the country; the King and his courtiers returned to Whitehall. Shops started to do business again, the law courts to function, the playhouses to stage performances" (FitzGerald, 26). The king and his court were soon engrossed in their empty, decadent lives, and the poor, though acknowledging that God had delivered them, returned to their old amusements. The plague had become a bitter memory.

Scarcely had the last plague-riddled bodies been buried when the Great Fire came, engulfing London in flames and destroying the entire old walled city. The fire had begun in a bakery near London Bridge and had spread out from there. Six-year-old Daniel

> saw the great red glow in the sky as the mediaeval and Tudor city, with its rabbit-warren of streets and alleys, disappeared in the flames and smoke. He saw the great commercial houses where the merchants and their households worked and slept grow red-hot before crumbling and crashing to the ground with a mighty roar. He watched with fascinated terror the flames as they devoured those abodes of wealth, commerce, and hospitality, licking their way through the gardens behind and the courtyards within, fanned all the time by the easterly breeze, cracking stones with the heat and sending them flying through the air, and causing a boiling stream of molten lead to flow along the gutters. He saw roofs and walls crashing down on every side. . . . He watched the frantic fire-fighters pouring buckets of water into the burning mass. He observed how "the despairing citizens looked on and saw the devastation of their dwellings, with a kind of stupidity." He watched the unending procession of refugees as they passed his Cripplegate doorway. (Backscheider, 4–6)

After five days, the inferno was contained. The Foes' house had been spared, but just barely. Backscheider notes that the conflagration destroyed 90 percent of all living accommodations in the city. With remarkable efficiency, the king and city council set about rebuilding London. Soon a new post office, a customhouse, and several government offices were established. In spite of this achievement, the devastation caused by the fire remained for more than thirty years, causing the people to be taxed again and again to pay for the cost of rebuilding.

Many people, including the Foes, regarded the fire and plague as signs of God's judgment on a sinful England, particularly the wicked and profane court of Charles II. To placate God, Mrs. Foe redoubled her efforts to teach her children the Bible and to instill in them the fear of the Lord, but more important, the fear of hell. "Hell in the first few years of dawning consciousness was a terrible reality to Daniel. It frightened him. It was drummed into him along with the Devil. Only those who lived virtuous and godly lives, renouncing the pomps and vanities of this wicked world and all the sinful lusts of the flesh— only those would be saved, and their business[es] prosper" (FitzGerald, 28).

It is hard for us in these enlightened days to conceptualize what it was like to live in a society where death was an ever-present likelihood. First of all, no one, not even doctors, knew what caused diseases to spread. Sanitation was unheard of: People dumped their raw sewage into the streets, there to mingle with the excretions left by horses and other animals passing by. People bathed only once a year, if that, and clothes would often be worn until they virtually fell off. And if there *was* an epidemic of any kind, it would be carried by doctors from one patient to the other, for none of them bothered to wash their hands between patients. The same was true for infections introduced during childbirth, which is why so many women died of complications— and why so many babies died in infancy. Every disease children contracted was likely to be fatal because there was no known way of stopping it, short of letting it run its course. Of every three children born, at best, one would live to adulthood. When one adds to this the terrible drain on men caused by continuous wars—keeping in mind the sad fact that, if they were wounded, the chances were excellent that the wound would be fatal—and the many who died on the dangerous seas, it was small wonder the population tended to either remain static or decrease. Not only did the people not bathe, but they mistakenly believed that disease was carried by fresh air; consequently, any germs or viruses shut up in those dark and gloomy houses—with too few windows as it was—were likely to dig in their heels and not leave until every human being in the house was infected.

Surrounded as the people were with ever-present death, it is not at all surprising that they talked and wrote so much about it. Three centuries later, we laugh at them and label them "morbid." Almost certainly, we'd have been morbid, too!

As for Daniel, as if all this were not enough, somewhere between 1668 and 1671 there came a fourth disaster: His mother died. Perhaps one can attribute Defoe's disinterest in beauty, nature, and the arts to this untimely removal of his mother from his life.

Annesley, Morton, and Foe

The most impressionable years of Defoe's life were colored by the brushes of three men: Samuel Annesley, Charles Morton, and James Foe. Dr.

Annesley was the hero of Defoe's childhood. His sermons, exhortations, and example became part of the very fiber of young Daniel's being. From childhood on, Annesley studied twenty chapters a day out of his Bible, so he knew it thoroughly. His sermons were distinguished by down-to-earth illustrations, anecdotes, and metaphors; by humor, and by clear prose. According to Backscheider, Annesley once compared one's conscience to a piece of gravel in the shoe, concluding with the simple admonition: "'There's nothing in the world for us to do, but to mind our duty'" (Backscheider, 13). Defoe admired Annesley for his devotion to God and his calling, his generosity toward others, and his preaching style.

Out of the pain of their being ostracized by society, the Nonconformists received an unexpected blessing. Now that their children were excluded from attending the university, they would have to find another way for them to be educated. Many of their youngsters, including fourteen-year-old Daniel, went to Morton's Academy in Newington Green. Charles Morton was as remarkable a man as Dr. Annesley, being both a preacher and an educator. The Great Fire of London had destroyed his income-producing property, and the king had taken away his pulpit, so Morton made his house into a meeting place and opened a one-man academy. It was illegal for a graduate of Oxford to teach anywhere but in Oxford or Cambridge—indeed, all graduates were forced to take an oath that they would not do so; thus people such as Morton who established their own Nonconformist schools were accused of perjury. This Stamford Oath was initiated in 1335 to keep rival universities and colleges from being established, and it was not abolished until 1827, almost half a millennium later. So, in effect, the Nonconformists had their hands tied.

For now, it was enough that Morton accepted Daniel into his school. Considered perhaps the greatest teacher in England, Morton and his academy quickly gained national stature. But, like Annesley, he would pay a heavy price for his success. He was excommunicated by the Church of England and arrested and imprisoned repeatedly. Eventually, Increase Mather lured him to the United States by offering him the presidency of Harvard.

Students at Morton's Academy could take a three-year law course or a five-year theology course. Defoe took theology. Unlike Oxford and Cambridge, Morton's curriculum was in English rather than in Latin, and it included rhetoric, logic, Latin grammar, arithmetic, geometry, astronomy, and music. After a year of philosophy and logic, students studied Aristotelian philosophy:

moral (political, economic, ethical), metaphysical, and natural (physics, biology, botany, and zoology) (Backscheider, 14–15).

Morton's students, and students at sister Nonconformist academies, were conspicuous for their freedom of inquiry; they were permitted to study a wide range of philosophical and theological material. Morton went beyond even that, introducing geography, history, and modern languages. And, breaking radically new ground (unlike universities of the day), he used the experimental approach—equipping laboratories for science instruction and, for good measure, incorporating the latest scientific research. Morton and his Nonconformist counterparts legitimized science instruction by noting that it revealed "God as manifested in the world." Morton even wrote a textbook for his students, *Compendium Physicae*, in which he presented the discoveries of William Harvey, Isaac Newton, Robert Hooke, William Gilbert, Pierre Gassendi, and René Descartes. So good was this textbook that Harvard would use it in its classrooms for more than thirty-five years.

Morton's curriculum was incredibly rigorous, considerably more difficult than Defoe would have had at Oxford or Cambridge, which were then notorious as places where England's elite sent their sons to have a good time, often returning home dissipated and minus the degree. For the rest of his life, Defoe would bless Morton for teaching him the glories of the English language rather than concentrating only on Latin; for making education practical rather than esoteric; and for teaching him to defend his views rigorously, both in speech and in writing.

Like Annesley, Morton enriched his instruction with fables, parables, allegories, stories, and romances. Defoe never forgot the impact these two men made on him: Rarely would he write much without interspersing entertaining, illustrative stories.

The third major influence on Defoe's life was exerted by his father, James Foe, who served as both father and mother for so many of Daniel's growing-up years. James helped his son to set lofty goals and so filled him with a love of the Bible and its rhythm that Defoe's prose would always mirror that of Scripture. His father, in spite of multiple reverses of fortune, found ways to secure a solid education for his son and supplied him with mentors who were both intellectually gifted and Spirit-led.

James was a member of the powerful ancient brotherhood of Freemen of the City of London and a member of an ancient livery company. Backscheider notes that "as such, he could practice his trade and vote 'in the City,' the one square mile that had grown behind its Roman wall to become the center of power, wealth, and commerce for the entire nation" (Backscheider, 22). A Freeman could vote for common councilmen, but only a liveryman could vote for the higher offices of the city—such as auditors, sheriffs, the Lord Mayor, and members of Parliament. Because liverymen represented the backbone of the nation's economy, they were usually free— for the time—to express themselves; and not surprisingly, they respected ability more than mere birth.

Because of his father's position, Daniel grew up with the ancient rituals of city elections, livery company meetings and dinners, processions on Lord Mayor's Day, and band drills in Finsbury Field. Few men could have passed the spirit of the city on to their sons better than James did. A master of a livery company had both administrative and ceremonial duties: He was judge of the company courts; he was the final authority on trade rules; he was the intermediary when the monarch requested funding for the nation's wars; and he accompanied the Lord Mayor by barge en route to taking the oath of office. Sadly, when Charles became king and instituted repressive acts against the Nonconformists, neither James nor Daniel could aspire to become Lord Mayor. Worse yet, the city grew fat on the fines levied on Nonconformist liverymen who were elected to the Lord Mayorship but who could not serve without violating their consciences. Nevertheless, both Foes, father and son, would fill high positions in that ancient fraternity.

No higher calling could Daniel imagine than to follow in his father's footsteps. So it was that Daniel too became first an apprentice and then a merchant, specializing in wholesale hosiery—this instead of becoming a minister.

Mary Tuffley

When Defoe was twenty-two years old, he decided it was time to look for a wife. Before long he set his sights on Mary Tuffley, the daughter of John Rawlins Tuffley, a well-to-do tradesman with considerable property. We have no picture of Mary, but if she was anything like the three daughters the Defoes would raise, she must have been a beauty in her youth. Mary was sixteen or seventeen when Defoe began his courtship. He managed to win out over his numerous rivals by dedicating a book, *The Historical Collections,* to his "Excellent," "Incomparable," and "Divine" lady, signing himself "The Meanest and Truest of all your Adorers and Servants." Two years later, Daniel and Mary were married. She brought with her a handsome dowry of 3,700 pounds, which her husband quickly spent.

This is a good place to bring up a woman's rights in seventeenth-century England—or, rather, the fact that she hadn't any. Whatever rights, whatever control of property she might have, all ended with marriage. Earle puts her sad condition this way:

> Women were not expected to be individuals; in law they were not supposed to live by themselves. . . . Unless they were widows, they were expected to spend their whole li[ves] in legal and physical subjection to a man, whether he be father, master, or husband. . . . The subjected woman had many duties, but few rights. She was expected to breed and rear children, as many as possible. . . . She was expected to work, not just to look after her master's or husband's household. . . . Ideally a woman or girl should never be idle. This was particularly true of the wives, daughters and servants of country folk. When they completed their household duties, if they ever did, they were not supposed to relax in the satisfying glow of a job well done but should immediately address themselves to their spinning wheels or their knitting, to earn a few more pennies for the family budget . . . , but work had another function. Tired women were more likely to be virtuous. For women were expected by society to be models of chastity and virtue, unlike their husbands, whose sins were laughed away as excusable trifles. (Earle, 243–44)

Once married, a woman could own nothing—not even the clothes on her back. In fact, theoretically, a man couldn't even give his wife a present because he'd merely be giving it to himself. Not only did the man have complete control over every asset his wife brought with her into the marriage, but he also had control over the children. She could not even make a contract. If he beat her and she screamed, no one would lift a finger, for beating was one of his rights. If a woman's husband died, the oldest male heir could evict her from her own house. At best, she might receive one-third of the estate—even if it was all hers to begin with! And if her husband were to wish her out of the way, there was little to stop him from locking her up, either in his own house (á la Rochester in *Jane Eyre*) or in an asylum.

On what basis was she kept in virtual slavery? Generally, because of the following: (1) The Bible declared that, because of her sin in Eden, the price she'd pay would be perpetual subjection to the man. (2) Because she was vain. (3) Because she was deceitful. (4) Because she was passionate rather than rational. (5) Because she was shamelessly wanton in terms of sexual appetite. (6) Because she was inherently stupid and totally incapable of making rational decisions on her own. In intelligence, she was considered halfway between a child and a man. A century or so later, in Victorian England, the only significant change in this view would be that a woman was a cold goddess rather than a wanton seductress. Because overwork and almost continuous pregnancy stripped them of their youth and beauty, women grew old before their time.

Divorce, in that society, wasn't even an option.

And there was marriage itself, based as it was on dowry instead of love. A woman, no matter how lovely, had little chance of a "good" marriage without money. Because these marriages were dynastic or financially based, love was merely an option that might or might not occur. Because of this sad state of affairs, in all but the poorest families, where they were unable to afford dowries, marriage was anything but happy.

Were Daniel and Mary happy? We don't know for sure. Did they marry for love as well as for money? We don't know that either. What we do know is that it was a tough marriage—on both sides. Throughout most of his married life, Defoe had to be on the road; he was in prison off and on as well. In short, he was away from his wife and children about half of the time, if not more. But apparently, in all his straying (he was not faithful to her), Mary remained the core of his life. Backscheider observes, "Defoe's *Collections* suggest that he married a woman he loved and respected. . . . Throughout his life, whenever he was away, she was the 'faithful steward' who would not misuse his stock 'One Penny,' the resourceful woman who could manage ten days without money, and the loving wife and mother. He kept in close touch with her [sometimes up to three letters in a week]" (Backscheider, 33).

The Duke of Monmouth

Defoe was twenty-five when Charles II died and James II became king. James was Catholic and most of his subjects were not. Had he been tolerant, humane, and kind, he might well have held the throne. But he was not. Worse yet, he was a firm believer in the divine right of kings—that kings could do no wrong and they were accountable to no one.

The first threat to James's sovereignty came from the Duke of Monmouth, the illegitimate son of Charles II. Monmouth had been a favorite of his father's, a hero in the Dutch war, and beloved by thousands of Englishmen. Dissenters especially felt they had little to lose by flocking to his standard—which Defoe did, leaving his bride of only months to fend for herself. The rebellion proved short-lived. Monmouth's troops were totally untried and poorly armed. Of the 3,000 who fought for the ill-fated duke, about a third died on the field; of the remaining 2,000 who tried to escape, within two weeks 751 had been captured—and more were caught later. Rewards were offered for turning in the rebels (five shillings or the rebel property, whichever was greater). For months, houses all over England continued to be searched. More than 850 rebels were sold into servitude in the colonies. On July 15, 1685, Monmouth was beheaded at Bulwark Gate, London. And those of his hapless followers who remained were whipped, burned, or executed (among the latter were at least four of Defoe's Morton Academy classmates). Not until mid-1686 did James finally issue a pardon for the few rebels who remained. Only twenty-eight besides Defoe were left.

The Glorious Revolution

In January 1687, James Foe presented Daniel for membership in the famed Butchers' Company. As a Freeman liveryman, Defoe rose rapidly in the ranks.

About this time, Defoe began writing pamphlets. The pamphlet filled a unique niche in Defoe's society. It was today's lead story in newspaper, magazine, radio, or television news. In those days, if you wanted to influence public opinion, you wrote a pamphlet (usually only one or two sheets long), then hawked it on street corners and sold it in bookshops. They were throwaways; consequently, few have survived. Defoe would go on to write more opinion-changing pamphlets than any other man of his time—or perhaps ever.

Meanwhile, King James continued in his self-destructive ways—almost as if he were determined to destroy any opportunities he had of surviving as a Catholic monarch in a predominantly Protestant country. Besides persecuting Protestants, he appointed—often quite forcibly—Catholics to a disproportionate number of key positions. He subverted the judicial processes by royal intimidation and viciously attacked the Anglican hierarchy by attempting to substitute Catholicism instead. Then, on June 10, 1688, the bells of London rang out the news that the king had a son. That was too much for the people! Seven eminent leaders sent a letter to William of Orange, the king's son-in-law and the premier Protestant leader in Europe, and asked him to come to England with an army. William landed and marched toward London; disaffected lords raised insurrections in the north. James, losing support on all sides, fled to France. After considerable negotiation, it was decided to crown William and his wife, Mary, as joint monarchs—but as empowered by Parliament, not by divine right.

On the first Lord Mayor's Day after the "Glorious Revolution" (so named because it reaffirmed the rights of the people and was accomplished without bloodshed), there was a grand parade honoring the new monarchs. Defoe marched with the other Dissenters, welcoming the change in government. The procession attended the king and queen from Whitehall to Guildhall, where a great feast was waiting for them.

Defoe had arrived. Perhaps down the line, if the full rights of Nonconformists were restored, *he* could become Lord Mayor of London. It was a heady feeling to be pointed out as one of the city's rising stars. Whenever he walked into one of the coffeehouses around Guildhall and the Exchange, he was noticed and admitted to the political debate.

Defoe's business continued to expand: into other English towns, into the colonies, into shipping. But then his father-in-law, who had been an astute business adviser to him, died. Never a good financial manager, Defoe's bills began to mount. Defoe—he added the French "De" to imply nobility—was unsurpassed at dreaming up concepts, ideas, and plans. But he was terrible at making them work and keeping track of details. In spite of England's war with France, which resulted in a considerable loss of shipping on both sides, Defoe continued to expand in international trade—and to borrow more money to pay for these ventures. In the process, he defrauded several people, including his long-suffering mother-in-law, Joan Tuffley. Defoe had built up this empire in order to support the façade that he was a young man with whom to be reckoned. In spite of his Puritan upbringing, he found that when backed against the wall financially, he would do things to people, even his wife and family, that would cause him regret and sleepless nights for the rest of his life.

Defoe's creditors finally lost patience with him, and his grand façade cracked down the middle. He had taken his wife's fortune and spent every pound. Worse yet, he was now bankrupt, owing much more than the 17,000 pounds for which he was held accountable. Defoe was so terrified of languishing in debtor's prison for the rest of his life that he went into hiding. At the outskirts of London was an old monastery called Whitefriars. In medieval times, it had been a sanctuary for criminals (a biblical city of refuge) where they were secure from pursuers—but only for a month. Defoe fled to it, most likely lodging among debtors like himself, thieves, highwaymen, prostitutes, and beggars.

From Whitefriars, he fled to various places, finally landing in Bristol. There he hid for several months, surfacing only on Sundays, when he would strut down the streets, "dressed in the height of fashion, with a fine flowing wig, and lace ruffles, and a sword at his side" (FitzGerald, 77). A number of times during this period he was arrested, booked, and brought to King's Bend, Fleet Prison, or Newgate Prison, until he, usually with Mary's help, could negotiate his way out.

There were no credit cards in those days; no easy way to recover financially once you were down. And even if you declared bankruptcy, you were still legally liable for all you owed. In those days, bankrupts were locked up and, in theory at least, could be kept in prison for the rest of their lives, or until all their debts, prison fines, and upkeep were paid off. Of course, being locked up in a prison didn't make the debt easy to repay. The conditions of prisons at that time were anything but pleasant: overcrowded, not enough food, bitterly cold in the winter, foul smelling, noisy, filled with ruthless criminals and brutal guards, overrunning with lice and rats. They were Dante's Inferno in real life. In Defoe's case, having been a prince of the city, the fall was much greater than for most of the others.

Meanwhile, everything the Defoes owned was garnished by Daniel's creditors. Their five servants were let go, and Mary took the children, including the new baby, and moved in with her mother in Kingsland.

The King and I

The Daniel Defoe who emerged from prison in 1692 was a different man than the one who had gone in. He had no illusions about the significance of his imprisonment. He would be tarred by the stigma for the rest of his life: "Bankrupt" would be tacked to the end of his name in much the same way as an academic degree would have been. He'd never be Lord Mayor of London now—or even an alderman, for that matter. He would also never again be the hail-fellow-well-met joiner he had been before he entered prison. The experience pushed him into a lonelier world than he had inhabited before.

But, with all this, it had given him something else: a new empathy with the down-and-outers—*especially* those whose liabilities exceeded their assets: the debtors. Even though debtors were in prison because they had little or no money, the prison keepers demanded garnish money; those who did not or could not pay were stripped, beaten, and tormented. Sometimes prisoners who did have money were tortured to death by guards determined to get it for themselves. The guards would even steal the prisoners' beef allowances and sell their bedding.

Defoe was lucky. With the assistance of his wife and highly placed friends, he was able to come to terms with his many creditors, but he would be in debt for the rest of his life. Piece by piece, job by job, he put together enough cash flow to keep him out of Newgate Prison and render him able to rejoin society. His biggest asset was his brick and tile factory in Tillbury, where he employed more than 100 workers. The rebuilding of London after the fire would continue for many years, so bricks were needed. That business alone netted Defoe 600 pounds a year. He was able to give his creditors about 1,000–2,000 pounds a year, thus earning back some of their respect. But because he "borrowed repeatedly, pieced loans together, promised profits from expansion, renegotiated agreements, . . . used courts to delay," one gets the impression that he was "a slippery, clever, reprehensible, and perhaps desperate man" (Backscheider, 66).

Throughout his life, Defoe used every sliver of time profitably. So, out of the long months in hiding to avoid imprisonment for debt, Defoe produced a work centuries ahead of its time, and one that would have a significant impact on thought-leaders of his age: *Essay on Projects*, published in 1698. This pamphlet included well-thought-out proposals for the improvement of seventeenth-century society: for example, ideas on reforming insurance plans, bankruptcy laws, the education system (including education for women), income tax laws, and labor; on increasing state control of capitalism, banking (he suggested one central Bank of England), taxation (be light on the poor and heavy on the wealthy), pensions, and charity lotteries; and on more humane treatment for the developmentally handicapped and mentally ill; on developing a national highway system (complete with exact measurements, materials used, ditches, side roads, signs, upkeep, policing).

FitzGerald paints a picture of Defoe entering the palace to propose his ideas to the king and his councilors:

> See how all eyes are turned upon him, the stranger, as he
> comes in with the determined air of a man of distinction.
> His face is surmounted by a magnificent wig; he wears a
> richly-laced cravat and a fine loose-flowing coat; and at his

side hangs a sword. In his hand he carries a rolled-up bundle of documents. So striking is his appearance that one is hardly aware of the large mole which disfigures his countenance. Certainly he has overcome all his old shyness and sense of inferiority on that account. He scans the courtiers, the ministers, before shaking hands with them. He knows that they too are contemplating him. He must impress them, overawe them, impose his personality upon them. When he talks he raises his voice so that it dominates the others. He wants Lord Halifax to hear what excellent French and Dutch he speaks, and how cleverly he can quote Virgil and Horace. He says quite casually, "I have written a great many sheets about the coin, about bringing in plate to the Mint, and about our standards", but all the while he is eyeing those to right and to left to see what effect his words have. He sees that he is the centre of all eyes, that the ministers are eager to hear more. He continues speaking. He says he has only refrained from publishing his views because there are already "so many great heads upon the subject". Lord Halifax smiles. Defoe has gained his end. . . . His self-confidence is stupendous. Call it impudence if you will, there is no denying his courage. There is no enterprise, he lets it be understood, that he cannot undertake. He contrives to talk on every subject like an expert. He has the manners of a diplomat. With consummate ease he unrolls financial schemes and displays a knowledge of figures which Halifax himself, the great financier, may well envy. The subject of State lotteries comes up for discussion. Defoe's advice is sought. He answers confidently the questions put to him. (FitzGerald, 79–80)

Two days after *Essay on Projects* hit the streets, Defoe unleashed *A Poor Man's Plea*. In it he asks why the rich are always trying to reform the poor but do nothing to reform themselves. In it is one of his all-time great lines, as relevant today as it was when it was written: "These are all cobweb laws, in which small flies are catched, and the great ones break through." Defoe goes on to point out numerous examples proving that the poor man receives one kind of justice and the rich man another.

Also in 1698, he wrote *An Argument for a Standing Army*, which endeared him to the king, who had been urging Parliament to give him one for a long time. At least partly as a result of the pamphlet, Parliament granted William such an army. What inspired the pamphlet was the latest news: The king of Spain had just died, and the throne was being offered to the Duc d'Anjou, King Louis XIV's grandson. Should France and Spain unite, there would be a monolithic state stretching from Portugal to Italy and, with the Spanish possessions in America, the greatest trading power in the world. To Defoe, economic power was far more important than political power, for in war, "it is not the longest sword, but the longest purse that wins." His arguments woke Parliament to the peril.

Also crucial to Defoe's ability to generate and share ideas was the government position he held from 1695 to 1699 as accountant to the commissioners of glass duty. As his influence and hopes soared, Defoe reveled in the glitter of royal life and the narcotic of power. He developed a friendship with the king, as well as deep relationships with other women, spending little time at home with his faithful wife and growing family.

Quietly but certainly, Defoe built an audience for what he had to say. In 1691, his good friend John Dunton had started a journal, initially called the *Athenian Gazette* (later changed to the *Athenian Mercury*), and asked Defoe to help him edit it. Thanks to their joint efforts, it became the first lively and successful nonpolitical journal in English history. Jonathan Swift also contributed to it. Defoe, always interested in growing, hit upon the idea of including things in the journal that women would be interested in. Up till this time, women were excluded from almost everything. So Defoe began a question and answer column, with questions like these: "What is platonic love?" "Is it lawful for a man to beat his wife?" "Is it possible for a tender relationship between persons of the opposite sex to be innocent?" "Why does a horse with a round fundament emit a square excrement?" "Shall Negroes rise at the last day?" That column became the most popular part of the journal.

Meanwhile, King William was not having an easy time of it. Mary had died—and she was heir to the throne, not he. Worse yet, they had no children. In those days, unless there was an heir, the death of a monarch meant bloody wars of succession. William's long war to contain France had been a severe drain on the economy, not to mention its devastating impact on shipping and trade. And, to top it off, he appeared cold, he was an introvert, he spoke English with an accent, and most intolerable of all—he was a Dutchman governing true-born Englishmen!

It was at this auspicious moment that Defoe published his rollicking and satiric *The True-Born Englishman*. Synthesizing it, FitzGerald commented, "True-born Englishman indeed! What is a true-born Englishman? They were the most mongrel race that ever walked upon the face of the earth. There was no such thing as a true-born Englishman—all were the offspring of foreigners"—of Romans, Picts, Celts, Angles, Saxons, Britons, Scots, Norwegians, Danes, and Normans, to name a few (FitzGerald, 109). The satire became a best-seller: Eighty thousand were sold on the streets, and by mid-century, it had gone through 50 printings. Not only did it make Defoe a household name, but it also discredited those who insisted on pure royal blood in England's monarchs.

The king, in fact, summoned Defoe to Hampton Court Palace and told him how much the poem had pleased him. The two men had a lot in common: They were both militant Protestants who loved the game of politics; and they were both progressive, seeing further into the future than most people. No matter what the subject, the king found that Defoe had mastered it. So, "at the age of forty-one Defoe found himself the confidential advisor to the King of England" (FitzGerald, 110–13).

These were heady days for Defoe. Now that his time had come, he would triumph over those who had put him down; at last he would make them pay. But it was not to be.

In the autumn of 1701, Defoe was "at the summit of his power, the prince of satirists, and the idol of the London populace" (FitzGerald, 116). But then a rapid succession of events occurred that toppled him from his lofty perch: On September 17, former King James II died in St. Germain, France, and a grieving Louis XIV unwisely announced that James's son was the new king of England. The Whigs and Tories (the two ruling parties at the time) were outraged at this announcement, and Defoe put words to their anger in his tongue-in-cheek *Reasons Against a War with France* (most of the reasons were *for* war). William became a lion and lined up a grand alliance against France, remodeled his ministry, dissolved Parliament (the new Parliament would be solidly behind him), and prepared for war.

Early in February 1702, Defoe galloped to Hampton Court with a plan that could change history and make his fortune: an ingenious military campaign in which England would seize control of Spain's South American colonies, thus dealing a terrible blow to the Franco-Spanish alliance. William prepared to implement them . . . and Defoe would be at the center.

But late in February, the king was galloping his horse across the palace grounds when the horse stumbled. The king fell and broke his collarbone.

Medical help was brought in, but to no avail. The king died on March 8. He was only fifty-two.

The Long Fall

William was succeeded by Anne, daughter of James II but a firm Protestant. Although great things happened during her reign, not much of it was due to her efforts. She loved and respected her husband, Prince George of Denmark; but when it came to producing an heir, Anne was not successful. None of her infants survived.

Anne was a narrow thinker and easily led. During the early part of her reign she was dominated by Sarah Churchill, Duchess of Marlborough; the latter part of her reign, she was led by her prime ministers. She was strong in her convictions, however: She detested Dissenters and Roman Catholics equally and adored the Anglican Church. Anne was a good woman, and she tried to be a good queen. England grew stronger during her reign, benefiting, if not from strong leadership, at least from homely virtues.

Throughout his life, Defoe displayed a talent for making enemies by saying the wrong things at the wrong times. With the publication of the satiric pamphlet *The Shortest Way with the Dissenters,* he proved himself true to form. The circumstances were inopportune for several reasons. First, Defoe had just lost his protector, King William, and the new monarch, Queen Anne, had expressed no sympathy for her predecessor or his views. In fact, everyone knew that she hated Dissenters. Second, as his power with King William had increased, Defoe had attracted a great deal of envy. Third, Defoe was still struggling to get out of bankruptcy.

And finally, not long before King William's death, Defoe had written a rather incendiary pamphlet, *An Enquiry Into the Occasional Conformity of Dissenters.* It had to do with Dissenters who felt that holding a position of power in London was worth compromising their beliefs. In order to become Lord Mayor of London, these men were willing to occasionally attend Anglican services. After everything Dissenters had gone through and given up, it angered Defoe that these men would be willing to do some fancy footwork to get the reward. Actually, the years had softened the stance of most Dissenters. Many of them, particularly the second and third generations, no longer wished to be martyrs. At any rate, when Defoe came out with *The Shortest Way,* Anglicans and Dissenters alike were still seething over *An Enquiry Into the Occasional Conformity of Dissenters.*

The problem was, what he had written was too good. It was one of the greatest examples of irony in the English language—it almost certainly inspired Swift's *A Modest Proposal.* The satire appeared to be deadly serious: an anonymous high churchman thundering about an end to pussyfooting tolerance against those dastardly Dissenters. These piddly fines levied on them for not coming to communion—much less the right church!—were accomplishing nothing! What was needed was good old-fashioned leadership, backed up with real courage. Hang these obnoxious Dissenters! Send them to the galleys! Crucify them! As for those spineless Dissenters who would do anything to become Lord Mayor . . . not a chance in the world they'd feel their faith was worth dying for! Have at them as well!

The very audacity of this supposed high churchman stunned London. The enemies of the Dissenters—and there were many—were jubilant: At last, they said, someone had told the truth. A strong hand! That's just what those pesky Nonconformists needed.

As for the Dissenters, they were panic-stricken. After all the time and effort they had put into trying to gain back respectability and full membership rights in the Chamber of Commerce, someone had exposed them. It was too much! If they could just catch the pious old prelate who had written the pamphlet, they would let him know exactly what they thought of him.

When the truth about who had actually written the satire leaked out— that it was none other than that unprincipled stooge Defoe—everyone, from the queen down, went looking for blood.

For the first time in his long and illustrious career, Defoe had alienated both sides equally. Thus there was no one he could go to for help when a month after he unleashed the pamphlet, a warrant for his arrest was issued by the secretary of state, the Earl of Nottingham. An accusation of sedition was far more serious than one of bankruptcy. To be imprisoned was horrible enough—but even that paled beside the likelihood that he would be pilloried as well. This time Defoe was almost paralyzed with terror. He remembered the other pamphleteers who had been accused of similar charges: They had been imprisoned, whipped, and put at hard labor; while in the pillory, they had been pelted with rotten food, street garbage, dung, dirt, and rocks. Sometimes those pilloried were stripped naked and even killed. What would happen to his family? What would happen to his now thriving businesses— especially the bedrock of his fortunes and the means to continue paying back his creditors: the brick and tile factory?

Events moved quickly: A reward of 50 pounds was offered for turning Defoe in; remaining copies of *The Shortest Way* were seized at his printer's, and the pamphlet was declared a "seditious publication" and burned publicly by the hangman (FitzGerald, 122). Defoe fled.

Meanwhile, faithful, long-suffering Mary was needed again. She served as intermediary for Defoe's pleas to the speaker of the house (they didn't yet call the head of the party a "prime minister") and the queen, abjectly begging them for another chance, even volunteering to serve as a soldier overseas at no pay. Mary, now with six children to care for (four daughters, two sons), and pregnant with the seventh, bravely forced herself into Nottingham's office with a petition from her husband—only to be humiliated by being offered a bribe to turn her husband in.

Defoe hid for four and a half months before he was caught and taken to Nottingham. Defoe already knew that all his books and papers had been confiscated, so he had nothing with which to defend himself. Nottingham was extremely harsh—almost brutal—in his interrogation. After seizing the writings Defoe had with him when he was arrested, Nottingham placed him under heavy guard and had him taken by coach to dreaded Newgate. Defoe was to be a resident of that hellhole for almost six months. Periodically, Nottingham had the prisoner hauled off to be grilled again.

Defoe's trial opened on July 7 "in a setting a visitor to London described as like the 'Judgment Hall of Pilate.' Visitors paid a shilling a seat and saw 'a vast concourse of people who made such a din that it was often impossible to hear either barristers or judges.' [Defoe] stood at the bar in front of the bench on which the lord mayor or chief magistrate sat with four assessors chosen from the twelve justices of the peace. Defoe did not face friends" (Backscheider, 108). Each of the judges had been the recipient, directly or indirectly, of Defoe's barbed prose, and they were now out for revenge. "The sentence was a savage one. But then, Defoe was a dangerous man—a Puritan intellectual, an enemy of the nobility and clergy, a Whig suspected of level-ling—not to say revolutionary—leanings. Away with the fellow! [Jail] him! Pillory him! Break his spirit—so as to frighten the wits out of any other Puritan intellectuals who may be minded to follow his example!" (FitzGerald, 123).

Defoe never had a chance, for the government had gradually been tightening the screws in its attempts to destroy freedom of the press. The court now insisted that *all* criticisms of the monarch, the government, or governing officials was "seditious libel." Juries were advised that the guilt or innocence of the defendant was irrelevant. The only question to be answered was "Is the defendant the author of the papers?" Basically, the trial was a farce.

Defoe was sentenced to pay 134 pounds (fines of 50–100 pounds were standard for heinous offenses), to be pilloried three times (this was almost unheard of—once was enough for a lifetime, if one made it through), and to be left in prison (most pamphleteers were released), and surety was required of all acts for seven years (two was the usual limit). Clearly, the judges had decided to throw the book at Defoe.

The prisoner was taken back to Newgate. Almost certainly, this period was the nadir of Defoe's lifetime. After he recovered some semblance of his normal self, he had his wife, friends, and intermediaries request that the pillory part of the sentence be softened. Since the seventh century, pillorying had been the means of publicly degrading thieves and tricksters. Later, in Anglo-Saxon times, others were added to the list of pillory victims: for example, those who sold or served spoiled food, loaded their dice, borrowed a child to beg with, lied, or kept dishonest scales. Later yet, the courts added perjurers, homosexuals, and rioters. The purpose was to "stigmatize and dishonor and to mark out an offender as unworthy of trust or respect," to be "shunned and avoided by all credible and honest men," to be made "infamous by law" (Backscheider, 116). A pilloried man was marked for life, as much as if he wore a scarlet letter on his chest. He could neither vote nor serve on a jury. On July 21, Defoe was brought before the queen at Windsor Castle on a writ of habeas corpus. Anne was angry at being brought into such a circus, for London was in an uproar. Defoe was grilled again, but to no avail.

Despite the public outcry, he was pilloried—three times. But FitzGerald tells us, it didn't quite have the desired effect:

> The last three days of July found Defoe standing in the pillory, exposed to the sun's heat and the rain—exposed also to the mob. His head, his arms, were locked in the wooden instrument of torture. Below him jostled the great mob of sightseers. What would they do to him, he wondered, as he gazed down upon them from his elevated position on the disgraceful platform. Would they pelt him with rotten eggs and stinking fish, as they were wont to bombard prisoners in his unhappy situation? Indeed, an offender put into the pillory was considered lucky if he escaped with his life from the shower of brickbats and paving-stones which were often hurled at him. But as Defoe stood there those July days a

remarkable thing happened. The crowd, the Cockney crowd, far from jeering at him, cheered him. Cheered him and drank his health in tankards of ale and stoups of wine; while the pretty flower-girls garlanded his pillory with flowers. . . . A ring of admirers grouped round the place of punishment handed his pamphlets among the onlookers. They found a ready sale for them. . . . Defoe had triumphed with a vengeance over his opponents. (FitzGerald, 124–25)

Of course it helped that his hot-off-the-press tract *A Hymn to the Pillory* was being hawked everywhere in his vicinity. In it, he had used his deadly quill with devastating effect. Not only did he show how unjust his sentence was, but he also turned the tables on his enemies: "Who should be in the pillory? Incompetent military commanders . . . , power-grabbing politicians, money-grubbing financiers, swindling stock-jobbers and brokers, profligate men of fashion, vicious lawyers and magistrates, fanatic Jacobites, drunken priests," and usurious landlords—THEY ought to be standing in the pillory (FitzGerald, 125). The people loved it!

Then it was back to Newgate, there to await "Her Majesty's pleasure"— whatever and whenever that might be. FitzGerald points out that even though Defoe was treated better than most of the other prisoners, he "did not shrink with loathing from the companionship of thieves, highwaymen, forgers, coiners, and pirates. He did not disdain the company of the pretty prostitutes" (FitzGerald, 127). Defoe not only admired the courage of these people, he also came to love them. And as was his custom, he used his time in prison to good advantage: "He spent many pleasant hours in listening to the tales of his adventurous fellow-prisoners" (FitzGerald, 127). His experiences at Newgate and Whitefriars gave him the scenes and the characters he later used in *Moll Flanders, Colonel Jack,* and his other realistic novels.

But with the passing of each dreadful day, and still no word on his future, Defoe began to despair. Was he to be locked up here in this evil-smelling sinkhole for the rest of his life? What about all those monstrous debts he still owed? And the brick factory at Tillbury—who was running it? Without proper supervision, it would go under. *Then* where would he be! What about Mary and the seven children? How would they survive? Defoe realized that this time he had done a superb job of sawing off the limb he had been sitting on. Short of a miracle, he was doomed.

Then he took stock of his assets. What did he possess that the other side might want? That it hadn't taken already, that is. Well, perhaps his writing. He sent Mary and some friends to negotiate for him. He wrote to Godolphin, the Lord Treasurer, and he wrote to Secretary of State Robert Harley, a rising star in English politics. He also wrote to the house speaker and his personal inquisitor, Nottingham.

Robert Harley was shrewd, and he saw Defoe's request as an opportunity to pick up a lot of talent cheaply. Defoe's gifts were the talk of the age: On the wrong side, he could be a deadly enemy; on the right side, a powerful friend. Harley decided to write Godolphin, insidiously noting that if Defoe "were let off fine-wise, and was willing to serve his Queen, he may do us service, and this may perhaps engage him better than any after rewards, and keep him under the power of an obligation" (FitzGerald, 127–29).

Godolphin agreed with Harley's assessment. Now he'd have to persuade the queen. He pointed out to her that Defoe was "the most popular man in the country at the moment" and that his writings went through printing after printing (FitzGerald, 129). At the moment, it just wasn't good press for her and the government. Finally, the queen saw the light. So, after five months in prison, Defoe was released, a free man.

A *free* man? Could he ever be completely free again? True, he would not be in prison, but there are other kinds of prisons besides those composed of iron bars. Up till now Defoe had prided himself on his core of integrity. It's true that he had said, written, and done things he was not proud of, but he had never compromised where his deepest ideals and principles were concerned. Now, for the sake of life, liberty, writing career, and family, he had given in. Where would it lead?

He was drained emotionally and physically. His experience during that harrowing year had aged him. Never again would he be as trusting as he had been, as willing to take risks, as brash, as foolhardy—as *young*. He no longer fully trusted even the Dissenters. He felt as if he had been silenced. More and more, he worked and traveled alone.

Just as Defoe had feared, his year's absence had destroyed his brick business. Without it, how could he keep his family alive and comfortable, as well as continue to pay his debts? At forty-four years of age, Defoe saw writing as his only hope of success. In 1704, he would publish over 400,000 words.

Backscheider points out that the prison experience had a profound impact on his writing, changing its purpose, focus, and tone. Instead of being personal, introspective, intense, and engaged, it became more impersonal, detached, and objectively professional.

Defoe put away forever his dreams of being a merchant prince and king's confidant. His future, he realized, was with a quill and bottle of ink. Yet he still believed that God was in control and had a divine plan for his life.

"He Who Gave Me the Brains Will Give Me the Bread"

Shortly after Defoe's release from Newgate, the third natural disaster of his lifetime occurred: the Great Storm. It proved to be the worst storm England had ever experienced. Defoe had already earned the titles of Father of Pamphleteering and Father of Propaganda. With the piece of investigative reporting he would do on the Great Storm, he would also become known as the Father of Journalism.

Defoe was in London when the storm hit. As a matter of fact, he barely escaped being killed by falling masonry. The streets were swamped with debris, and the barometer was so low, Defoe was certain the children had been playing with it. For two days and nights, the wind howled as buildings collapsed all around his house. When he went down to the coastal cities, which had been hit even harder than London, he saw wreckage of ships everywhere and heard stories of heroic rescue attempts. Out of it all came the book *The Great Storm*. It could be considered one of the earliest (if not *the* earliest) disaster stories.

Gradually, Defoe became acquainted with his new employer/probation officer, Robert Harley, now speaker of the house and de facto ruler of England. Little did anyone realize that the rule of a weak queen, followed by the rule of several kings who could barely speak English, would lead to the end of royal power and the beginning of parliamentary democracy. At the beginning, Defoe was obsequious with Harley, almost to the point of groveling, but as time went on, his tone changed to that of a colleague, and later yet, a friend.

One of the things Harley wanted Defoe to do was to continue influencing public opinion. To accomplish that, Defoe needed a publication; hence *The Review* was established. The magazine ran for nine years, with issues coming out three times a week. Defoe wrote all the copy himself. Readers loved his question and answer column, "The Scandal Club," a mix of familiar situations, firm morality, common sense, and biting satire. Early circulation was 400–500, each copy being read by ten to fifteen people. Amazingly, even though Defoe lived on the road and had to send his copy by mail, he managed to meet his deadlines.

The next thing Harley wanted of Defoe was for him to serve as one of his secret agents. If Harley was to govern effectively, he had to know what was happening across the country and what people thought about issues. In the eighteenth century, politicians didn't have the convenience of polls and instantaneous reporting, as they do today. In fact, it was difficult for even government leaders to find out what was happening in the nations they were governing.

Since Defoe loved to travel, his new assignment was an exciting challenge. He visited every corner of England by horseback, developing a support system of individuals who would keep him updated on local developments between his visits. In each place, by getting acquainted with people in pubs and coffeehouses, Defoe discovered who the key thought-leaders were, and which government officials were most admired, which least, and why. Over time, Harley became a far more effective prime minister because of these enlightening reports from Defoe, knowing whom to reward and whom to pass over.

For five years, Defoe traveled around England, spending little time with his wife and children. When he did remain in one place for any length of time, he would write from 8:00 in the morning until noon, and then from 2:00 in the afternoon until 9:00 at night. Normally, it took five to seven hours on horseback to reach the next town, allowing Defoe the evenings to talk politics in clubhouses with dissenting ministers or Harley's other agents. Usually, Defoe would spend only one night in each town. He distributed his own published works wherever he went.

In 1706, Harley sent him on the most significant mission of his life: to move to Scotland until such time as Scotland and England would agree to become one nation. The 372-mile horse ride from London to Edinburgh took ten to fourteen days, with nights spent at inns along the way. Since most of the Scots were not interested in giving up their independence and were suspicious of all Englishmen right then, Defoe's position was dangerous. If it came out that he was a spy, he would have been lucky to get out of Scotland alive.

Defoe found Edinburgh fascinating. High Street he pronounced clean and pleasant, although he considered the little streets "very steepy and troublesome, and . . . nasty." Because the terrain was rocky, there was little available water, thus severely limiting sanitary facilities: "Each family kept its 'excrements and foul water' in large vessels until 10:00 P.M., when the bells of St. Giles signaled that it was time to dump them into the open street" (Backscheider, 211).

When the Scot and English commissioners arrived, everyone got down to business. The debates were long and heated, lasting fourteen to sixteen hours a day. Harley, his associate leaders, and the queen were afraid that if the two kingdoms did not join, Scotland might be swallowed up by France. Defoe did everything he could to help turn the tide toward union. In the streets, the coaches of the commissioners would often be stoned, for the Scots were furious when they discovered that union would mean the end of their independent parliament. But Harley had the votes he needed, so on January 6, 1707, the final vote was taken, and thus was born the United Kingdom.

Harley kept Defoe in Scotland for a while afterward. Backscheider notes that "Defoe's activities and contacts in Scotland were astonishing. His power to penetrate diverse groups ranks him among the greatest spies of all time" (Backscheider, 232).

When he finally returned to London, Defoe had been away from home for an entire year. While he was absent, his father had died; and soon after his return, his daughter Martha took sick and died as well.

Harley resigned in 1708 and was replaced by Godolphin, who promptly sent Defoe back to Scotland. In 1710, Harley was back in office again.

The Harley years taught Defoe a great deal. According to FitzGerald, Harley and Defoe came to depend on each other; gradually, this dependence developed into a friendship. The two men had many characteristics in common: both were shifty and secretive; both were tolerant and kindly; and both had had a Puritan upbringing. There was one difference, however, and this difference cemented the two men's relationship: "Harley was a statesman of power and consequence, but a slovenly and confused writer. Defoe was an undischarged bankrupt—and a writer of genius! . . . Harley, the statesman who spoke poorly and who could not write, employed the journalist of genius to travel round England and report; and, in the *Review*, to preach the cause of national unity to win the war. Defoe performed his task to perfection" (FitzGerald, 135–36).

On the Continent, some of the greatest battles of the age were being fought as the allies gradually trimmed the French empire back to size and, in the process, kept France and Spain from uniting into one monolithic power. Everywhere blood continued to flow.

Meanwhile, Defoe, the secret agent, was traveling around Britain, feeling the pulse of the kingdom. At each town, he would visit the coffeehouses, the fairs, the markets, and the Dissenters' chapels, watching, listening, and sending reports back to Harley. It was dangerous work: Because many suspected that Defoe was not the person he appeared to be, he had several close calls.

Defoe's *Review* continued to gain in popularity. Its articles were widely read and discussed. Literary historians have made much of the *Tattler* and the *Spectator,* but those two magazines lasted only a short time, whereas the *Review* spanned almost a decade. FitzGerald maintains that "there has been nothing quite like the *Review* since. Writing with incomparable brilliancy of method and vivacity of style, Defoe ranged over every conceivable subject—the war, the peace, religious toleration, national unity, trade, industry, and employment. The amount of sheer physical work involved—quite apart from the mental effort—dazzles one; for every word had to be written by hand with a quill pen" (FitzGerald, 138).

The Review wasn't the only magazine for which Defoe was writing. He simultaneously submitted poetry, stories, and pamphlets to other publications as well. Off and on—part of the time with Godolphin—Defoe would help Harley with his articles and speeches, until Harley resigned for the last time in 1714, having worked far longer than the mandated seven years of servitude with the government. Today we may thank Harley for a good share of the Defoe letters that have survived, for he valued authors like Defoe and Swift and preserved their communications in what has become known as the Harleian Collection.

Shambles

Defoe's fortunes took a turn for the worse again when Queen Anne died unexpectedly on August 1, 1714. Shortly after her successor, George Ludwig, Elector of Hanover and founder of the Hanoverian (or House of Windsor) dynasty, arrived in England, another war on the press began. Since Defoe was considered the champion of the opposition party and the most prominent political writer in the country, he found himself at the center of the conflict. Without the support of Queen Anne or Harley, Defoe was defenseless against his enemies, who quickly moved in to denounce him as an unprincipled mercenary. The charge was unfair because neither Harley nor Godolphin had ever taken that kind of control of Defoe's pen. This time, however, the smear worked.

Defoe's tendency to do foolish things at times of peril held true again. With a witch hunt on, Defoe published a defense of the Harley government at the same time the lords were in the process of impeaching prominent members of his administration and Harley himself had been imprisoned in the Tower of London.

As for George I, he had been one of the most powerful leaders in Europe before he came to England. He was methodical, deliberate, economical, cautious, and definitely not a man to be crossed. As a matter of fact, he had his former wife locked up in a remote German castle—and there she would stay.

So, once again, Defoe was in danger of being imprisoned for "seditious libel." But now he was older, fifty-four, and no longer had the reserves he once had. With the death of Queen Anne, he had felt freed from his shackles. At last he could be his own man again. But clearly the situation had not changed. He could choose prison or accommodation. Again he chose the latter. This time the directive was more devious: He was to worm his way into an extremist opposition publication, Nathaniel Mist's *Weekly Journal* (or *Saturday's Evening Post)* and help to tone it down. Mist was a strange man who was always being hauled off to prison for the extremist positions he took. Strangely enough, the partnership worked: During Defoe and Mist's long association together, *Saturday's Post* became the most popular journal in the nation, with a weekly circulation of about 10,000 copies. However, years later when Mist found out the real reason Defoe had been hired for the magazine, he tried to kill him with his sword.

A Second Wind

Defoe wrote his best, and most enduring, works in the final years of his life. Through the years, he had always found a new direction out of the ashes of defeat. Thus he concluded that out of disaster, God always points us to a better way. Defoe began to experiment as he never had before—with new points of view, different kinds of narrators, different kinds of characters and characterizations, different literary forms.

Somewhere between 1714 and 1717, Defoe began thinking about doing something that had never been done before: writing a story in plain English prose so that everyone could understand and enjoy it. It would be a story about life—especially about the loneliness of life. And since Bunyan had set his *Pilgrim's Progress* in England, Defoe would go farther away, perhaps even travel around the world. And instead of a prison of iron bars, his character would be cast on a deserted island in the middle of the ocean. *That* certainly would be a prison! He'd name the protagonist after his childhood friend: Timothy Cruso. Except "Timothy" wasn't quite right. He'd have to come up with a better first name.

Once Defoe unleashed his alter ego, Robinson Crusoe, and put himself in his place, absolutely alone on an island, something began to happen: The story became increasingly real to him. Defoe couldn't have Crusoe do or say anything uncharacteristic, for he saw every reader saying to himself as he read, "Yes! If I were in Crusoe's place, that's exactly what I would have thought/said/done."

Though he himself couldn't travel the world, there were plenty of resources Defoe could use to provide the information he needed. He reread William Daumpier's book *A New Voyage Around the World*, published in 1703, which related the story of an Indian marooned for three years on San Fernando Island. Speaking of San Fernando Island, wasn't that the one that Alexander Selkirk had been left on for four years, until Captain Cook rescued him? That tale was in *A Voyage to the South Sea, and Around the World*, published in 1712. Then there was Captain Woodes Rogers's book *A Cruising Voyage Around the World*, also published in 1712. Two other good voyage books were Daniel Beckman's *Voyage to and from the Island of Borneo*, published in 1718; and James Janeway's *Legacy to His Friends,* published in 1674. The latter dealt with God's providence, something most writers ignored. And then there were a number of travel books such as *Hakluyt's Voyages* that would help when Crusoe got off the island and made up for lost time by *really* traveling.

When Defoe delivered the finished manuscript to William Taylor at Sign of the Ship in Paternoster Row, April 25, 1719, he did not do so with pride. He knew *Robinson Crusoe* was good, but this kind of story would be looked down on by so many people. Well, the 100-pound payment would cover quite a few bills.

Sadly for the Defoe family, 100 pounds was all Defoe ever received for the book. It would be others who would make a fortune from it. The first printing in late April was for 1,000 copies; by May 9, a second printing had been done; by June 6, a third printing was ordered. Within a year, *Robinson Crusoe* had been translated into French, German, and Dutch. By the end of the nineteenth century, 181 years later, it had come out in more than 700 different editions—today, that number is well over 1,000. Without question, it is one of the best-selling books of all time.

The second part of the book, *The Farther Adventures of Robinson Crusoe,* was published in August 1719. Many editions include only the first part of the story: Crusoe's life on the island.

The third part, *Serious Reflections During the Life and Surprising Adventures of Robinson Crusoe, with His Vision of the Angelick World,* was first published in 1720. Since it is heavily philosophical and moralistic, it has rarely been included as part of the standard text.

The Fireworks at the End

In the nine-year period beginning with 1719, Defoe unleashed one blockbuster after another. *Robinson Crusoe* was followed by *The Life, Adventures, and Pyracies of the Famous Captain Singleton* in 1720. This is a powerful book that holds its own with its illustrious predecessor; it covers the parts of the known world *Robinson Crusoe* missed. It must have been heady reading in 1720, for there is excitement on virtually every page. Captain Singleton represents the bridge from the spiritual Robinson Crusoe to the darker characters to come. Most likely, he is based on Will Atkins, the bold troublemaker on Crusoe's island.

In Defoe's day, pirates were everywhere. In fact, in some parts of the world, they actually outnumbered legitimate merchants. Defoe knew a number of them personally—and occasionally one would wander home alive. Defoe read every book he could find that described their lives. *Captain Singleton* represents a lifetime of distilling information about pirates. As was true with *Robinson Crusoe*, early editions of the book sported detailed maps. Amazingly, *Captain Singleton* didn't survive. I'm sure there must be copies somewhere, but in all my years of haunting old bookstores, I've never stumbled on one.

Captain Singleton was actually preceded (by one month) by another major book, which today is even scarcer than *Captain Singleton*—*Memoirs of a Cavalier* (1720). Defoe had been doing research most of his life on one of his personal military heroes, Sweden's Gustavus Adolphus. When he wrote *Memoirs*, he had just reviewed an earlier tour de force, *The History of Wars*, in which he noted a big difference between the egocentric Charles XII and the devout Protestant Gustavus Adolphus, Charles' grandfather. The first part of *Memoirs of a Cavalier* follows the campaigns of Gustavus Adolphus; the second part details the defeat of the Royalists in 1640. The book vividly portrays the misery civil wars leave in their wake. Our protagonist, the Cavalier, eventually is forced to kill those he earlier fought to protect and who would have died for him. Leadership on both sides is "pitifully inept." In retirement, the Cavalier's memories are bitter, burning, and melancholy as he looks back at all the bloodshed on behalf of Gustavus Adolphus, whose empire is now only a memory; on Cromwell's Protectorate, which didn't last a dozen years; and on Charles XII's meaningless death. At the end, Defoe asks this rhetorical question: *For what?* H. G. Wells, in the best-selling history book of the century, *The Outline of History,* made this statement: "The earliest chapters of Defoe's *Memoirs of a Cavalier,* with its vivid description of the massacre and burning of Magdeburg, will give the reader a far better idea of the warfare of this time than any formal history" (FitzGerald, 183).

During this period, Defoe began two monumental works that in themselves would have brought fame enough for a lifetime: *Atlas Maritimus,* a huge, oversized geography book, which he began in 1722 but did not publish until 1728; and *A Tour Thro' the Whole Island of Great Britain,* a three-volume work published in 1724, 1725, and 1726.

The *Atlas Maritimus* came out at a time when people everywhere were so interested in geography and maps that it was almost a rage. Royal patents for books were rarely granted but so much expense went into this work that such a patent was imperative in order to keep it from being pirated. The book was endorsed by three admirals and by the legendary Oxford scientist Edmund Halley (only Isaac Newton was more famous at that time). Some of the greatest names of the time were among the subscribers for the landmark work (one of the publishing events of the age).

England held its breath when the plague again headed north across the Continent. Through almost barbaric containment measures, it was stopped at Marseilles, just across the English Channel. But the interest it aroused was too high for an opportunist like Defoe to resist. He went back to his childhood and recreated the terrible plague of 1665; he titled the work *A Journal of the Plague Year.* The book is so powerful that it has remained in print through the centuries and remains a classic even today. Walter Allen, in his best-selling *The English Novel* (New York: E. P. Dutton, 1954), states that *A Journal of the Plague Year* is "perhaps the most convincing re-creation of an historical event ever written" (29).

Also in 1722 came *The Fortunes and Misfortunes of Moll Flanders,* considered by some scholars to be Defoe's greatest book, and by many others, to be one of the most powerful novels ever written. In Defoe's London, there were few career options for a woman. She might be a maid in a tavern, a domestic, or if she was educated, possibly a governess. If she was poor, as most were, without a dowry, she'd have a hard time finding a husband. These young women soon found out that being a servant or working in a tavern was an open invitation to seduction. For a tragically large number of them, the only alternative to starvation was to become a street prostitute.

By 1720, women criminals were showing up more frequently in court.

The war in Europe had ended, and the troops were returning home. The few jobs women had held while the men were away were given back to them; and the depressed economy and 30 percent inflation rate got rid of many more jobs. Tens of thousands of women, like Moll Flanders, were sent to the colonies (such as America) in order to help them find new lives: From 1580 to 1650, eighty thousand women were sent to America alone; from 1651 to 1700, ninety thousand more were sent. By 1722, of those convicted at Old Bailey, close to 8 percent were executed; of the remaining 92 percent, 70 percent were shipped out. During the years 1718–1775, Maryland and Virginia alone took 30,000 British women.

Many people, including Defoe, wondered if the treatment accorded these women was morally any worse than the custom of selling one's daughter into a loveless marriage by means of a dowry. Defoe got to know these women well when he was in prison, and he developed a great pity for them: To him, they were poor, lost souls, victims of circumstances beyond their control, valiantly searching for meaning in life. FitzGerald maintains that

> *Moll Flanders* is more subtle, more complex than *Robinson Crusoe*. Moll, the pathetic heroine, so human and lovable, is a much more complicated character than the simple, open-mouthed, manly mariner of York. She is the victim both of heredity and of environment, a magnificently alive common girl, caught in the meshes of her too responsive temperament, her seducer's egoism, and the monster, the lumpish monster, of capitalist society that makes her an outcast. She is both the victim and the product of that society which disowns her. In tracing her fortunes and misfortunes Defoe delves much more deeply into the springs of human behaviour than he does in *Robinson Crusoe*, and the outcome is perhaps the most remarkable example of pure realism in literature. (FitzGerald, 188)

The History of Colonel Jack, also published in 1722, is a story of another rogue with a conscience: a pirate of the highways. At this stage of Defoe's career, crime in England was apparently completely out of control, and justice was only an abstract term. Defoe knew how little sense it made to house side by side in Newgate a father unable to pay his debts, a starving woman who killed a bird on a noble's estate, a journalist who offended the wrong people in a pamphlet he wrote, a prostitute who got caught in the act (the aristocrat with her wasn't even booked), a desperate mother who stole a loaf of bread to feed her starving children, an embezzler, a pickpocket, a rapist, and a murderer. There were more than 100 offenses for which one could receive the death penalty.

Like Dickens after him, Defoe was a voice crying in the wilderness: a plea for a more humane way of administering justice. And Colonel Jack was another in a long line of sympathetic character sketches. During this same period (mid-1720s), Defoe interviewed real-life criminals such as Jack Sheppard (1724), Jonathon Wild (1725), and Rob Roy (1723) and wrote character sketches of them as well.

The last of Defoe's great novels was *Roxana* (1724), the grimmest book of all because it lacked hope and optimism. Lady Roxana and her alter ego, Amy, sink into evil. To punish Roxana, Defoe creates two hellhounds: "Susan, the abandoned child of her body, and Amy, the rejected product of her secret thoughts" (Backscheider, 310).

Of these last two books, *Colonel Jack* is rarely seen today, but *Roxana*, that brooding study of evil, has remained in print.

Not Going Gently Into That Good Night

For years, Defoe suffered from bladder stones. Finally, in 1725, he agreed, in despair, to have them removed. The operation was horrible. First of all, the instruments they used were frightening. Second, given the nature of the operation, Defoe had to be strapped to the table with his wrists tied to his ankles; once he was secured, three strong orderlies held him in position to keep his bent legs apart. Third, they used no anesthetic. Fourth, since the doctors didn't clean their instruments between patients, operations, besides being excruciatingly painful, often resulted in months of continued pain as infection spread, many times leading to putrefaction and death. Defoe thought it would have been better to be hanged and be done with it.

Defoe had no fear of death. To him, death was merely "a passing out of life." In 1727, he noted that he was "soon to come before" the great judge of his life and intentions. All his life Defoe had daily talked with God as with a friend; and he faithfully attended church every Sunday. He was confident that God, in spite of Defoe's many mistakes, would understand and forgive him, knowing that he had tried to do what was right.

On April 24, 1731, while hiding from a creditor, Defoe was felled by a stroke. He was buried in Bunham Fields with at least 100,000 other Dissenters, such as John Bunyan, George Fox, Isaac Watts, and the Cromwell family.

So ended the life of Daniel Defoe, the Father of Journalism, the Father of Propaganda, the Father of the Novel. In his lifetime, with only a quill and an ink bottle by his side, he had written as much, perhaps, as anyone who has ever lived.

One last letter brings Defoe's life full circle. It was written to Henry Baker, who was married to Defoe's youngest and favorite daughter, Sophie:

> I am near my journey's end, and am hastening to the place where the weary are at rest, and where the wicked cease to trouble; be it that the passage is rough, and the day stormy, by what way soever He please to bring me to the end of it, I desire to finish life with this temper of soul in all cases: *Te Deum Laudamus*. . . . It adds to my grief that I must never see the pledge of your mutual love, my little grandson. Give him my blessing, and may he be to you both your joy in youth, and your comfort in age, and never add a sigh to your sorrow. But alas! that is not to be expected. Kiss my Soph[ie] once more for me; and if I must see her no more, tell her [that her] father loved her above all his comforts, to his last breath. (FitzGerald, 238–39)

Joseph Leininger Wheeler, Ph.D.
The Grey House
Conifer, Colorado

WORKS BY OR ATTRIBUTED TO DANIEL DEFOE

NOTE: Unless otherwise indicated, place of publication is London. Dates are as printed on the title pages and may be Old Style. This bibliography is taken from Paula R. Backscheider's *Daniel Defoe: His Life* (Baltimore and London: Johns Hopkins University Press, 1989). Reprinted by permission of the publisher.

An Account of the Conduct of Robert Earl of Oxford. 1715.

An Account of the Great and Generous Actions of James Butler. [1715].

An Account of the Late Horrid Conspiracy to Depose Their Present Majesties K. William and Q. Mary, to Bring in the French and the Late King James, and Ruine the City of London. 1691.

An Account of the Proceedings Against the Rebels. 1716.

The Advantages of the Present Settlement, and the Great Danger of a Relapse. 1689.

The Advantages of Peace and Commerce; with Some Remarks on the East-India Trade. 1729.

Advertisement from Daniel De Foe, to Mr. Clark. [Edinburgh, 1710].

Advice to the People of Great Britain, with Respect to Two Important Points of Their Future Conduct: I. What They Ought to Expect from the King; II. How They Ought to Behave by Him. 1714.

"The Age of Wonders." 1710.

The Anatomy of Exchange-Alley. 1719.

And What If the Pretender Should Come? Or Some Considerations of the Advantages and Real Consequences of the Pretender's Possessing the Crown of Great Britain. 1713.

The Annals of King George, Year the Second. 1717.

The Annals of King George, Year the Third. 1718.

An Answer to a Paper Concerning Mr. De Foe, Against His History of the Union. Edinburgh, 1708.

An Answer to a Question That No Body Thinks of, Viz. But What If the Queen Should Die? 1713.

An Answer to the Late K. James's Last Declaration. 1693.

An Apology for the Army. 1715.

The Apparent Danger of an Invasion. 1701.

An Appeal to Honour and Justice. 1715. In *The Shortest-Way with the Dissenters and Other Pamphlets.* Shakespeare Head edition. Oxford: Blackwell, 1974.

An Argument Shewing That a Standing Army, with Consent of Parliament, Is Not Inconsistent with a Free Government. 1698.

Applebee's Original Weekly Journal. See *Original Weekly Journal.*

Arguments About the Alteration of Triennial Elections of Parliament. 1716.

Armageddon: Or, the Necessity of Carrying on the War. [1711].

Atlantis Major. 1711.

Atlas Maritimus & Commercialis. 1728.

Augustus Triumphans. 1728.

The Ballad: Or, Some Scurrilous Reflections in Verse . . . with the Memorial, Alias Legion Reply'd to Paragraph by Paragraph. [1701].

The Ballance of Europe: Or, An Enquiry Into the Respective Dangers of Giving the Spanish Monarchy to the Emperour as Well as to King Phillip. 1711.

The Ban[bur]y Apes: Or, The Monkeys Chattering to the Magpye. [1710].

A Brief Explanation of a Late Pamphlet, Entitled The Shortest Way with the Dissenters. [1703].

A Brief Historical Account of the Lives of the Six Notorious Street-Robbers, Executed at Kingston. 1726. In vol. 16 of *Romances and Narratives by Daniel Defoe,* edited by George A. Aitken. London: Dent, 1905.

A Brief History of the Poor Palatine Refugees, Lately Arrived in England. 1709.

A Brief Reply to the History of Standing Armies in England. 1698.

A Brief State of the Question, Between the Printed and Painted Callicoes and the Woollen and Silk Manufacture. 1719.

A Brief Survey of the Legal Liberties of the Dissenters. 1714.

Caledonia. Edinburgh, 1706.

The Candidate: Being a Detection of Bribery and Corruption as It Is Just Now in Practice All Over Great Britain. 1715.

Captain Singleton. 1720. Shakespeare Head edition. Oxford: Blackwell, 1974.

The Case of Dissenters as Affected by the Late Bill Proposed in Parliament for Preventing Occasional Conformity. 1703.

The Case of Mr. Law, Truly Stated, in Answer to a Pamphlet, Entitul'd A Letter to Mr. Law. 1721.

The Character of the Late Dr. Samuel Annesley. 1697.

Chicken Feed Capons. 1731.

Colonel Jack. 1723. Shakespeare Head edition. Oxford: Blackwell, 1974.

A Collection of Miscellany Letters. 4 vols. 1722, 1727.

A Collection of the Writings of the Author of The True-Born Englishman. 1703.

Commentator. 1 Jan.–16 Sept. 1720.

The Compleat English Gentleman. Edited by Karl D. Bülbring. London: David Nutt, 1890.

The Complete English Tradesman. 1726.

A Condoling Letter to The Tattler: *On Account of the Misfortunes of Isaac Bickerstaff, Esq.* [1710].

The Conduct of Christians Made the Sport of Infidels. 1717.

The Conduct of Parties in England, More Especially of Those Whigs Who Now Appear Against the New Ministry and a Treaty for Peace. 1712.

The Conduct of Robert Walpole, Esq. 1717.

Conjugal Lewdness. 1727. Edited by Maximillian E. Novak. Gainesville, Fla.: Scholars' Facsimiles & Reprints, 1967.

Considerations in Relation to Trade Considered. [Edinburgh], 1706.

Considerations on the Present State of Affairs in Great Britain. 1718.

Considerations Upon the Eighth and Ninth Articles of the Treaty of Commerce and Navigation. 1713.

The Consolidator. 1705. Edited by Malcolm J. Bosse. New York: Garland, 1972.

A Continuation of Letters Written by a Turkish Spy at Paris. 1718.

Daily Post. 3 Oct. 1719–c. 27 Apr. 1725.

The Danger and Consequences of Disobliging the Clergy. 1717.

The Danger of Court Differences. 1717.

The Danger of the Protestant Religion Consider'd. 1701.

Daniel Defoe's Hymn for the Thanksgiving. 1706.

The Defection Farther Considered. 1718.

A Defence of the Allies. 1712.

A Dialogue Between a Dissenter and the Observator. 1703.

Director. 5 Oct. 1720–16 Jan. 1721.

The Dissenter[s] Misrepresented and Represented. [1704].

The Dissenters Answer to the High-Church Challenge. 1704. In *A Second Volume of the Writings of the Author of* The True-Born Englishman. 1705.

The Dissenters in England Vindicated. [Edinburgh, 1707].

[*Dormer's News Letter.* June 1716–Aug. 1718?]

The Double Welcome: A Poem to the Duke of Marlboro. 1705.

Due Preparations for the Plague as Well for Soul as Body. 1722.

The Dyet of Poland: A Satyr. 1705.

The Dyet of Poland, A Satyr. Consider'd Paragraph by Paragraph. 1705.

An Effectual Scheme for the Immediate Preventing of Street Robberies. 1731.

An Elegy on the Author of The True-Born Englishman. 1704.

An Encomium Upon the Parliament. 1699.

The Englishman's Choice, and True Interest. 1694.

An Enquiry Into Occasional Conformity, Shewing That the Dissenters Are in No Way Concerned in It. 1702.

An Enquiry Into the Danger and Consequences of a War with the Dutch. 1712.

An Enquiry Into the Disposal of the Equivalent. Edinburgh, 1706.

An Enquiry Into the Occasional Conformity of Dissenters, in Cases of Preferment. 1697.

An Enquiry Into the Occasional Conformity of Dissenters Shewing That the Dissenters Are No Way Concern'd in It. 1702. In *A True Collection of the Writings of the Author of* The True-Born Englishman. 1703.

An Enquiry Into the Real Interest of Princes. 1712.

An Essay at a Plain Exposition of That Difficult Phrase A Good Peace. 1711.

An Essay at Removing National Prejudices Against a Union with Scotland, To Be Continued During the Treaty Here. Part I. 1706.

An Essay at Removing National Prejudices Against a Union with Scotland, To Be Continued During the Treaty Here. Part II. 1706.

An Essay, at Removing National Prejudices Against a Union with Scotland, Part III. [Edinburgh], 1706.

An Essay on the History and Reality of Apparitions. 1727.

An Essay on the History of Parties, and Persecution in Britain: Beginning with a Brief Account of the Test-Act and an Historical Enquiry Into the Reasons, the Original and the Consequences of the Occasional Conformity of Dissenters. 1711.

An Essay on the Late Storm. 1704.

An Essay on the Regulation of the Press. 1704. Edited by J. R. Moore. Luttrell Society Reprints, no. 7. Oxford: Blackwell, 1948.

An Essay on the South-Sea Trade. 1711.

An Essay on the Treaty of Commerce with France. 1713.

An Essay Upon Projects. 1697. Menston, Eng.: Scholar, 1969.

An Essay Upon Publick Credit. 1710.

Every-body's Business Is No-body's Business. 1725.

The Experiment: Or, The Shortest Way with the Dissenters Exemplified. 1705.

An Expostulatory Letter, to the B[ishop] of B[angor]. [1717].

Faction in Power: Or, The Mischiefs and Dangers of a High-Church Magistracy. 1717.

Fair Payment No Spunge. 1717.

The Family Instructor, in Three Parts, with a Recommendatory Letter by the Reverend Mr. S. Wright. Newcastle, 1715.

The Family Instructor, in Three Parts . . . The Second Edition. Corrected by the Author. 1715.

The Family Instructor, in Two Parts. I. Relating to Family Breaches, and Their Obstructing Religious Duties. II. To the Great Mistake of Mixing the Passions in the Managing and Correcting of Children. . . . Vol. II. 1718.

The Farther Adventures of Robinson Crusoe. 1719. Shakespeare Head edition. Oxford: Blackwell, 1974.

The Fears of the Pretender Turn'd Into the Fears of Debauchery. 1715.

The Felonious Treaty. 1711.

A Fifth Essay, at Removing National Prejudices. [Edinburgh], 1607 (for 1707).

The Fortunate Mistress: Or, A History of the Life and Vast Variety of Fortunes of Mademoiselle de Beleau, Afterwards Call'd the Countess de Wintelsheim, in Germany. Being the Person Known by the Name of the Lady Roxana. [1724]. Shakespeare Head edition. Oxford: Blackwell, 1974.

The Fortunes and Misfortunes of the Famous Moll Flanders, &c. 1721. Shakespeare Head edition. Oxford: Blackwell, 1974.

The Four Years Voyages of Capt. George Roberts. 1726.

The Fourth Essay, at Removing National Prejudices. [Edinburgh], 1706.

The Free-holders Plea Against Stock-Jobbing Elections of Parliament Men. 1701.

A Friendly Epistle by Way of Reproof from One of the People Called Quakers. 1715.

A Further Search Into the Conduct of the Allies. 1712.

A General History of Discoveries and Improvements. Oct. 1725–Jan. 1726; 1727.

A General History of the Pyrates. 1724. Edited by Manuel Schonhorn. Columbia: University of South Carolina Press, 1972.

The Great Law of Subordination Consider'd. 1724.

Hannibal at the Gates. 1712.

Hanover or Rome. 1715.

His Majesty's Obligations to the Whigs Plainly Proved. 1715.

An Historical Account of the Bitter Sufferings, and Melancholly Circumstances of the Episcopal Church in Scotland, Under the Barbarous Usage and Bloody Persecution of the Presbyterian Church Government. Edinburgh, 1707.

An Historical Account of the Voyages and Adventures of Sir Walter Raleigh. 1719.

"Historical Collections: Or, Memoirs of Passages Collected from Several Authors." William Andrews Clark Library, UCLA. Manuscript. 1682.

A History of the Clemency of Our English Monarchs. 1717.

The History of the Kentish Petition. 1701.

The History of the Remarkable Life of John Sheppard. [1724].

The History of the Union of Great Britain. Edinburgh, 1709.

The History of the Wars, of His Late Majesty Charles XII. King of Sweden. 1720.

The History of the Wars, of His Present Majesty Charles XII. King of Sweden. 1715.

The Honour and Prerogative of the Queen's Majesty Vindicated and Defended Against the Unexampled Insolence of the Author of the Guardian, in a Letter from a Country Whig to Mr. Steele. 1713.

An Humble Proposal to the People of England, for the Encrease of Their Trade, and Encouragement of Their Manufactures. 1729.

A Hymn to Peace. 1706.

A Hymn to the Pillory. 1703. In *The Shortest Way with the Dissenters and Other Pamphlets*. Shakespeare Head edition. Oxford: Blackwell, 1974.

A Hymn to Victory. 1704.

The Immorality of the Priesthood. 1715.

An Impartial Enquiry Into the Conduct of the Right Honourable Charles Lord Viscount T[ownshend]. 1717.

An Impartial History of the Life and Actions of Peter Alexowitz, the Present Czar of Muscovy. 1723.

Instructions from Rome, in Favour of the Pretender. [1710].

A Journal of the Earl of Marr's Proceedings. [1716].

A Journal of the Plague Year. 1722. Shakespeare Head edition. Oxford: Blackwell, 1974.

A Journeye to the World in the Moon. [1705].

Jure Divino: A Satyr in Twelve Books. 1706.

The Just Complaint of the Poor Weavers. 1719.

The Justice and Necessity of Restraining the Clergy. 1715.

A Justification of the Dutch. 1712.

The King of Pirates. 1712. Vol. 8 of *The Works of Daniel Defoe,* edited by G. H. Maynadier. Boston: Brainard, 1904.

The Lay-Man's Sermon Upon the Late Storm. 1704.

The Layman's Vindication of the Church of England. 1716.

Legion's Humble Address to the Lords. [1704].

Legion's Memorial. [1701].

Legion's New Paper. 1702.

A Letter from a Dissenter in the City to a Dissenter in the Country, Advising Him to a Quiet and Peaceable Behaviour in This Present Conjuncture. 1710.

A Letter from a Member of the House of Commons. 1713.

A Letter from Mr. Reason. [Edinburgh, 1706].

A Letter from One Clergy-Man to Another. 1716.

A Letter from Some Protestant Dissenting Laymen. 1718.

A Letter from the Man in the Moon. [1705].

A Letter to a Dissenter from His Friend at the Hague, Concerning the Penal Laws and the Test. [1688].

A Letter to a Merry Young Gentleman. 1715.

A Letter to Mr. How. 1701.

A Letter to Mr. Steele. 1714.

A Letter to the Author of the Flying-Post. 1718.

A Letter to the Dissenters. 1713, 1714.

A Letter to the Dissenters. 1719.

The Letters of Daniel Defoe. Edited by George H. Healey. 1955. Oxford: Clarendon Press, 1969.

The Life and Strange Surprising Adventures of Robinson Crusoe. 1719.

The Life of Jonathan Wild. 1725.

The Livery Man's Reasons, Why He Did Not Give His Vote for a Certain Gentleman Either to Be Lord Mayor, or Parliament Man for the City of London. 1701.

Manufacturer. 13 Oct. 1719–17 Feb. 1720. Introduced by Robert N. Gosselink. Delmar, N.Y.: Scholars' Facsimiles & Reprints, 1978.

The Master Mercury. Introduced by Frank Ellis and Henry Snyder. ARS no. 184. Los Angeles: Clark Library, 1977.

"Meditaçons." Huntington Library. Manuscript. 1681.

The Meditations of Daniel Defoe Now First Published. Edited by George Harris Healey. Cummington, Mass.: Cummington, 1946.

Memoirs of a Cavalier. [1720]. Shakespeare Head edition. Oxford: Blackwell, 1974.

The Memoirs of an English Officer. 1728. In *Memoirs of an English Officer and Two Other Short Novels.* Introduced by J. T. Boulton. London: Gollancz, 1970.

Memoirs of Count Tariff, &c. 1713.

Memoirs of John, Duke of Melfort. 1714.

The Memoirs of Majr. Alexander Ramkins. 1719. In *Memoirs of an English Officer and Two Other Short Novels.* Introduced by J. T. Boulton. London: Gollancz, 1970.

Memoirs of Publick Transactions in the Life and Ministry of His Grace the D. of Shrewsbury. 1718.

Memoirs of Some Transactions During the Late Ministry of Robert, E. of Oxford. 1717.

Memoirs of the Church of Scotland. 1717.

Memoirs of the Conduct of Her Late Majesty and Her Last Ministry. 1715.

Memoirs of the Life and Eminent Conduct of That Learned and Reverend Divine, Daniel Williams, D. D. 1718.

A Memorial to the Nobility of Scotland, Who Are to Assemble in Order to Choose the Sitting Peers for the Parliament of Great Britain. Edinburgh, 1708.

Mercator: Or, Commerce Retrieved. 26 May 1713–20 July 1714.

Mercurius Brittanicus. Jan. 1718–March 1719.

Mercurius Politicus. May 1716–Oct. 1720.

Minutes of the Negotiations of Monsr. Mesnager. 1717.

The Mock-Mourners: A Satyr. 1702.

A Modest Vindication of the Present Ministry. 1707.

More Reformation: A Satyr Upon Himself, by the Author of The True-Born Englishman. 1703.

More Short-Ways with the Dissenters. 1704.

A Narrative of All the Robberies, Escapes, &c of John Sheppard. 1724. In Vol. 16 of *Romances and Narratives by Daniel Defoe,* edited by George A. Aitken. London: Dent, 1905.

A New Discovery of an Old Intreague. 1691.

A New Family Instructor. 1727.

A New Map of the Laborious and Painful Travels of Our Blessed High Church Apostle. 1710.

A New Test of the Church of England's Honesty. 1704.

A New Test of the Church of England's Loyalty. 1702.

A New Test of the Sence of the Nation. 1710.

No Queen, or No General. 1712.

Novels and Selected Writings. 2d ed. Shakespeare Head edition. Oxford: Blackwell, 1974.

Observations on the Fifth Article of the Treaty of Union. [Edinburgh, 1706].

Of Royall Education: A Fragmentary Treatise. Edited by Karl D. Bülbring. London: Nutt, 1985.

On the Fight at Ramellies. Review 3 (1706): 242–44.

The Original Power of the Collective Body of the People of England. 1702.

Original Weekly Journal (later called *Applebee's Original Weekly Journal*). 25 June 1720–14 May 1726 (and occasionally thereafter).

The Pacifactor: A Poem. 1700.

Parochial Tyranny. [1727].

Passion and Prejudice. Edinburgh, 1707.

Peace, or Poverty. 1712.

Peace Without Union. 1703.

The Pernicious Consequences of the Clergy's Intermeddling with Affairs of State. [1714?].

"The Petition of Dorothy Distaff." *Mercurius Politicus,* Dec. 1719.

A Plan of the English Commerce. 1728, 1730. Shakespeare Head edition. Oxford: Blackwell, 1974.

The Political History of the Devil. 1726.

The Poor Man's Plea. 1698.

Preface to *De Laune's Plea for the Non-Conformists.* 1706.

Preface to *De Laune's Plea for the Non-Conformists.* In *Dr. Sacheverell's Recantation.* 1709.

The Present Negotiations of Peace Vindicated. 1712.

The Present State of Jacobitism Considered. 1701.

The Present State of the Parties in Great Britain. 1712.

The Protestant Jubilee. 1714.

The Protestant Monastery. 1727.

The Quarrel of the School-Boys at Athens. 1717.

Queries Upon the Bill Against Occasional Conformity. [1704].

The Question Fairly Stated, Whether Now Is Not the Time to Do Justice to the Friends of the Government as Well as to Its Enemies? 1717.

Reasons Against a War with France. 1701.

Reasons Against Fighting: Being an Enquiry Into This Great Debate, Whether It Is Safe for Her Majesty, or Her Ministry, to Venture an Engagement with the French. 1712.

Reasons Against the Succession of the House of Hanover. 1713.

Reasons for a Peace: Or, The War at an End. 1711.

Reasons for Im[peaching] the L[or]d H[igh] T[reasure]r. [1714].

Reasons Why a Party Among Us, and Also Among the Confederates, Are Obstinately Bent Against a Treaty of Peace with the French at This Time. 1711.

Reasons Why This Nation Ought to Put a Speedy End to This Expensive War. 1711.

Reflections Upon the Late Great Revolution. 1689.

Reformation of Manners. 1702.

Religious Courtship. 1722.

Remarks on the Bill to Prevent Frauds Committed by Bankrupts. 1706.

Remarks on the Speeches of William Paul Clerk and John Hall. 1716.

The Remedy Worse Than the Disease. 1714.

A Reply to a Pamphlet Entituled, the L[or]d H[aversham]'s Vindication. 1706.

A Reply to a Traiterous Libel Entituled English Advice to the Freeholders of Great Britain. 1715.

A Reply to the Remarks Upon the Lord Bishop of Bangor's Treatment of the Clergy and Convocation. 1717.

The Representation Examined: Being Remarks on the State of Religion in England. 1711.

The Reproof to Mr. Clark, and a Brief Vindication of Mr. De Foe. [Edinburgh, 1710].

A Re-Representation: Or, A Modest Search After the Great PLUNDERERS of the NATION. 1711.

Resignacion. 1708. In Frank Ellis, "Defoe's 'Resignacion' and the Limitations of Mathematical Plainness." 1985.

The Review. 9 vols. 19 Feb. 1704–11 June 1713. Edited by A. W. Secord. 22 vols. New York: Columbia University Press, 1938.

The Royal Progress: Or, A Historical View of the Journeys or Progresses, Which Several Great Princes Have Made to Visit Their Dominions. 1724.

Royal Religion: Being Some Enquiry After the Piety of Princes. 1704.

The Scot's Narrative Examin'd. 1709.

The Scots Nation and Union Vindicated; from the Reflections Cast on Them, in an Infamous Libel, Entitl'd the Publick Spirit of the Whigs. 1714.

A Scots Poem: Or, A New-Years Gift, from a Native of the Universe, to His Fellow-Animals in Albania. Edinburgh, 1707.

A Seasonable Warning and Caution Against the Insinuations of Papists and Jacobites. 1712.

A Second, and More Strange Voyage to the World in the Moon. [1705].

Second Thoughts Are Best: Or, A Further Improvement of a Late Scheme to Prevent Street Robberies. 1729.

A Second Volume of the Writings of the Author of The True-Born Englishman. 1705.

The Secret History of the October Club. 1711.

The Secret History of the October Club. . . . Part II. 1711.

The Secret History of State Intrigues. 1715.

The Secret History of the Scepter. 1715.

The Secret History of the White Staff. 1715.

The Secret History of the White Staff. . . . [Pt. I.] 1714.

The Secret History of the White Staff. . . . Pt. II. 1714.

The Secret History of the White Staff. . . . Pt. III. 1715.

Secret Memoirs of a Treasonable Conference at S[omerset] House. 1717.

Secret Memoirs of the New Treaty of Alliance with France. 1716.

A Serious Inquiry Into This Grand Question, Whether a Law to Prevent the Occasional Conformity of Dissenters Would Not Be Inconsistent with the Act of Toleration. 1704.

Serious Reflections During the Life and Surprising Adventures of Robinson Crusoe, with His Vision of the Angelick World. 1720. Vol. 3 of *The Works of Daniel Defoe,* edited by G. H. Maynadier. New York: Crowell, 1903.

A Short Letter to the Glasgow-men. [Edinburgh, 1706].

A Short Narrative of the Life and Actions of His Grace John, D. of Marlborough. 1711.

A Short View of the Present State of the Protestant Religion. Edinburgh, 1707.

The Shortest Way to Peace and Union. 1703.

The Shortest Way with the Dissenters: Or, Proposals for the Establishment of the Church. 1702. In *The Shortest Way with the Dissenters.* Shakespeare Head edition. Oxford: Blackwell, 1974.

The Sincerity of the Dissenters Vindicated. 1703.

The Six Distinguishing Characters of a Parliament-Man. 1700.

Some Considerations on a Law for Triennial Parliaments. 1716.

Some Considerations on the Reasonableness and Necessity of Encreasing and Encouraging the Seamen. 1728.

Some Considerations Upon Street-Walkers. [1726].

Some Methods to Supply the Defects of the Late Peace. [1715].

Some Persons Vindicated Against the Author of the Defection. 1718.

Some Reasons Offered by the Late Ministry in Defence of Their Administration. 1715.

Some Reflections on a Pamphlet Lately Publish'd Entitl'd An Argument Shewing That a Standing Army Is Inconsistent with a Free Government. 1697.

Some Remarks on the First Chapter in Dr. Davenant's Essays. 1703.

Some Thoughts of an Honest Tory in the Country. 1716.

Some Thoughts Upon the Subject of Commerce with France. 1713.

The Spanish Descent. 1702.

[A Speech of a Stone Chimney-Piece]. [1711].

A Speech Without Doors. 1710.

The Storm: Or, A Collection of the Most Remarkable Casualties and Disasters Which Happen'd in the Late Dreadful Tempest, Both by Sea and Land. 1704.

Street-Robberies Consider'd. [1728].

A Strict Enquiry Into the Circumstances of a Late Duel. 1713.

Strike While the Iron's Hot: Or, Now Is the Time to Be Happy. 1715.

The Succession of Spain, Considered. 1711.

The Succession to the Crown of England, Considered. 1701.

A Supplement to the Faults on Both Sides. 1710.

A System of Magick. 1727.

"To the Athenian Society." In *The History of the Athenian Society,* by Charles Gildon. [1692].

To the Honourable, the C—s of England Assembled in P—t. 1704.

A Tour thro' the Whole Island of Great Britain. 1724–27. Introduction by G.D.H. Cole. 2 vols. New York: Kelley, 1968.

The Trade of Britain Stated. [Edinburgh, 1707].

The Trade of Scotland with France, Consider'd. 1713.

The Trade to India Critically and Calmly Consider'd. 1720.

Treason Detected, in an Answer to That Traiterous and Malicious Libel, Entitled English Advice to the Freeholders of England. 1715.

A True Account of the Proceedings at Perth. 1716.

The True and Genuine Account of the Life and Actions of the Late Jonathan Wild. 1725. In vol. 16 of *Romances and Narratives by Daniel Defoe,* edited by George A. Aitken. London: Dent, 1905.

The True-Born Englishman. 1700.

The True-Born Englishman. Rev. ed. 1716.

A True Collection of the Writings of the Author of The True-Born Englishman. 1703.

A WORD TO THE READER

*T*he *Farther Adventures of Robinson Crusoe* is a troubling book because it is an honest one. In it, Daniel Defoe faithfully re-creates the violence and injustices of the seventeenth and eighteenth centuries. It was a time when the plague swept repeatedly through nations, leaving millions of corpses behind; it was a time when men, women, and children could be forced from their homes and sold into slavery; it was a time when thousands of women died in childbirth, when only one in three children survived to adulthood, when the majority of men lived, and died, on battlefields. It was a time when people faced the realities of life daily.

Sadly, many people today, particularly among the media, perceive Christians as unwilling or unable to accept these realities. They believe that we deliberately close ourselves off from the world's ugliness, thinking that if we don't know it's there, it won't affect us. But if Christians really believed this, we would not read our Bibles. After all, the Scriptures cover a particularly bloody period in human history, and biblical writers didn't sugarcoat or shy away from discussing topics such as wars, slavery, idolatry, cannibalism, adultery, pride, incest, and treachery. They realized that God gave us minds capable of dealing with life in a fallen world, because God knows that is how we will be able to grow in compassion and wisdom. Our consciences are not V-chips that block evil from our too-impressionable souls; rather, they are divine prisms through which we are to discern good from bad, truth from lies.

It is no coincidence that many great Christians were worldly in the sense of being well educated and well read—for example, Moses, Daniel, Paul, Augustine, Luther, Bonhoeffer, C. S. Lewis. They knew what life could offer—the good and the bad—so when they chose to serve God and His ways, their decisions were well informed: They understood exactly what they were doing. These saints of the church would recognize that if one would truly understand a classic work of literature, it is essential to first understand the world in which the author wrote, for no human being writes in a vacuum: We are all products of our age.

With that in mind, the educated Christian will wish to read *The Farther Adventures of Robinson Crusoe* side by side with history books dealing with the seventeenth and eighteenth centuries. Trading in drugs and liquor? The Western powers did it then and still do it today. Violence? Defoe's world truly was one of violence; but actual violence and vicarious media violence are far more omnipresent today than back then. Hangings? Hangings and executions were public spectacles centuries ago; today, however, we can watch the process in the privacy of our living rooms on primetime television shows. Massacres? They occurred in Defoe's time, but our daily news reveals that they continue to happen today. Slavery? Americans would retain slavery for another century and a half after Defoe wrote this book. Religious persecution? It was certainly more widespread a few centuries ago, but headlines every day reveal to us that this is a problem that refuses to go away. Prejudice is not easily eradicated. Even the relatively enlightened Defoe evidenced prejudice in his fictional put-downs of tribal peoples, the Chinese, Muscovites, and the Greek Orthodox Church, which he ridiculed or excoriated in earlier pronouncements in the Crusoe saga.

We live in a fallen world, and for us to have a positive impact on it, we must first understand how it works. Books such as *The Farther Adventures of Robinson Crusoe* provide powerful vehicles for helping us do just that.

JLW

I farmed my own land

Chapter 1

WANDERLUST

That homely proverb, used on so many occasions in England, namely, "That what is bred in the bone will not go out of the flesh," was never more verified than in the story of my life. Anyone would think that after thirty-five years' affliction and a variety of unhappy circumstances that few men, if any, ever went through before, and after nearly seven years of peace and enjoyment in the fullness of all things, grown old, and when, if ever, it might be allowed me to have had experience of every state of middle life, and to know which was most adapted to make a man completely happy—I say, after all this, anyone would have thought that the native propensity to rambling, which I gave an account of in my first setting out in the world[1] to have been so predominant in my thoughts, should be worn out, the volatile part be fully evacuated, or at least condensed, and I might, at sixty-one years of age, have been a little inclined to stay at home and have done venturing life and fortune anymore.

Nay, further, the common motive of foreign adventures was taken away in me, for I had no fortune to make; I had nothing to seek: If I had gained ten thousand pounds, I had been no richer, for I had already sufficient for me and for those I had to leave it to. And what I had was visibly increasing, for

---

1. See *Robinson Crusoe* in Focus on the Family's Great Stories Collection, published by Tyndale House Publishers, Wheaton, Illinois, 1997.

1

having no great family, I could not spend the income of what I had, unless I would set up for an expensive way of living, such as a great family, servants, equipage, gaiety, and the like, which were things I had no notion of, or inclination to; so that I had nothing, indeed, to do but to sit still and fully enjoy what I had got and see it increase daily upon my hands. Yet all these things had no effect upon me—or at least not enough to resist the strong inclination I had to go abroad again, which hung about me like a chronic distemper. In particular, the desire of seeing my new plantation on the island, and the colony I left there, ran in my head continually. I dreamed of it all night, and my imagination ran upon it all day. It was uppermost in all my thoughts, and my fancy worked so steadily and strongly upon it that I talked of it in my sleep. In short, nothing could remove it out of my mind: It even broke so violently into all my discourses that it made my conversation tiresome, for I could talk of nothing else; all my discourse ran into it, even to impertinence; and I saw it myself.

I have often heard persons of good judgment say that all the stir people make in the world about ghosts and apparitions is owing to the strength of imagination and the powerful operation of fancy in their minds; that there is no such thing as a spirit appearing or a ghost walking; that people's poring affectionately upon the past conversation of their deceased friends so realizes it to them that they are capable of fancying, upon some extraordinary circumstances, that they see them, talk to them, and are answered by them, when, in truth, there is nothing but shadow and vapor in the thing, and they really know nothing of the matter.

For my part, I know not to this hour whether there are any such things as real apparitions, specters, or walking of people after they are dead; or whether there is anything in the stories they tell us of that kind more than the product of vapors, sick minds, and wandering fancies. But this I know: that my imagination worked up to such a height and brought me into such excess of vapors, or what else I may call it, that I actually supposed myself often upon the spot at my old castle behind the trees and saw my old Spaniard, Friday's father, and the reprobate sailors I left upon the island—nay, I fancied I talked with them and looked at them steadily, though I was broad awake, as at persons just before me. This I did till I often frightened myself with the images my fancy represented to me. One time, in my sleep, I had the villainy of the three pirate sailors so lively related to me by the first Spaniard and Friday's father that it was surprising; they told me how they barbarously attempted to murder all the Spaniards and that they set fire to the provisions they had laid up, on purpose to distress and starve them—things that I had never heard of and that, indeed, were never all of them true in fact. But it was so warm in my imagination and so realized to me that, to the hour I saw them, I could not be persuaded but that it was, or would be, true. Also, how I resented it when the Spaniard complained to me; and how I brought them to justice, tried them, and ordered them all three to be hanged. What there was really in this shall be seen in its place; for however I came to form such things in my dream, and what secret converse of spirits injected it, yet there was, I say, much of it true. I own that this dream had nothing in it literally and specifically true, but the general part was so true—the base, villainous behavior of these three hardened rogues was such, and had been so much worse than all I can describe, that the dream had too much similitude of the fact. And as I would afterward have punished them severely, so, if I had hanged them all, I had been much in the right and even should have been justified both by the laws of God and man.

But to return to my story. In this kind of temper, I lived some years. I had no enjoyment of my life, no pleasant hours, no agreeable diversion, but what had something or other of this in it; so that my wife, who saw my mind wholly bent upon it, told me very seriously one night that she believed there was some secret, powerful impulse of Providence upon me that had determined me to go thither again; and that she found nothing hindered my going but my being tied to a wife and children. She told me that it was true she could not think of parting with me; but as she was assured that if she was dead it would be the first thing I would do, it seemed to her that the thing was determined above, and she would not be the only obstruction. So, if I thought fit and resolved to go . . . (Here she found me very intent upon her words and that I looked very earnestly at her, so that it a little disordered her, and she stopped. I asked her why she did not go on and say out what she was going to say. But I perceived that her heart was too full and some tears stood in her eyes.)

"Speak out, my dear," said I. "Are you willing I should go?"

"No," said she very affectionately, "I am far from willing. But if you are resolved to go," said she, "rather than I would be the only hindrance, I will go with you; for though I think it a most preposterous thing for one of your years and in your condition, yet if it must be," said she, again weeping, "I would not leave you; for, if it be of Heaven, you must do it; there is no resisting it. And if Heaven make it your duty to go, He will also make it mine to go with you, or otherwise dispose of me, that I may not obstruct it."

This affectionate behavior of my wife's brought me a little out of the vapors, and I began to consider what I was doing. I corrected my wandering fancy and began to argue with myself sedately what business I had, after threescore years, and after such a life of tedious sufferings and disasters and closed in so happy and easy a manner—I say, what business had I to rush into new hazards and put myself upon adventures fit only for youth and poverty to run into?

Settling Down

With those thoughts I considered my new engagement: that I had a wife, one child born, and my wife then great with child of another; that I had all the world could give me and had no need to seek hazard for gain; that I was declining in years and ought to think rather of leaving what I had gained than of seeking to increase it; that as to what my wife had said of its being an impulse from Heaven and that it should be my duty to go, I had no notion of that. After many of these cogitations, I struggled with the power of my imagination, reasoned myself out of it (as I believe people may always do in like cases if they will), and, in a word, I conquered it. I composed myself with such arguments as occurred to my thoughts and which my present condition furnished me plentifully with, and particularly, as the most effectual method, I resolved to divert myself with other things and to engage in some business that might effectually tie me up from any more excursions of this kind; for I found that thing return upon me chiefly when I was idle and had nothing to do, nor anything of moment immediately before me. To that purpose, I bought a little farm in the county of Bedford and resolved to remove myself thither. I had a little convenient house upon it, and the land about it, I found, was capable of great improvement. It was in many ways suited to my inclination, which delighted in cultivating, managing, planting, and improving of land; and particularly, being an inland county, I was removed from conversing among sailors and things relating to the remote parts of the world.

In a word, I went down to my farm, settled my family, bought plows, harrows, a cart, wagon, horses, cows, and sheep, and, setting seriously to work, became in one-half year a mere country gentleman. My thoughts were entirely taken up in managing my servants, cultivating the ground, enclosing, planting, etc.; and I lived, as I thought, the most agreeable life that nature was capable of directing, or that a man always led to misfortunes was capable of retreating to.

I farmed upon my own land. I had no rent to pay and was limited by no articles; I could pull up or cut down as I pleased; what I planted was for myself, and what I improved was for my family. Having thus left off the thoughts of wandering, I had not the least discomfort in any part of life as to this world. Now I thought indeed that I enjoyed the middle state of life, which my father so earnestly recommended to me, and lived a kind of heavenly life, something like what is described by the poet, upon the subject of a country life:

> Free from vices, free from care,
> Age has no pain, and youth no snare.

But in the middle of all this felicity, one blow from unseen Providence unhinged me at once and not only made a breach upon me inevitable and incurable, but drove me, by its consequences, into a deep relapse of the wandering disposition, which, as I may say, being born in my very blood, soon recovered its hold of me and, like the returns of a violent distemper, came on with an irresistible force upon me. This blow was the loss of my wife. It is not my business here to write an elegy upon my wife, give a character of her particular virtues, and make my court to the sex by the flattery of a funeral sermon. She was, in a few words, the stay of all my affairs, the center of all my enterprises, the engine that, by her prudence, reduced me to that happy compass I was in, from the most extravagant and ruinous project that filled my head; and did more to guide my rambling genius than a mother's tears, a father's instructions, a friend's counsel, or all my own reasoning powers could do. I was happy in listening to her and in being moved by her entreaties and, to the last degree, desolate and dislocated in the world by the loss of her. When she was gone, the world looked awkwardly around me. I was as much a stranger in it, in my thoughts, as I was in the Brazils, when I first went on shore there; and as much alone, except for the assistance of servants, as I was on my island. I knew neither what to think nor what to do. I saw the world busy around me; one part laboring for bread, another part squandering in vile excesses or empty pleasures, equally miserable, because the end they proposed still fled from them; for the men of pleasure every day surfeited of their vice and heaped up work for sorrow and repentance; and the men of labor spent their strength in daily struggling for bread to maintain the vital strength they labored with; so living in a daily circulation of sorrow, living but to work, and working but to live, as if daily bread were the only end of wearisome life, and a wearisome life the only occasion of daily bread.

This put me in mind of the life I lived in my kingdom, the island—where

I suffered no more corn to grow, because I did not want it, and bred no more goats, because I had no more use for them; where the money lay in the drawer till it grew moldy and had scarcely the favor to be looked upon in twenty years.

All these things, had I improved them as I ought to have done, and as reason and religion had dictated to me, would have taught me to search further than human enjoyments for a full felicity; and that there was something which certainly was the reason and end of life, superior to all these things, and which was either to be possessed, or at least hoped for, on this side of the grave.

But my sage counselor was gone: I was like a ship without a pilot that could only run afore the wind. My thoughts ran all away again into the old life: My head was quite turned with the whimsies of foreign adventures; and all the pleasant, innocent amusements of my farm, my garden, my cattle, and my family, which before entirely possessed me, were nothing to me, had no relish, and were like music to one that has no ear, or food to one that has no taste. In a word, I resolved to leave off housekeeping, lease out my farm, and return to London; and in a few months after, I did so.

London

When I came to London, I was still as uneasy as I was before. I had no relish for the place, no employment in it, nothing to do but to saunter about like an idle person, of whom it may be said he is perfectly useless in God's creation, and it is not one farthing's matter to the rest of his kind whether he be dead or alive. This also was the thing that, of all circumstances of life, I was most averse to, who had been all my days used to an active life; and I would often say to myself, "A state of idleness is the very dregs of life." Indeed, I thought I was much more suitably employed when I was twenty-six days making a deal-board.[2]

It was now the beginning of the year 1693, when my nephew, whom, as I have observed before, I had introduced to the sea and had made him commander of a ship, was come home from a short voyage to Bilbao, being the first he had made. He came to me and told me that some merchants of his acquaintance had been proposing that he undertake a voyage for them to the East Indies and to China as private traders.

"And now, Uncle," said he, "if you will go to sea with me, I will engage

---

2. Hand-hewn plank board. All boards in those days were made by hand, a very time-consuming operation.

to land you upon your old habitation on the island; for we are to touch at the Brazils."

Nothing can be a greater demonstration of a future state, and of the existence of an invisible world, than the concurrence of second chances with the ideas of things that we form in our minds in secret and have not communicated to any in the world.

My nephew knew nothing of how serious my wanderlust fever was, and I knew nothing of what he had in his thoughts to say. In fact, on that very morning before he came to me, I had, with a great deal of confusion of thought and revolving every part of my circumstances in my mind, come to this resolution: that I would go to Lisbon and consult with my old sea captain; and if it seemed to make sense, I would go and see the island again and find out what was become of my people there. I had pleased myself with the thoughts of peopling the place and carrying inhabitants from hence, getting a patent for the possession, and I know not what all—when, in the middle of all this, in comes my nephew, as I have said, with his project of carrying me thither on his way to the East Indies.

I paused awhile at his words, and looking steadily at him, I said, "What devil sent you on this unlucky errand?"

My nephew stared as if he had been frightened at first; but perceiving that I was not much displeased with the proposal, he recovered himself.

"I hope it may not be an unlucky proposal, sir," said he. "I dare say you would be pleased to see your new colony there, where you once reigned with more felicity than most of your brother monarchs in the world."

In a word, the scheme hit so exactly with my mood—that is to say, the prepossession I was under and of which I have said so much—that I told him, in a few words, if he agreed with the merchants, I would go with him, but I would not promise to go any farther than my own island.

"Why, sir," said he, "you don't want to be left there again, I hope?"

"Why," said I, "can you not take me up again on your return?"

He told me it would not be possible to do so, that the merchants would never allow him to come that way with a laden ship of such value, it being a month's sail out of his way—and might be three or four. "Besides, sir, if I should miscarry," said he, "and not return at all, then you would be reduced to the condition you were in before."

This made sense, but we both found out a remedy for it, which was, to carry a framed sloop on board the ship, which being taken in pieces and shipped on board the ship might, by the help of some carpenters, whom we

It was all to no avail

agreed to carry with us, be set up again on the island and finished fit to go to sea in a few days.

I was not long resolving, for, indeed, the importunities of my nephew joined so effectually with my inclination that nothing could oppose me. On the other hand, my wife being dead, nobody concerned themselves about persuading me one way or the other, except my ancient good friend the widow, who earnestly struggled with me to consider my years, my easy circumstances, and the needless hazards of a long voyage—and above all, my young children. But it was all to no avail: I had an irresistible desire for the voyage; and I told her I thought there was something so uncommon in the impressions I had on my mind that it would be a kind of resisting Providence if I should attempt to stay at home—after which she ceased her objections and joined with me, not only in making provision for my voyage, but also in settling my family affairs for my absence and providing for the education of my children.

Preparations for Departure

In order to do this, I made my will and settled the estate I had in such a manner for my children, and placed in such hands, that I was perfectly at ease and satisfied they would have justice done them, whatever might befall me. As for their education, I left it wholly to the widow, with a sufficient maintenance to herself for her care—all which she richly deserved, for no mother could have taken more care in their education or understood it better. And as she lived till I came home, I also lived to thank her for it.

My nephew was ready to sail about the beginning of January 1695; and I, with my man Friday, went on board in the Downs on the 8th, having, besides that sloop, which I mentioned before, a very considerable cargo of all kinds of necessary things for my colony, which, if I did not find in good condition, I resolved to leave so.

First, I carried with me some servants, whom I purposed to place there as inhabitants, or at least to set on work there, upon my account, while I stayed, and either to leave them there or carry them forward, as they should appear willing. Particularly, I carried two carpenters, a smith, and a very handy, ingenious fellow who was a cooper by trade and was also a general mechanic; for he was dexterous at making wheels and hand mills to grind corn, was a good turner, and a good pot maker; he also made anything that was proper to make of earth or of wood—in a word, we called him our Jack-of-all-trades. With these I carried a tailor, who had offered himself to go a passenger to the East Indies with my nephew but afterward consented to stay on our new plantation, and who proved a most necessary, handy fellow, as could be desired, in many other businesses besides that of his trade; for, as I observed formerly, necessity arms us for all employments.

My cargo, as near as I can recollect, for I have not kept account of the particulars, consisted of a sufficient quantity of linen and some English thin stuffs for clothing the Spaniards that I expected to find there; and enough of them as, by my calculation, might comfortably supply them for seven years. If I remember right, the materials I carried for clothing them, with gloves, hats, shoes, stockings, and all such things as they could want for wearing, amounted to over two hundred pounds, including some beds, bedding, and household stuff—particularly, kitchen utensils, with pots, kettles, pewter, brass, etc.; and near a hundred pounds more in ironwork, nails, tools of every kind, staples, hooks, hinges, and every necessary thing I could think of.

I carried also a hundred spare arms, muskets, and fusils, besides some pistols, a considerable quantity of shot of all sizes, three or four tons of lead, and two pieces of brass cannon; and because I knew not what time and what extremities I was providing for, I carried a hundred barrels of powder, besides swords, cutlasses, and the iron part of some pikes and halberds; so that, in short, we had a large magazine of all sorts of stores. And I made my nephew carry two small quarterdeck guns more than he wanted for his ship, to leave behind if there was occasion; that when we came there, we might build a fort and man it against all sorts of enemies; and, indeed, I at first thought there would be need enough for all, and much more, if we hoped to maintain our possession of the island, as shall be seen in the course of the story.

I had no such bad luck on this voyage as I had been used to meet with and, therefore, shall have the less occasion to interrupt the reader, who, perhaps, may be impatient to hear how matters went with my colony. Yet some odd accidents, crosswinds, and bad weather happened on this first setting out that made the voyage longer than I expected it at first; and I, who had never made but one voyage—my first voyage to Guinea, in which I might be said to come back again, as the voyage was at first designed—began to think the same ill fate attended me and that I was born to be never content with being on shore and yet to be always unfortunate at sea.

Contrary winds first put us to the northward, and we were obliged to put in at Galway, in Ireland, where we lay wind-bound two-and-twenty days; but we had this satisfaction with the disaster: that provisions here were exceedingly cheap and in the utmost plenty; so that while we lay here, we never touched the ship's stores but rather added to them. Here, also, I took in several live hogs and two cows with their calves, which I resolved, if I had a good passage, to put on shore on my island; but we found occasion to dispose otherwise of them.

Chapter 2

DISASTER AT SEA

We set out on the 5th of February from Ireland and had a very fair gale of wind for some days. As I remember, it might be about the 20th of February, late in the evening, when the mate, having the watch, came into the roundhouse and told us he saw a flash of fire and heard a gun fired; and while he was telling us of it, a boy came in and told us the boatswain heard another. This made us all run out upon the quarterdeck, where, for a while, we heard nothing. But in a few minutes, we saw a very great light and found that there was some very terrible fire at a distance. Immediately, we had recourse to our reckonings, in which we all agreed that there could be no land that way in which the fire showed itself, no, not for five hundred leagues, for it appeared at west-northwest. Upon this, we concluded it must be some ship on fire at sea; and as by our hearing the noise of guns just before, we concluded that it could not be far off. We stood directly toward it and were presently satisfied we should discover it, because the farther we sailed, the greater the light appeared; though, the weather being hazy, we could not perceive anything but the light for a while. In about half an hour's sailing, the wind being fair for us, though not much of it, and the weather clearing up a little, we could plainly discern that it was a great ship on fire in the middle of the sea.

I was most deeply touched with this disaster, though not at all acquainted with the persons engaged in it. I presently recollected my former circumstances and what condition I was in when taken up by the Portuguese captain, and how much more deplorable the circumstances of the poor creatures belonging to that ship must be, if they had no other ship in company with them. Upon this, I immediately ordered that five guns should be fired, one soon after another, so that, if possible, we might give notice to them that there was help for them at hand and that they might endeavor to save themselves in their boat; for though we could see the flames of the ship, yet they, it being night, could see nothing of us.

The ship blew up in the air

We lay by some time upon this, only driving as the burning ship drove, waiting for daylight; when, suddenly, to our great horror, though we had reason to expect it, the ship blew up in the air. Immediately—that is to say, in a few minutes—all the fire was out: that is to say, the rest of the ship sank. This was a terrible and, indeed, an afflicting sight, for the sake of the poor men, who, I concluded, must be either all destroyed in the ship, or be in the utmost distress in their boat in the middle of the ocean, which, at present, as it was dark, I could not see. However, to direct them as well as I could, I caused lights to be hung out in all parts of the ship where we could, and which we had lanterns for, and kept firing guns all the night long, letting them know by this that there was a ship not far off.

About eight o'clock in the morning, we discovered the ship's boats by the help of our perspective glasses[1] and found there were two of them, both thronged with people and deep in the water. We perceived they rowed, the wind being against them; that they saw our ship and did their utmost to make us see them.

---

1. Telescope.

We immediately spread our ancient,[2] to let them know we saw them, and hung a waft[3] out, as a signal for them to come on board. Then we made more sail, standing directly to them. In little more than half an hour, we came up with them and, in a word, took them all in, being no less than sixty-four men, women, and children, for there were a great many passengers.

Upon inquiry, we found it was a French merchant ship of three hundred tons, homeward-bound from Quebec on the river of Canada. The master gave us a long account of the distress of his ship: how the fire began in the steerage by the negligence of the steersman; but on his crying out for help, it was, as everybody thought, entirely put out. But they soon found that some sparks of the first fire had got into some part of the ship so difficult to come at that they could not effectually quench it; and afterward getting in between the timbers and within the ceiling of the ship, it proceeded into the hold and resisted all the skill and all the application they were able to exert.

They had no more to do then but to get into their boats, which, to their great comfort, were pretty large, being their longboat and a great shallop, besides a small skiff, which was of no great service to them other than to get some fresh water and provisions into her after they had secured their lives from the fire. They had, indeed, small hope of their lives by getting into these boats, at that distance from land; only, as they said, they thus escaped from the fire, and there was a possibility that some ship might happen to be at sea and might take them in. They had sails, oars, and a compass and were preparing to make the best of their way back to Newfoundland, the wind blowing pretty fair, for it blew an easy gale at southeast by east. They had as much provision and water as, with sparing it so as to be next door to starving, might support them about twelve days, in which, if they had no bad weather and no contrary winds, the captain said he hoped he might get to the banks of Newfoundland and might perhaps take some fish to sustain them till they might go on shore. But there were so many chances against them in all these cases: such as storms to overset and founder them; rains and cold to benumb and perish their limbs; contrary winds to keep them off course and starve them; that it would have been next to miraculous had they escaped.

In the midst of their consternation, everyone being hopeless and ready to despair, the captain, with tears in his eyes, told me they were suddenly overjoyed by hearing a gun fire—and after that four more: These were the five

---

2. The word, derived from the French *enseigne*, for a flag or the man who carries it.
3. A signal flag.

guns that I caused to be fired at first seeing the light. This revived their hearts and gave them notice, which, as before, I desired it should: that there was a ship at hand for their help. It was upon the hearing of these guns that they took down their masts and sails—the sound coming from the windward—and resolved to lie by till morning. Some time after this, hearing no more guns, they fired three muskets, one a considerable while after another; but these, the wind being contrary, we never heard.

Some time after that they were still more agreeably surprised with seeing our lights, and hearing the guns, which, as I have said, I caused to be fired all the rest of the night. This set them to work with their oars, to keep their boats ahead, at least, that we might the sooner come up with them; and, at last, to their inexpressible joy, they found we saw them.

It is impossible for me to express the many gestures, the strange ecstasies, the variety of postures, with which these poor delivered people expressed the joy of their souls at so unexpected a deliverance. Grief and fear are easily described; sighs, tears, groans, and a very few motions of the head and hands, make up the sum of its variety; but an excess of joy, a surprise of joy, has a thousand extravagances in it. There were some in tears; some raging and tearing themselves, as if they had been in the greatest agonies of sorrow; some stark raving and downright lunatic; some ran about the ship stamping with their feet, others wringing their hands; some were dancing, some singing, some laughing, more crying, many struck dumb, unable to speak a word; others sick and vomiting; several swooning or ready to faint; and a few were crossing themselves and giving God thanks.

I would not wrong them either. There might be many who were thankful afterward, but the passion was too strong for them at first, and they were not able to master it. They were thrown into ecstasies and a kind of frenzy—and it was but a very few who were composed and serious in their joy.

Perhaps, also, the situation may have been affected by the particular circumstance of the nation they belonged to: I mean the French, whose temper is allowed to be more volatile, more passionate, and more sprightly and their spirits more fluid than those of other nations. I am not philosopher enough to determine the cause; but nothing I had ever seen before came up to it. The ecstasies poor Friday, my trusty savage, was in, when he found his father in the boat, came the nearest to it; and the surprise of the master and his two companions, whom I delivered from the villains who set them on shore on the island, came a little way toward it—but nothing could possibly compare to this, either that I saw in Friday, or anywhere else in my life.

Gratitude of the Saved

It is further observable that these extravagances did not show themselves, as described, in different persons only, but the entire range of emotions would appear, in a short succession of moments, in one and the same person. A man that we saw this minute dumb and, as it were, stupid and confounded, would the next minute be dancing and halloing like an antic;[4] and the next moment be tearing his hair or pulling his clothes to pieces and stamping them under his feet like a madman; in a few moments after we would have him all in tears, then sick and swooning, and, had not immediate help been had, he would in a few minutes have been dead. Thus it was, not with one or two, or ten or twenty, but with the greatest part of them; and if I remember right, our surgeon was obliged to let blood[5] of about thirty of them.

There were two priests among them: one an old man, and the other a young man; and that which was strangest was, the oldest man was the worst. As soon as he set his foot on board our ship and saw himself safe, he dropped down stone dead to all appearances—not the least sign of life could be perceived in him. Our surgeon immediately applied proper remedies to recover him and was the only man on the ship who believed he was not dead. At length he opened a vein in his arm, having first chafed and rubbed the part, so as to warm it as much as possible. Upon this, the blood, which only dropped at first, flowed freely. In three minutes after, the man opened his eyes; and a quarter of an hour after that, he spoke, grew better, and in a little time became quite well. After the blood was stopped, he walked about, told us he was perfectly well, took a dram of cordial that the surgeon gave him, and had come to himself. About a quarter of an hour after this, they came running into the cabin to the surgeon—who was bleeding a French woman that had fainted—and told him the priest was gone stark mad. It seems he had begun to revolve the change of his circumstances in his mind, and again this put him into an ecstasy of joy. His spirits whirled about faster than the vessels could convey them, the blood grew hot and feverish, and the man was as fit for Bedlam[6] as any creature that ever was in it. The surgeon would not bleed him again in that condition, but gave him something to doze and put him to sleep—which, after some time, operated upon him, and he awoke the next morning perfectly composed and well.

The younger priest behaved with great command of his passions and was

---

4. A clown or mountebank.
5. Bleeding the ill was a common medical practice then.
6. London insane asylum.

really an example of a serious, well-governed mind. At his first coming on board the ship, he threw himself flat on his face, prostrating himself in thankfulness for his deliverance, in which I unhappily and unnecessarily disturbed him, really thinking he had been in a swoon. But he spoke calmly, thanked me, told me he was giving God thanks for his deliverance, begged me to leave him a few moments, and that, next after his Maker, he would give me thanks also.

I was heartily sorry that I disturbed him, and not only left him but kept others from disturbing him also. He continued in that posture about three minutes or so after I left him, then came to me, as he had said he would, and, with a great deal of seriousness and affection, but with tears in his eyes, thanked me, who had, under God, given him and so many miserable creatures their lives. I told him I had no need to tell him to thank God for it, rather than me, for I had seen that he had done that already; but I added that it was nothing but what reason and humanity dictated to all men and that we had as much reason as he to give thanks to God, who had blessed us so far as to make us the instruments of His mercy to so many of His creatures.

After this the young priest applied himself to his countrymen: labored to compose them; persuaded, entreated, argued, reasoned with them, and did his utmost to keep them within the exercise of their reason. With some he had success, though others for a time lost all self-control.

I cannot help committing this to writing, as perhaps it may be useful to those into whose hands it may fall, for guiding them in the extravagances of their passions. For if an excess of joy can carry us out to such a length beyond the reach of our reason, what will not the extravagances of anger, rage, and a provoked mind carry us to? And, indeed, here I saw reason for keeping an exceeding watch over our passions of every kind: as much for joy and satisfaction as for sorrow and anger.

We were somewhat unnerved by these extravagances among our new guests, for the first day. But after they had retired to lodgings provided for them as well as our ship would allow, and they had slept heartily—as most of them did, being fatigued and frightened—they were quite another sort of people the next day.

Nothing of good manners, or civil acknowledgments for the kindness shown them, was wanting. The French, it is known, are naturally apt enough to exceed that way. The captain and one of the priests came to me the next day and desired to speak with me and my nephew. The commander began to consult with us what should be done with them. First, they told us we had saved their lives, so all they had was little enough return to us for that kindness received. The captain said they had saved some money and some things of value in their boats, caught hastily out of the flames, and if we would accept it, they were ordered to make an offer of it all to us; they only desired to be set on shore somewhere in our way, where, if possible, they might get a passage to France. My nephew wished to accept their money at first and to consider what to do with them afterward, but I overruled him in that part, for I knew what it was to be set on shore in a strange country. And if the Portuguese captain that took me up at sea had served me so, and taken all I had for my deliverance, I must have starved, or have been as much a slave at the Brazils as I had been at Barbary, the mere being sold to a Mahometan excepted; and perhaps a Portuguese is not a much better master than a Turk, if not, in some cases, much worse.

I therefore told the French captain that we had taken them up in their distress, it was true, but that it was our duty to do so, as we were fellow creatures, and we would desire to be so delivered, if we were in the like or any other extremity; that we had done nothing for them but what we believed they would have done for us, if we had been in their situation, and they in ours; but that we took them up to save them, not to plunder them, and it would be a most barbarous thing to take that little from them which they had saved out of the fire and then set them on shore and leave them; that this would be first to save them from death and then kill them ourselves—save them from drowning and abandon them to starving; and, therefore, I would not let the least thing be taken from them. As to setting them on shore, I told them, indeed, that was exceedingly difficult, for the ship was bound to the East Indies. And though we were driven out of our course to the westward a very great way, and perhaps were directed by Heaven on purpose for their deliverance, yet it was impossible for us deliberately to change our course on their particular account; nor could my nephew, the captain, answer so to the freighters, with whom he was under charter to pursue his voyage by way of Brazil. All I knew we could do for them was to put ourselves in the way of meeting with other ships homeward bound from the West Indies and get them a passage, if possible, to England or France.

The first part of the proposal was so generous and kind, they could not but be very thankful for it; but they were in very great consternation, especially the passengers, at the notion of being carried away to the East Indies. They then entreated me that as I was driven so far to the westward before I met with them, I would, at least, keep on the same course to the banks of Newfoundland, where it was probable I might meet with some ship or sloop that they might hire to carry them back to Canada, from whence they came.

I thought this was but a reasonable request on their part, and therefore I inclined to agree to it; for, indeed, I considered that to carry this whole company to the East Indies would not only be an intolerable severity upon the poor people, but would be ruining our whole voyage, by their devouring all our provisions. So I thought it no breach of charter party but what an unforeseen accident made absolutely necessary to us, and in which no one could say we were to blame; for the laws of God and nature would have forbid that we should refuse to take up two boats full of people in such a distressed condition; and the nature of the thing, as well respecting ourselves as the poor people, obliged us to set them on shore somewhere or other for their deliverance. So I consented that we would carry them to Newfoundland, if wind and weather would permit; and if not, that I would carry them to Martinique, in the West Indies.

The wind continued fresh easterly, but the weather was pretty good; and as the winds had continued in the points between northeast and southeast a long time, we missed several opportunities of sending them to France; for we met several ships bound to Europe, whereof two were French, from St. Christopher's; but they had been so long beating up against the wind that they dared not take in passengers, for fear of lacking provisions for the voyage, as well for themselves as for those they should take in; so we were obliged to go on. It was about a week after this that we made the Banks of Newfoundland, where, to shorten my story, we put all our French people on board a bark, which they hired at sea there, to put them on shore and afterward to carry them to France, if they could get provisions to victual themselves with. When I say all the French went on shore, I should remember that the young priest I spoke of, hearing we were bound to the East Indies, desired to go on the voyage with us and to be set on shore on the coast of Coromandel, which I readily agreed to, for I wonderfully liked the man, and had very good reason, as will appear afterward. Also, four of the seamen entered themselves on our ship and proved very useful fellows.

Making for the West Indies

From hence we directed our course for the West Indies, steering away south and south by east for about twenty days together, sometimes with little or no wind at all; when we met with another subject for our humanity to work upon, almost as deplorable as that before.

It was in the latitude of 27 degrees 5 minutes north, on the 19th day of March 1695, when we spied a sail, our course southeast and by south. We soon perceived it was a large vessel and that she bore up to us. We could not at first know what to make of her, till, after coming a little nearer, we found she had lost her main topmast, foremast, and bowsprit; and presently she fired a gun as a signal of distress. The weather was pretty good, wind at north-northwest, a fresh gale, and we soon came to speak with her.

We found her a ship of Bristol, bound home from Barbados, but she had been blown out of the road[7] at Barbados a few days before she was ready to sail, by a terrible hurricane, while the captain and chief mate were both gone on shore; so that, besides the terror of the storm, they had no one on board qualified to bring the ship home. They had been already nine weeks at sea and had met with another terrible storm after the hurricane was over, which had blown them so far off course they knew not where they were—worse yet, during that storm, they had lost their masts. They told us they expected to have seen the Bahama Islands, but were then driven away again to the southeast, by a strong gale of wind at north-northwest, the same that blew now; and having no sails to work the ship with but a main course and a kind of square sail upon a jury foremast, which they had set up, they could not lie near the wind, but were endeavoring to stand away for the Canaries.

The Starving Crew

But that which was worst of all was that they were almost starved for want of provisions, besides the fatigues they had undergone. Their bread and meat were quite gone; they had not one ounce left on the ship and had had none for eleven days. The only relief they had was that their water was not all spent, and they had about half a barrel of flour left; they had sugar enough; some succades, or sweetmeats, they had at first, but they were all devoured; and they had seven casks of rum.

There was a youth, and his mother, and a maidservant on board, who were passengers and, thinking the ship was ready to sail, unhappily came on board the evening before the hurricane began. Having no provisions of their own left, they were in a more deplorable condition than the rest, for the seamen, being reduced to such an extreme necessity themselves, had no compassion, we may be sure, for the poor passengers; and they were, indeed, in such a condition that their misery is very hard to describe.

I had perhaps not known this part, if my curiosity had not led me (the weather being fair, and the wind abated) to go on board the ship. The second mate, who upon this occasion commanded the ship, had been on board our ship, and he told me they had three passengers in the great cabin that were in a deplorable condition.

---

7. Main shipping channel.

"Nay," said he, "I believe they are dead, for I have heard nothing of them for above two days, and I was afraid to inquire after them . . . for I had nothing to relieve them with."

We immediately applied ourselves to give them what relief we could spare; and, indeed, I had so far overruled things with my nephew that I would have victualed them, though we had gone away to Virginia, or any other part of the coast of America, to have supplied ourselves; but there was no necessity for that.

But now they were in a new danger, for they were afraid of eating too much, even of that little we gave them. The mate, or commander, brought six men with him in his boat; but these poor wretches looked like skeletons and were so weak that they could hardly sit to their oars. The mate himself was very ill and half-starved, for he declared he had reserved nothing from the men and went share and share alike with them in every bit they ate.

I cautioned him to eat sparingly but set meat before him immediately. He had not

The mate brought six men with him

eaten three mouthfuls before he began to be sick, so he stopped awhile. Our surgeon mixed him something with some broth, which he said would be to him both food and physic; and after he had taken it, he grew better. In the meantime, I forgot not the men: I ordered victuals to be given them, and the poor creatures rather devoured than ate it. They were so exceedingly hungry that they were in a manner ravenous and had no command over themselves; and two of them ate with so much greediness that they were in danger of losing their lives the next morning.

The sight of these people's distress was very moving to me and brought to mind the terrible prospect of my first coming on shore on my island, where I had never the least mouthful of food, or any prospect of procuring any; besides the hourly apprehensions I had of being made the food of other creatures. But all the while the mate was thus relating to me the miserable condition of the ship's company, I could not put out of my thought the story he had told me of the three poor creatures in the great cabin: namely, the mother, her son, and the maidservant, whom he had heard nothing of for two or three days, and whom, he seemed to confess, they had wholly neglected, their own extremities being so great—by which I understood that they had really given them no food at all and that therefore they must be perished and be all lying dead, perhaps, on the floor or deck of the cabin.

As I therefore kept the mate, whom we then called "Captain," on board with his men to refresh them, so I also forgot not the starving crew that were left on board. I ordered my own boat to go on board the ship and, with my mate and twelve men, to carry them a sack of bread and four or five pieces of beef to boil. Our surgeon charged the men to cause the meat to be boiled while they stayed and to keep guard in the cook-room, to prevent the men taking it to eat raw, or taking it out of the pot before it was well boiled, and then to give every man but a very little at a time. By this caution he preserved the men, who would otherwise have killed themselves with that very food that was given them on purpose to save their lives.

At the same time, I ordered the mate to go into the great cabin and see what condition the poor passengers were in; and if they were alive, to comfort them and give them what refreshment was proper. The surgeon gave him a large pitcher, with some of the prepared broth that he had given the mate that was on board, and which he did not question would restore them gradually.

I was not satisfied with this, but, as I said above, having a great mind to see the scene of misery that I knew the ship itself would present me with, in a more truthful manner than I could have it by report, I took the captain of the ship, as we now called him, with me and went myself, a little after, in their boat.

I found the poor men on board almost in a tumult, trying to get the victuals out of the boiler before it was ready. But the mate observed his orders and kept a good guard at the cook-room door; and the men he placed there, after using all possible persuasion for them to have patience, kept them off by force. However, he caused some biscuit cakes to be dipped in the pot and softened with the liquor of the meat, which they called brewis, and gave them every one some to stay their stomachs and told them it was for their own safety that he was obliged to give them but little at a time. But it was all in vain; and had I not come on board, and their own commander and officers with me, and with wise counsel and some threats also of giving them no more, I believe they would have broken into the cook-room by force and torn the meat out of the furnace; for words are indeed of very small force to a hungry belly. However, we pacified them and fed them gradually and cautiously at first, and the next time gave them more, and at last filled their bellies, and the men did well enough.

But the misery of the poor passengers in the cabin was of another nature and far beyond the rest, for as, first, the ship's company had so little for themselves, it was but too true that they had kept them very low at the start and at last totally neglected them, so that for six or seven days it might be said they had received really no food at all, and for several days before very little. The poor mother, who, as the men reported, was a woman of sense and good breeding, had spared all she could so affectionately for her son that at last she entirely sank under it; and when the mate of our ship went in, she sat upon the floor or deck, with her back up against the sides, between two chairs, which were lashed fast, and her head sunk between her shoulders, like a corpse, though not quite dead. My mate said all he could to revive and encourage her and, with a spoon, put some broth into her mouth. She opened her lips and lifted up one hand, but could not speak. Yet she understood what he said and made signs to him, intimating that it was too late for her, but pointed to her child, as if she would have said, *Please take care of him!* However, the mate, who was exceedingly moved at the sight, endeavored to get some of the broth into her mouth and, as he said, got two or three spoonfuls down; though I question whether he could be sure of it or not—but it was too late, and she died that same night.

The youth, who was preserved at the price of his most affectionate

I found the poor men on board almost in a tumult

mother's life, was not so far gone; yet he lay in a cabin bed, as one stretched out with hardly any life in him. He had a piece of an old glove in his mouth, having eaten up the rest of it. However, being young and having more strength than his mother, the mate got something down his throat, and he gradually began to revive; though by giving him, sometime after, but two or three extra spoonfuls, he was very sick and brought it up again.

But the next care was the poor maid. She lay all alone upon the deck, close to her mistress, just like one who had fallen down with a stroke, and struggled for life. Her limbs were distorted; one of her hands was clasped around the frame of the chair, and she gripped it so hard that we could not easily make her let it go; her other arm lay over her head, and her feet lay both together, set fast against the frame of the cabin table. In short, she lay just like one in the agonies of death, and yet she was alive, too.

The poor creature was not only starved with hunger and terrified with the thoughts of death, but, as the men told us afterward, was brokenhearted for her mistress, whom she saw dying for two or three days before and whom she loved most tenderly.

We knew not what to do with this poor girl, for when our surgeon, who was a man of very great knowledge and experience, had, with great application, recovered her as to life, he had her upon his hands still; for she was little less than distracted for a considerable time after.

Whoever shall read these memorandums must consider that visits at sea are not like a journey into the country, where sometimes people stay a week or a fortnight at a place. Our business was to relieve this distressed ship's crew but not lie by for them; and though they were willing to steer the same course with us for some days, yet we could carry no sail, to keep pace with a ship that had no masts. However, as their captain begged of us to help him to set up a main topmast and a kind of topmast to his jury foremast, we did, as it were, lie by him for three or four days. Then, having given him five barrels of beef, a barrel of pork, two hogsheads of biscuit, and a proportion of peas, flour, and what other things we could spare; and taking three casks of sugar, some rum, and some pieces of eight from them in return, we left them, taking on board with us, at their own earnest request, the youth and the maid and all their goods.

The young lad was about seventeen years of age; a pretty, well-bred, modest, and sensible youth, greatly dejected with the loss of his mother; and, as it seems, he had lost his father but a few months before at Barbados. He begged of the surgeon to speak to me to take him out of the ship, for he said the cruel fellows had murdered his mother. And, indeed, so they had, that is to say, passively; for they might have spared a small sustenance to the poor helpless widow that might have preserved her life, though it had been but just enough to keep her alive. But hunger knows no friend, no relation, no justice, no right, and therefore is remorseless and capable of no compassion.

The surgeon told him how far we were going and that it would carry him away from all his friends and put him, perhaps, in as bad circumstances almost as those we found him in—that is to say, starving in the world. He said it mattered not whither he went, if he was but delivered from the terrible crew that he was among; that the captain (by which he meant me, for he could know nothing of my nephew) had saved his life, and he was sure would not hurt him; and as for the maid, he was sure, if she came to herself, she would be very thankful for it, let us carry them where we would. The surgeon represented the case so earnestly to me that I yielded, and we took them both on board, with all their goods, except eleven hogsheads of sugar, which could not be removed or come at; and as the youth had a bill of lading for them, I made his commander sign a document, obliging himself to go as soon as he came to Bristol, to one Mr. Rogers (a merchant there), to whom the youth said he was related, and to deliver a letter that I wrote to him and all the goods he had belonging to the deceased widow; which I suppose was not done, for apparently the ship never did get to Bristol, but was probably lost at sea, being in so disabled a condition and so far from any land that I am of opinion the first storm she met with afterward, she most likely foundered in the sea, for she was leaky and had damage in her hold when we met with her.

Chapter 3

BACK HOME

I was now in the latitude of 19 degrees 32 minutes and had hitherto a tolerable voyage as to weather, though, at first, the winds had been contrary. I shall trouble nobody with the little incidents of wind, weather, currents, etc., on the rest of our voyage; but, to shorten my story, shall observe that I came to my old habitation, the island, on the 10th of April 1695. It was with no small difficulty that I found the place, for as I came to it and went from it before on the south and east side of the island, coming from the Brazils, so now, coming in between the main and the island and having no chart for the coast, nor any landmark, I did not know it when I saw it, or know whether I saw it or not.

We beat about a great while and went on shore on several islands in the mouth of the great river Oronooque, but without success. But this I learned by my coasting the shore: that I was under one great mistake before—namely, that the continent which I thought I saw from the island I lived on was really no continent but a long island, or rather a ridge of islands, reaching from one to the other side of the extended mouth of that great river; and that the savages who came to my island were not properly those that we call Caribbees, but islanders and other barbarians of the same kind who inhabited nearer to our side than the rest.

In short, I visited several of these islands to no purpose; some I found were inhabited, and some were not. On one of them I found some Spaniards and thought they had lived there; but speaking with them, I found they had a sloop lying in a small creek hard by and came thither to make salt and to catch some pearl mussels if they could. But they belonged to the Isla de Trinidad, which lay farther north, in the latitude of 10 and 11 degrees.

Thus, coasting from one island to another, sometimes with the ship, sometimes with the Frenchmen's shallop (which we had found a convenient boat

I came fair on the south side of my island

and therefore kept her with their very goodwill), at length I came fair on the south side of my island and presently knew the very countenance of the place. So I brought the ship safely to an anchor, broadside with the little creek where my old habitation was.

As soon as I saw the place, I called for Friday and asked him if he knew where he was. He looked about a little and presently, clapping his hands, cried, "Oh, yes! Oh, there—oh, yes; oh, there!" pointing to our old habitation. He fell dancing and capering like a mad fellow, and I had much ado to keep him from jumping into the sea to swim ashore to the place.

"Well, Friday," said I, "do you think we shall find anybody here or no? And do you think we shall see your father?"

The fellow stood mute as a stock a good while; but when I named his father, the poor affectionate creature looked dejected, and I could see the tears run down his face very plentifully.

"What is the matter, Friday?" said I. "Are you troubled because you may see your father?"

"No, no," said he, shaking his head, "no see him more. No, never more see him again."

"Why so, Friday?" said I. "How do you know that?"

"Oh no, oh no," said Friday. "He long ago die, long ago. He much old man."

"Well, well," said I, "Friday, you don't know. But shall we see anyone else, then?"

The fellow, it seemed, had better eyes than I, and he pointed to the hill just above my old house; and though we lay half a league off, he cried out, "Me see, me see, yes, yes, me see much man there, and there, and there!"

I looked, but I saw nobody—no, not with a perspective glass, which was, I suppose, because I could not find the right place; for the fellow was right, as I found upon inquiry the next day; and there were five or six men all together, who stood to look at the ship, not knowing what to think of us.

As soon as Friday told me he saw people, I caused the English ancient to be spread and fired three guns, to give them notice we were friends. In about half a quarter of an hour after we perceived a smoke arise from the side of the creek; so I immediately ordered a boat out, taking Friday with me. Hanging out a white flag, or a flag of truce, I went directly on shore, taking with me the young friar I mentioned, to whom I had told the story of my living there and the manner of it and every particular, both of myself and those I left there, and who was, on that account, extremely desirous to go with me. We had, besides, about sixteen men well armed, just in case we had found any new guests there that we did not know of; but we had no need of weapons.

Ancient Haunts

As we went on shore upon the tide, near high water, we rowed directly into the creek. The first man I fixed my eye upon was the Spaniard whose life I had saved and whom I knew by his face perfectly well. As to his habit, I shall describe it afterward. I ordered nobody to go on shore at first but myself; but there was no keeping Friday in the boat, for the affectionate creature had spied his father at a great distance, a good way off from the Spaniards, where, indeed, I saw nothing of him; and if they had not let him go ashore, he would have jumped into the sea. He was no sooner on shore, but he flew away to his father, like an arrow out of a bow. It would have made any man shed tears, in spite of the firmest resolution, to have seen the first transports of this poor fellow's joy when he came to his father: how he embraced him, kissed him, stroked his face, took him up in his arms, set him down upon a tree, and lay down by him; then stood and looked at him, as anyone would look at a strange picture, for a quarter of an hour together; then lay down on the ground and stroked his legs and kissed them, and then got up again and stared at him. One would have thought the fellow bewitched. But it would have made a dog laugh the next day to see how differently he expressed filial love. In the morning, he walked along the shore, and again with his father, several hours, always leading him by the hand, as if he had been a lady; and every now and then he would come to a boat to fetch something or other for him, either a lump of sugar, a dram, a biscuit cake, or something or other that was good. In the afternoon his frolics ran another way, for then he would set the old man down upon the ground and dance about him, making a thousand antic postures and gestures. All the while he did this he would be talking to him and telling him one story or another of his travels and of what happened to him abroad, to divert him. In short, if the same filial affection was to be found in Christians to their parents in our part of the world, one would be tempted to say there would hardly be any need of the fifth commandment.

But this is a digression: I return to my landing. It would be endless to take notice of all the ceremonies and civilities that the Spaniards received me with. The first Spaniard, whom, as I said, I knew very well, was he whose life I had saved. He came toward the boat, attended by one more, carrying a flag of truce also. He not only did not know me at first, but he had no inkling, no notion, of its being me that was come, till I spoke to him.

"Seignior," said I in Portuguese, "do you not know me?"

At which he spoke not a word, but, giving his musket to the man who was with him, he threw up his arms and, saying something in Spanish that I did not perfectly hear, came forward and embraced me, telling me it was inexcusable not to know that face again that he had once seen as if an angel from Heaven sent to save his life. He said an abundance of very handsome things, as a well-bred Spaniard always knows how; then, beckoning to the person that attended him, he bade him go and call out his comrades. He then asked me if I would walk to my old habitation, where he would give me possession of my own house again, and where I should see they had made but mean improvements; so I walked along with him. But, alas, I could no more find the place again than if I had never been there, for they had planted so many trees and placed them in such a position, so thick and close to one another, and in ten years' time they were grown so big, that, in short, the place was inaccessible, except by such windings and blind ways as they themselves only, who made them, could find.

I asked them what reasons there were for all these fortifications; he told me I would say there was need enough of it when they had given me an account how they had passed their time since their arriving on the island, especially after they had the misfortune to find that I was gone. He told me he could

"Seignior, do you not know me?"

not but have some satisfaction in my good fortune when he heard that I was gone in a good ship, and that he had oftentimes a strange presentiment that one time or other he should see me again. But nothing that ever befell him in his life, he said, was so surprising and afflicting to him at first as his terrible disappointment when he came back to the island and found I was not there.

The Spaniard's Tale

As to the three barbarians (so he called them) that were left behind, and of whom, he said, he had a long story to tell me, the Spaniards all thought themselves much better off among the savages, only that their number was so small.

"And," said he, "had they been strong enough, we had been all long ago in purgatory." With that he crossed himself on the breast. "But, sir," said he, "I hope you will not be displeased when I shall tell you how, forced by necessity, we were obliged for our own preservation to disarm them and make them our subjects, as they would not be content with being moderately our masters, but would be our murderers."

I answered that I had been afraid of that when I left them there, and nothing troubled me more at my parting from the island but that they had not come back that I might have put them in possession of everything first and left the Englishmen in a state of subjection, as they deserved. But if they had been reduced to do it to them, then I would be very glad and be far from finding any fault with it, for I knew they were a parcel of refractory, ungovernable villains and were fit for any manner of mischief.

While I was saying this, the man came whom he had sent back, and with him eleven more. In the dress they were in, it was impossible to guess what nation they were of, but he made all clear both to them and to me.

First, he turned to me and, pointing to them, said, "These, sir, are some of the gentlemen who owe their lives to you."

Then, turning to them and pointing to me, he let them know who I was; upon which they all came up, one by one, not as if they had been sailors and ordinary fellows, and the like, but really as if they had been ambassadors or noblemen, and I a monarch or great conqueror. Their behavior was, to the last degree, obliging and courteous, and yet mixed with a manly, majestic gravity, which very well became them. In short, they had so much more manners than I that I scarcely knew how to receive their civilities, much less how to return them in kind.

The history of their coming to, and conduct on, the island after my going away is so very remarkable and has so many incidents, which the former part of my story will help to understand, and which will, in most of the particulars, refer to the account I have already given, that I cannot but commit them, with great delight, to the reading of those who come after me.

I shall collect the facts historically, as near as I can gather them out of my memory, from what they related to me and from what I met with in my conversing with them and with the place.

In order to do this succinctly, and as intelligibly as I can, I must go back to the circumstances in which I left the island and in which the persons were of whom I am to speak. First, it is necessary to repeat that I had sent away Friday's father and the Spaniard (the two whose lives I had rescued from the savages) in a large canoe to the main, as I then thought it, to fetch over the Spaniard's companions that he left behind him, in order to save them from the like calamity that he had been in and in order to succor them for the present; and that, if possible, we might together find some way for our deliverance afterward.

When I sent them away, I had no visible appearance of, or the least room to hope for, my own deliverance, any more than I had twenty years before— much less had I any foreknowledge of what afterward happened, I mean, of an English ship coming on shore there that would end up fetching me off. And it could not be but a very great surprise to them when they came back, not only to find that I was gone but to find three strangers left on the spot, possessed of all that I had left behind me, which would otherwise have been their own.

The first thing, however, that I inquired into, that I might begin where I left off, was of their own part; and I desired the Spaniard would give me a particular account of his voyage back to his countrymen with the boat, when I sent him to fetch them over. He told me there was little of interest in that part, for nothing remarkable happened to them on the way, having had very calm weather and a smooth sea. As for his countrymen, it could not be doubted, he said, but that they were overjoyed to see him (it seems he was the principal man among them, the captain of the vessel they had been shipwrecked in having been dead some time). They were, he said, the more surprised to see him because they knew he was fallen into the hands of the savages, who, they were satisfied, would devour him, as they did all the rest of their prisoners; that when he told them the story of his deliverance, and in what manner he was furnished for carrying them away, it was like a dream to them, and their astonishment, he said, was somewhat like that of Joseph's brethren when he told them who he was and the story of his exaltation in Pharaoh's court. But when he showed them the arms, the powder, the ball, and provisions that he brought them for their journey or voyage, they were restored to themselves, took a just share of the joy of their deliverance, and immediately prepared to come away with him.

Their first business was to get canoes, and in this they were obliged to be a little devious honesty-wise and to trespass upon the kindness of their friendly savages, "borrowing" two large canoes, or *periaguas,* on pretense of going out a-fishing, or for pleasure. In these they came away the next morning. It seems they wasted no time in getting themselves ready; for they had no baggage, neither clothes, nor provisions, nor anything in the world but what they had on them, and a few roots to eat, which they used to make their bread.

They were in all three weeks' absent; and in that time, unluckily for them, I had the occasion offered for my escape, as I mentioned in the other part, and to get off from the island, leaving three of the most impudent, hardened, ungovernable, disagreeable villains behind me that any man could desire to meet with—to the poor Spaniards's great grief and disappointment, you may be sure.

The only just thing the rogues did was that when the Spaniards came ashore, they gave my letter to them and gave them provisions and other relief, as I had ordered them to do. Also, they gave them the long paper of directions that I had left with them, containing the particular methods that I took for managing every part of my life there: the way I baked my bread, bred up tame goats, and planted my corn; how I cured my grapes, made my pots, and, in a word, everything I did. All this being written down, they gave it to the Spaniards (two of them understood English well enough). Nor did they refuse to accommodate the Spaniards with anything else, for they agreed very well for some time. They gave them an equal admission into the house, or cave, and they began to live very sociably. The head Spaniard, who had seen pretty much of my methods, and Friday's father together managed all their affairs. As for the Englishmen, they did nothing but ramble about the island, shoot parrots, and catch tortoises; and when they came home at night, the Spaniards provided their suppers for them.

The Spaniards would have been satisfied with this had the others but let them alone, which, however, they could not find in their hearts to do long; but like the dog in the manger, they would not eat themselves, neither would they let the others eat. The differences, nevertheless, were at first but trivial and such as are not worth relating, but at last it broke out into open war. It began with all the rudeness and insolence that can be imagined—without reason, without provocation, contrary to nature, and, indeed, to common sense. Though, it is true, the first relation of it came from the Spaniards themselves, whom I may call the accusers, yet when I came to examine the fellows, they could not deny a word of it.

A Mutiny

But before I come to the particulars of this part, I must supply a defect in my earlier account; and this was, I forgot to set down, among the rest, that just as we were weighing the anchor to set sail, there happened a little quarrel on board of our ship, which I was once afraid would have turned to a second mutiny. Nor was it appeased till the captain, rousing up his courage and taking us all to his assistance, parted them by force, and making two of the most refractory fellows prisoners, he laid them in irons. As they had been active in the former disorders and let fall some ugly, dangerous words, the second time he threatened to carry them in irons to England and have them hanged there for mutiny and running away with the ship. This, it seems, though the captain did not intend to do it, frightened some other men on the ship; and some of them had put it into the heads of the rest that the captain only gave them good words for the present, till they could come to some English port, and that then they should be all put into jail and tried for their lives. The mate got intelligence of this and acquainted us with it; upon which it was desired that I, who still passed for a great man among them, should go down with the mate and satisfy the men, and tell them that they might be assured, if they behaved well the rest of the voyage, all they had done for the time past should be pardoned. So I went, and after passing my honor's word to them, they appeared easy, and the more so when I caused the two men that were in irons to be released and forgiven.

But this mutiny had brought us to an anchor for that night. The wind also falling calm the next morning, we found that our two men who had been laid in irons had stolen each of them a musket and some other weapons (what powder or shot they had we knew not) and had taken the ship's pinnace, which was not yet hauled up, and run away with her to their companions in roguery on shore. As soon as we found this, I ordered the longboat on shore with twelve men and the mate, and away they went to seek the rogues. But they could neither find them nor any of the rest, for they all fled into the woods when they saw the boat coming on shore. The mate was at once resolved, in justice to their roguery, to have destroyed their plantations, burned all their household stuff and furniture, and left them to shift without it. But having no orders, he let it all alone, left everything as he found it, and, bringing the pinnace away, came on board without them. These two men made their number five; but the other three villains were so much more wicked than they that after they had been two or three days together, they turned the two newcomers out of doors to shift for themselves and would have nothing to do with them; nor could they, for a good while, be persuaded to give them any food. As for the Spaniards, they were not yet come.

When the Spaniards came first on shore, the business began to go forward. The Spaniards would have persuaded the three English brutes to have taken in their countrymen again that, as they said, they might be all one family, but they would not hear of it. So the two poor fellows lived by themselves; and finding nothing but industry and application would make them live comfortably, they pitched their tents on the north shore of the island, but a little more to the west, to be out of danger of the savages, who always landed on the east parts of the island.

Here they built them two huts—one to lodge in and the other to lay up their magazines and stores in. The Spaniards having given them some corn for seed and some of the peas that I had left them, they dug, planted, and enclosed, after the pattern I had set for them all, and began to live pretty well. Their first crop of corn was on the ground; and though it was but a little bit of land that they had dug up at first, having had but a little time, yet it was enough to relieve them and find them with bread and other eatables. One of the fellows being the cook's mate of the ship was very ready at making soup, puddings, and such other preparations as the rice and the milk and such little flesh as they got furnished him to do.

They were going on in this little thriving position when the three unnatural rogues, their own countrymen, too, in mere humor and to insult them, came and bullied them. They told them the island was theirs, that the governor (meaning me) had given them the possession of it, and nobody else had any right to it, and that they should build no houses upon their ground unless they would pay rent for them.

Quarrels

The two men, thinking they were jesting at first, asked them to come in, sit down, and see what fine houses they were that they had built and to tell them what rent they demanded. One of them merrily said that if they were the ground landlords, he hoped that if they built tenements upon their land and made improvements, they would, according to the custom of landlords, grant a long lease; and he desired they would get a scrivener to draw up the agreement. One of the three, cursing and raging, told them they should see they were not in jest; and going to a little place at a distance, where the honest men had made a fire to dress their victuals, he took a firebrand and clapped it to the outside of their hut and very fairly set it on fire. It would have been all burned down in a few minutes if one of the two had not run to the fellow, thrust him away, and trod the fire out with his feet, and that not without some difficulty, too.

The fellow was in such a rage at the honest man's thrusting him away that he returned upon him, with a pole he had in his hand, and had not the man avoided the blow very nimbly and run into the hut, he would have ended his days at once. His comrade, seeing the danger they were both in, ran in after him, and immediately they came both out with their muskets, and the man that was first struck at with the pole knocked the fellow down that began the quarrel, with the stock of his musket, and that before the other two could come to help him. Then, seeing the rest come at them, they stood together and, presenting the other ends of their pieces to them, bade them stand off.

The others had firearms with them, too; but one of the two honest men, bolder than his comrade and made desperate by his danger, told them, if they offered to move hand or foot, they were dead men, and boldly commanded them to lay down their arms. They did not, indeed, lay down their arms, but seeing him so resolute, it brought them to a parley, and they consented to take their wounded man with them and be gone; and, indeed, it seems the fellow was wounded sufficiently with the blow. However, they were much in the wrong, since they had the advantage, that they did not disarm them effectually, as they might have done, and have gone immediately to the Spaniards and given them an account how the rogues had treated them; for the three villains studied nothing but revenge, and every day gave them some intimation that they did so.

But not to crowd this part with an account of the lesser part of their rogueries, their greater evils included tricks such as treading down their crops; shooting three young kids and a she-goat, which the poor men had got to breed up tame for their store; and, in a word, plaguing them night and day in this manner. It forced the two men to such a desperation that they resolved to fight them all three the first time they had a fair opportunity. In order to do this, they resolved to go to the castle, as they called it (that was

They bade them stand off

my old dwelling), where the three rogues and the Spaniards all lived together at that time, intending to have a fair battle, and the Spaniards should stand by to see fair play. So they got up in the morning before day and came to the place and called the Englishmen by their names, telling a Spaniard who answered that they wanted to speak with them.

It happened that the day before, two of the Spaniards, having been in the woods, had seen one of the two Englishmen, whom, for distinction, I called the honest men, and he had made a sad complaint to the Spaniards of the barbarous usage they had met with from their three countrymen and how they had ruined their plantation, and destroyed their corn that they had labored so hard to bring to harvest, and killed the milch goat and their three kids, which was all they had provided for their sustenance; and that if he and his friends, meaning the Spaniards, did not assist them again, they should be starved. When the Spaniards came home at night, and they were all at supper, one of them took the freedom to reprove the three Englishmen, though in very gentle and mannerly terms, and asked them how they could be so cruel, they being harmless, inoffensive fellows; that they were putting themselves in a way to subsist by their labor and that it had cost them a great deal of pains to bring things to such perfection as they were then in.

One of the Englishmen returned very briskly, "What had they to do there? They came on shore without leave, and they should not plant or build upon the island. It was none of their ground."

"Why," said the Spaniard very calmly, "Seignior Inglese, they must not starve."

The Englishman replied, like a rough-hewn tarpaulin, "They might starve. They should not plant nor build in that place."

"But what must they do then, Seignior?" said the Spaniard.

Another of the brutes returned, "Do? They should be servants and work for us."

"But how can you expect that of them?" said the Spaniard. "They are not bought with your money; you have no right to make them servants."

The Englishman replied, "The island is ours. The governor has given it to us, and no man has anything to do here but ourselves." With that, he swore by his Maker that they would go and burn all their new huts; they should build none upon their land.

"Why, Seignior," said the Spaniard, "by the same rule, we must be your servants, too."

"Aye," said the bold dog, "and so you shall, too, before we have done with you," mixing two or three oaths in the proper intervals of his speech.

The Spaniard only smiled at that and made him no answer.

However, this little discourse had heated them; and starting up, one said to the other (I think it was he they called Will Atkins), "Come, Jack, let's go, and have t'other brush with them. We'll demolish their castle, I'll warrant you. They shall plant no colony in our dominions."

Upon this, they went all trooping away, with every man a gun, a pistol, and a sword, and muttered some insolent things among themselves of what they would do to the Spaniards, too, when opportunity offered. But the Spaniards, it seems, did not so perfectly understand them as to know all the particulars—only that, in general, they threatened them hard for taking the two Englishmen's part.

Whither they went, or how they bestowed their time that evening, the Spaniards said they did not know; but it seems they wandered about the country for part of the night, and then, lying down in the place that I used to call my bower, they were weary and overslept themselves. The case was this: They had resolved to stay till midnight and so to take the two poor men when they were asleep, and as they acknowledged afterward, they intended to set fire to their huts while they were in them and either burn them there or murder them as they came out. As malice seldom sleeps very soundly, it was very strange they should not have been kept awake.

However, as the two men had also a design upon them, as I have said, though a much fairer one than that of burning and murdering, it happened, and very luckily for them all, that they were up and gone abroad before the bloody-minded rogues came to their huts.

Chapter 4

CIVIL WAR ON THE ISLAND

When they came there and found the men gone, Atkins, who, it seems, was the most insolent of the three, called out to one of his comrades, "Ha, Jack, here's the nest, but the birds are flown." They mused awhile, to think what should be the occasion of their being gone abroad so soon, and concluded presently that the Spaniards had warned them of their attack. With that they shook hands and swore to one another that they would be revenged on the Spaniards. As soon as they had made this bloody bargain, they fell to work with the poor men's habitation. They did not set fire, indeed, to anything, but they pulled down both their houses and pulled them so limb from limb that they left not the least stick standing, or scarce any sign on the ground where they stood. They tore all their little collected household stuff into pieces and threw everything about in such a manner that the poor men afterward found some of their things a mile away from their habitation. When they had done this, they pulled up all the young trees that the poor men had planted; pulled up an enclosure they had made to secure their cattle and their corn; and, in a word, sacked and plundered everything as completely as a horde of Tartars would have done.

The two men were, at this juncture, gone to find them out and had resolved to fight them wherever they had been, though they were but two to three; so that, had they met, there certainly would have been bloodshed among them, for they were all very stout, resolute fellows, to give them their due.

A Knockdown Blow

But Providence took more care to keep them asunder than they themselves could do to meet; for, as if they had dogged one another, when the three were gone thither, the two were here; and afterward, when the two went back to find them, the three were come to the old habitation again—we shall see

The Spaniard, with one blow of his fist, knocked him down

their different conduct presently. When the three came back like violent creatures, flushed with the rage that the work they had been about had put them
into, they came up to the Spaniards and told them what they had done by
way of scoff and bravado.

One of them stepping up to one of the Spaniards, as if they had been a
couple of boys at play, took hold of his hat as it was upon his head, and
giving it a twirl about, jeered in his face, saying, "And you, Seignior Jack
Spaniard, shall have the same sauce, if you do not mend your manners."

The Spaniard, who, though a quiet, civil man, was as brave a man as could
be and, withal, a strong, well-made man, looked at him for a good while and
then, having no weapon in his hand, stepped gravely up to him and, with
one blow of his fist, knocked him down, as an ox is felled with a poleax; at
which one of the rogues, as insolent as the first, fired his pistol at the
Spaniard immediately. He missed his body, indeed, for the bullets went

through his hair, but one of them touched the top of his ear, and he bled pretty much. The blood made the Spaniard believe he was more hurt than he really was, and that put him into some heat, for before he acted all in a perfect calm; but now, resolving to go through with his work, he stooped and took the fellow's musket whom he had knocked down and was just going to shoot the man who had fired at him when the rest of the Spaniards, being in the cave, came out and, calling to him not to shoot, stepped in, secured the other two, and took their arms from them.

When they were thus disarmed and found they had made all the Spaniards their enemies, as well as their own countrymen, they began to cool and, giving the Spaniards more conciliatory words, would have had their arms again. But the Spaniards, considering the feud that was between them and the other two Englishmen and that it would be the best method that they could take to keep them from killing one another, told them they would do them no harm; and if they would live peaceably, they would be very willing to assist and associate with them as they did before; but that they could not think of giving them their arms again, while they appeared so resolved to do mischief with them to their own countrymen and had even threatened them all to make them their servants.

The rogues were now no more capable to hear reason than to act with reason. But being refused their arms, they went raving away and raging like madmen, and they threatened what they would do, though they had no firearms. But the Spaniards, despising their threats, told them they should take care how they offered any injury to their plantation or cattle; for if they did, they would shoot them as they would ravenous beasts, wherever they found them; and if they fell into their hands alive, they should certainly be hanged. However, this was far from cooling them, but away they went, raging and swearing like furies of hell. As soon as they were gone, the two men came back, in passion and rage enough also, though of another kind; for having been at their plantation, and finding it all demolished and destroyed, as above, it will easily be supposed they had provocation enough. They could scarcely have room to tell their tale, the Spaniards were so eager to tell them theirs; and it was strange enough to find that three men should thus bully nineteen and receive no punishment at all.

The Spaniards, indeed, despised them and especially, having thus disarmed them, made light of their threatenings; but the two Englishmen resolved to have their redress against them, what pains soever it cost to get it. But the Spaniards interposed here, too, and told them that as they had disarmed them, they could not consent that they (the two) should pursue them with firearms and perhaps kill them.

"But," said the grave Spaniard, who was their governor, "we will endeavor to make them do you justice, if you will leave it to us; for there is no doubt but they will come to us again, when their passion is over, being not able to subsist without our assistance. We promise you to make no peace with them without having a full satisfaction for you. And, upon this condition, we hope you will promise to use no violence with them, other than in your own defense."

The two Englishmen yielded to this very awkwardly and with great reluctance; but the Spaniards protested that they did it only to keep them from bloodshed and to make them all safe at last.

"For," said they, "we are not so many of us. Here is room enough for us all, and it is a great pity that we should not be all good friends."

At length they did consent and waited for the issue of the thing, living for some days with the Spaniards, for their own habitation was destroyed.

Humble Pie

In about five days' time, the three vagrants, tired with wandering and almost starved with hunger, having chiefly lived on turtles' eggs all that while, came back to the grove; and finding my Spaniard, who, as I have said, was the governor, and two more with him walking by the side of the creek, they came

They came up in a submissive, humble manner

up in a very submissive, humble manner and begged to be received again into the family. The Spaniards used them civilly but told them they had acted so unnaturally to their countrymen and so very grossly to them (the Spaniards) that they could not come to any conclusion without consulting the two Englishmen and the rest; however, they would go to them and discuss it, and they should know in half an hour. It may be guessed that they were very hard put to it; for, it seems, as they were to wait this half hour for an answer, they begged they would send them out some bread in the meantime, which they did, sending at the same time a large piece of goat's flesh and a boiled parrot, which they ate very heartily, for they were hungry enough.

After half an hour's consultation, they were called in, and a long debate ensued, their two countrymen charging them with the ruin of all their labor and intent to murder them; all which they admitted before and therefore could not deny now. Upon the whole, the Spaniards acted the moderators between them; and as they had obliged the two Englishmen not to hurt the three while they were naked and unarmed, so they now obliged the three to go and rebuild their fellows' two huts, one to be of the same and the other of larger dimensions than they were before; to fence their ground again where they had pulled up their fences, plant trees in place of those pulled up, dig up the land again for planting corn where they had spoiled it, and, in a word, to restore everything to the same state as they found it as near as they could; for entirely it could not be, the season for the corn and the growth of the trees and hedges not being possible to be recovered.

Well, they submitted to all this; and as they had plenty of provisions given them all the while, they grew very orderly, and the whole society began to live pleasantly and agreeably together again. Only, these three fellows could never be persuaded to work—I mean for themselves—except now and then a little, just as they pleased; however, the Spaniards told them plainly that if they would but live sociably and friendly together and study the good of the whole plantation, they would be content to work for them and let them walk about and be as idle as they pleased; and thus, having lived pretty well together for a month or two, the Spaniards gave them arms again and gave them liberty to go abroad with them as before.

It was not above a week after they had these arms and went abroad before the ungrateful creatures began to be as insolent and troublesome as ever. However, an accident happened right after this that endangered the safety of them all, and they were obliged to lay by all private resentments and look to the preservation of their lives.

It happened one night that the Spaniard governor, as I call him—that is to say, the Spaniard whose life I had saved—who was now the captain, or leader, or governor of the rest—found himself very uneasy in the night and could by no means get any sleep. He was perfectly well in body, as he told me the story, only found his thoughts tumultuous; his mind ran upon men fighting and killing one another; but he was broad awake and could not by any means get any sleep. In short, he lay a great while, but growing more and more uneasy, he resolved to rise. As they lay, being so many of them, on goatskins laid thick upon such couches and pads as they made for themselves, and not in hammocks and ship beds as I did, who was but one, so they had little to do, when they were willing to rise, but to get upon their feet and perhaps put on a coat, such as it was, and their pumps, and they were ready for going any way that their thoughts guided them. Being thus got up, he looked out; but it being dark, he could see little or nothing; the trees that I had planted, as in my former account is described, and which were now grown tall, intercepted his sight, so that he could only look up and see that it was a clear starlight night. Hearing no noise, he returned and laid him down again. But it was as before: He could not sleep, nor could he compose himself to anything like rest; but his thoughts were to the last degree uneasy, and he knew not for what.

Having made some noise with rising and walking about, going out and coming in, another of them waked, and calling, asked who it was that was up. The governor told him how it had been with him.

"Say you so?" said the other Spaniard. "Such things are not to be slighted, I assure you. There is certainly some mischief working near us." Presently, he asked him, "Where are the Englishmen?"

"They are all in their huts," said he, "safe enough."

It seems the Spaniards had kept possession of the main apartment and had made a place for the three Englishmen, who, since their last mutiny, were always quartered by themselves, so they could not easily attack the rest.

"Well," said the Spaniard, "there is something in it, I am persuaded, from my own experience. I am satisfied our spirits embodied have converse with and receive intelligence from the spirits unembodied and inhabiting the invisible world; and this friendly notice is given for our advantage, if we knew how to make use of it. Come," said he, "let us go and look abroad; and if we find nothing at all in it to justify the trouble, I'll tell you a story to the purpose that shall convince you of the justice of my proposing it."

In a word, they went out to go up to the top of the hill, where I used to go; but they being strong and a good company, not alone, as I was, used none of my cautions, to go up by the ladder, and pulling it up after them, to go up a second stage, to the top, but were going around through the grove, unconcerned and unwary, when they were surprised with seeing a light as of fire, a very little way off from them, and hearing the voices of men—not of one or two, but of a great number.

An Error of Judgment

In all the discoveries I had made of the savages landing on the island, it was my constant care to prevent them making the least discovery of there being any inhabitant upon the place; and when by any occasion they came to know it, they felt it so effectually that they who got away were scarcely able to give any account of it; for we disappeared as soon as possible. Nor did ever any that had seen me escape to tell anyone else, except it was the three savages in our last encounter, who jumped into the boat; of whom, I mentioned, I was afraid they should go home and bring more help. Whether it was the consequence of the escape of those men that so great a number came now together, or whether they came ignorantly, and by accident, on their usual bloody errand, the Spaniards could not, it seems, understand; but, whatever it was, it should have been their business either to have concealed themselves, or not to have seen them at all, much less to have let the savages have seen that there were any inhabitants in the place; or to have fallen upon them so effectually as that not a man of them should have escaped, which could only have been by getting in between them and their boats. But this presence of mind was wanting to them, which was the ruin of their tranquility for a great while.

We need not doubt but that the governor and the man with him, surprised with this sight, ran back immediately and raised their fellows, giving them an account of the imminent danger they were all in, and they again as readily took the alarm. But it was impossible to persuade them to stay close within where they were, but they must all run out to see how things stood.

While it was dark, indeed, they were well enough, and they had opportunity enough, for some hours, to view them by the light of three fires they had made at a distance from one another. What they were doing they knew not, and what to do themselves they knew not. For, first, the enemy were too many; and, secondly, they did not keep together but were divided into several parties and were on shore in several places.

The Spaniards were in no small consternation at this sight. As they found

They were surprised with seeing a light

that the fellows ran straggling all over the shore, they made no doubt but,
first or last, that some of them would discover upon their habitation, or upon
some other place where they would see the token of inhabitants; and they
were in great perplexity also for fear about their flock of goats, which would
have meant little less than starving them, if they should have been destroyed.
So the first thing they resolved upon was to dispatch three men away before
it was light, two Spaniards and one Englishman, to drive all the goats away
to the great valley where the cave was and, if need were, to drive them into

the very cave itself. Could they have seen the savages all together in one body, and at a distance from their canoes, they resolved, if there had been a hundred of them, to have attacked them. But that could not be obtained, for they were some of them two miles off from the others and, as it appeared afterward, were of two different nations.

After having mused a great while on the course they should take and beating their brains in considering their present circumstances, they resolved at last, while it was still dark, to send the old savage, Friday's father, out as a spy, to learn, if possible, something concerning them—as what they came for, what they intended to do, and the like. The old man readily undertook it; and stripping himself quite naked, as most of the savages were, away he went. After he had been gone an hour or two, he brought word that he had been among them undiscovered; that he found they were two parties and of several nations who had war with one another and had had a great battle in their own country; and that both sides, having had several prisoners taken in the fight, were, by mere chance, landed all on the same island, for the devouring of their prisoners and making merry. But their coming so by chance to the same place had spoiled all their mirth—they were in a great rage at one another and were so near that he believed they would fight again as soon as daylight began to appear. But he did not perceive that they had any notion of anybody being on the island but themselves. He had hardly made an end of telling his story, when they could perceive, by the unusual noise they made, that the two little armies were engaged in a bloody fight.

Fight Between the Savages

Friday's father used all the arguments he could to persuade our people to lie close and not be seen. He told them their safety consisted in it and that they had nothing to do but lie still, and the savages would kill one another, and then the rest would go away; and it was so to a tittle. But it was impossible to prevail, especially upon the Englishmen. Their curiosity was so importunate upon their prudence that they must needs run out and see the battle. However, they used some caution, too. They did not go openly, just by their own dwelling, but went farther into the woods and placed themselves to advantage, where they might securely see them fight and, as they thought, not be seen by them. But it seems the savages *did* see them, as we shall find hereafter.

The battle was very fierce; and, if I might believe the Englishmen, one of them said he could perceive that some of them were men of great bravery, of invincible spirits, and of wise judgment in guiding the fight. The battle, they said, was fought two hours before they could guess which party would be beaten; but then that party which was nearest our people's habitation began to appear weakest, and after some time more, some of them began to fly. This put our men again into a great consternation, lest any one of those that fled should run into the grove before their dwelling for shelter and thereby involuntarily discover the place; and that, by consequence, the pursuers would do the like in search of them. Upon this, they resolved that they would stand armed within the wall, and whoever came into the grove, they resolved to sally over the wall and kill them, so that, if possible, not one should return to give an account of it. They ordered also that it should be done with their swords, or by knocking them down with the stocks of their muskets, but not by shooting them, for fear of raising an alarm by the noise.

As they expected, it fell out: Three of the routed army fled for life and, crossing the creek, ran directly into the place, not in the least knowing whither they went, but running as into a thick wood for shelter. The scout they kept to look abroad gave notice of this within with this addition, to our men's great satisfaction, namely, that the conquerors had not pursued them or seen which way they were gone. Upon this, the Spaniard governor, a man of humanity, would not suffer them to kill the three fugitives, but sending three men out by the top of the hill, ordered them to go around, come in behind them, and surprise and take them prisoners; which was done. The residue of the conquered people fled to their canoes and got off to sea; the victors retired, made no pursuit, or very little, but drawing themselves into a body together, gave two great screaming shouts, which they supposed was by way of triumph—and so the fight ended. The same day, about three o'clock in the afternoon, they also marched to their canoes. And thus the Spaniards had the island again free to themselves, their fright was over, and they saw no savages for several years after.

After they were all gone, the Spaniards came out of their den, and viewing the field of battle, they found about two-and-thirty men dead on the spot; some were killed with great long arrows, some of which were found sticking in their bodies; but most of them were killed with great wooden swords, sixteen or seventeen of which they found in the field of battle, and as many bows, with a great many arrows. These swords were strange, great unwieldy things, and they must be very strong men that used them. Most of those men that were killed with them had their heads mashed to pieces, as we may say, or, as we call it in English, their brains knocked out, and several their arms and legs broken; so that it is evident they fight with inexpressible rage and fury. We found not one man that was not stone dead; for either they stay by their enemy till they have killed him, or they carry all the wounded men that are not quite dead away with them.

This deliverance tamed our Englishmen for a great while; the sight had filled them with horror, and the consequences appeared terrible to the last degree, especially upon supposing that some time or other they should fall into the hands of those creatures, who would not only kill them as enemies, but kill them for food, as we kill our cattle. They professed to me that the thoughts of being eaten up like beef and mutton, though it was supposed it was not to be till they were dead, had something in it so horrible that it nauseated their very stomachs, made them sick when they thought of it, and filled their minds with such unusual terror that they were not themselves for some weeks after. This, as I said, tamed even the three English brutes I have been speaking of; and for a great while after they were tractable and went about the common business of the whole society well enough—planted, sowed, reaped, and began to be all naturalized to the country. But some time after this they fell into such unwise measures again and brought them into a great deal of trouble.

The Three Prisoners

They had taken three prisoners, as I observed; and these three being lusty, stout young fellows, they made them servants and taught them to work for them; and as slaves they did well enough. But they did not take their measures with them as I did by my man Friday, namely, to begin with them upon the principle of having saved their lives and then instruct them in the rational principles of life, much less of religion—civilizing and training them by kind usage and affectionate arguments. But as they gave them their food every day, so they gave them their work, too, and kept them fully employed in drudgery enough. But they failed in this by it: that they never had them to assist them and fight for them as I had my man Friday, who was as true to me as the very flesh upon my bones.

But to come to the family part. Being all now good friends—for common danger, as I said above, had effectually reconciled them—they began to consider their general circumstances. The first thing that came under consideration was whether, seeing that the savages particularly haunted that side of the island and that there were more remote and retired parts of it equally adapted to their way of living and manifestly to their advantage, they should not rather move their habitation and plant in some more proper place for their safety and especially for the security of their cattle and corn.

Upon this, after long debate, it was concluded that they would not remove their habitation, because, some time or other, they thought they might hear from their governor again, meaning me; and if I should send anyone to seek them, I should be sure to direct them to that side, where, if they should find the place demolished, they would conclude the savages had killed us all and we were gone, and so our supply would go, too. But as to their corn and cattle, they agreed to remove them into the valley where my cave was, where the land was as proper for both and where, indeed, there was land enough. However, upon second thoughts, they altered one part of their resolution, too, and resolved only to remove part of their cattle thither and plant part of their corn there; and so if one part was destroyed, the other might be saved.

And one part of prudence they used, which it was very well they did: They never trusted those three savages, whom they had taken prisoners, with knowing anything of the plantation they had made in that valley, or of any cattle they had there, much less of the cave there, which they kept, in case of necessity, as a safe retreat; and thither they carried also the two barrels of powder that I had sent them at my coming away.

But while they resolved not to change their habitation, yet they agreed that as I had carefully covered it first with a wall or fortification, and then with a grove of trees, so seeing their safety consisted entirely in their being concealed, of which they were now fully convinced, they set to work to cover and conceal the place yet more effectually than before. For this purpose, as I planted trees, or rather thrust in stakes, which in time all grew up to be trees, for some good distance before the entrance into my apartments, they went on in the same manner and filled up the rest of that whole space of ground from the trees I had set quite down to the side of the creek, where, as I said, I landed my floats, and even into the very ooze where the tide flowed in, not so much as leaving any place to land, or any sign that there had been any landing thereabouts. These stakes also being of a wood very quick to grow, as I have noted formerly, they took care to have them generally much larger and taller than those that I had planted; and as they grew apace, so they planted them so very thick and close together that, when they had been three or four years grown, there was no piercing with the eye any considerable way into the plantation. As for that part which I had planted, the trees were grown as thick as a man's thigh, and among them they placed so many other shorter ones, and so thick, that, in a word, it stood like a palisade a

They were surprised with seeing Indians coming ashore

quarter of a mile thick, and it was next to impossible to penetrate it but with a little army to cut it all down—for a little dog could hardly get between the trees, they stood so close.

But this was not all; for they did the same by all the ground to the right and to the left, and around even to the side of the hill, leaving no way, not so much as for themselves, to come out but by the ladder placed up to the side of the hill, and then lifted up and placed again from the first stage up to the top. And when the ladder was taken down, nothing but what had wings or witchcraft to assist it could come at them. This was excellently well contrived; nor was it less than what they afterward found occasion for, which served to convince me that as human prudence has the authority of Providence to justify it, so it has doubtless the direction of Providence to set it to work; and if we listened carefully to the voice of it, I am persuaded we might prevent many of the disasters that our lives are now, by our own negligence, subjected to.

I return to the story. They lived two years after this in perfect retirement and had no more visits from the savages. They had, indeed, an alarm given them one morning, which put them into a great consternation; for some of the Spaniards being out early one morning on the west side, or rather end, of the island (which was that end where I never went, for fear of being discovered), they were surprised with seeing more than twenty canoes of Indians just coming on shore. They made the best of their way home in hurry enough, and giving the alarm to their comrades, they kept close all that day and the next, going out only at night to make their observation; but they had the good luck to be mistaken, for wherever the savages went, they did not land that time on the island but pursued some other design.

Another Broil

And now they had another broil with the three Englishmen. One of them, a most turbulent fellow, being in a rage at one of the three slaves, whom I mentioned they had taken, because the fellow had not done something right that he bid him do and seemed a little untractable in his showing him, drew a hatchet out of a frog-belt,[1] in which he wore it by his side, and fell upon the poor savage, not to correct him, but to kill him. One of the Spaniards, who was nearby, seeing him give the fellow a barbarous cut with the hatchet, which he aimed at his head but struck into his shoulder, so that he thought he had cut the poor creature's arm off, ran to him and, entreating him not to murder the poor man, placed himself between him and the savage to prevent the mischief. The fellow, being enraged the more at this, struck at the Spaniard with his hatchet and swore he would serve him as he intended to serve the savage; which the Spaniard perceiving, avoided the blow, and with a shovel that he had in his hand (for they were all working in the field about their cropland), knocked the brute down. Another of the Englishmen, running at the same time to help his comrade, knocked the Spaniard down. Then two Spaniards more came in to help their man, and a third Englishman fell in upon them. They had none of them any firearms or any other weapons but hatchets and other tools, except this third Englishman; he had one of my rusty cutlasses, with which he made at the two last Spaniards and wounded them both. This fray set the whole family in an uproar; with more help coming in, they took the three Englishmen prisoners.

The next question was, what should be done with them? They had been so often mutinous and were so very violent, so desperate, and so idle withal, they knew not what course to take with them, for they were mischievous to the highest degree and cared not what hurt they did to any man; so that, in short, it was not safe to live with them.

---

1. A belt with loops in which to carry wedge-shaped chisels and other related tools.

He placed himself between him and the savage

The Spaniard who was governor told them, in so many words, that if they had been of his own country, he would have hanged them; for all laws and all governors were to preserve society, and those who were dangerous to the society ought to be expelled from it. But as they were Englishmen, and it was to the generous kindness of an Englishman that they all owed their preservation and deliverance, he would use them with all possible leniency and would leave them to the judgment of the other two Englishmen, who were their countrymen.

One of the two honest Englishmen stood up and said they desired it might not be left to them—"for," said he, "I am sure we ought to sentence them to the gallows"; and with that he gave an account how Will Atkins, one of the three, had proposed to have all the five Englishmen join together and murder all the Spaniards when they were in their sleep.

When the Spaniard who was governor heard this, he called to Will Atkins, "How, Seignior Atkins, would you murder us all? What have you to say to that?"

The hardened villain was so far from denying it that he said it was true and swore they would do it still before they had done with them.

"Well, but Seignior Atkins," said the Spaniard, "what have we done to you that you will kill us? And what would you get by killing us? And what must we do to prevent your killing? Must we kill you, or you will kill us? Why will you put us to the necessity of this, Seignior Atkins?" said the Spaniard very calmly and smiling.

Seignior Atkins was in such a rage at the Spaniard's making a jest of it that, had he not been held by three men and withal had no weapon near him, it was thought that he would have attempted to kill the Spaniard in the middle of all the company. This harebrained attitude obliged them to consider seriously what was to be done; the two Englishmen and the Spaniard who saved the poor savage were of the opinion that they should hang one of the three, as an example to the rest, and that particularly it should be he that had twice attempted to commit murder with his hatchet. Indeed, there was some reason to believe that he had done it, for the poor savage was in such a miserable condition with the wound he had received that it was thought he could not live. But the Spaniard who was governor still said no; it was an Englishman that had saved all their lives, and he would never consent to put an Englishman to death, though he had murdered half of them; nay, he said, if he had been killed himself by an Englishman and had time left to speak, it should be that they should pardon him.

Chapter 5

A DANGEROUS
EXPEDITION

This was so positively insisted on by the Spaniard who was governor that
there was no gainsaying it; and as merciful counsels are most apt to
prevail where they are so earnestly pressed, so they all came into it. But then
it was to be considered what should be done to keep them from doing the
mischief they designed, for all agreed, governor and all, that means were to
be used for preserving the society from danger. After a long debate, it was
agreed, first, that the three should be disarmed and not permitted to have
either gun, powder, shot, sword, or any weapon and that they should be
turned out of their society and left to live where they would, and how they
could, by themselves; but that none of the rest, either Spaniards or English,
should converse with them, speak with them, or have anything to do with
them; and that they should be forbidden to come within a certain distance
of the place where the rest dwelt. And if they offered to commit any disorder, so as to spoil, burn, kill, or destroy any of the corn, plantings, buildings,
fences, or cattle belonging to the society, they should die without mercy, and
they would shoot them wherever they could find them.

The governor, a man of great humanity, musing upon the sentence,
considered a little upon it; and turning to the two honest Englishmen, he
said, "Hold. You must reflect that it will be long ere they can raise corn and
cattle of their own, and they must not starve. We must therefore allow them
provisions."

So he caused to be added that they should have a proportion of corn given
them to last them eight months, and for seed to sow, by which time they
might be supposed to raise some of their own; that they should have six
milch goats, four he-goats, and six kids given them, as well for present subsis-

tence as for a store; and that they should have tools given them for their work in the fields, such as six hatchets, an adze, a saw, and the like; but they should have none of these tools or provisions unless they would swear solemnly that they would not hurt or injure any of the Spaniards with them or their fellow Englishmen.

Thus they dismissed them from their society and turned them out to shift for themselves. They went away sullen and refractory, as neither content to go away, nor to stay; but as there was no remedy, they went, pretending to go and choose a place where they would settle themselves; and some provisions were given them, but no weapons.

About four or five days after, they came again for some victuals and gave the governor an account where they had pitched their tents and marked themselves out a habitation and plantation, and it was a very convenient place indeed, on the remotest northeastern part of the island, much about the place where I providentially landed in my first voyage, when I was driven out to sea, the Lord knows whither, in my foolish attempt to sail around the island.

The Kindness of the Spaniards

Here they built themselves two handsome huts and contrived them in a manner like my first habitation, being close under the side of a hill, having some trees growing already on three sides of it, so that by planting others it would be very easily covered from sight, unless carefully searched for. They desired some dried goatskins for beds and covering, which were given them; and upon giving their word that they would not disturb the rest, or injure any of their plantations, they gave them hatchets and what other tools they could spare, some peas, barley, and rice for sowing, and, in a word, anything they wanted, except arms and ammunition.

They lived in this separate condition about six months and had got in their first harvest, though the quantity was but small, the parcel of land they had planted being but little; for, indeed, having all their plantation to cultivate, they had a great deal of work upon their hands. When they came to make boards and pots, and such things, they were quite out of their element and could make nothing of it; and when the rainy season came on, for want of a cave in the earth, they could not keep their grain dry, and it was in great danger of spoiling. This humbled them much, so they came and begged the Spaniards to help them, which they very readily did. In four days they worked a great hole in the side of the hill for them, big enough to secure their corn and other things from the rain. But it was a poor place, at best, compared with mine, and especially as mine was then, for the Spaniards had greatly enlarged it and made several new apartments in it.

About three-quarters of a year after this separation, a new frolic took these rogues, which, together with the former villainy they had committed, brought mischief enough upon them and had very near been the ruin of the whole colony. The three new associates began, it seems, to be weary of the laborious life they led, and that without hope of bettering their circumstances. A whim took them that they would make a voyage to the continent, from whence the savages came, and would see if they could seize upon some prisoners among the natives there and bring them home, so as to make them do the laborious part of the work for them.

The project was not so preposterous, if they had gone no further. But they did nothing, and proposed nothing, but had either mischief in the design or mischief in the event. And if I may give my opinion, they seemed to be under a blast from Heaven; for if we will not allow a visible curse to pursue visible crimes, how shall we reconcile the events of things with the divine justice? It was certainly an apparent vengeance on their crime of mutiny and piracy that brought them to the state they were in; and they showed not the least remorse for the crime, but added new villainies to it, such as the piece of monstrous cruelty of wounding a poor slave because he did not, or perhaps could not, understand how to do what he was directed, and to wound him in such a manner as made him a cripple all his life, and in a place where no surgeon or medicine could be had for his cure; and what was still worse, the murderous intent—or, to do justice to the crime, the intentional murder—for such to be sure it was, as was afterward the formed design they all laid, to murder the Spaniards in cold blood and in their sleep.

But I leave observing and return to the story. The three fellows came down to the Spaniards one morning and in very humble terms desired to be admitted to speak with them. The Spaniards very readily heard what they had to say, which was this: that they were tired of living in the manner they did, and that they were not handy enough to make the necessaries they wanted, and that having no help, they found they should be starved. But if the Spaniards would give them leave to take one of the canoes that they came over in and give them arms and ammunition proportioned to their defense, they would go over to the main and seek their fortunes, and so deliver them from the trouble of supplying them with any other provisions.

The Spaniards were glad enough to get rid of them, but very honestly represented to them the certain destruction they were running into; they told them they had suffered such hardships upon that very spot, that they could, without any spirit of prophecy, tell them they would be starved or murdered, and bade them consider it.

The men replied audaciously that they should be starved if they stayed here, for they could not work and would not work, and they could but be starved abroad; and if they were murdered, there was an end of them. In short, they insisted importunately upon their demand, declaring they would go, whether they gave them any arms or no.

The Spaniards told them, with great kindness, that if they were resolved to go, they should not go like naked men and be in no condition to defend themselves; and that, though they could ill spare their firearms, having not enough for themselves, yet they would let them have two muskets, a pistol, and a cutlass, and each man a hatchet, which they thought was sufficient for them. In a word, they accepted the offer; and having baked bread enough to serve them a month, and given them as much goats' flesh as they could eat while it was sweet, and a great basket of dried grapes, a pot of fresh water, and a young kid alive, they boldly set out in a canoe for a voyage over the sea, where it was at least forty miles broad.

The boat, indeed, was a large one and would very well have carried fifteen or twenty men, and therefore was rather too big for them to manage; but as they had a fair breeze and flood tide with them, they did well enough. They had made a mast of a long pole and a sail of four large dried goatskins, which they had sewed or laced together; and away they went merrily enough. The Spaniards called after them, *"Bon veyajo!"*[1] and no man ever thought of seeing them anymore.

The Spaniards were often saying to one another, and to the two honest Englishmen who remained behind, how quietly and comfortably they lived, now these three turbulent fellows were gone. As for their coming again, that was the remotest thing from their thoughts that could be imagined; when, behold, after two-and-twenty-days' absence, one of the Englishmen, being abroad upon his planting work, saw three strange men coming toward him at a distance, with guns upon their shoulders.

Away ran the Englishman, as if he were bewitched; he came frightened and amazed to the Spaniard who was governor and told him they were all undone, for there were strangers upon the island, but he could not tell who they were.

The Spaniard, pausing awhile, said to him, "How do you mean—you cannot tell who? They are the savages, to be sure."

---

1. "Bon voyage!"

He saw three strange men coming toward him

"No, no," said the Englishman, "they are men in clothes, with arms."

"Nay, then," said the Spaniard, "why are you so concerned? If they are not savages, they must be friends, for there is no Christian nation upon earth but will do us good rather than harm."

While they were debating thus, the three Englishmen came and, standing without the wood, which was newly planted, halloed to them. They presently knew their voices, and so all the wonder ceased. But now the wonder was turned into another question: *What could be the matter, and what made them come back again?*

It was not long before they brought the men in, and inquiring where they had been and what they had been doing, the men gave them a full account of their voyage in a few words: They reached the land in two days, or something less; but finding the people alarmed at their coming and prepared with bows and arrows to fight them, they dared not go on shore but sailed on to the northward six or seven hours, till they came to a great opening, by which they perceived that the land they saw from our island was not the main but an island. Upon entering that opening of the sea, they saw another island on the right hand, north, and several more west; and being resolved to land somewhere, they put over to one of the islands that lay west and went boldly on shore. They found the people very courteous and friendly to them, and they gave them several roots and some dried fish and appeared very sociable. The women, as well as the men, were very willing to supply them with anything they could get for them to eat and brought it to them a great way upon their heads.

They continued here four days and inquired as well as they could of them, by signs, what nations were this way and that way, and they were told of several fierce and terrible peoples that lived almost every way, who, as they made known by signs to them, used to eat men. But as for themselves, they said, they never ate men or women, except only such as they took in wars;[2] and then, they admitted, they made a great feast and ate their prisoners.

A Curious Exchange

The Englishmen inquired when they had had a feast of that kind, and they told them about two moons ago, pointing to the moon and to two fingers; and that their great king had two hundred prisoners now, which he had taken in his war, and they were feeding them to make them fat for the next feast. The Englishmen seemed mighty desirous of seeing those prisoners; but the others mistaking them, thought they were desirous to have some of them to carry away for their own eating. So they beckoned to them, pointing to the setting of the sun and then to the rising, which was to signify that the next morning at sunrising they would bring some for them. Accordingly, the next morning they brought down five women and eleven men and gave them to the Englishmen to carry away with them on their voyage, just as we would bring so many cows and oxen down to a seaport town to victual a ship.

As brutish and barbarous as these fellows were at home, their stomachs turned at this sight, and they did not know what to do. To refuse the prisoners would have been the highest affront to the savage gentry that could be offered them; and what to do with them they knew not. However, after some debate they resolved to accept them. In return, they gave the savages that brought them one of their hatchets, an old key, a knife, and six or seven of their bullets—which, though they did not understand their use, they seemed particularly pleased with. Then tying the poor creatures' hands behind them, they dragged the prisoners into the boat for our men.

The Englishmen were obliged to come away as soon as they had them, or else they that gave them this noble present would certainly have expected that they should have gone to work with them, have killed two or three of

---

2. If men of a given tribe or village were defeated, their women and children became the property of the victors.

them the next morning, and perhaps have invited the donors to dinner. But having taken their leave, with all the respect and thanks that could well pass between people, where, on either side, they understood not one word they could say, they put off with their boat and came back toward the first island. When they arrived, they set eight of their prisoners at liberty, there being too many of them for their occasion.

In the voyage they endeavored to have some communication with their prisoners, but it was impossible to make them understand anything. Nothing they could say to them, or give them, or do for them but was looked upon as going to murder them. They first of all unbound them, but the poor creatures screamed at that, especially the women, as if they had just felt the knife at their throats; for they immediately concluded they were unbound on purpose to be killed. If they gave them anything to eat, it was the same thing: They then concluded it was for fear they should be reduced in flesh and so not be fat enough to kill. If they looked at one of them more particularly, the party concluded it was to see whether he or she was fattest and fittest to kill first. Nay, after they had brought them quite over, and began to use them kindly, and treat them well, still they expected every day to make a dinner or supper for their new masters.

When the three wanderers had given this unaccountable history or journal of their voyage, the Spaniard asked them where their new family was; and being told that they had brought them on shore, put them into one of their huts, and were come up to beg some victuals for them, they (the Spaniards) and the other two Englishmen, that is to say, the whole colony, resolved to go all down to the place and see them. They did so, and Friday's father with them.

When they came into the hut, there they sat, all bound; for when they had brought them on shore, they bound their hands, that they might not take the boat and make their escape; there, I say, they sat, all of them stark naked. First, there were three men, lusty, comely fellows, well-shaped, with straight and fair limbs, about thirty to thirty-five years of age; and five women, whereof two might be from thirty to forty; two more not above four- or five-and-twenty; and the fifth, a tall, comely maiden, about sixteen or seventeen. The women were well-favored, agreeable persons, both in shape and features, only tawny; and two of them, had they been perfectly white, would have passed for very handsome women, even in London itself, having pleasant, agreeable countenances and of a very modest behavior—especially when they came afterward to be clothed and dressed, as they called it, though that dress was very indifferent, it must be confessed.

The sight, you may be sure, was something uncouth to our Spaniards, who were, to give them a just character, men of the best behavior, of the most calm, sedate tempers and perfect good humor, and, in particular, of the most modesty that ever I met with. I say, the sight was very uncouth to see three naked men and five naked women, all together bound and in the most miserable circumstances that human nature could be supposed to be, namely, to be expecting every moment to be dragged out and have their brains knocked out, and then to be eaten up like a calf that is killed for a dainty.

The first thing they did was to cause the old Indian, Friday's father, to go in and see, first, if he knew any of them, and then if he understood any of their speech. As soon as the old man came in, he looked seriously at them but knew none of them; neither could any of them understand a word he said, or a sign he could make, except one of the women. However, this was enough to answer the end, which was to satisfy them that the men into whose hands they were fallen were Christians; that they abhorred eating men or women; and that they might be sure they would not be killed. As soon as they were assured of this, they discovered such a joy, and by such awkward gestures, several ways, as is hard to describe; for it seems they were of several nations.

The woman who was their interpreter was bid, in the next place, to ask them if they were willing to be servants and to work for the men who had brought them away to save their lives, at which they all fell a-dancing, and presently one fell to taking up this, and another that, anything that lay next, to carry on their shoulders to intimate they were willing to work.

Marriage of the Englishmen

The governor, who found that having women among them would presently be attended with some inconvenience and might occasion some strife and perhaps blood, asked the three men what they intended to do with these women, and how they intended to use them, whether as servants or as wives? One of the Englishmen answered, very boldly and readily, that they would use them as both; to which the governor said, "I am not going to restrain you from it—you are your own masters as to that. But this I think is but just, for avoiding disorders and quarrels among you, and I desire it of you for that reason only—namely, that you will all engage that if any of you take any of these women as a wife that he shall take but one; and that, having taken one, none else shall touch her; for though we cannot marry any one of you, yet it is but reasonable that, while you stay here, the woman any of you takes shall be maintained by the man that takes her and should be his wife—

I mean," said he, "while he continues here, and that none else shall have anything to do with her."

All this appeared so just that everyone agreed to it without any difficulty. Then the Englishmen asked the Spaniards if they designed to take any of them. But every one of them answered, "No." Some of them said they had wives in Spain, and the others did not like women that were not Christians; and all together declared that they would not touch one of them, which was an instance of such virtue as I have not met with in all my travels. On the other hand, to be short, the five Englishmen took them every one a wife— that is to say, a temporary wife. And so they set up a new form of living, for the Spaniards and Friday's father lived in my old habitation, which they had enlarged exceedingly within. The three servants who were taken in the last battle of the savages lived with them; and these carried on the main part of the colony, supplied all the rest with food, and assisted them in anything as they could, or as they found necessity required.

A Marriage Lottery

But the wonder of the story was, how five such refractory, ill-matched fellows should agree about these women, and that two of them should not choose the same woman, especially seeing two or three of them were, without comparison, more attractive than the others. But they took a good way enough to prevent quarreling among themselves, for they set the five women by themselves in one of their huts, and they went all into the other hut and drew lots among them who should choose first.

He that drew to choose first went away by himself to the hut where the poor naked creatures were and fetched out her he chose; and it was worth observing that he that chose first took her that was reckoned the homeliest and oldest of the five, which made mirth enough among the rest; and even the Spaniards laughed at it. But the fellow considered better than any of them that it was application and business they were to expect assistance in, as much as in anything else; and she proved the best wife of all the parcel.

When the poor women saw themselves set in a row thus, and fetched out one by one, the terrors of their condition returned upon them again, and they firmly believed they were now going to be devoured. Accordingly, when the English sailor came in and fetched out one of them, the rest set up a most lamentable cry and hung about her, and took their leave of her with such agonies and affection as would have grieved the hardest heart in the world. Nor was it possible for the Englishmen to satisfy them that they were not to

They drew lots among them

be immediately murdered, till they fetched the old man, Friday's father, who immediately let them know that the five men, who were to fetch them out one by one, had chosen them for their wives.

When they had done, and the fright the women were in was a little over, the men went to work, and the Spaniards came and helped them. In a few hours they had built them every one a new hut or tent for their lodging apart, for those they had already were crowded with their tools, household stuffs, and provisions. The three wicked ones had pitched farthest off, and the two honest ones nearer, but both on the north shore of the island, so that they continued separated as before; and thus my island was peopled in three places, and, as I might say, three towns were begun to be built.

And here it is very well worth observing that, as it often happens in the world (what the wise ends of God's providence are, in such a disposition of things, I cannot say), the two honest fellows had the two worst wives; and the three reprobates, that were scarcely worth hanging, that were fit for nothing, and neither seemed born to do themselves good nor anyone else, had three clever, diligent, careful, and ingenious wives; not that the first two were bad wives, as to their temper or humor, for all the five were most willing, quiet, passive, and subjected creatures, rather like slaves than wives—but my meaning is, they were not alike capable, ingenious, or industrious, or alike clean and neat.

Another observation I must make, to the honor of a diligent application on one hand, and to the disgrace of a slothful, negligent, idle temper on the other, is that when I came to the place and viewed the several improvements, plantings, and management of the several little colonies, the two men had so far outdone the three that there was no comparison. They had, indeed, both of them as much ground laid out for corn as they wanted, and the reason was because, according to my rule, nature dictated that it was to no purpose to sow more corn than they wanted; but the difference of the cultivation, of the planting of the fences, and, indeed, of everything else, was easy to be seen at first view.

The two men had innumerable young trees planted about their huts, so that when you came to the place, nothing was to be seen but a wood; and though they twice had had their plantation demolished—once by their own countrymen and once by the enemy, as shall be shown in its place—yet they had restored all again, and everything was thriving and flourishing about them. They had grapes planted in order and managed like a vineyard, though they had themselves never seen anything of that kind; and, by their good ordering of their vines, their grapes were as good again as any of the others. They had also found themselves out a retreat in the thickest part of the woods, where, though there was not a natural cave, as I had found, yet they made one with incessant labor of their hands, and where, when the mischief that followed happened, they secured their wives and children so as they could never be found—they having, by sticking innumerable stakes and poles of wood that, as I said, grew so rapidly, made the grove impassable, except in some places, where they climbed up to get over the outside part and then went on by ways of their own leaving.

As to the three reprobates, as I justly call them, though they were much civilized by their settlement compared with what they were before, and were not so quarrelsome, having not the same opportunity, yet one of the certain companions of a profligate mind never left them and that was their idleness. It is true, they planted corn and made fences; but Solomon's words were never better verified than in them—"I went by the vineyard of the slothful, and it was all overgrown with thorns"—for when the Spaniards came to view their crop, they could not see it in some places for weeds, and the hedge had several gaps in it where the wild goats had got in and eaten up the corn. Perhaps here and there a dead bush was crammed in to stop them out for the present, but it was only shutting the stable door after the steed was stolen; whereas, when they looked on the colony of the other two, there was the very face of industry and success upon all they did. There was not a weed to be seen in all their corn, or a gap in any of their hedges; and they, on the other hand, verified Solomon's words in another place, that "the diligent hand maketh rich"; for everything grew and thrived, and they had plenty within and without. They had more tame cattle than the others, more utensils and necessaries within doors, and yet more pleasure and diversion, too.

It is true, the wives of the three were very handy and clean within doors; and having learned the English ways of dressing[3] and cooking from one of the other Englishmen, who, as I said, was a cook's mate on board the ship, they dressed their husbands' victuals very nicely and well; whereas the others could not be brought to understand it; but then the husband, who, as I say, had been cook's mate, did it himself. But as for the husbands of the three wives, they loitered about, fetched turtles' eggs, and caught fish and birds— in a word, anything but labor—and they fared accordingly. The diligent lived well and comfortably, and the slothful hard and beggarly; and so, I believe, generally speaking, it is all over the world.

But I now come to a scene different from all that had happened before, either to them or to me, and the origin of the story was this: Early one morning, there came on shore five or six canoes of Indians or savages—call them which you please—and there is no room to doubt they came upon the old errand of feeding upon their slaves. But that part was now so familiar to the Spaniards, and to our men, too, that they did not concern themselves about it as I did. Having been made sensible, by their experience, that their only business was to lie concealed, and that if they were not seen by any of the savages they would go off again quietly when their business was done, having, as yet, not the least notion of there being any inhabitants on the island—I say, having been made sensible of this, they had nothing to do but give notice to all the three plantations to keep within doors and not show themselves, only placing a scout in a proper place to give notice when the boats went to sea again. This was, without doubt, very right. But a disaster spoiled all these measures and made it known among the savages that there were inhabitants there, which, in the end, caused the destruction of almost

3. Preparing food.

the whole colony. After the canoes with the savages were gone off, the Spaniards peeped abroad again; and some of them had the curiosity to go to the place where they had been, to see what they had been doing. Here, to their great surprise, they found three savages left behind and lying fast asleep upon the ground. It was supposed they had either been so gorged with their inhuman feast that, like beasts, they were fallen asleep when the others went, or they had wandered into the woods, and did not come back in time to be taken in.

A Discovery

The Spaniards were greatly surprised at this sight and perfectly at a loss what to do. The governor, as it happened, was with them, and his advice was asked, but he professed he knew not what to do. As for slaves, they had enough already; and as to killing them, there were none of them inclined to do that. The Spaniard who was governor told me they could not think of shedding innocent blood, for as to them, the poor creatures had done them no

There lay the fellows fast asleep

wrong, invaded none of their property, and they thought they had no just quarrel against them to take away their lives. And here I must, in justice to these Spaniards, observe that let the accounts of Spanish cruelty in Mexico and Peru be what they will, I never met with seventeen men of any nation whatsoever, in any foreign country, who were so universally modest, temperate, virtuous, so very good-humored, and so courteous as these Spaniards. As to cruelty, they had nothing of it in their very nature: no inhumanity, no barbarity, no outrageous passions. Yet all of them were men of great courage and spirit. Their temper and calmness had appeared in their bearing the insufferable usage of the three Englishmen; and their justice and humanity appeared now in the case of the savages, as above. After some consultation, they resolved upon this: that they would lie still awhile longer, till, if possible, these three men might be gone. But then the governor recollected that the three savages had no boat; and if they were left to roam about the island, they would certainly discover that there were inhabitants in it, and so they should be undone that way. Upon this, they went back again, and there lay the fellows fast asleep still. So they resolved to awaken them and take them prisoners; and they did so. The poor fellows were strangely frightened when they were seized upon and bound—afraid, like the women, that they should be murdered and eaten, for it seems those people think all the world does as they do, eating men's flesh. But they were soon made easy as to that, and away they carried them.

It was very happy for them that they did not carry them home to their castle—I mean, to my palace under the hill; but they carried them first to the bower, where was the chief of their country work, such as keeping the goats, planting the corn, etc.; and afterward they carried them to the habitation of the two Englishmen.

Here they were set to work, though it was not much they had for them to do; and whether it was by negligence in guarding them, or that they thought the fellows could not fend for themselves, I know not, but one of them ran away and, taking to the woods, was never heard of anymore.

They had good reason to believe he got home again soon after in some other boats or canoes of savages who came on shore three or four weeks afterward and who, carrying on their revels as usual, went off in two days' time. This thought terrified them exceedingly, for they concluded, not without good cause indeed, that if this fellow came home safe among his comrades, he would certainly give them an account that there were people on the island, and also how few and weak they were; for this savage, as observed before, had never been told, and it was very happy he had not, how many there were, or where they lived; nor had he ever seen or heard the fire of any of their guns, much less had they shown him any of their other retired places, such as the cave in the valley, or the new retreat that the two Englishmen had made, and the like.

The first testimony they had that this fellow had given intelligence of them was, that about two months after this, six canoes of savages, with about seven, eight, or ten men in a canoe, came rowing along the north side of the island, where they never used to come before, and landed, about an hour after sunrise, at a convenient place, about a mile from the habitation of the two Englishmen, where this escaped man had been kept. As the Spaniard who was governor said, had they been all there, the damage would not have been so much, for not a man of them would have escaped; but the case differed now very much, for two men to fifty was too much odds. The two men had the happiness to discover them about a league off, so that it was more than an hour before they landed; and as they landed a mile from their huts, it was some time before they could come at them. Now, having great reason to believe that they were betrayed, the first thing they did was to bind the two slaves who were left and cause two of the three men whom they brought with the women (who, it seems, proved very faithful to them) to lead them, with their two wives and whatever they could carry away with them, to their retired places in the woods (which I have spoken of above), and there to bind the two fellows hand and foot, till they heard further.

In the next place, seeing the savages were all come on shore, and that they had bent their course directly that way, they opened the fences where the milch cows were kept and drove them all out; leaving their goats to straggle in the woods whither they pleased, that the savages might think they were all bred wild. But the rogue who came with them was too cunning for that and gave them an account of it all, for they went directly to the place.

When the two poor frightened men had secured their wives and goods, they sent the other slave they had of the three who came with the women, and who was at their place by accident, away to the Spaniards with all speed to give them the alarm and desire speedy help, and, in the meantime, they took their arms and what ammunition they had and retreated toward the place in the wood where their wives were sent; keeping at a distance yet so that they might see, if possible, which way the savages took.

They saw all their huts and household stuff flaming up together

Chapter 6

WAR WITH THE SAVAGES

They had not gone far when, from a rising ground, they saw the little army of their enemies come on directly to their habitation and, in a moment more, could see all their huts and household stuff flaming up together, to their great grief and mortification; for they had a very great loss, to them irretrievable, at least for some time. They kept their station for a while, till they found the savages, like wild beasts, spread themselves all over the place, rummaging every way and every place they could think of, in search of prey; and in particular for the people, of whom now it plainly appeared they had intelligence.

The two Englishmen, seeing this, thinking themselves not secure where they stood, because it was likely some of the wild people might come that way, and they might come too many together, thought it proper to make another retreat about half a mile farther—believing, as it afterward happened, that the farther they strolled, the fewer would be together.

Their next halt was at the entrance into a very thick-grown part of the

71

woods, where an old trunk of a tree stood, which was hollow and vastly large. In this tree they both took their standing, resolving to see there what might offer. They had not stood there long before two of the savages appeared, running directly that way, as if they already had noticed where they stood and were coming up to attack them; and a little way farther they espied three more coming after them, and five more beyond them, all coming the same way; besides which, they saw seven or eight more at a distance, running another way. In a word, they ran every way, like sportsmen beating for their game.

The poor men were now in great perplexity whether they should stand and keep their posture or fly; but after a very short debate with themselves, they considered that if the savages ranged the country thus before help came, they might perhaps find out their retreat in the woods, and then all would be lost. So they resolved to stand them there, and if they were too many to deal with, then they would get up to the top of the tree, from whence they doubted not to defend themselves, fire excepted, as long as their ammunition lasted, though all the savages that were landed, which was near fifty, were to attack them.

Having resolved upon this, they next considered whether they should fire at the first two or wait for the three, and so take the middle party, by which the two and the five that followed would be separated. At length they resolved to let the first two pass by, unless they should spy them in the tree and come to attack them. The first two savages confirmed them also in this resolution, by turning a little from them toward another part of the wood; but the three, and the five after them, came forward directly to the tree, as if they had known the Englishmen were there. Seeing them come so straight toward them, they resolved to take them in a line as they came; and as they resolved to fire but one at a time, perhaps the first shot might hit them all three. For that purpose the man who was to fire put three or four small bullets into his piece; and having a fair loophole, as it were, from a broken hole in the tree, he took a sure aim, without being seen, waiting till they were within about thirty yards of the tree, so that he could not miss.

While they were thus waiting, and the savages came on, they plainly saw that one of the three was the runaway savage that had escaped from them. They both knew him distinctly and resolved that, if possible, he should not escape, though they should both fire. So the other stood ready with his piece, that if he did not drop at the first shot, he should be sure to have a second. But the first was too good a marksman to miss his aim; for as the savages kept near one another, a little behind in a line, he fired and hit two of them directly. The foremost was killed outright, being shot in the head; the second, who was the runaway Indian, was shot through the body and fell but was not quite dead. The third had a little scratch in the shoulder, perhaps by the same ball that went through the body of the second; and being dreadfully frightened, though not so much hurt, he sat down upon the ground, screaming and yelling in a hideous manner.

The five that were behind, more frightened with the noise than sensible of the danger, stood still at first; for the woods made the sound a thousand times bigger than it really was, the echoes rattling from one side to another, and the fowls rising from all parts, screaming, and every sort making a different noise, according to their kind; just as it was when I fired the first gun that perhaps was ever shot off on the island.

However, all being silent again, and they not knowing what the matter was, came on unconcerned, till they came to the place where their companions lay in a condition miserable enough. Here the poor ignorant creatures, not sensible that they were within reach of the same mischief, stood all together over the wounded man, talking and, as may be supposed, inquiring of him how he came to be hurt, and who, it is very rational to believe, told them that a flash of fire first and, immediately after that, thunder from their gods had killed those two and wounded him. This, I say, is rational, for nothing is more certain than that, as they saw no man near them, so they had never heard a gun in all their lives, nor so much as heard of a gun; neither knew they anything of killing and wounding at a distance with fire and bullets. If they had, one might reasonably believe they would not have stood so unconcerned to view the fate of their fellows without some apprehensions of their own.

Our two men—though, as they confessed to me, it grieved them to be obliged to kill so many poor creatures, who, at the same time, had no notion of their danger—having them all thus in their power, and the first having to load his piece again, resolved to let fly both together among them. Singling out, by agreement, which to aim at, they shot together and killed, or very much wounded, four of them. The fifth, frightened even to death, though not hurt, fell with the rest; so that our men, seeing them all fall together, thought they had killed them all.

A Wrong Step

The belief that the savages were all killed made our two men come boldly out of the tree before they had charged their guns, which was a wrong step;

and they were under some surprise when they came to the place and found no less than four of them alive, and two of them wounded very little, and one not at all. This obliged them to fall upon them with the stocks of their muskets. First they made sure of the runaway savage, who had been the cause of all the mischief, and of another who was hurt in the knee, and put them out of their pain. Then the man who was not hurt at all came and kneeled down to them, with his two hands held up, and made piteous moans to them, by gestures and signs, for his life, but could not say one word to them that they could understand. However, they made signs to him to sit down at the foot of a tree hard by, and one of the Englishmen, with a piece of rope-twine that he had by great chance in his pocket, tied his two hands behind him, and there they left him. With what speed they could, they made after the other two, who were gone before, fearing they, or any of them, should find their way to the covered place in the woods, where their wives and the few goods they had left lay. They came once in sight of the two men, but it was at a great distance; however, they had the satisfaction to see them cross over a valley toward the sea, quite the contrary way from that which led to their retreat, which they were afraid of; and being satisfied with that, they went back to the tree where they left their prisoner, who, as they supposed, was delivered by his comrades, for he was gone, and the two pieces of rope-twine, with which they had bound him, lay just at the foot of the tree.

They were now in as great concern as before, not knowing what course to take, or how near the enemy might be, or in what number; so they resolved to go away to the place where their wives were, to see if all was well there and to reassure them, who were in fright enough to be sure; for though the savages were their own countrymen, yet they were most terribly afraid of them, and perhaps the more for the knowledge they had of them.

When they came there, they found the savages had been in the wood and very near that place, but had not found it; for it was indeed inaccessible, from the trees standing so thick, unless the persons seeking it had been directed by those who knew it, which these were not. They found, therefore, everything very safe, only the women in a terrible fright. While they were here, they had the comfort to have seven of the Spaniards come to their assistance. The other ten, with their servants and old Friday (I mean Friday's father), were gone in a body to defend their bower and the corn and cattle that were kept there, in case the savages should have roved over to that side of the country; but they did not spread so far. With the seven Spaniards came one of the three savages who, as I said, were their prisoners formerly; and with them also came the savage whom the Englishman had left with bound hands at the tree; for it seems they came that way, saw the slaughter of the seven men, and unbound the eighth and brought him along with them; where, however, they were obliged to bind him again, as they had done the two others who were left when the third ran away.

The prisoners now began to be a burden to them; and they were so afraid of their escaping that they were once resolving to kill them all, believing they were under an absolute necessity to do so for their own preservation. However, the Spaniard who was governor would not consent to it but ordered, for the present, that they should be sent out of the way, to my old cave in the valley, and be kept there, with two Spaniards to guard them and give them food for their subsistence, which was done; and they were bound there hand and foot for that night.

Ruin

When the Spaniards came, the two Englishmen were so encouraged that they could not satisfy themselves to stay any longer there; but taking five of the Spaniards and themselves, with four muskets and a pistol among them and two stout quarterstaves, away they went in quest of the savages. And first they came to the tree where the men lay who had been killed; but it was easy to see that some more of the savages had been there, for they had attempted to carry their dead men away and had dragged two of them a good way but had given it up. From thence they advanced to the first rising ground, where they had stood and seen their camp destroyed, and where they had the mortification still to see some of the smoke; but neither could they here see any of the savages. They then resolved, though with all possible caution, to go forward toward their ruined plantation. But a little before they came thither, coming in sight of the seashore, they saw plainly the savages all embarking again in their canoes in order to be gone. They seemed very sorry, at first, that there was no way to come at them, to give them a parting blow; but upon the whole, they were very well satisfied to be rid of them.

The poor Englishmen being now twice ruined and all their improvements destroyed, the rest all agreed to come and help them to rebuild and assist them with needful supplies. Their three countrymen, who were not yet noted for having the least inclination to do any good, yet as soon as they heard of it (for they, living remote eastward, knew nothing of the matter till all was over), came and offered their help and assistance and did very helpful work for several days to restore their habitations and make necessaries for them. And thus in a little time they were set upon their legs again.

About two days after this they had the further satisfaction of seeing three of the savages' canoes come driving on shore and, at some distance from them, two drowned men, by which they had reason to believe that they had met with a storm at sea, which had overset some of them; for it had blown very hard the night after they went off.

However, as some might miscarry, so, on the other hand, enough of them escaped to inform the rest, as well of what they had done as of what had happened to them and to whet them on to another enterprise of the same nature, which they, it seems, resolved to attempt, with sufficient force to carry all before them; for except what the first man had told them of inhabitants, they could say little of it of their own knowledge, for they never saw one man; and the fellow being killed that had affirmed it, they had no other witness to confirm it to them.

It was five or six months after this before they heard any more of the savages, in which time our men were in hopes they had either forgot their former bad luck or given over hopes of better; when, on a sudden, they were invaded by a most formidable fleet of no less than eight-and-twenty canoes, full of savages, armed with bows and arrows, great clubs, wooden swords, and such like engines of war; and they brought such numbers with them that, in short, it put all our people into the utmost consternation.

The Fight Continued

As they came on shore in the evening and at the easternmost side of the island, our men had that night to consult and consider what to do. In the first place, knowing that their being entirely concealed was their only safety before and would be much more so now, while the number of their enemies would be so great, they therefore resolved, first of all, to take down the huts that were built for the two Englishmen and drive away their goats to the old cave; because they supposed the savages would go directly thither, as soon as it was day, to play the old game over again, though they did not now land within two leagues of it. In the next place, they drove away all the flocks of goats they had at the old bower, as I called it, which belonged to the Spaniards, and, in short, left as little appearance of inhabitants anywhere as was possible. The next morning early they posted themselves, with all their force, at the plantation of the two men to await for their coming. As they guessed, so it happened: These new invaders, leaving their canoes at the east end of the island, came ranging along the shore directly toward the place, to the number of two hundred and fifty, as near as our men could judge. Our

These new invaders came ranging along the shore

army was but small, indeed; but that which was worse, they had no arms for all their number either. The whole account, it seems, stood thus: first, as to men, seventeen Spaniards, five Englishmen, old Friday (or Friday's father), the three slaves taken with the women, who proved very faithful, and three other slaves, who lived with the Spaniards. To arm these, they had eleven muskets, five pistols, three fowling pieces (five of the muskets and fowling pieces had been taken from me by the mutinous seamen whom I reduced), two swords, and three old halberds.

To their slaves they did not give either musket or fusil; but they had each a halberd, or a long staff, like a quarterstaff, with a great spike of iron fastened into each end of it, and by his side a hatchet; also every one of our men had a hatchet. Two of the women could not be prevailed upon, but they would come into the fight, and they had bows and arrows, which the Spaniards had taken from the savages when the first action happened, which I have spoken of, where the Indians fought with one another; and the women had hatchets, too.

The governor, whom I described so often, commanded the whole; and Will Atkins, who, though a dreadful fellow for wickedness, was a most daring, bold fellow, commanded under him. The savages came forward like lions; and our men, which was the worst of their fate, had no advantage in their situation; only that Will Atkins, who now proved a most useful fellow, with six men was planted just behind a small thicket of bushes as an advance guard, with orders to let the first of them pass by and then fire into the middle of them, and as soon as he had fired, to make his retreat as nimbly as he could around a part of the wood and so come in behind the Spaniards where they stood, having a thicket of trees before them.

When the savages came on, they ran straggling about every way in clusters in no particular order, and Will Atkins let about fifty of them pass by him. Then, seeing the rest come in a very thick throng, he ordered three of his men to fire, having loaded their muskets with six or seven bullets apiece, about as big as large pistol bullets. How many they killed or wounded they knew not, but the consternation and surprise was inexpressible among the savages; they were frightened to the last degree to hear such a dreadful noise and see their men killed and others hurt, but see nobody that did it. In the middle of their fright, Will Atkins and his other three let fly again among the thickest of them; and in less than a minute, the first three being loaded again, gave them a third volley.

Had Will Atkins and his men retired immediately, as soon as they had fired, as they were ordered to do, or had the rest of the body been at hand to have poured in their shot continually, the savages would have been effectually routed; for the terror that was among them came principally from this: that they were killed by the gods with thunder and lightning and could see nobody that hurt them. But Will Atkins, staying to load again, discovered the deception: Some of the savages who were at a distance spying them came upon them behind; and though Atkins and his men fired at them also two or three times and killed above twenty, retiring as fast as they could, yet they wounded Atkins himself and killed one of his fellow Englishmen with their arrows, as they did afterward one Spaniard and one of the Indian slaves who came with the women. This slave was a most gallant fellow and fought most desperately, killing five of them with his own hand, having no weapon but one of the armed staves and a hatchet.

Our men being thus hard-pressed, with Atkins wounded and three other men killed, the rest retreated to a rising ground in the wood; and the Spaniards, after firing three volleys upon them, retreated also; for their number was so great and they were so desperate that though above fifty of them were killed and more than as many wounded, yet they came on in the teeth of our men, fearless of danger, and shot their arrows like a cloud. And it was observed that their wounded men, who were not quite disabled, were made ferocious by their wounds and fought like madmen.

When our men retreated, they left the Spaniard, the Englishman, and the slave who were killed behind them; and the savages, when they came up to them, killed them over again in a wretched manner, breaking their arms, legs, and heads, with their clubs and wooden swords, like true savages. But finding our men were gone, they did not seem to pursue them, but drew themselves up in a ring, which is, it seems, their custom, and shouted twice in token of their victory; after which, they had the mortification to see several of their wounded men fall, dying with the mere loss of blood.

The Spaniard who was governor having drawn his little body up together upon a rising ground, Atkins, though he was wounded, would have had them march and charge again altogether at once.

But the Spaniard replied, "Seignior Atkins, you see how their wounded men fight. Let them alone till morning. All the wounded men will be stiff and sore with their wounds and faint with the loss of blood, and so we shall have the fewer to engage."

This advice was good, but Will Atkins replied merrily, "That is true, Seignior, and so shall I, too; and that is the reason I would go on while I am warm."

"Well, Seignior Atkins," said the Spaniard, "you have behaved gallantly and done your part. We will fight for you if you cannot come on; but I think it best to stay till morning."

So they waited.

But as it was a clear moonlight night, and they found the savages in great disorder about their dead and wounded men, and a great noise and hurry among them where they lay, they afterward resolved to fall upon them in the night; especially if they could come to give them but one volley before they were discovered. This they had a fair opportunity to do, for one of the Englishmen in whose quarter it was where the fight began led them around between the woods and the seaside westward, and then turning short south, they came so near where the thickest of them lay that, before they were seen or heard, eight of them fired in upon them and did dreadful execution upon them. In half a minute or more, eight others fired after them, pouring in their small shot in such a quantity that an abundance were killed and wounded; and all this while they were not able to see who hurt them or which way to fly.

Victory

The Spaniards charged again with the utmost expedition and then divided themselves into three bodies and resolved to fall in among them altogether. They had in each body eight persons, that is to say, twenty-two men and the two women, who, by the way, fought desperately. They divided the firearms equally in each party, as well as the halberds and staves. They would have had the women kept back, but they said they were resolved to die with their husbands. Having thus formed their little army, they marched out from among the trees and came up to the teeth of the enemy, shouting and halloing as loud as they could. The savages stood all together but were in the utmost confusion, hearing the noise of our men shouting from three quarters together. They would have fought if they had seen us; for as soon as we came near enough to be seen, some arrows were shot, and poor old Friday was wounded, though not mortally. But our men gave them no time but, running up to them, fired among them three ways and then fell in with the butt ends of their muskets, their swords, armed staves, and hatchets, and laid about them so well that, in a word, they set up a dismal screaming and howling, flying to save their lives which way soever they could.

Our men were tired with the execution and killed or mortally wounded in the two fights about one hundred and eighty of them. The rest, being frightened out of their wits, scoured through the woods and over the hills, with all the speed fear and nimble feet could help them to; and as we did not trouble ourselves much to pursue them, they got all together to the seaside where they landed and where their canoes lay. But their disaster was not at an end yet; for it blew a terrible storm of wind that evening from the sea so that it was impossible for them to go off. Nay, the storm continuing all night, when the tide came up, their canoes were most of them driven by the surge of the sea so high upon the shore that it required infinite toil to get them off; and some of them were even dashed to pieces against the beach or against one another.

Our men, though glad of their victory, yet got little rest that night; but having refreshed themselves as well as they could, they resolved to march to that part of the island where the savages were fled and see what posture they were in. This necessarily led them over the place where the fight had been, and where they found several of the poor creatures not quite dead and yet past recovering life—a sight disagreeable enough to generous minds, for a truly great man, though obliged by the law of battle to destroy his enemy, takes no delight in his misery. However, there was no need to give any orders

Their savages dispatched these poor creatures with their hatchets

in this case, for their own savages, who were their servants, dispatched these poor creatures with their hatchets.

At length they came in view of the place where the more miserable remains of the savages' army lay, where there appeared about a hundred still; their posture was generally sitting upon the ground, with their knees up toward their mouths, and their heads put between their hands, leaning down upon the knees.

When our men came within two musket shots of them, the governor ordered two muskets to be fired, without ball, to alarm them; this he did that by their countenance he might know what to expect, whether they were still in heart to fight or were so heartily beaten as to be dispirited and discouraged, and so he might manage accordingly. This stratagem worked: for as soon as the savages heard the first gun and saw the flash of the second, they started up upon their feet in the greatest consternation imaginable; and as our men advanced swiftly toward them, they all ran screaming and yelling away, with a kind of howling noise, which our men did not understand and had never heard before; and thus they ran up the hills into the country.

Chapter 7

THE GOVERNOR
BRINGS GIFTS

At first our men had much rather the weather had been calm, and they had all gone away to sea; but they did not then consider that this might probably have been the occasion of their coming again in such multitudes as not to be resisted, or, at least, to come so many and so often as would quite desolate the island and starve them. Will Atkins, therefore, who, notwithstanding his wound, kept always with them, proved the best counselor in this case. His advice was to take the advantage that offered and step in between them and their boats and so deprive them of the capacity of ever returning anymore to plague the island.

They consulted long about this; and some were against it for fear of making the wretches fly to the woods and live there desperate, and so they should have to hunt them like wild beasts, be afraid to stir out about their business, and have their plantations continually rifled, all their tame goats destroyed, and, in short, be reduced to a life of continual distress.

Will Atkins told them they had better have to do with a hundred men than with a hundred nations; that as they must destroy their boats, so they must destroy the men, or be all of them destroyed themselves. In a word, he showed the necessity of it so plainly that they all agreed to it. So they went to work immediately with the boats, and getting some dry wood together from a dead tree, they tried to set some of them on fire, but they were so wet that they would not burn. However, the fire so burned the upper part that it soon made them unfit for use in the sea as boats. When the Indians saw what they were about, some of them came running out of the woods and, coming as near as they could to our men, kneeled down and cried, "Oa, Oa, Waramokoa!" and some other words of their language, which none of the others understood anything of. But as they made pitiful gestures and strange noises, it was easy to understand they begged to have their boats spared and that they would be gone and never come there again. But our men were now satisfied that they had no way to preserve themselves or to save their colony but effectually to prevent any of these people from ever going home again—depending upon this, that if even so much as one of them got back into their country to tell the story, the colony was undone. So letting them know that they should not have any mercy, they fell to work with their canoes and destroyed every one that the storm had not destroyed before. At the sight, the savages raised a hideous cry in the woods, which our people heard plain enough, after which they ran about the island like distracted men, so that, in a word, our men did not really know what at first to do with them. Nor did the Spaniards, with all their prudence, consider that while they made those people thus desperate, they ought to have kept a good guard at the same time upon their plantations; for though it is true, they had driven away their cattle, and the Indians did not find out their main retreat—I mean my old castle at the hill, nor the cave in the valley—yet they found out my plantation at the bower and pulled it all to pieces, and all the fences and planting about it; trod all the corn underfoot, tore up the vines and grapes, being just then almost ripe, and did our men an inestimable damage, though to themselves not one farthing's worth of service.

Though our men were able to fight them upon all occasions, yet they were in no condition to pursue them or hunt them up and down; for as they were too nimble of foot for our men when they found them single, so our men durst not go abroad single, for fear of being surrounded with their numbers. The best was, they had no weapons; for though they had bows, they had no arrows left, nor any materials to make any; nor had they any edge-tool or weapon among them.

The extremity and distress they were reduced to was great and indeed deplorable. But at the same time, our men were also brought to very bad circumstances by them; for though their retreats were preserved, yet their provision was destroyed and their harvest spoiled, and what to do or which way to turn themselves, they knew not. The only refuge they had now was the stock of cattle they had in the valley by the cave and some little corn that grew there and the plantation of the three Englishmen, Will Atkins and his comrades, who were now reduced to two—one of them being killed by an arrow, which struck him on the side of his head, just under the temples, so that he never spoke more; and it was very remarkable that this was the same barbarous fellow that cut the poor savage slave with his hatchet and who afterward intended to have murdered the Spaniards.

I looked upon their case to have been worse at this time than mine was at any time, after I first discovered the grains of barley and rice and got into the manner of planting and raising my corn and my tame cattle; for now they had, as I may say, a hundred wolves upon the island that would devour everything they could come at, yet could be hardly come at themselves.

When they saw what their circumstances were, the first thing they concluded was that they would, if possible, drive them up to the farther part of the island, southwest, so that if any more savages came on shore they might not find one another; then, that they would daily hunt and harass them and kill as many of them as they could come at, till they had reduced their number. If they could at last tame them and bring them to anything, they would give them corn and teach them how to plant and live upon their daily labor.

In order to do this, they so followed them and so terrified them with their guns that in a few days, if any of them fired a gun at an Indian, if he did not hit him, yet he would fall down for fear. So dreadfully frightened they were that they kept out of sight farther and farther, till, at last—our men following them and almost every day killing or wounding some of them—they kept up in the woods or hollow places so much that it reduced them to the utmost misery for want of food. Many were afterward found dead in the woods, without any hurt, absolutely starved to death.

When our men found this, it made their hearts relent, and pity moved them, especially the Spaniard who was governor, who was the most gentlemanlike, generous-minded man that I ever met with in my life. He proposed, if possible, to take one of them alive and bring him to understand what they meant, so far as to be able to act as interpreter and go among them and see if they might be brought to some conditions that might be depended upon to save their lives and do us no harm.

It was some while before any of them could be taken; but being weak and half-starved, one of them was at last surprised and made a prisoner. He was sullen at first and would neither eat nor drink; but finding himself kindly used, and victuals given to him, and no violence offered him, he at last grew tractable and came to himself. They brought Old Friday to him, who talked often with him and told him how kind the others would be to them all; that they would not only save their lives but give them part of the island to live in, provided they would give satisfaction that they would keep in their own

They ate their provisions thankfully

bounds and not come beyond it to injure or prejudice others; and that they should have corn given them to plant and make it grow for their bread, and some bread given them for their present subsistence. Old Friday bade the fellow go and talk with the rest of his countrymen and see what they said to it; assuring them that, if they did not agree immediately, they should all be destroyed.

The poor wretches, thoroughly humbled and reduced in number to about thirty-seven, agreed with the proposal at the first offer and begged to have some food given them; upon which, twelve Spaniards and two Englishmen, well armed, with three Indian slaves and Old Friday, marched to the place where they were. The three Indian slaves carried to them a large quantity of bread, some rice boiled up to cakes and dried in the sun, and three live goats; and they were ordered to go to the side of a hill, where they sat down, ate their provisions very thankfully, and were the most faithful fellows to their words that could be thought of; for, except when they came to beg victuals and directions, they never came out of their bounds. And there they lived when I came to the island, and I went to see them.

Teaching the Savages

They had taught them to plant corn, make bread, breed tame goats, and milk them. They lacked nothing but wives, and they soon would have been a nation. They were confined to a neck of land, surrounded with high rocks behind them and a plain lying toward the sea before them, on the southeast corner of the island. They had land enough, and it was very good and fruitful—about a mile and a half broad, and three or four miles in length.

Our men taught them to make wooden spades, such as I made for myself, and gave to them twelve hatchets and three or four knives; and there they lived, the most subjected,[1] innocent creatures that ever were heard of.

After this, the colony enjoyed a perfect tranquility, with respect to the savages, till I came to revisit them, which was about two years after. Now and then, some canoes of savages still came on shore for their triumphal, unnatural feasts; but as they were of several nations, and perhaps had never heard of those that came before or the reason of it, they did not make any search or inquiry after their countrymen—and if they had, it would have been very hard to have found them out.

Thus, I think, I have given a full account of all that happened to them till my return—at least, all that was worth notice. The Indians or savages were wonderfully civilized by them, and they frequently went among them; but

---

1. Totally under the dominion of others.

they forbade, on pain of death, any of the Indians coming to them, because they would not have their settlement betrayed again. One thing was very remarkable, namely, that they taught the savages to make wickerwork, or baskets, but they soon outdid their masters; for they made abundance of most ingenious things in wickerwork, particularly of all sorts of baskets, sieves, birdcages, cupboards, etc.; also chairs to sit on, stools, beds, couches, and abundance of other things; being very ingenious at such work, when they were once put in the way of it.

The New House

My coming was a particular relief to these people, because we furnished them with knives, scissors, spades, shovels, pickaxes, and all things of that kind which they could want. With the help of those tools, they were so very handy that they came at last to build up their huts or houses very handsomely, raddling or working it up like basketwork all the way around—which was a very extraordinary piece of ingenuity and looked very odd, but was an exceeding good fence, as well against heat as against all sorts of vermin. Our men were so taken with it that they got the wild savages to come and do the like for them, so that when I came to see the two Englishmen's colonies, they looked, at a distance, as if they all lived like bees in a hive.

As for Will Atkins, who was now become a very industrious, useful, and sober fellow, he had made himself such a tent of basketwork as, I believe, was never seen. It was one hundred and twenty paces around on the outside, as I measured it by my steps; the walls were as close worked as a basket, in panels or squares of thirty-two in number, and very strong, standing about seven feet high; in the middle was another not above twenty-two paces around but built stronger, being octagon in its form, and in the eight corners stood eight very strong posts. Around the top of this, he laid strong pieces, pinned together with wooden pins, from which he raised a pyramid for a roof of eight rafters—very handsome, I assure you, and joined together very well, though he had no nails and only a few iron spikes, which he made himself, too, out of the old iron that I had left there. Indeed, this fellow showed abundance of ingenuity in several things that he had no knowledge of. He made himself a forge, with a pair of wooden bellows to blow the fire; he made himself charcoal for his work; and he formed out of the iron crows[2] a middling good anvil to hammer upon. In this manner he made many things, but especially hooks, staples, spikes, bolts, and hinges. But to return to the

---

2. Crowbars.

house: After he had pitched the roof of his innermost tent, he worked it up between the rafters with basketwork, so firm, and thatched that over again so ingeniously with rice straw, and over that a large leaf of a tree, which covered the top, so that his house was as dry as if it had been tiled or slated. Indeed, he owned that the savages had made the basketwork for him. The outer circuit was covered as a lean-to, all around this inner apartment, and long rafters lay from the thirty-two angles to the top posts of the inner house, being about twenty feet distant, so that there was a space like a walk within the outer wicker-wall and without the inner, near twenty feet wide.

The inner place he partitioned off with the same wickerwork, but much fairer, and divided into six apartments, so that he had six rooms on a floor, and out of every one of these there was a door—first into the entry, or coming into the main tent, another door into the main tent, and another door into the space or walk that was around it, so that walk was also divided into six equal parts, which served not only for a retreat but to store up any necessaries that the family had occasion for. These six spaces not taking up the whole circumference, what other apartments the outer circle had were thus ordered: As soon as you were in at the door of the outer circle, you had a short passage straight before you to the door of the inner house; but on either side was a wicker partition and a door in it, by which you went first into a large room, or storehouse, twenty feet wide and about thirty feet long, and through that into another not quite so long, so that in the outer circle there were ten handsome rooms, six of which were only to be come at through the apartments of the inner tent and which served as closets or retiring-rooms to the respective chambers of the inner circle; and four large warehouses, or barns, or what you please to call them, which went through one another, two on either hand of the passage, that led through the outer door to the inner tent.

Such a piece of basketwork, I believe, was never seen in the world, nor a house or tent so neatly contrived, much less so built. In this great beehive lived the three families, that is to say, Will Atkins and his companion; the third was killed, but his wife remained with three children, for she was, it seems, big with child when he died. The other two were not at all backward to give the widow her full share of everything—I mean as to their corn, milk, grapes, etc., and when they killed a kid or found a turtle on the shore—so that they all lived well enough; though, it was true, they were not so industrious as the other two, as has been observed already.

One thing, however, cannot be omitted, namely, that as for religion, I do

In this great beehive lived the three families

not know that there was anything of that kind among them. They often, indeed, put one another in mind that there was a God by the very common method of seamen: swearing by His name. Nor were their poor ignorant savage wives much better for having been married to Christians, as we must call them; for as they knew very little of God themselves, so they were utterly incapable of entering into any discourse with their wives about a God, or to talk anything to them concerning religion.

The utmost of all the improvement that I can say the wives had made from them was that they had taught them to speak English pretty well; and most of their children, who were near twenty in all, were taught to speak English, too, from their first learning to speak, though they at first spoke it in a very broken manner, like their mothers. None of these children were above six years old when I came thither, for it was not much above seven years since they had fetched these five savage ladies over; but they had all been pretty fruitful, for they had all children, more or less. I think the cook's mate's wife was big of her sixth child; and the mothers were all a good sort of well-governed, quiet, laborious women, modest and decent, helpful to one another, mighty observant and subject to their masters (I cannot call them husbands), and wanted nothing but to be well instructed in the Christian religion and to be legally married; both which were happily brought about afterward by my means, or at least in consequence of my coming among them.

Having thus given an account of the colony in general, and pretty much of my runagate English, I must say something of the Spaniards, who were the main body of the family and in whose story there are some incidents also remarkable enough.

The Spaniards' Story

I had a great many discourses with them about their circumstances when they were among the savages. They told me readily that they had no instances to give of their application or ingenuity in that country; that they were a poor, miserable, dejected handful of people; that if means had been put into their hands, they had yet so abandoned themselves to despair, and so sunk under the weight of their misfortune, that they thought of nothing but starving. One of them, a grave and sensible man, told me he was convinced they were in the wrong; that it was not the part of wise men to give themselves up to their misery, but always to take hold of the helps that reason offered, as well for present support as for future deliverance. He told me that grief was the most senseless, insignificant passion in the world, for it regarded only things past, which were generally impossible to be recalled or to be remedied, but had no views of things to come and had no share in anything that looked like deliverance, but rather added to the affliction than proposed a remedy. Upon this he repeated a Spanish proverb, which, though I cannot repeat in just the same words that he spoke it in, yet I remember I made it into an English proverb of my own, thus:

> In trouble to be troubled,
> Is to have your trouble doubled.

He ran on then in remarks upon all the little improvements I had made in my solitude (my unwearied application, as he called it), and how I had made a condition, which in its circumstances was at first much worse than theirs, a thousand times more happy than theirs was, even now when they were all together. He told me it was remarkable that Englishmen had a greater presence of mind in their distress than any people that ever he met with; that their unhappy nation and the Portuguese were the worst men in the world to struggle with misfortunes; for their first step in dangers, after the common efforts were over, was to despair, lie down under it, and die, without rousing their thoughts up to proper remedies for escape.

I told him their case and mine differed exceedingly, that they were cast upon the shore without necessaries, without supply of food or present sustenance till they could provide for it. It was true I had this disadvantage and discomfort: that I was alone. But then the supply I had providentially thrown into my hands, by the unexpected driving of the ship on shore, was such a help as would have encouraged any creature in the world to have applied himself as I had done.

"Seignior," said the Spaniard, "had we poor Spaniards been in your case, we should never have got half those things out of the ship, as you did. Nay," said he, "we should never have found means to have got a raft to carry them, or to have got the raft on shore without boat or sail. And how much less should we have done if any of us had been alone!"

Well, I desired him to abate his compliments and go on with the history of their coming on shore and where they had landed. He told me they unhappily had landed at a place where there were people without provisions. Had they had the common sense to put off to sea again and gone to another island a little farther on, there they would have found provisions, though no people—there being an island that way, as they had been told; that is to say, the Spaniards of Trinidad had frequently been there and had filled the island with goats and hogs at several times, where they had bred in such multitudes, and where turtles and seafowls were in such plenty, that they could have been in no want of flesh, though they had found no bread. Here, on the island where they had originally landed, they were only sustained with a few roots and herbs, which they understood not, and which had no substance in them, and which the inhabitants gave them sparingly enough; and they could treat them no better, unless they would turn cannibals and eat men's flesh, which was the great dainty of their country.

They gave me an account how many ways they strove to civilize the savages they were with and to teach them rational customs in the ordinary way of living, but in vain; and how they retorted it upon them as unjust that they, who came there for assistance and support, should attempt to set up for instructors of those that gave them food—intimating, it seems, that none should set up for the instructors of others but those who could live without them.

They gave me dismal accounts of the extremities they were driven to: how sometimes they were many days without any food at all, the island they were upon being inhabited by a sort of savage that lived more indolently and for that reason were less supplied with the necessaries of life than they had reason to believe others were in the same part of the world. Yet they found that these savages were less ravenous and voracious than those who had better supplies of food. Also, they added, they could not but see with what demonstrations of wisdom and goodness the governing providence of God directs the events of things in this world, which, they said, appeared in their circumstances; for if, pressed by the hardships they were under and the barrenness of the country where they were, they had searched after a better to live in, they had then been out of the way of the relief that happened to them by my means.

They then gave me an account of how the savages whom they lived among expected them to go out with them into their wars. It was true that as they had firearms with them, had they not had the disaster to lose their ammunition, they could have been serviceable not only to friends but also have made themselves terrible both to friends and enemies. But being without powder and shot, and yet in a condition that they could not in reason deny to go out with their landlords to their wars, when they came into the field of battle, they were in a worse condition than the savages themselves, for they had neither bows nor arrows, nor could they use those the savages gave them. They could do nothing but stand still and be wounded with arrows, till they came up to the teeth of their enemy. Then, indeed, the three halberds they had were of use to them, and they would often drive a whole little army before them with those halberds and sharpened sticks put into the muzzles of their muskets. But, for all this, they were sometimes surrounded with multitudes and in great danger from their arrows, till at last they found the way to make themselves large targets of wood, which they covered with skins of wild beasts, whose names they knew not, and these covered them from the arrows of the savages. Notwithstanding these, they were sometimes in great danger: Five of them were once knocked down together with the clubs of the savages, which was the time when one of them was taken prisoner, that is to say, the Spaniard whom I relieved. At first they thought he had been killed, but when they afterward heard he was taken prisoner, they were under the greatest grief imaginable and would willingly have all ventured their lives to have rescued him.

They told me that when they were so knocked down, the rest of their company rescued them and stood over them fighting till they were come to themselves—all but he who they thought had been dead. Then they made their way with their halberds and pieces, standing close together in a line, through a body of above a thousand savages, beating down all that came in their way. They got the victory over their enemies, but to their great sorrow, because it was with the loss of their friend, whom the other party, finding alive, carried off, with some others, as I gave an account before.

They described, most affectionately, how they were surprised with joy at the return of their friend and companion in misery, who they thought had been devoured by wild beasts of the worst kind—wild men. And yet, how more and more surprised they were with the account he gave them of his errand and that there was a Christian in any place near, much more one that was able, and had humanity enough, to contribute to their deliverance.

They described how they were astonished at the sight of the relief I sent them and the appearance of loaves of bread—things they had not seen since their coming to that miserable place; how often they crossed it and blessed it as bread sent from heaven; and what a reviving cordial it was to their spirits to taste it, as also the other things I had sent for their supply. After all, they would have told me something of the joy they were in at the sight of a boat and pilots to carry them away to the person and place from whence all these new comforts came, but it was impossible to express it by words; for their excessive joy naturally driving them to unbecoming extravagances, they had no way to describe them but by telling me they bordered upon lunacy, having no way to give vent to their feelings suitable to the sense that was upon them—in some it worked one way, and in some another; some of them, through a surprise of joy, would burst into tears, others be stark mad, and others immediately faint. This discourse extremely affected me and called to my mind Friday's ecstasy when he met his father and the poor people's ecstasy when I took them up at sea after their ship was on fire; the joy of the mate of the ship when he found himself delivered in the place where he expected to perish; and my own joy, when, after twenty-eight years' captivity, I found a good ship ready to carry me to my own country. All these things made me more sensible of the relation of these poor men and more affected with it.

The Governor Makes an Appeal

Having thus given a view of the state of things as I found them, I must relate some of the things I did for these people and the condition in which I left them. It was their opinion—and mine, too—that they would be troubled no more with the savages, or if they were, they would be able to cut them off, if they were twice as many as before; so they had no concern about that. Then I entered into a serious discourse with the Spaniard, whom I called "Governor," about their stay on the island; for as I was not come to carry any of them off, so it would not be just to carry off some and leave others, who, perhaps, would be unwilling to stay if their strength was diminished. On the other hand, I told them I came to establish them there, not to remove them. Then I let them know that I had brought with me relief of sundry kind for them; that I had been at a great expense to supply them with all things necessary, as well for their convenience as their defense; and that I had such and such particular persons with me, as well to increase and recruit their number, as by the particular necessary employments that they were bred to, being artificers, to assist them in those things in which at present they were in want.

They were all together when I talked thus to them; and before I delivered to them the stores I had brought, I asked them, one by one, if they had entirely forgot and buried their first animosities that had been among them and would shake hands with one another and engage in a strict friendship and union of interest, so there might be no more misunderstandings and jealousies.

Will Atkins, with abundance of frankness and good humor, said they had met with affliction enough to make them all sober, and enemies enough to make them all friends; that, for his part, he would live and die with them and was so far from designing anything against the Spaniards that he owned they had done nothing to him but what his own mad humor made necessary and what he would have done, and perhaps worse, in their case; and that he would ask them pardon, if I desired it, for the foolish and brutish things he had done to them; and that he was very willing and desirous of living in terms of entire friendship and union with them and would do anything that lay in his power to convince them of it. As for going to England, he cared not if he did not go thither these twenty years.

The Spaniards said they had, indeed, at first disarmed and excluded Will Atkins and his two countrymen for their ill conduct, as they had let me know, and they appealed to me for the necessity they were under to do so. But Will Atkins had behaved himself so bravely in the great fight they had with the savages and on several occasions since, and he had shown himself so faithful to, and concerned for, the general interest of them all, that they had forgotten all that was past and thought he merited as much to be trusted with arms and supplied with necessaries as any of them. They had testified their satisfaction in him by committing the command to him next to the

We made a splendid feast

governor himself; and as they had entire confidence in him and all his countrymen, so they acknowledged they had merited that confidence by all the methods that honest men could merit to be valued and trusted. They most heartily embraced the occasion of giving me this assurance that they would never have any interest separate from one another.

Upon these frank and open declarations of friendship, we appointed the next day to dine all together; and, indeed, we made a splendid feast. I caused the ship's cook and his mate to come on shore and dress our dinner, and the old cook's mate we had on shore assisted. We brought on shore six pieces of good beef and four pieces of pork, out of the ship's provisions, with our punch bowl, and materials to fill it. In particular, I gave them ten bottles of French claret and ten bottles of English beer—things that neither the Spaniards nor the English had tasted for many years, and which it may be supposed they were very glad of. The Spaniards added to our feast five whole kids, which the cooks roasted; and three of them were sent covered up close on board the ship to the seamen, so that they might feast on fresh meat from on shore, as we did with their salt meat from on board.

My Cargo of Goods

After this feast, at which we were very innocently merry, I brought my cargo of goods. That there might be no dispute about dividing, I showed them that there was a sufficiency for them all, desiring that they might all take an equal quantity of the goods that were for wearing—that is to say, equal when made up. As, first, I distributed linen sufficient to make every one of them four shirts and, at the Spaniard's request, afterward made them up six; these were exceedingly comfortable to them, having been what they had long since forgot the use of, or what it was to wear them. I allotted the thin English stuffs, which I mentioned before, to make everyone a light coat like a frock, which I judged fittest for the heat of the season, cool and loose; and ordered that whenever they decayed, they should make more, as they thought fit; the like for pumps, shoes, stockings, hats, etc.

I cannot express what pleasure, what satisfaction, rested upon the countenances of all these poor men when they saw the care I had taken of them and how well I had furnished them. They told me I was a father to them, and that having such a correspondent as I was in so remote a part of the world, it would make them forget that they were left in a desolate place. And they all voluntarily gave me their word not to leave the place without my consent.

Then I presented to them the people I had brought with me, particularly

I allotted the English stuffs to make everyone a light coat

the tailor, the smith, and the two carpenters, all of them most necessary people; but, above all, my general artificer, whom they could not name anything that was more useful to them. The tailor, to show his concern for them, went to work immediately and, with my leave, made them every one a shirt, the first thing he did. What was still more, he taught the women not only how to sew and stitch and use the needle, but made them assist in making the shirts for their husbands and for all the rest.

As to the carpenters, I scarce need mention how useful they were; for they took to pieces all my clumsy, unhandy things and made clever, convenient tables, stools, bedsteads, cupboards, lockers, shelves, and everything they wanted of that kind. But to let them see how nature made artificers at first, I carried the carpenters to see Will Atkins' basket-house, as I called it; and they both owned they never saw an instance of such natural ingenuity before, nor anything so regular and so handily built, at least of its kind.

One of them, when he saw it, after musing a good while, turned about to me and said, "I am sure that man has no need of us. You need do nothing but give him tools."

Then I brought them out all my store of tools and gave every man a digging spade, a shovel, and a rake, for we had no harrows or plow; and to every separate place a pickax, a crowbar, a broadax, and a saw—always appointing that as often as any were broken or worn out, they should be supplied, without grudging, out of the general stores that I left behind. Nails, staples, hinges, hammers, chisels, knives, scissors, and all sorts of ironwork they had without reserve, as they required; for no man would take more than he needed, and he must be a fool that would waste or spoil them on any account whatever. For the use of the smith, I left two tons of unwrought iron for a supply.

My magazine of powder and arms that I brought them was such, even to profusion, that they could not but rejoice at them; for now they could march, as I used to do, with a musket upon each shoulder, if there was occasion, and would be able to fight a thousand savages, if they had but some little advantages of situation, which also they could not miss, if they had occasion.

I carried on shore with me the young man whose mother was starved to death, and the maid also. She was a sober, well-educated, religious young woman and behaved so gently that everyone gave her a good word. She had, indeed, an unhappy life with us, there being no woman on the ship but herself, but she bore it with patience. After a while, seeing things so well ordered and in so fine a way of thriving upon my island, and considering that they had neither business nor acquaintance in the East Indies, or reason for taking so long a voyage, both of them came to me and desired I would give them leave to remain on the island and be entered among my family, as they called it. I agreed to this readily; and they had a little plot of ground allotted to them, where they had three tents or houses set up, surrounded with a basketwork, palisaded like Atkins', adjoining to his plantation. Their tents were contrived so that they had each of them a room apart to lodge in and a middle tent like a great storehouse, to lay their goods in and to eat and drink in. And now the other two Englishmen removed their habitation to the same place; and so the island was divided into three colonies, and no more—namely, the Spaniards, with Old Friday and the first servants, at my old habitation under the hill, which was, in a word, the capital city. They had so enlarged and extended their works, as well under as on the outside of the hill, that they lived, though perfectly concealed, yet comfortably at large.

Never was there such a city in a wood, and so hid, in any part of the world; for I verily believe that a thousand men might have ranged the island for a month, and if they had not known there was such a thing and looked on purpose for it, they would not have found it; for the trees stood so thick and so close and grew so fast woven one into another that nothing but cutting them down first could discover the place. Only the two narrow entrances where they went in and out could be found, which was not very easy: One of them was close down to the water's edge on the side of the creek, and it was afterward above two hundred yards to the place; and the other was up a ladder, twice, as I have already described it. They had also a large wood, thickly planted, on the top of the hill, containing above an acre, which grew apace and concealed the place from all discovery there, with only one narrow place between two trees, not easily to be discovered, to enter on that side.

The only colony was that of Will Atkins, where there were four families of Englishmen (I mean those I had left there, with their wives and children), three savages that were slaves, the widow and the children of the Englishman who was killed, and the young man and the maid (by the way, we made a wife of her before we went away). There were also the two carpenters and the tailor, whom I brought with me for them; also the smith, who was a very necessary man to them, especially as a gunsmith, to take care of their arms; and my other man, whom I called Jack-of-all-trades, who was in himself as good almost as twenty men, for he was not only a very ingenious fellow but a very merry fellow, and before I went away we married him to the honest maid that came with the youth in the ship I mentioned before.

Chapter 8

THE FRENCH PRIEST

And now I speak of marrying, it brings me naturally to say something of the French ecclesiastic that I had brought with me out of the ship's crew whom I took up at sea. It is true this man was a Roman Catholic, and perhaps it may give offense to some hereafter if I leave anything extraordinary upon record of a man whom, before I begin, I must (to set him out in just colors) represent in terms very much to his disadvantage, at least where Protestants are concerned: First, he was a Papist; secondly, a Popish priest; and thirdly, a French Popish priest. But justice demands of me to give him a due character; and I must say, he was a grave, sober, pious, and most religious person—exact in his life, extensive in his charity, and exemplary in almost everything he did. What, then, can anyone say against being very sensible of the value of such a man, notwithstanding his profession? Though it may be my opinion, perhaps, as well as the opinion of others who shall read this, that he was mistaken.

The first hour that I began to converse with him after he had agreed to go with me to the East Indies, I found reason to delight exceedingly in his conversation; and he first began with me about religion in the most obliging manner imaginable.

"Sir," said he, "you have not only under God" (and at that he crossed his chest) "saved my life, but you have admitted me to go on this voyage in your ship and, by your obliging civility, have taken me into your family, giving me an opportunity of free conversation. Now, sir, you see by my habit what my profession is, and I guess by your nation what yours is. I may think it is my duty, and doubtless it is so, to use my utmost endeavors, on all occasions, to bring all the souls I can to the knowledge of the truth and to embrace the Catholic doctrine; but as I am here under your permission and in your family, I am bound in justice to your kindness, as well as in decency and good manners, to be under your government; and therefore I shall not, without your leave, enter into any debate on the points of religion in which we may not agree, further than you shall give me leave."

I told him his carriage was so modest that I could not but acknowledge it; that it was true we were such people as they called heretics but that he was not the first Catholic I had conversed with, without falling into inconveniences or carrying the questions to any height in debate; that he should not find himself the worse used for being of a different opinion from us, and if we did not converse without any dislike on either side, it should be his fault, not ours.

He replied that he thought all our conversation might be easily separated from disputes; that it was not his business to debate principles with every man he conversed with; and that he rather desired me to converse with him as a gentleman than as a religionist; and that if I would give him leave at any time to discourse upon religious subjects, he would readily comply with it and that he did not doubt but I would allow him also to defend his own opinions as well as he could; but that, without my leave, he would not break in upon me with any such thing. He told me, further, that he would not cease to do all that became him, in his office as a priest, as well as a private Christian, to procure the good of the ship and the safety of all that was on her; and though, perhaps, we would not join with him, and he could not pray with us, he hoped he might pray for us, which he would do upon all occasions. In this manner we conversed; and as he was of the most obliging, gentlemanlike behavior, so he was, if I may be allowed to say so, a man of good sense and, as I believe, of great learning.

He gave me a most diverting account of his life and of the many extraordinary events of it; of many adventures that had befallen him in the few years that he had been abroad in the world. Particularly, it was very remarkable that on the voyage he was now engaged in, he had the misfortune to be five times shipped and unshipped and never to go to the place whither any of the ships he was in at first were headed. His first intent was to have gone to Martinique, and he went on board a ship bound thither at St. Malo. But being forced into Lisbon by bad weather, the ship received some damage by running aground in the mouth of the river Tagus and was obliged to unload her cargo there. Finding a Portuguese ship there bound to the Madeiras and ready to sail, and supposing he should easily meet with a vessel there bound to Martinique, he went on board, in order to sail to the Madeiras. But the master of the Portuguese ship, being but an indifferent mariner, had been off his reckoning, and they drove to Fyal;[1] where, however, he happened to find

---

1. Faial, an island near the Portuguese islands of Azores.

a very good market for his cargo, which was corn. Therefore he resolved not to go to the Madeiras but to load salt at the Isle of May and go away to Newfoundland. The priest had no remedy in this exigency but to go with the ship, and he had a pretty good voyage as far as the Banks (so they call the place where they catch the fish), where, meeting with a French ship bound from France to Quebec, in the river of Canada,[2] and from thence to Martinique to carry provisions, he thought he should have an opportunity to complete his first design. But when he came to Quebec, the master of the ship died, and the vessel proceeded no farther. So on the next voyage, the priest shipped himself for France in the ship that was burned when we took them up at sea, and then shipped with us for the East Indies, as I have already said. Thus he had been disappointed in five voyages, all, as I may call it, in one voyage, besides what I shall have occasion to mention further of him.

But I shall not make digression into other men's stories, which have no relation to my own; I return to what concerns our affairs on the island. The priest came to me one morning (for he lodged among us all the while we were upon the island), and it happened to be just when I was going to visit the Englishmen's colony, at the farthest part of the island—I say, he came to me and told me, with a very grave countenance, that he had for two or three days desired an opportunity of some discourse with me, which he hoped would not be displeasing to me, because he thought it might in some measure correspond with my general design, which was the prosperity of my new colony, and perhaps might put it, at least more than he yet thought it was, in the way of God's blessing.

I looked a little surprised at the last part of his discourse and turned a little short. "How, sir," said I, "can it be said that we are not in the way of God's blessing, after such visible assistances and deliverances as we have seen here and of which I have given you a large account?"

"If you had pleased, sir," said he with a world of modesty and yet great readiness, "to have heard me, you would have found no room to have been displeased, much less to think so hard of me, that I should suggest that you have not had wonderful assistances and deliverances; and I hope, on your behalf, that you are in the way of God's blessing and your design is exceedingly good and will prosper. But, sir, though it were more so than is even possible to you, yet there may be some among you that are not equally right in their actions, and you know that in the story of the children of Israel, one Achan in the camp removed God's blessing from them and turned His hand

2. Today it's known as the St. Lawrence Seaway.

so against them that six-and-thirty of them, though not concerned in the crime, were the objects of divine vengeance and bore the weight of that punishment."

I was sensibly touched with his discourse and told him his inference was so just, and the whole design seemed so sincere and was really so religious in its own nature, that I was very sorry I had interrupted him and begged him to go on. In the meantime, because it seemed that what we both had to say might take up some time, I told him I was going to the Englishmen's plantations and asked him to go with me, and we might discourse of it by the way. He told me he would the more willingly wait on me thither, because it was partly about that which he desired to speak to me. So we walked on, and I pressed him to be free and plain with me in what he had to say.

"Why, then, sir," said he, "be pleased to give me leave to lay down a few propositions, as the foundation of what I have to say, that we may not differ in the general principles, though we may be of some differing opinions in the practice of particulars. First, sir, though we differ in some of the doctrinal articles of religion (and it is very unhappy it is so,

We walked on

especially in the case before us, as I shall show afterward), yet there are some general principles in which we both agree—that there is a God and that this God, having given us some stated general rules for our service and obedience, we ought not willingly and knowingly to offend, either by neglecting to do what He has commanded, or by doing what He has expressly forbidden. And let our different religions be what they will, this general principle is readily owned by us all: that the blessing of God does not ordinarily follow presumptuous sinning against His command; and every good Christian will be naturally concerned to prevent any that are under his care from living in a total neglect of God and His commands. It is not your men being Protestants, whatever my opinion may be of such, that discharges me from being concerned for their souls and from endeavoring, if it lies before me, that they should live in as little distance from enmity with their Maker as possible, especially if you give me leave to meddle so far in your circuit."

I could not yet imagine what he aimed at and told him I granted all he had said. I thanked him that he would so far concern himself for us and begged he would explain the particulars of what he had observed, so that like Joshua, to take his own parable, I might put away the accursed thing from us.

"Why, then, sir," said he, "I will take the liberty you give me. There are three things that, if I am right, must stand in the way of God's blessing upon your endeavors here, and which I should rejoice, for your sake and their own, to see removed. And, sir, I promise myself that you will fully agree with me in them all, as soon as I name them—especially because I shall convince you that every one of them may, with great ease and very much to your satisfaction, be remedied. First, sir," said he, "you have here four Englishmen who have fetched women from among the savages, and have taken them as their wives, and have had many children by them all, and yet are not married to them after any stated legal manner, as the laws of God and man require. Therefore they are yet, in the sense of both, no less than fornicators, if not living in adultery. To this, sir, I know you will object that there was no clergyman or priest of any kind, or any profession, to perform the ceremony; nor any pen and ink, or paper, to write down a contract of marriage and have it signed between them. And I know also, sir, what the Spanish governor has told you—I mean, of the agreement that he obliged them to make when they took those women, namely, that they should choose them out by consent and keep separately to them—which, by the way, is nothing of a marriage, no agreement with the women as wives, but only an agreement among themselves to keep them from quarreling. But, sir, the essence of the sacrament of matrimony" (so he called it, being a Roman) "consists not only in the mutual consent of the parties to take one another as man and wife, but in the formal and legal obligation that there is in the contract to compel the man and woman, at all times, to own and acknowledge each other; obliging the man to abstain from all other women, to engage in no other contract while these subsist, and, on all occasions, as ability allows, to provide honestly for them and their children; and to oblige the women to the same or like conditions, mutatis mutandis, on their side. Now sir," said he, "these men may, when they please or when occasion presents, abandon these women, disown their children, leave them to perish, and take other women and marry them while these are living." Here he added with some warmth, "How, sir, is God honored in this unlawful liberty? And how shall a blessing succeed your endeavors in this place, however good in themselves and however sincere in your design, while these men, who at present are your subjects, under your absolute government and dominion, are allowed by you to live in open adultery?"

I confess I was struck with the thing itself, but much more with the convincing arguments he supported it with; for it was certainly true that, though they had no clergyman upon the spot, yet a formal contract on both sides, made before witnesses and confirmed by any token that they had all agreed to be bound by, though it had been but breaking a stick between them, engaging the men to own these women for their wives upon all occasions and never to abandon them or their children, and the women to the same with their husbands, had been an effectual lawful marriage in the sight of God; and it was a great neglect that it was not done. But I thought to have got off my young priest by telling him that all that part was done when I was not there and that they had lived so many years with them now that if it was adultery, it was past remedy; nothing could be done in it now.

"Sir," said he, "begging your pardon for such freedom, you are right in this, that it being done in your absence, you could not be charged with that part of the crime. But, I beseech you, flatter not yourself that you are not, therefore, under an obligation to do your utmost now to put an end to it. How can you think but that, let the time past lie on whom it will, all the guilt for the future will lie entirely upon you? Because it is certainly in your power now to put an end to it, and in nobody's power but yours."

I was so dull still that I did not understand him right; but I imagined that by putting an end to it, he meant that I should part them and not suffer them to live together any longer. I said to him I could not do that by any means, for that would put the whole island into confusion. He seemed surprised that I should so far mistake him.

"No, sir," said he, "I do not mean that you should now separate them but legally and effectually marry them. And as, sir, my way of marrying them may not be easy to reconcile them to, though it will be effectual, even by your own laws, so your way may be as well before God and as valid among men. I mean by a written contract, signed by both man and woman and by all the witnesses present, which all the laws of Europe would decree to be valid."

I was amazed to see so much true piety and so much sincerity of zeal, besides the unusual impartiality in his discourse as to his own party or church, and such true warmth for preserving the people that he had no knowledge of or relation to; I say, for preserving them from transgressing the laws of God, the like of which I had, indeed, not met with anywhere. But recollecting what he had said of marrying them by a written contract, which I knew he would stand to, I returned it back upon him and told him I granted all that he had said to be just and on his part very kind; that I would discourse with the men upon the point now, when I came to them; and I knew no reason why they should scruple to let him marry them all, which I knew well enough would be granted to be as authentic and valid in England as if they were married by one of our own clergymen. What was afterward done in this matter, I shall speak of by itself.

I then pressed him to tell me what was the second complaint that he had to make, acknowledging that I was very much his debtor for the first and thanked him heartily for it. He told me he would use the same freedom and plainness in the second and hoped I would take it as well; and this was that notwithstanding these English subjects of mine, as he called them, had lived with these women almost seven years, had taught them to speak English and even to read it, and that they were, as he perceived, women of tolerable understanding and capable of instruction, yet they had not, to this hour, taught them anything of the Christian religion—no, not so much as to know that there was a God, or a worship, or in what manner God was to be served, or that their own idolatry, and worshiping they knew not whom, was false and absurd. This, he said, was an unaccountable neglect and what God would certainly call them to account for, and perhaps at last take the work out of their hands. He spoke this very affectionately and warmly.

"I am persuaded," said he, "had those men lived in the savage country whence their wives came, the savages would have taken more pains to have brought them to be idolaters and to worship the devil than any of these men, so far as I can see, have taken with them to teach them the knowledge of the true God. Now, sir," said he, "though I do not acknowledge your religion, or you mine, yet we would be glad to see the devil's servants, and the subjects of his kingdom, taught to know the general principles of the Christian religion; that they might, at least, hear of God and a Redeemer, and of the resurrection, and of a future state—things that we all believe; that they might, at least, be so much nearer coming into the bosom of the true Church than they are now, in the public profession of idolatry and devil worship."

The Work of Conversion

I could hold back no longer: I took him in my arms and embraced him with an excess of emotion.

"How far," said I to him, "have I been from understanding the most essential part of a Christian, namely, to love the interest of the Christian Church, and the good of other men's souls! I scarcely have known what belongs to the being of a Christian."

"Oh, sir! Do not say so," replied he. "This thing is not your fault."

"No," said I. "But why did I never lay it to heart as well as you?"

"It is not too late yet," said he. "Be not too anxious to condemn yourself."

"But what can be done now?" said I. "You see I am going away."

"Will you give me leave to talk with these poor men about it?"

"Yes, with all my heart," said I. "And I will oblige them to give heed to what you say, too."

"As to that," said he, "we must leave them to the mercy of Christ. But it is your business to assist them, encourage them, and instruct them; and if you give me leave and God His blessing, I do not doubt but the poor ignorant souls shall be brought home to the great circle of Christianity, if not into the particular faith we all embrace, and that even while you stay here."

Upon this, I said, "I shall not only give you leave, but give you a thousand thanks for it." What followed I shall mention in its place.

I now pressed him for the third article in which we were to blame.

"Why, really," said he, "it is of the same nature. And I will proceed, asking your leave, with the same plainness as before. It is about your poor savages, who are, as I may say, your conquered subjects. It is a maxim, sir, that is, or ought to be, received among all Christians, of what church or pretended church soever, that the Christian knowledge ought to be propagated by all possible means and on all possible occasions. It is on this principle that our Church sends missionaries into Persia, India, and China; and that our clergy, even of the superior sort, willingly engage in the most hazardous voyages and the most dangerous residence among murderers and barbarians, to teach them the knowledge of the true God and to bring them over to embrace the Christian faith. Now, sir, you have such an opportunity here to have thirty-six to thirty-seven poor savages brought over from a state of idolatry to the knowledge of God, their Maker and Redeemer, that I wonder how you can pass such an occasion of doing good that is really worth the expense of a man's whole life."

The French Priest's Zeal

I was now struck dumb indeed and had not one word to say. I had here the spirit of true Christian zeal for God and religion before me, let his particular principles be of what kind soever. As for me, I had not so much as entertained a thought of this in my heart before, and I believe I should not have thought of it; for I looked upon these savages as slaves and people whom, had we not had any work for them to do, we would have used as such, or would have been glad to have transported them to any other part of the world; for our business was to get rid of them, and we would all have been satisfied if they had been sent to any country, just so they had never seen their own. I was confounded at his discourse and knew not what answer to make to him.

He looked earnestly at me, seeing me in some confusion. "Sir," said he, "I shall be very sorry if what I have said gives you any offense."

"No, no," said I, "I am offended with nobody but myself. But I am perfectly confounded, not only to think that I should never have taken any notice of this before, but with reflecting what notice I am able to take of it now. You know, sir," said I, "what circumstances I am in. I am bound to the East Indies in a ship freighted by merchants and to whom it would be an insufferable piece of injustice to detain their ship here, the men lying all this while at victuals and wages on the owners' account. It is true, I agreed to be allowed twelve days here, and if I stay more, I must pay three pounds sterling per diem demurrage; nor can I stay upon demurrage above eight days more, and I have been here thirteen already; so that I am perfectly unable to engage in this work, unless I would suffer myself to be left behind here again; in which case, if this single ship should miscarry in any part of her voyage, I should be in just the same condition that I was left in here at first and from which I have been so wonderfully delivered."

He owned the case was very hard upon me as to my voyage, but he laid it home upon my conscience whether the blessing of saving thirty-seven souls was not worth venturing all I had in the world for. I was not so sensible of that as he was.

He made me a very low bow

I replied to him thus: "Why, sir, it is a valuable thing, indeed, to be an instrument in God's hand to convert thirty-seven heathens to the knowledge of Christ; but as you are an ecclesiastic and are given over to the work, so it seems so naturally to fall into the way of your profession. How is it, then, that you do not rather offer yourself to undertake it than press me to do it?"

Upon this he faced about just before me as he walked along, and bringing me to a full stop, he made me a very low bow.

"I most heartily thank God and you, sir," said he, "for giving me so evident a call to so blessed a work; and if you think yourself discharged from it and desire me to undertake it, I will most readily do it and think it a happy reward for all the hazards and difficulties of such a broken, disappointed voyage as I have met with that I am dropped at last into so glorious a work."

I discovered a kind of rapture in his face while he spoke this to me: His eyes sparkled like fire, his face glowed, and his color came and went, as if he had been falling into fits. In a word, he was fired with the joy of being embarked in such a work. I paused a considerable while before I could know what to say to him, for I was really surprised to find a man of such sincerity and zeal, and carried out in his zeal beyond the ordinary rate of men, not of his profession only, but even of any profession whatsoever. But after I had considered it awhile, I asked him seriously if he was in earnest and that he would venture, on the single consideration of an attempt to convert those poor people, to be locked up on an unplanted island for, perhaps, his life and at last might not know whether he should be able to do them good or not.

He turned short upon me and asked me what I called a venture. "Pray, sir," said he, "what do you think I consented to go on your ship to the East Indies for?"

"Nay," said I, "that I know not, unless it was to preach to the Indians."

"Doubtless it was," said he, "and do you think, if I can convert these thirty-seven men to the faith of Jesus Christ, it is not worth my time, though I should never be fetched off the island again? Nay, is it not infinitely of more worth to save so many souls than my life is, or the life of twenty more of the same profession? Yes, sir," said he, "I would give Christ and the Blessed Virgin thanks all my days if I could be made the happy instrument of saving the souls of those poor men, though I were never to get my foot off this island or see my native country anymore. But since you will honor me with putting me into this work, for which I will pray for you all the days of my life, I have one humble petition to you besides."

"What is that?" said I.

"Why," said he, "it is that you will leave your man Friday with me to be my interpreter to them and to assist me; for without some help I cannot speak to them, or they to me."

I was sensibly touched at his requesting Friday, because I could not think of parting with him, and that for many reasons: He had been the companion of my travels; he was not only faithful to me but sincerely affectionate to the last degree; and I had resolved to do something considerable for him if he outlived me, as it was probable he would. Then I knew that as I had bred Friday up to be a Protestant, it would quite confound him to bring him to embrace another religion; and he would never, while his eyes were open, believe that his old master was a heretic and would be damned; and this might in the end ruin the poor fellow's principles and so turn him back again to his first idolatry. However, a sudden thought relieved me in this strait, and it was this: I told him I could not say that I was willing to part with Friday on any account whatever, though a work that to him was of more value than his life ought to be to me of much more value than the keeping or parting with a servant. But, on the other hand, I was persuaded that Friday would by no means agree to part with me, and I could not force him to it without his consent, without manifest injustice, because I had promised I would never send him away, and he had promised me that he would never leave me unless I sent him away.

He seemed very much concerned at it, for he had no rational access to these poor people, seeing he did not understand one word of their language, nor they one of his. To remove this difficulty, I told him Friday's father had learned Spanish, which I found he also understood, and he should serve him as an interpreter. So he was much better satisfied, and nothing could deter him from staying and endeavoring to convert them. But Providence gave another very happy turn to all this.

I come back now to the first part of his objections. When we came to the Englishmen, I sent for them all together, and after some account given them of what I had done for them, namely, what necessary things I had provided for them, and how they were distributed, which they were very sensible of and very thankful for, I began to talk to them of the scandalous life they led and gave them a full account of the notice the clergyman had taken of it. Arguing how unchristian and irreligious a life it was, I first asked them if they were married men or bachelors. They soon explained their condition to me and showed that two of them were widowers and the other three were single men, or bachelors. I asked them with what conscience they could take these women, and call them their wives, and have so many children by them, and not be lawfully married to them.

They all gave me the answer I expected, namely, that there was nobody to marry them; that they agreed before the governor to keep them as their wives and to maintain them and own them as their wives; and they thought, as things stood with them, they were as legally married as if they had been married by a parson and with all the formalities in the world.

I told them that no doubt they were married in the sight of God and were bound in conscience to keep them as their wives; but that the laws of men being otherwise, they might desert the poor women and children hereafter; and that their wives, being poor desolate women, friendless and moneyless, would have no way to help themselves. I therefore told them that, unless I was assured of their honest intent, I could do nothing for them but would take care that what I did should be for the women and children without them; and that unless they would give me some assurances that they would marry the women, I could not think it was convenient they should continue together as man and wife; for that it was both scandalous to men and offensive to God, who they could not think would bless them if they went on thus.

All this went on as I expected; and they told me, especially Will Atkins, who now seemed to speak for the rest, that they loved their wives as well as if they had been born in their own native country and would not leave them on any account whatever; and they did verily believe that their wives were as virtuous and as modest and did, to the utmost of their skill, as much for them and for their children as any women could possibly do; and they would not part with them on any account. And Will Atkins, speaking just for himself, added that if any man would take him away and offer to carry him home to England and make him captain of the best man-of-war in the navy, he would not go with him if he might not carry his wife and children with him; and if there was a clergyman on the ship, he would be married to her now with all his heart.

This was just as I would have it. The priest was not with me at that moment, but was not far off. So to try him further, I told him I had a clergyman with me, and if he was sincere, I would have him married the next morning and bade him consider of it and talk with the rest. Atkins said, as for himself, he need not consider it at all, for he was very ready to do it and was glad I had a minister with me, and he believed they would be all willing also. I then told him that my friend, the minister, was a Frenchman and could not speak English, but I would act the clerk between them. He never so much as asked me whether he was a Papist or Protestant, which was, indeed, what I was afraid of. So we parted: I went back to my clergyman, and Will Atkins went in to talk with his companions. I desired the French gentleman not to say anything to them till the business was thoroughly agreed upon, and I told him what answer the men had given me.

Chapter 9

WILL ATKINS FINDS GOD

Before I went from their quarter, they all came to me and told me they had been considering what I had said. They were glad to hear I had a clergyman in my company, and they were very willing to give me the satisfaction I desired and to be formally married as soon as I pleased; for they were far from desiring to part with their wives and that they meant nothing but what was very honest when they chose them. So I appointed them to meet me the next morning. In the meantime, they should let their wives know the meaning of the marriage law, and that it was not only to prevent any scandal, but also to assure them that they should not forsake them, whatever might happen.

The women were easily made sensible of the meaning of the thing and were very well satisfied with it, as, indeed, they had reason to be. So they failed not to attend all together at my apartment the next morning, where I brought out my clergyman. Though he had not on a minister's gown, after the manner of England, or the habit of a priest, after the manner of France, yet having a black vest something like a cassock, with a sash around it, he did not look very unlike a minister. As for his language, I was his interpreter. But the seriousness of his behavior to them, and the scruples he made of marrying the women, because they were not baptized and professed Christians, gave them an exceeding reverence for his person; and there was no need, after that, to inquire whether he was a clergyman or not. Indeed, I was afraid his scruples would have been carried so far as that he would not have married them at all; nay, notwithstanding all I was able to say to him, he resisted me, though graciously, yet very firmly, and at last absolutely refused to marry them, unless he had first talked with the men and the women, too. Though at first I was a little reluctant, yet at last I agreed to it with a good will, perceiving the sincerity of his design.

They all came to me

When he came to them, he let them know that I had acquainted him with
their circumstances and with the present design; that he was very willing to
perform that part of his function and marry them, as I had desired; but that
before he could do it, he must take the liberty to talk with them. He told
them that in the sight of all men and in the purview of the laws of society,
they had lived all this while in open fornication and that it was true that
nothing but the consenting to marry, or effectually separating them from one
another, could now put an end to it. But there was a difficulty in it, too, with
respect to the laws of Christian matrimony, which he was not fully satisfied
with: that of marrying one who is a professed Christian to a savage, an idol-
ater, and a heathen—one who is not baptized. Yet he did not see that there
was time left to endeavor to persuade the women to be baptized, or to profess
the name of Christ, whom they had, he doubted, heard nothing of and without which they could not be baptized. He told them he assumed they were
but indifferent Christians themselves; that they had but little knowledge of
God or of His ways, and therefore he could not expect that they had said

much to their wives on that subject yet. But unless they would promise him to use their influence with their wives to persuade them to become Christians and would, as well as they could, instruct them in the knowledge and belief of the God that made them and to worship Jesus Christ that redeemed them, he could not marry them; for he would have no hand in joining Christians with savages. Nor was it consistent with the principles of the Christian religion and, indeed, it was expressly forbidden in God's law.

They heard all this very attentively, and I delivered it very faithfully to them from his mouth, as near his own words as I could, only sometimes adding something of my own to convince them just how it was and that I was of his mind; and I always very faithfully distinguished between what I said from myself and what were the clergyman's words. They told me it was very true what the gentleman said: that they were very indifferent Christians themselves and that they had never talked to their wives about religion.

"Lord, sir," said Will Atkins, "how should we teach them religion? Why, we know nothing ourselves. Besides, sir," said he, "should we talk to them of God and Jesus Christ, and heaven and hell, it would make them laugh at us and ask us what we believe ourselves. And if we should tell them that we believe all the things we speak of to them, such as of good people going to heaven and wicked people to the devil, they would ask us where we intend to go ourselves, who believe all this and are such wicked fellows as indeed we are. Why, sir, 'tis enough to give them a surfeit of religion at first hearing; folks must have some religion themselves before they pretend to teach other people."

"Atkins," said I to him, "though I am afraid that what you say has too much truth in it, yet can you not tell your wife she is in the wrong; that there is a God, and a religion, better than her own; that her gods are idols; that they can neither hear nor speak; that there is a great Being that made all things and that can destroy all that He has made; that He rewards the good and punishes the bad; and that we are to be judged by Him at last for all we do here? You are not so ignorant, but even nature itself will teach you that all this is true; and I am satisfied you know it all to be true and believe it yourself."

"That is true, sir," said Atkins. "But how can I say anything to my wife of all this, when she will tell me immediately it cannot be true?"

"Not true!" said I. "What do you mean by that?"

"Why, sir," said he, "she will tell me it cannot be true that this God I shall tell her of can be just, or can punish or reward, since I am not punished and sent to the devil—I who have been such a wicked creature as she knows I have been, even to her and to everybody else; and that I should be suffered to live, who have been always acting so contrary to what I must tell her is good and to what I ought to have done."

"Why, truly, Atkins," said I, "I am afraid thou speakest too much truth."

With that I informed the clergyman of what Atkins had said, for he was impatient to know.

"Oh," said the priest, "tell him there is one thing that will make him the best minister in the world to his wife, and that is repentance; for none teach repentance like true penitents. He wants nothing but to repent, and then he will be so much the better qualified to instruct his wife. He will then be able to tell her that there is not only a God and that He is the just rewarder of good and evil, but that He is a merciful Being and, with infinite goodness and long-suffering, forbears to punish those that offend. Waiting to be gracious and willing not the death of a sinner, but rather that he should return and live, He oftentimes suffers wicked men to go a long time and even reserves damnation to the general day of retribution. It is a clear evidence of God and of a future state that righteous men receive not their reward, nor wicked men their punishment, till they come into another world. This will lead him to teach his wife the doctrine of the resurrection and of the last judgment. Let him but repent himself, and he will be an excellent preacher of repentance to his wife."

Will Atkins Has Scruples

I repeated all this to Atkins, who looked very serious all the while and who, we could easily perceive, was more than ordinarily affected with it.

When being eager and hardly suffering me to make an end, he said, "I know all this, master, and a great deal more. I have not the impudence to talk thus to my wife, when God and my conscience know, and my wife will be an undeniable evidence against me, that I have lived as if I had never heard of a God or future state, or anything about it. And to talk of my repenting, alas!" (and with that he fetched a deep sigh, and I could see that the tears stood in his eyes) " 'Tis past all that with me."

"Past it, Atkins?" said I. "What doest thou mean by that?"

"I know well enough what I mean," said he. "I mean 'tis too late, and that is too true."

I told the clergyman, word for word, what he said. The poor, zealous priest—I must call him so, for, be his opinion what it will, he had certainly a most singular affection for the good of other men's souls, and it would be hard to think he had not the like for his own—I say, this affectionate man could not refrain from tears.

Recovering himself, he said to me, "Ask him but one question. Is he sorry that it is too late; or is he troubled and wishes it were not so?"

I put the question fairly to Atkins; and he answered with a great deal of passion, "How could any man be at ease in a condition that must certainly end in eternal destruction? That he was far from being at ease about it, but that, on the contrary, he believed it would one time or other ruin him."

"What do you mean by that?" said I.

"Why," said he, "I believe I shall one time or another cut my throat—to put an end to the terror of it."

The clergyman shook his head, with great concern on his face, when I told him all this.

Turning quickly to me upon it, he said, "If that be his case, we may assure him it is not too late; Christ will give him repentance. But pray," said he, "explain this to him: that as no man is saved but by Christ, and the merit of His passion procuring divine mercy for him, how can it be too late for any man to receive mercy? Does he think he is able to sin beyond the power or reach of divine mercy? Pray tell him there may be a time when provoked mercy will no longer strive, and when God may refuse to hear, but that it is never too late for men to ask mercy. We who are Christ's servants are commanded to preach mercy at all times, in the name of Jesus Christ, to all those that sincerely repent. So it is never too late to repent."

I told Atkins all this, and he heard me with great earnestness. But it seemed as if he turned over the discussion to the rest, for he said to me he would go and have some talk with his wife. So he went out awhile, and we talked to the rest. I perceived they were all stupidly ignorant as to matters of religion, as much as I was when I went rambling away from my father. Yet there were none of them reluctant to hear what had been said, and all of them seriously promised that they would talk with their wives about it and do their best to persuade them to turn Christians.

The clergyman smiled upon me when I reported what answer they gave, but said nothing a good while. At last, shaking his head, he said, "We that are Christ's servants can go no further than to exhort and instruct; and when men comply, submit to the reproof, and promise what we ask, 'tis all we can do; we are bound to accept their good words. But believe me, sir," said he, "whatever you may have known of the life of that man you call Will Atkins, I believe he is the only sincere convert among them. I will not despair of the rest, but that man is apparently struck with the sense of his past life, and I doubt not, when he comes to talk of religion to his wife, he will talk himself effectually into it; for attempting to teach others is sometimes the best way of teaching ourselves. I know a man who, having nothing but a summary notion of religion himself, and being wicked and profligate to the last degree in his life, made a thorough reformation in himself by laboring to convert a Jew. If that poor Atkins begins but once to talk seriously of Jesus Christ to his wife, I'd stake my life for it that he talks himself into a thorough convert, makes himself a penitent—and who knows what may follow?"

The Conversion

Upon this discourse, however, and their promising, as above, to endeavor to persuade their wives to embrace Christianity, the priest married the other three couples; but Will Atkins and his wife were not yet come in. After this, my clergyman, waiting awhile, was curious to know where Atkins was gone.

Turning to me, he said, "I entreat you, sir, let us walk out of your labyrinth here and look. I dare say we shall find this poor man somewhere or other talking seriously to his wife and teaching her already something of religion."

I began to be of the same mind; so we went out together, and I led him a way that none knew but myself, where the trees were so very thick that it was not easy to see through the thicket of leaves and far harder to see in than

Atkins and his tawny wife sitting under a bush

to see out. Coming to the edge of the wood, I saw Atkins and his tawny wife sitting under the shade of a bush, very eager in discourse. I stopped short till my clergyman came up to me, and then, having shown him where they were, we stood and looked very steadily at them a good while. We observed him very earnest with her, pointing up to the sun, and to every quarter of the heavens, and then down to the earth, then out to the sea, then to himself, then to her, to the woods, to the trees.

"Now," said the clergyman, "you see my words are made good. The man preaches to her. Mark him now: He is telling her that our God has made him and her, and the heavens, the earth, the sea, the woods, the trees, etc."

"I believe he is," said I.

Immediately, we perceived Will Atkins start upon his feet, fall down on his knees, and lift up both his hands. We supposed he said something, but we could not hear him; it was too far for that. He did not continue kneeling half a minute, but came and sat down again by his wife and talked to her again. We perceived then the woman was very attentive, but whether she said anything to him we could not tell. While the poor fellow was upon his knees, I could see the tears run plentifully down my clergyman's cheeks, and I could hardly forbear myself. But it was a great affliction to us both that we were not near enough to hear anything that passed between them. However, we could come no nearer for fear of disturbing them; so we resolved to see an end of this piece of still conversation, and it spoke loud enough to us without the help of voice.

He sat down again, as I have said, close by her and talked again earnestly to her, and two or three times we could see him embrace her most passionately; another time we saw him take out his handkerchief and wipe her eyes and then kiss her again with a kind of transport very unusual. After several of these things, we saw him suddenly jump up again and lend her his hand to help her up, when immediately leading her by the hand a step or two, they both kneeled down together and continued so about two minutes.

My friend could bear it no longer but cried out aloud, "St. Paul! St. Paul! Behold, he prayeth!"

I was afraid Atkins would hear him, therefore I entreated him to constrain himself awhile that we might see an end to the scene, which to me, I must confess, was the most affecting that I ever saw in my life. Well, he strove with himself for a while, but was in such raptures to think that the poor heathen woman was become a Christian that he was not able to contain himself: He wept several times, then throwing up his hands and crossing his breast, said a number of things by the way of giving God thanks for so miraculous a testimony of the success of our endeavors. Some he spoke softly, and I could not well hear others; some in Latin, some in French. Then two or three times the tears would interrupt him so that he could not speak at all. But I begged that he would contain himself and let us more narrowly and fully observe what was before us, which he did for a time, the scene not being near ended yet; for after the poor man and his wife were risen again from their knees, we observed him talking still eagerly to her, and we observed by her emotion that she was greatly affected with what he said, by her frequently lifting up her hands, laying her hand to her breast, and such other postures as express the greatest seriousness and attention. This continued about half an hour, and then they walked away so we could see no more of them in there.

I took this interval to say to the clergyman, first, that I was glad to see the particulars we had both been witness to: that though I was hard enough of belief in such cases, yet I began to think that it was all very sincere here, both in the man and his wife, however ignorant they might both be, and I hoped such a beginning would yet have a more happy end. "And who knows," said I, "but these two may in time, by instruction and example, work upon some of the others?"

"*Some* of them?" said he, turning quickly upon me. "Aye, upon *all* of them. Depend upon it, if those two savages—for he has been but little better as you relate it—should embrace Jesus Christ, they will never leave till they work upon all the rest: for true religion is naturally communicative, and he that is once made a Christian will never leave a pagan behind him, if he can help it."

I owned it was a most Christian principle to think so, and a testimony of true zeal, as well as a generous heart, in him. "But, my friend," said I, "will you give me leave to state one difficulty here? I cannot tell how to object the least thing against that affectionate concern which you show for the turning of the poor people from their paganism to the Christian religion. But how does this comfort you, while these people are, in your account, out of the pale of the Catholic Church, without which you believe there is no salvation, so that you esteem these but heretics, as effectually lost as the pagans themselves?"

To this he answered with abundance of candor: "Sir, I am a Catholic of the Roman Church and a priest of the order of St. Benedict, and I embrace all the principles of the Roman faith. But yet, if you will believe me, and that I do not speak in compliment to you, or in respect to my circumstances and your civilities—I say, nevertheless, I do not look upon you, who call yourselves reformed, without some charity: I dare not say (though I know it is our opinion in general) that you cannot be saved. I will by no means limit the mercy of Christ so far as to think that He cannot receive you into the bosom of His Church, in a manner to us unperceivable; and I hope you have the same charity for us. I pray daily for your being all restored to Christ's Church, by whatsoever method He, who is all-wise, is pleased to direct. In the meantime, surely you will allow it consists with me, as a Roman, to distinguish far between a Protestant and a pagan; between one that calls on Jesus Christ, though in a way that I do not think is according to the true faith, and a savage or a barbarian, that knows no God, no Christ, no Redeemer; and if you are not within the pale of the Catholic Church, we hope you are nearer being restored to it than those who know nothing of God or of His Church. I rejoice, therefore, when I see this poor man, who, you say, has been a profligate and almost a murderer, kneel down and pray to Jesus Christ, as we suppose he did, though not fully enlightened; believing that God, from whom every such work proceeds, will sensibly touch his heart and bring him to the further knowledge of that truth in His own time. And if God shall influence this poor man to convert and instruct the ignorant savage, his wife, I can never believe that he shall be cast away himself. And have I not reason, then, to rejoice the nearer any are brought to the knowledge of Christ, though they may not be brought quite home into the bosom of the Catholic Church just at the time when I may desire it, leaving it to the goodness of Christ to perfect His work in His own time and in His own way? Certainly, I would rejoice if all the savages in America were brought, like this poor woman, to pray to God, though they were all to be Protestants at first, rather than they should continue pagans or heathens; firmly believing that He that had bestowed the first light on them would further illuminate them with a beam of His heavenly grace and bring them into the pale of His Church in His own time."

I was astonished at the sincerity and temper of this pious Papist, as much as I was oppressed by the power of his reasoning; and it presently occurred to me that if such a devotion was universal, we might be all Catholic Christians, whatever church or particular profession we joined in; that a spirit of charity would soon work us all up into right principles. And as the clergyman thought that the like charity would make us all Catholics, so I told him I believed, had all the members of his Church the like moderation, they would soon all be Protestants. And there we left that part; for we never disputed at all.

However, I talked to him another way, and taking him by the hand, I said, "My friend, I wish all the clergy of the Romish Church were blessed with such moderation and had an equal share of your charity. I am entirely of your opinion; but I must tell you that if you should preach such doctrine in Spain or Italy, they would put you into the Inquisition."

"It may be so," said he. "I know not what they would do in Spain or Italy, but I will not say they would be the better Christians for that severity; for I am sure there is no heresy in abounding with charity."

Our Talk with Atkins

As Will Atkins and his wife were gone, our business there was over, so we went back our own way. When we came back, we found them waiting to be called in. Observing this, I asked my clergyman if we should reveal to him that we had seen him under the bush or not; and it was his opinion we should not but that we should talk to him first and hear what he would say to us. So we called him in alone, nobody being in the place but ourselves, and I began with him thus:

"Atkins," said I, "prithee what education had you? What was your father?"

"A better man than ever I shall be, sir. My father was a clergyman."

We called him in alone

"What education did he give you?"

"He would have taught me well, sir, but I despised all education, instruction, or correction, like a beast as I was," Atkins replied.

"It is true, Solomon says, 'He that despises reproof is brutish.' "

"Aye, sir, I was brutish indeed, for I murdered my father. For God's sake, sir, talk no more about that. Sir, I murdered my poor father."

"Ha! A murderer!"

Here the priest started (for I interpreted every word he spoke) and looked pale: It seems he believed that Will had really killed his father.

"No, no, sir; I do not understand him so," I said quickly. "Atkins, explain yourself. You did not kill your father, did you, with your own hands?"

"No, sir, I did not cut his throat, but I cut the thread of all his comforts and shortened his days. I broke his heart by the most ungrateful, unnatural return for the most tender and affectionate treatment that ever father gave or child could receive."

"Well, I did not ask you about your father to extort this confession. I pray God give you repentance for it and forgive that and all your other sins. I asked you because I see that though you have not much learning, yet you are not so ignorant as some are in things that are good; that you have known more of religion, a great deal, than you have practiced."

"Though you, sir, do not extort the confession that I make about my father, conscience does. Whenever we come to look back upon our lives, the sins against our indulgent parents are certainly the first to touch us; the wounds they make lie deepest, and the weight they leave will lie heaviest upon the mind, of all the sins we can commit."

"You talk too feelingly and sensibly for me, Atkins. I cannot bear it."

"*You* bear it, master! I dare say you know nothing of it."

"Yes, Atkins; every shore, every hill, nay, I may say every tree on this island, is witness to the anguish of my soul for my ingratitude to, and bad usage of, a good, tender father, a father much like yours, by your description. And I murdered my father as well as you, Atkins. But I think, for all that, my repentance is short of yours, too, by a great deal."

I would have said more, if I could have restrained my emotions; but I thought this poor man's repentance was so much sincerer than mine that I was going to leave off the discourse and retire; for I was surprised with what he had said and thought that instead of my going about to teach and instruct him, the man was made a teacher and instructor to me in a most surprising and unexpected manner.

I laid all this before the young clergyman, who was greatly affected with it and said to me, "Did I not say, sir, that when this man was converted, he would preach to us all? I tell you, sir, if this one man be made a true penitent, there will be no need of me here. He will make Christians of all on the island."

But having a little composed myself, I renewed my discourse with Will Atkins. "But Will," said I, "how comes the sense of this matter to touch you just now?"

"Sir, you have set me about a work that has struck a dart through my very soul: I have been talking about God and religion to my wife, in order, as you directed me, to make a Christian of her, and she has preached such a sermon to me as I shall never forget while I live."

"No, no," I said, "it is not your wife who has preached to you; but when you were speaking to her about religion, conscience has flung it back upon you."

"Aye, sir," Atkins replied, "and with such force as is not to be resisted."

"Pray, Will, let us know what passed between you and your wife, for I know something of it already."

"Sir, it is impossible to give you a full account of it. I am too full to hold it and yet have no tongue to express it. But let her have said what she will, though I cannot give you an account of it, this I can tell you: that I have resolved to amend and reform my life."

"But tell us some of it," said I. "How did you begin, Will? For this has been an extraordinary case, that is certain. She has preached a sermon, indeed, if she has wrought this upon you."

"Why, I first told her the nature of our laws about marriage and what the reasons were that men and women were obliged to enter into such compacts as it was neither in the power of one nor the other to break; that otherwise, order and justice could not be maintained, and men would run from their wives and abandon their children, mix confusedly with one another, and neither families be kept entire nor inheritances be settled by legal descent."

"You talk like a man of law, Will. Could you make her understand what you meant by inheritance and families? They know no such things among the savages, but marry anyhow, without regard to relation, consanguinity, or family—brother and sister, nay, as I have been told, even the father and the daughter, and the son and the mother."

"I believe, sir, you are misinformed. My wife assures me to the contrary, and that they abhor it. Perhaps, for any further relations, they may not be so exact as we are; but she tells me never in the near relationship you speak of."

"Well, what did she say to what you told her?"

"She said she liked it very well, as it was much better than in her country."

"But did you tell her what marriage was?"

"Aye, aye. There began all our dialogue. I asked her if she would be married to me our way. She asked me what way that was. I told her marriage was appointed by God; and here we had a strange talk together, indeed— as ever man and wife had, I believe."

This dialogue between Will Atkins and his wife I took down in writing, just after he told it me, which was as follows.

Will Atkins and His Wife

Wife: "Appointed by your God! Why, have you a God in your country?"

W.A.: "Yes, my dear, God is in every country."

Wife: "No your God in my country. My country have the great old Benamuckee god."

W.A.: "Child, I am very unfit to show you who God is. God is in heaven and made the heaven and the earth, the sea, and all that is in them."

Wife: "No makee de earth; no your God makee de earth; no makee my country."

Will Atkins laughed a little at her expression of God not making her country.

Wife: "No laugh; why laugh me? This nothing to laugh."

He was justly reproved by his wife, for she was more serious than he at first.

W.A.: "That's true, indeed. I will not laugh anymore, my dear."

Wife: "Why, you say your God makee all?"

W.A.: "Yes, child, our God made the whole world, and you, and me, and all things; for He is the only true God; and there is no God but Him. He lives forever in heaven."

Wife: "Why you no tell me long ago?"

W.A.: "That's true, indeed; but I have been a wicked wretch and have not only forgotten to acquaint you with anything before, but have lived without God in the world myself."

Wife: "What, have you a great God in your country, you no know Him? No say O! to Him? No do good thing for Him? That no possible."

W.A.: "It is true, though, for all that. We live as if there was no God in heaven, or that He had no power on earth."

Wife: "But why God let you do so? Why He no makee you good live?"

W.A.: "It is all our own fault."

Wife: "But you say me He is great, much great, have much great power, can makee kill when He will, why He no makee kill when you no serve Him? No say O! to Him, no be good mans?"

W.A.: "That is true. He might strike me dead; and I ought to expect it, for I have been a wicked wretch, that is true. But God is merciful and does not deal with us as we deserve."

Wife: "But then you do not tell God thankee for that, too?"

W.A.: "No, indeed, I have not thanked God for His mercy, any more than I have feared God for His power."

Wife: "Then your God no God. Me no think believe He be such one, great much power strong: no makee kill you, though you make Him much angry."

W.A.: "What? Will my wicked life hinder you from believing in God? What a dreadful creature I am! And what a sad truth it is that the horrid lives of Christians hinder the conversion of heathens!"

Wife: "How me think you have great much God up there" (she pointed up to heaven) "and yet no do well, no do good thing? Can He tell? Sure He no tell what you do?"

W.A.: "Yes, yes, He knows and sees all things. He hears us speak, sees what we do, knows what we think, though we do not speak."

Wife: "What? He no hear you curse, swear, speak de great damn?"

W.A.: "Yes, yes, He hears it all."

Wife: "Where be then the much great power strong?"

W.A.: "He is merciful, that is all we can say for it; and this proves Him to be the true God. He is God and not man, and therefore we are not consumed."

Here Will Atkins told us he was struck with horror, to think how he could tell his wife so clearly that God sees, and hears, and knows the secret thoughts of the heart, and all that we do, and yet that he had dared to do all the vile things he had done.

Wife: "Merciful! What you call that?"

W.A.: "He is our Father and Maker, and He pities and spares us."

Wife: "So then He never makee kill, never angry when you do wicked? Then He no good Himself, or no great able."

W.A.: "Yes, yes, my dear, He is infinitely good and infinitely great and able to punish, too; and sometimes, to show His justice and vengeance, He lets fly His anger to destroy sinners and make examples; many are cut off in their sins."

Wife: "But no makee kill you yet; then He tell you, maybe, that He no makee you kill. So you makee de bargain with Him, you do bad thing, He no be angry at you when He be angry at other mans."

W.A.: "No, indeed, my sins are all presumptions upon His goodness; and He would be infinitely just if He destroyed me, as He has done other men."

Wife: "Well, and yet no kill, no makee you dead. What you say to Him for that? You no tell Him thankee for all that, too?"

W.A.: "I am an unthankful, ungrateful dog, that is true."

Wife: "Why He no makee you much good better? You say He makee you."

W.A.: "He made me as He made all the world. It is I who have deformed myself and abused His goodness and made myself an abominable wretch."

Wife: "I wish you makee God know me. I no makee Him angry—I no do bad, wicked thing."

Here Will Atkins said his heart sank within him, to hear a poor, untaught creature desire to be taught to know God, and he such a wicked wretch that he could not say one word to her about God, but what the reproach of his own behavior would make most irrational to her and hard to believe—nay, that already she had told him that she could not believe in God, because he, who was so wicked, was not destroyed.

W.A.: "My dear, you mean, you wish I could teach you to know God, not God to know you; for He knows you already, and every thought in your heart."

Wife: "Why, then He know what I say to you now: He know me wish to know Him. How shall me know who makee me?"

W.A.: "Poor creature! He must teach thee: I cannot teach thee. I will pray to Him to teach thee to know Him and forgive me, who is unworthy to teach thee."

The poor fellow was in such an agony at her desiring him to make her know God and her wishing to know Him that he said he fell down on his knees before her and prayed to God to enlighten her mind with the saving knowledge of Jesus Christ, and to pardon his sins, and accept of his being the unworthy instrument of instructing her in the principles of religion—after which he sat down by her again, and their dialogue went on. This was the time when we saw him kneel down and hold up his hands.

Wife: "What you put down the knee for? What you hold up the hand for? What you say? Who you speak to? What is all that?"

W.A.: "My dear, I bow my knees in token of my submission to Him that made me. I said O! to Him, as you call it, and as your old men do to their idol Benamuckee; that is, I prayed to Him."

Wife: "What you say O! to Him for?"

W.A.: "I prayed to Him to open your eyes and your understanding, that you may know Him and be accepted by Him."

Wife: "Can He do that, too?"

W.A.: "Yes, He can; He can do all things."

Wife: "But now He hear what you say?"

W.A.: "Yes. He has bid us pray to Him and promised to hear us."

Wife: "Bid you pray? When He bid you? How He bid you? What you hear Him speak?"

W.A.: "No, we do not hear Him speak; but He has revealed Himself in many ways to us."

Here he was at a great loss to make her understand that God has revealed Himself to us by His Word and what His Word was; but at last he told it to her thus:

W.A.: "God has spoken to some good men in former days, even from heaven, by plain words; and God has inspired good men by His Spirit, and they have written all His laws down in a book."

Wife: "Me no understand that. Where is book?"

W.A.: "Alas, my poor creature, I have not this book; but I hope I shall one time or other get it for you and help you to read it."

Here he embraced her with great affection, but with inexpressible grief that he had not a Bible.

Wife: "But how you makee me know that God teachee them to write that book?"

W.A.: "By the same rule that we know Him to be God."

Wife: "What rule? What way you know Him?"

W.A.: "Because He teaches and commands nothing but what is good, righteous, and holy and intends to make us perfectly good, as well as perfectly happy; and because He forbids, and commands us to avoid, all that is wicked, that is evil in itself or evil in its consequence."

Wife: "That me would understand, that me fain see. If He teachee all good thing, He makee all good thing, He give all thing, He hear me when I say O! to Him, as you do just now; He makee me good, if I wish to be good; He spare me, no makee kill me, when I no be good—all this you say He do, yet He be great God. Me take, think, believe Him to be great God: Me say O! to Him with you, my dear."

Here the poor man could forbear no longer but raised her up and made her kneel by him. Then he prayed to God aloud to instruct her in the knowl-

The man made her kneel by him

edge of Himself, by His Spirit; and that by some good providence, if possible, she might, some time or other, come to have a Bible so that she might read the Word of God and be taught by it to know Him. This was the time that we saw him lift her up by the hand and saw him kneel down by her, as above.

They had several other discourses, it seems, after this, too long to be set down here; and particularly, she made him promise that since he confessed his own life had been a wicked, abominable course of provocations against God that he would reform it and not make God angry anymore, lest He should make him dead, as she called it, and then she would be left alone and never be taught to know this God better; and lest he should be miserable, as he had told her wicked men would be, after death.

This was a strange account and very affecting to us both, but particularly to the young clergyman. He was, indeed, wonderfully surprised with it, but under the greatest affliction imaginable that he could not talk to her, that he could not speak English, to make her understand him; and as she spoke but very broken English, he could not understand her. However, he turned to me and told me that he believed that there must be more to do with this woman than to marry her. I did not understand him at first; but at length he explained himself, namely, that she ought to be baptized. I agreed with him in that part readily and wished it to be done right away.

"No, no. Hold, sir," said he. "Though I would have her be baptized, by all means, for I must observe that Will Atkins, her husband, has indeed brought her, in a wonderful manner, to be willing to embrace a religious life and has given her just ideas of the being of God, of His power, justice, and mercy; yet I desire to know of him if he has said anything to her of Jesus Christ and of the salvation of sinners; of the nature of faith in Him and redemption by Him; of the Holy Spirit, the resurrection, the last judgment, and the future state."

I called Will Atkins again and asked him. The poor fellow fell immediately into tears and told us he had said something to her of all those things but that he was himself so wicked a creature, and his own conscience so reproached him with his horrid, ungodly life, that he trembled at the apprehensions that her knowledge of him should lessen the attention she should give to those things and make her rather condemn religion than receive it; but he was assured, he said, that her mind was so disposed to receive due impressions of all those things and that if I would but discourse with her, it would quickly become apparent to me that my labor would not be lost upon her.

Accordingly, I called her in, and placing myself as interpreter between my religious priest and the woman, I entreated him to begin with her; but surely such a sermon was never preached by a Popish priest in these latter ages of the world; and, as I told him, I thought he had all the zeal, all the knowledge, all the sincerity of a Christian, without the error of a Roman Catholic; and that I took him to be such a clergyman as the Roman bishops were before the Church of Rome assumed spiritual sovereignty over the consciences of men. In a word, he brought the poor woman to embrace the knowledge of Christ and of redemption by Him, not with wonder and astonishment only, as she did the first notions of a God, but with joy and faith; with an affection and a surprising degree of understanding, scarcely to be imagined, much less to be expressed—and, at her own request, she was baptized.

When he was preparing to baptize her, I entreated him that he would perform that office with some caution, that the man might not perceive he was of the Roman Church, if possible, because of other ill consequences that might attend a difference among us in that very religion which we were instructing the other in. He told me that as he had no consecrated chapel, nor proper things for the office, I should see he would do it in a manner that I should not know by it that he was a Roman Catholic myself, if I had not known it before; and so he did, for saying only some words over to himself in Latin, which I could not understand, he poured a whole dishful of water upon the woman's head, pronouncing in French, very loud, "Mary" (which was the name her husband desired me to give her, for I was her godfather), "I baptize thee in the name of the Father, and of the Son, and of the Holy Ghost," so that none could know anything by it what religion he was of. He gave the benediction afterward in Latin, but either Will Atkins did not know but it was French, or else did not take notice of it at that time.

Another Wedding

As soon as this was over, we married them. After the marriage was over, he turned to Will Atkins and in a very affectionate manner exhorted him, not only to persevere in that good disposition he was in, but to support the convictions that were upon him by a resolution to reform his life; told him it was in vain to say he repented if he did not forsake his crimes; reminded him how God had honored him with being the instrument of bringing his wife to the knowledge of the Christian religion and that he should be careful he should not dishonor the grace of God; and that if he did, he would see the heathen a better Christian than himself—the savage converted, and the instrument cast away. He said a great many good things to them both; and then, recommending them to God's goodness, gave them the benediction again, I repeating everything to them in English. This ended the ceremony. I think it was the most deeply moving day to me that ever I passed in my whole life.

But my clergyman had not done yet: His thoughts hung continually upon the conversion of the thirty-seven savages, and fain he would have stayed upon the island to have undertaken it. But I convinced him, first, that his undertaking was impracticable in itself; and, secondly, that perhaps I would put it into a way of being done in his absence to his satisfaction.

Having thus brought the affairs of the island to a close, I was preparing to go on board the ship, when the young man I had taken out of the famished ship's company came to me and told me he understood I had a clergyman with me and that I had caused the Englishmen to be married to the savages; that he had a match, too, which he desired might be finished before I went, between two Christians, which he hoped would not be disagreeable to me.

I knew this must be the young woman who was his mother's servant, for there was no other Christian woman on the island; so I began to persuade him not to do anything of that kind rashly, or because he found himself in solitary circumstances. I reminded him that he had some considerable substance in the world, and good friends, as I understood by himself, and the maid also; that the maid was not only poor and a servant but was unequal to him, she being six- or seven-and-twenty years old, and he not above seventeen or eighteen; that he might very probably, with my assistance, make a remove from this wilderness and come into his own country again; and that then it would be a thousand to one but he would repent his choice, and the dislike of that circumstance might be disadvantageous to both. I was going to say more, but he interrupted me, smiling, and told me, with a great deal of modesty, that I mistook in my guesses; that he had nothing of that kind

in his thoughts; and he was very glad to hear that I had an intent of putting
them in a way to see their own country again; and nothing should have made
him think of staying there, but that the voyage I was going on was so exceedingly long and hazardous and would carry him quite out of the reach of all
his friends; that he had nothing to desire of me, but that I would settle him
in some little property on the island where he was, give him a servant or two
and some few necessaries, and he would live here like a planter, waiting the
good time when, if ever I returned to England, I would redeem him; and
hoped I would not be unmindful of him when I came to England—that he
would give me some letters to his friends in London, to let them know how
good I had been to him and in what part of the world and what circumstances I had left him in; and he promised me that whenever I redeemed
him, the plantation and all the improvements he had made upon it, let the
value be what it would, should be wholly mine.

His discourse was very prettily delivered, considering his youth, and was
the more agreeable to me, because he told me positively the match was not
for himself. I gave him all possible assurances that if I lived to come safely to
England, I would deliver his letters and do his business effectually and that
he might depend I should never forget the circumstances I had left him in.
But still I was impatient to know who was the person to be married; upon
which he told me it was my Jack-of-all-trades and his maid, Susan. I was
most agreeably surprised when he named the match; for, indeed, I thought
it very suitable. The character of that man I have given already; and as for the
maid, she was a very honest, modest, sober, and religious young woman; had
a very good share of sense, was agreeable enough in her person, spoke very
handsomely and to the purpose, always with decency and good manners, and
was neither too backward to speak when appropriate, nor impertinently
forward when it was not her business; very handy and housewifely and an
excellent manager; fit, indeed, to have been governess to the whole island;
and she knew very well how to behave in every respect.

The match being proposed in this manner, we married them the same day.
As I was father at the altar and gave her away, so I gave her a portion; for I
appointed her and her husband a handsome large space of ground for their
plantation. Indeed, this match and the proposal of the young gentleman—
to give him a small property on the island—resulted in my parceling it out
among them, that they might not quarrel afterward about their situation.

This sharing out the land to them I left to Will Atkins, who was now
grown a sober, grave, managing fellow, perfectly reformed, exceedingly pious

We married them the same day

and religious; and, as far as I may be allowed to speak positively in such a case, I verily believe he was a true penitent. He divided things so justly, and so much to everyone's satisfaction, that they only desired one general writing under my hand for the whole, which I caused to be drawn up and signed and sealed, setting out the bounds and situation of every man's plantation and testifying that I gave them thereby severally a right to the whole possession and inheritance of the respective plantations or farms, with their improvements, to them and their heirs, reserving all the rest of the island as my own property and a certain rent for every particular plantation after eleven years, if I, or anyone from me or in my name, came to demand it, producing an attested copy of the same writing.

As to the government and laws among them, I told them I was not capable of giving them better rules than they were able to give themselves; only I made them promise me to live in love and good fellowship with one another. And so I prepared to leave them.

One thing I must not omit, and that is that being now settled in a kind of commonwealth among themselves and having much business in hand, it was odd to have seven-and-thirty Indians live in a nook of the island independent and, indeed, unemployed; for, excepting the providing themselves with food, which they had difficulty enough to do, they had no manner of business or property to manage. I proposed, therefore, to the Spaniard who was governor that he should go to them with Friday's father and propose to them to remove and either plant for themselves or be taken into their several families as servants, to be maintained for their labor, but without being absolute slaves; for I would not permit them to make them slaves by force, by any means; because they had their liberty given them by capitulation, as it were articles of surrender, which they ought not to break.

They most willingly embraced the proposal and came all very cheerfully along with him. So we allotted them land and plantations, which three or four accepted of, but all the rest chose to be employed as servants in the several families we had settled. Thus my colony was in a manner settled as follows: The Spaniards possessed my original habitation, which was the capital city, and extended their plantations all along the side of the brook, which followed the creek that I have so often described, as far as my bower; and as they increased their holdings, it went always eastward. The English lived in the northeast part, where Will Atkins and his comrades began, and came on southward and southwest, toward the back part of the Spaniards; and every plantation had a great addition of land to take in, if they found occasion, so that they need not jostle one another for want of room. All the east end of the island was left uninhabited, that if any of the savages should come on shore there only for their usual customary barbarities, they might come and go. If they disturbed nobody, nobody would disturb them. No doubt but they were often ashore and went away again, for I never heard that the planters were ever attacked or disturbed anymore.

Converting the Savages

I was now reminded that I had hinted to my friend the clergyman that the work of converting the savages might perhaps be set on foot in his absence to his satisfaction, and I told him that now I thought that it would come to pass—for the savages, being thus divided among the Christians, if they would but every one of them do their part with those that came under their hands, I hoped it might have a very good effect.

He agreed presently in that, if they did their part. "But how," said he, "shall we obtain that of them?"

I told him we would call them all together and leave the matter in their charge, or go to them, one by one—whichever he thought best. So we divided it: he to speak to the Spaniards, who were all Papists, and I to speak to the English, who were all Protestants. We recommended it earnestly to them and made them promise that they would never make any distinction of Papist or Protestant in their exhorting the savages to turn Christians, but teach them the general knowledge of the true God and of their Savior Jesus Christ; and they likewise promised us that they would never have any differences or disputes one with another about religion.

When I came to Will Atkins' house (I may call it so, for no such house, or such a piece of basketwork, I believe was standing in the whole world other than his), there I found that the young woman I have just mentioned and Will Atkins' wife were become intimates. This prudent, religious young woman had perfected the work Will Atkins had begun; and though it was not more than four days after what I have related, yet the newly baptized savage woman was made such a Christian as I have seldom heard of in all my life.

It came next to me in the morning before I went to them that among all the needful things I had to leave with them, I had not left them a Bible—in which I showed less consideration for them than my good friend the widow did for me when she sent me the cargo of a hundred pounds from Lisbon, wherein she packed up three Bibles and a prayer book. However, the good woman's charity had a greater impact than ever she imagined, for they were reserved for the comfort and instruction of those that made much better use of them than I had done.

I took one of the Bibles in my pocket, and I came to Will Atkins' tent, or house, and found the young woman and Atkins' baptized wife had been discussing religion together—for Will Atkins told it to me with a great deal of joy. I asked if they were together now, and he said yes; so I went into the house, and he with me, and we found them together very earnestly in discourse.

"Oh, sir," said Will Atkins, "when God has sinners to reconcile to Himself, and aliens to bring home, He never lacks a messenger: My wife has got a new instructor. I knew I was unworthy, as I was incapable of that work; that young woman has been sent hither from heaven. She is enough to convert a whole island of savages."

The young woman blushed and rose up to go away, but I desired her to sit still. I told her she had a good work upon her hands, and I hoped God would bless her in it.

A Present to Will Atkins

We talked a little, and I did not perceive that they had any book among them, though I did not ask; but I put my hand into my pocket and pulled out my Bible.

"Here," said I to Atkins, "I have brought you an assistant that perhaps you had not before."

The man was so confounded that he was not able to speak for some time; but recovering himself, he took it with both his hands, and turning to his wife, he said, "Here, my dear. Did I not tell you our God, though He lives above, could hear what we have said? Here's the book I prayed for when you and I kneeled down under the bush. Now God has heard us and sent it."

When he had said so, the man fell into such transports of passionate joy that between the joy of having it and giving God thanks for it, the tears ran down his face like those of a crying child.

The woman was surprised and was like to have run into a mistake that none of us were aware of, for she firmly believed God had sent the book upon her husband's petition. It is true that providentially it

"I have brought you an assistant"

was so and might be taken so in a consequent sense; but I believe it would have been no difficult matter at that time to have persuaded the poor woman to have believed that an express messenger came from heaven on purpose to bring that individual book. But it was too serious a matter to suffer any delusion to take place, so I turned to the young woman and told her we did not desire to impose upon the new convert in her first and more simple understanding of things and begged her to explain to her that God may be very properly said to answer our petitions, when, in the course of His providence, such things are in a particular manner brought to pass as we petitioned for: but we do not generally expect returns from heaven in a miraculous and particular manner, and it is a mercy that it is not so.

This the young woman did afterward effectually, so that there was, I assure you, no priestcraft used here; and I should have thought it one of the most unjustifiable frauds in the world to have had it so. But Will Atkins' surprise of joy was wonderful to see—and there we may be sure was no delusion. Surely no man was ever more thankful in the world for anything of its kind than he was for the Bible; nor, I believe, never any man was more glad of a Bible from a better principle: that though he had been a most profligate creature—headstrong, violent, and desperately wicked—yet this man is a standing rule to us all for the well instructing of children, namely, that parents should never give up in their teaching and instructing, nor ever despair of the success of their endeavors, let the children be ever so refractory, or, to appearance, resistant to instruction; for, if ever God, in His providence, touches the conscience of such, the force of their education returns upon them, and the early instruction of parents is not lost, though it may have been many years laid asleep, but some time or other they may reap the benefit of it. Thus it was with this poor man. However ignorant he was of religion and Christian knowledge, he found that he had someone to deal with now more ignorant than himself and that the least part of the instruction of his good father that now came to his mind was of use to him.

Among the rest, it occurred to him, he said, how his father used to insist so much on the inexpressible value of the Bible and the privilege and blessing of it to nations, families, and persons, but he never entertained the least notion of its worth till now. When conversing with heathens, savages, and barbarians, he wanted the help of the written oracle for his assistance.

The young woman was glad of it also for the present occasion, though she had one and so had the youth, on board our ship, among their goods, which were not yet brought on shore. And now, having said so many things of this young woman, I cannot omit telling one story more of her and myself, which has something in it very instructive and remarkable.

Chapter 10

THE LAST OF THE ISLAND

I have related to what extremity the poor young woman was reduced—how her mistress was starved to death and died on board that unhappy ship we met at sea, and how the ship's company were reduced to the last extremity. The gentlewoman, and her son, and this maid were first treated unkindly as to provisions and at last totally neglected and starved—that is to say, brought to the last extremity of hunger. One day, being discoursing with her on the hardships they suffered, I asked her if she could describe, by what she had felt, what it was to starve and how it appeared. She told me she believed she could and told her tale very distinctly thus:

"First, sir," said she, "we had for some days fared exceedingly hard and suffered very great hunger; but at last we were wholly without food of any kind, except sugar and a little wine and water. The first day after I had received no food at all, I found myself, toward evening, first empty and sick at the stomach, and nearer night much inclined to yawning and sleep. I lay down on the couch in the great cabin to sleep and slept about three hours and awakened a little refreshed, having taken a glass of wine when I lay down. After being about three hours awake, it being about five o'clock in the morning, I found myself empty and my stomach sickish, and I lay down again but could not sleep at all, being very faint and ill; and thus I continued all the second day with a strange variety—first hungry, then sick again, with retchings to vomit. The second night, being obliged to go to bed again without any food, more than a draught of fresh water, and being asleep, I dreamed I was at Barbados and that the market was mightily stocked with provisions and that I bought some for my mistress and went and dined very heartily. I thought my stomach was as full after this as it would have been after a good dinner; but when I awakened, I was exceedingly sunk in my spirits to find myself in the extremity of famine. The last glass of wine we had, I put sugar in and drank it, because of its having some spirit to supply nourishment, but there being no substance in the stomach for the digesting office to work upon, I found the only effect of the wine was to raise disagreeable fumes from the stomach into the head; and I lay, as they told me, stupid and senseless, as one drunk, for some time. The third day, in the morning, after a night of strange, confused, and inconsistent dreams and rather dozing than sleeping, I awaked ravenous and violently hungry; and I question, had not my understanding returned and conquered it, whether, if I had been a mother and had had a little child with me, its life would have been safe or not. This lasted about three hours, during which time I was twice as raging mad as any creature in Bedlam, as my young master told me and as he can now inform you.

"In one of those fits of lunacy or distraction I fell down and struck my face against the corner of a pallet bed, in which my mistress lay, and with the blow the blood gushed out of my nose. The cabin boy bringing me a little basin, I sat down and bled into it a great deal. As the blood came from me, I came to myself, and the violence of the flame or fever I was in abated, and so did the ravenous part of the hunger. Then I grew sick and retched to vomit but could not, for I had nothing in my stomach to bring up.

"After I had bled some time, I swooned, and they all believed I was dead; but I came to myself soon after and then had a most dreadful pain in my stomach not to be described—not like the colic, but a gnawing, eager pain for food; and toward night it turned into a kind of earnest wishing or longing for food—something like, as I suppose, the longing of a woman with child. I took another draught of water with sugar in it; but my stomach loathed the sugar and brought it all up again. Then I took a draught of water without sugar, and that stayed with me. I laid me down upon the bed, praying most heartily that it would please God to take me away; and composing my mind in hopes of it, I slumbered awhile, and then waking, thought myself dying, being light with vapors from an empty stomach. I recommended my soul then to God and earnestly wished that somebody would throw me into the sea.

"All this while my mistress lay by me, just, as I thought, dying but bearing it with much more patience than I—giving the last bit of bread she had left to her child, my young master, who would not have taken it, but she obliged him to eat it; and I believe it saved his life.

"Toward the morning I slept again, and when I awoke, I fell into a violent passion of crying, and after that I had a second fit of violent hunger. I got up ravenous and in a most dreadful condition. Had my mistress been dead, as much as I loved her, I am certain I should have eaten a piece of her flesh with as much relish and unconcern as ever I did eat the flesh of any creature appointed for food; and once or twice I was going to bite my own arm. At last I saw the basin in which was the blood I had bled at my nose the day before: I ran to it and swallowed it with such haste, and such a greedy appetite, as if I wondered that nobody had taken it before and afraid it should be taken from me now. After it was down, though the thoughts of it filled me with horror, yet it checked the fit of hunger, and I took another draught of water and was composed and refreshed for some hours after. This was the fourth day; and thus I kept up till toward night, when, within the compass of three hours, I had all the several circumstances over again, one after another: namely, sick, sleepy, eagerly hungry, pain in the stomach, then ravenous again, then sick, then lunatic, then crying, then ravenous again, and so every quarter of an hour, and my strength wasted exceedingly. At night I lay me down, having no comfort but in the hope that I should die before morning.

"All this night I had no sleep, but the hunger was now turned into a disease; and I had a terrible colic and spasms, because of wind, instead of food, having found its way into the bowels. In this condition I lay till morning, when I was surprised by the cries and lamentations of my young master, who called out to me that his mother was dead. I lifted myself up a little, for I had not strength to rise, but found she was not dead, though she was able to give very little signs of life.

"I had then such convulsions in my stomach, for want of some sustenance, as I cannot describe, with such frequent throes and pangs of appetite, as nothing but the tortures of death can imitate. In this condition I was when I heard the seamen above cry out, 'A sail! A sail!' and halloo and jump about as if they were distracted.

"I was not able to get off from the bed, and the mistress much less; and my young master was so sick that I thought he had been dying. So we could not open the cabin door, or get any account what it was that occasioned such confusion; nor had we had any conversation with the ship's company for two days, they having told us that they had not a mouthful of anything to eat on the ship; and this they told us afterward, they thought we had been dead. It was this dreadful condition we were in when you were sent to save our lives; and how you found us, sir, you know as well as I, and better, too."

This was her own story and as truthful an account of starving to death as, I confess, I have ever met with. I am the rather apt to believe it to be a true account, because the youth gave me an account of a good part of it; though I must own, not so distinct and so full of feeling as the maid's is—and the rather, because it seems his mother fed him at the price of her own life. But the poor maid, though her constitution being stronger than that of her mistress (who was further along in years and a weakly woman, too, thus she might struggle harder with it)—I say, the poor maid might be supposed to feel the extremity somewhat sooner than her mistress, who might be expected to keep the last bit of food herself rather than parting with it to relieve the maid. There is no question, as the case is here related, but that had our ship, or some other, not so providentially met them, a few days more would have ended all their lives, unless they had prevented it by eating one another; and that even, as their case stood, would have served them but a little while, they being five hundred leagues from any land, or any possibility of relief, other than in the miraculous manner it happened—but this is by the way. I return to my disposition of things among the people.

We Leave the Island

First, it is to be observed here, that for many reasons I did not think fit to let them know anything of the sloop I had framed, and which I thought of setting up among them; for I found, at least at my first coming, such seeds of division among them that I saw plainly, had I set up the sloop and left it among them, they would, upon every light disagreement, have separated and gone away from one another; or perhaps have turned pirates and so made the island a den of thieves, instead of a plantation of sober and religious people, as I intended it. Nor did I leave the two pieces of brass cannon that I had on board, or the two extra quarterdeck guns that my nephew took, for the same reason: I thought it was enough to equip them for a defensive war against any that should invade them, but not to set them up for an offensive war, or to go abroad to attack others; which, in the end, would only bring ruin and destruction upon them. I reserved the sloop, therefore, and the guns for their service another way, as I shall observe in its place.

Having now done with the island, I left them all in good circumstances and in a flourishing condition and went on board my ship again on the 6th of May, having been about twenty-five days among them; and as they were all resolved to stay upon the island till I came to remove them, I promised to send them further relief from the Brazils, if I could possibly find an opportunity;

We gave them a salute of five guns

and particularly I promised to send them some cattle, such as sheep, hogs, and cows. As to the two cows and calves that I brought from England, we had been obliged, by the length of our voyage, to kill them at sea, for want of hay to feed them.

The next day, giving them a salute of five guns at parting, we set sail and arrived at the bay of All Saints in the Brazils in about twenty-two days, meeting nothing remarkable in our passage but this: that about three days after we had sailed, being becalmed and the current setting strong to the east-northeast, running, as it were, into a bay or gulf on the land side, we were driven something out of our course, and once or twice our men cried out, "Land to the eastward!" But whether it was the continent or islands we could not tell by any means. But the third day, toward evening, the sea smooth and the weather calm, we saw the sea, as it were, covered toward the land with something very black. Not being able to discover what it was till after some time, our chief mate, going up the mainshrouds[1] a little way and looking at them with a perspective,[2] cried out it was an army. I could not imagine what he meant by an army and answered in obvious disbelief.

1. Sets of ropes leading down from the head of the mast; their purpose was to relieve some of the lateral strain.
2. Perspective glasses, or telescope.

"Nay, sir," said he, "don't be angry, for 'tis an army, and a fleet, too; for I believe there are a thousand canoes, and you may see them paddle along, for they are coming toward us apace."

I was a little surprised then, indeed, and so was my nephew, the captain; for he had heard such terrible stories of them on the island, and having never been on those seas before, he could not tell what to think of it but said two or three times that we should all be devoured. I must confess, considering we were becalmed and the current set strong toward the shore, I liked it the worse; however, I bade them not be afraid but bring the ship to an anchor as soon as we came so near as to know that we must engage them.

The weather continued calm, and they came on apace toward us; so I gave orders to come to an anchor and furl all our sails. As for the savages, I told my men they had nothing to fear from them but fire, and therefore they should get their boats out and fasten them, one close by the head and the other by the stern, and man them both well, and wait the issue in that posture. This I did that the men in the boats might be ready with sheets and buckets to put out any fire these savages might endeavor to fix to the outside of the ship.

In this posture we lay by for them, and in a little while they came up with us; but never was such a horrid sight seen by Christians. Though my mate was much mistaken in his calculation of their number, yet when they came up we reckoned about a hundred and twenty-six canoes; some of them had sixteen or seventeen men in them, and some more, and the least six or seven.

When they came nearer to us, they seemed to be struck with wonder and astonishment, as at a sight that doubtless they had never seen before; nor could they at first, as we afterward understood, know what to make of us. They came boldly up, however, very near to us, and seemed to go about to surround us; but we called to our men in the boats not to let them come too near them. This very order brought us to an engagement with them, without designing it; for five or six of the large canoes came so near our longboat that our men gestured with their hands to keep them back, which they understood very well and went back. But at their retreat about fifty arrows came on board us from those boats, and one of our men in the longboat was very much wounded. However, I called to them not to fire by any means; but we handed down some deal boards into the boat, and the carpenter presently set up a kind of fence, like waste boards, to protect them from the arrows of the savages, if they should shoot again.

Death of Friday

About half an hour afterward, the savages all came up in a body astern of us and so near that we could easily discern what they were, though we could not tell their design; and I easily found they were some of my old friends, the same sort of savages that I had been used to engage with. In a short time more, they rowed a little farther out to sea, till they came directly broadside with us and then rowed down straight upon us, till they came so near that they could hear us speak. Upon this I ordered all my men to keep close, lest they should shoot any more arrows, and we made all our guns ready. But being so near as to be within hearing, I made Friday go out upon the deck and call out aloud to them in his language, to know what they meant; which accordingly he did. Whether they understood him or not, I knew not, but as soon as he had called to them, six of them who were in the foremost or nighest boat to us turned their canoes from us and, stooping down, showed us their naked backs. Whether this was a defiance or challenge, or whether it was done in mere contempt or as a signal to the rest, we knew not; but immediately Friday cried out they were going to shoot, and unhappily for him, poor fellow, they let fly about three hundred of their arrows and, to my inexpressible grief, killed poor Friday, no other man being in their sight. The poor fellow was shot with no less than three arrows, and about three more fell very near him; such unlucky for us marksmen they were!

I was so enraged at the loss of my trusty old servant and companion that I immediately ordered five guns to be loaded with small shot, and four with great, and gave them such a broadside they had never heard in their lives before, to be sure. They were not above half a cable's length off when we fired, and our gunners took their aim so well

They killed poor Friday

I gave them a broadside

that three or four of their canoes were overset, as we had reason to believe, by one shot only.

The ill manners of turning up their bare backs to us gave us no great offense; neither did I know for certain whether that which would pass for the greatest contempt among us might be understood so by them or not. Therefore, in return, I had only resolved to have fired four or five guns at them with powder only, which I knew would frighten them sufficiently. But when they shot at us directly with all the fury they were capable of, and especially as they had killed my poor Friday, whom I so deeply loved and valued and who, indeed, so well deserved my esteem, I thought myself not only justified before God and man, but would have been very glad if I could have overset every canoe there and drowned every last one of them.

I can neither tell how many we killed nor how many we wounded at this broadside, but surely such a fright and hurry never were seen among such a multitude; there were thirteen or fourteen of their canoes split and overset in all, and the men all set a-swimming. The rest, frightened out of their wits, scoured away as fast as they could, taking but little care to save those whose boats were split or spoiled with our shot, so I suppose that many of them were lost. And our men took up one poor fellow swimming for his life, about an hour after they were all gone.

The small shot from our cannon must needs have killed and wounded a great many; but, in short, we never knew how it went with them, for they fled so fast that, in three hours or thereabouts, we could not see more than three or four straggling canoes. Nor did we ever see the rest anymore, for a breeze of wind springing up the same evening, we weighed anchor and set sail for the Brazils.

Under Sail Again

We had a prisoner, indeed, but the creature was so sullen that he would neither eat nor speak, and we all fancied he would starve himself to death. But I found a way to cure him, for I made them take him into the longboat and make him believe they would toss him into the sea again and so leave him where they found him, if he would not speak. When that threat failed, they really *did* throw him into the sea and came away from him. Then he followed them, for he swam like a cork, and called to them in his tongue, though they knew not one word of what he said. At last, they took him in again, and then he began to be more tractable; nor had I even intended to have him drowned.

We were now under sail again, but I was the most disconsolate creature alive for want of my man Friday and would have been very glad to have gone back to the island, to have taken one of the rest from thence for my occasion, but it could not be: so we went on. We had one prisoner, as I have said, and it was a long time before we could make him understand anything; but, in time, our men taught him some English, and he began to be a little tractable. Afterward, we inquired what country he came from, but could make nothing of what he said; for his speech was so odd, all gutturals, and he spoke in the throat in such a hollow, odd manner that we could never understand a word of it. We were all of the opinion that they might speak that language just as well if they were gagged as otherwise; nor could we perceive that they had any occasion either for teeth, tongue, lips, or palate, but formed their words just as a hunting horn forms a tune with an open throat. He told us, however, some time after, when we had taught him to speak a little English, that they had been going with their kings to fight a great battle. When he said "kings," we asked him how many kings. He said that they were five nation (we could not make him understand the plural *s)* and that they all joined to go against two nation. We asked him what made them come up to us. He said, "To makee te great wonder look." Here it is to be observed that all those natives, as also those of Africa, when they learn English, always add two *e*'s at the end of the words where we use one; and they place the accent upon them, as mak-*e,* tak-*e,* and the like; nay, I could hardly make Friday leave it off, though at last he did.

And now, I come back to that unfortunate fellow Friday one more time—and I must take my last leave of him. Poor, honest Friday! We buried him with all the decency and solemnity possible, by putting him into a coffin and dropping him into the sea; and I caused them to fire eleven guns for him. So ended the life of the most grateful, faithful, honest, and most affectionate servant that ever a man had.

We went now away with a fair wind for Brazil; and in about twelve days' time we made land, in the latitude of 5 degrees south of the line, being the northeasternmost land of all that part of America. We kept on south by east, in sight of the shore four days, when we made Cape St. Augustine, and in three days came to an anchor off the bay of All Saints, the place of my deliverance, from whence came both my good and evil fate.

Never ship came to this port that had less business than I had, and yet it was with great difficulty that we were admitted to hold the least correspondence on shore: Not my partner himself, who was alive and made a great figure among them; not my two merchant-trustees; not the fame of my wonderful preservation on the island, could obtain me that favor. But my partner, remembering that I had given five hundred moidores to the prior of the monastery of the Augustines and two hundred and seventy-two to the poor, went to the monastery and obliged the prior that then was there to go to the governor and get leave for me personally, with the captain and one more, besides eight seamen, to come on shore, but no more; and this upon condition, absolutely capitulated for, that we should not offer to land any goods out of the ship or to carry any person away without license. They were so strict with us, as to landing any goods, that it was with extreme difficulty that I got on shore three bales of English goods, such as fine broadcloths, stuffs, and some linen, which I had brought as a present to my partner.

He was a very generous, openhearted man. Though, like me, he began with little at first, and though he knew not that I had the least design of giving him anything, he sent me on board a present of fresh provisions, wine, and sweetmeats, worth above thirty moidores, including some tobacco and three or four fine medals of gold. But I was even with him in my present, which, as I have said, consisted of fine broadcloths, English stuffs, lace, and fine Hollands; also, I delivered him about the value of one hundred pounds sterling, in the same goods, for other uses. I obliged him to set up the sloop, which I had brought with me from England, as I have said, for the use of my colony, in order to send the refreshments I intended to my plantation.

Accordingly, he got hands and finished the sloop in a very few days, for she was already framed; and I gave the master of her such instructions that he could not miss the place; nor did he, as I had an account from my partner afterward. I got him soon loaded with the small cargo I sent them; and one of our seamen who had been on shore with me there offered to go with the sloop and settle there, upon my letter to the governor, to allot him a sufficient quantity of land for a plantation and giving him some clothes and tools for his planting work, which he said he understood, having been an old planter in Maryland and a buccaneer into the bargain. I encouraged the fellow by granting all he desired; and, as an addition, I gave him the savage whom we had taken prisoner of war, to be his slave and ordered the governor to give him his share of everything he wanted with the rest.

When we came to fit this man out, my old partner told me there was a certain very honest fellow, a Brazilian planter of his acquaintance, who had fallen into the displeasure of the Church. "I know not what the matter is with him," said he, "but, on my conscience, I think he is a heretic in his heart, and he has been obliged to conceal himself for fear of the Inquisition." This planter would be very glad of such an opportunity to make his escape, with his wife and two daughters; and if I would let them go to my island and allot them a plantation, my partner would give them a small stock to begin with—for the officers of the Inquisition had seized all his effects and estate, and he had nothing left but a little household stuff and two slaves. "And," added my partner, "though I hate his principles, yet I would not have him fall into their hands, for he will be assuredly burned alive if he does."

I granted this presently and joined my Englishman with them; and we concealed the man and his wife and daughters on board our ship, till the sloop put out to go to sea. Then, having put all their goods on board some time before, we put them on board the sloop after she was got out of the bay.

Our seaman was mightily pleased with this new partner; and their stocks, indeed, were much alike, rich in tools, in preparations, and a farm—but nothing to begin with, except as above. However, they carried over with them what was worth all the rest: some materials for planting sugarcanes, with some plants of canes, which he—I mean the Portuguese man—understood very well.

Among the rest of the supplies sent to my tenants on the island, I sent them by the sloop three milch cows and five calves, about twenty-two hogs, among them three sows big with pig, two mares, and a stone horse. For my Spaniards, according to my promise, I engaged three Portuguese women to go and recommended it to them to marry them and use them kindly. I could have procured more women, but I remembered that the poor persecuted man had two daughters and that there were but five of the Spaniards that wanted wives—the rest had wives of their own, though in another country.

All this cargo arrived safely and, as you may easily suppose, was very welcome to my old inhabitants, who were now, with this addition, between sixty and seventy people, besides little children, of which there were a great many. I found letters at London from them all, by way of Lisbon, when I came back from England, of which I shall also take some notice immediately.

The Last of the Island

I have now done with the island and all manner of discourse about it, and whoever reads the rest of my memorandums would do well to turn his thoughts entirely from it and expect to read of the follies of an old man, not warned by his own misfortunes, much less by those of other men, to beware; not cooled by almost forty years' miseries and disappointments; not satisfied with prosperity beyond expectation, nor made cautious by afflictions and distress beyond belief.

I had no more business to go to the East Indies than a man at full liberty has to go to the turnkey at Newgate and desire him to lock him up among the prisoners there and starve him. Had I taken a small vessel from England and gone directly to my island; had I loaded her, as I did the other vessel, with all the necessaries for the plantation and for my people and taken a patent from the government here to have secured my property in subjection only to that of England; had I carried over cannon and ammunition, servants and people to plant, and taken possession of the place, fortified and strengthened it in the name of England, and increased it with people, as I might easily have done; had I then settled myself there and sent the ship back laden with good rice, as I might also have done in six months' time, and ordered my friends to have fitted her out again for our supply—had I done this and stayed there myself, I had at least acted like a man of common sense. But I was possessed of a wandering spirit and scorned all advantages. I pleased myself with being the patron of the people I placed there and doing for them, in a kind of haughty, majestic way, like an old patriarchal monarch, providing for them as if I had been father of the whole family, as well as of the plantation. But I never so much as pretended to plant in the name of any government or nation, or to acknowledge any prince, or to call my people subjects to any one nation more than another. Nay, I never so much as gave the place a name, but left it as I found it, belonging to nobody and the people under no discipline or government but my own; who, though I had influence over them as a father and benefactor, had no authority or power to act or command one way or other, further than voluntary consent moved them to comply. Yet even this, had I stayed there, would have done well enough. But as I rambled from them and came there no more, the last letters I had from any of them were by my partner's means, who afterward sent another sloop to the place and who sent me word, though I had not the letter till I got to London, several years after it was written, that they went on but poorly and were discontent with their long stay there; that Will Atkins was dead; that five of the Spaniards were come away; and though they had not been much molested by the savages, yet they had had some skirmishes with them; and that they begged of him to write to me to think of the promise I had made to fetch them away that they might see their country again before they died.

But I was gone on a wild goose chase indeed! And they that will have any more of me must be content to follow me into a new variety of follies, hard-ships, and wild adventures, wherein the justice of Providence may be duly observed; and we may see how easily Heaven can gorge us with our own desires, make the strongest of our wishes be our affliction, and punish us most severely with those very things that we think it would be our utmost happiness to be allowed in. Whether I had business or no business, away I went. It is no time now to enlarge upon the reason or absurdity of my own conduct, but to come to the history—I was embarked for the voyage, and on the voyage I went.

I shall only add a word or two concerning my honest Popish clergyman; for let their opinion of us, and all other heretics in general, as they call us, be as uncharitable as it may, I verily believe this man was very sincere and wished the good of all men. Yet I believe he was upon the reserve in many of his expressions, to prevent giving me offense; for I scarcely heard him once call on the Blessed Virgin or mention St. Jago or his guardian angel, though so common with the rest of them. However, I say, I had not the least doubt of his sincerity and pious intentions, and I am firmly of the opinion that if the rest of the Popish missionaries were like him, they would strive to visit even the poor Tartars and Laplanders, where they have nothing to give them, as well as flocking to India, Persia, China, etc., the most wealthy of the heathen countries; for if they expected to bring no gains to their Church by it, it may well be admired how they came to admit the Chinese Confucius into the calendar of the Christian saints.

Chapter 11

MASSACRE

A ship being ready to sail for Lisbon, my pious priest asked me leave to go thither, being still, as he observed, bound never to finish any voyage he began. How happy it had been for me if I had gone with him! But it was too late now: all things Heaven appoints for the best. Had I gone with him, I had never had so many things to be thankful for, and the reader had never heard of the second part of the travels and adventures of Robinson Crusoe; so I must here leave exclaiming of myself and go on with my voyage.

From the Brazils, we made directly over the Atlantic Sea to the Cape of Good Hope. We had a tolerable good voyage, our course generally southeast, with now and then a storm and some contrary winds. But my disasters at sea were at an end—my future rubs and cross events were to befall me on shore, that it might appear the land was as well prepared to be our scourge as the sea.

Our ship was on a trading voyage and had a supercargo[1] on board, which was to direct all her motions after she arrived at the Cape, only being limited to a certain number of days for stay, by charter party, at the several ports she was to go to. This was none of my business; neither did I meddle with it— my nephew, the captain, and the supercargo adjusting all those things between them as they thought fit.

We stayed at the Cape no longer than was needful to take in fresh water, but made the best of our way for the coast of Coromandel. We were, indeed, informed that a French man-of-war of fifty guns and two large merchant ships were gone for the Indies; and as I knew we were at war with France, I had some apprehensions of them. But they went their own way, and we heard no more of them.

I shall not pester the reader with a tedious description of places, journals of our voyages, variations of the compass, latitudes, trade winds, etc.; it is

---

1. Merchant ship officer.

enough to name the ports and places that we touched at, and what occurred to us upon our passage from one to another. We touched first at the island of Madagascar, where, though the people are fierce and treacherous and very well armed with lances and bows, which they use with inconceivable dexterity, yet we fared very well with them awhile. They treated us very civilly; and for some trifles that we gave them, such as knives, scissors, etc., they brought us eleven good fat bullocks of a middling size, which we took in, partly for fresh provisions for our present spending and the rest to salt for the ship's use.

We were obliged to stay here some time after we had furnished ourselves with provisions; and I, who was always so curious to look into every nook of the world wherever I came, went on shore as often as I could. It was on the east side of the island that we went on shore one evening; and the people—who, by the way, are very numerous—came thronging about us and stood gazing at us at a distance. But as we had traded freely with them and had been kindly used, we thought ourselves in no danger. When we saw the people, we cut three boughs out of a tree and stuck them up at a distance from us; which, it seems, is a mark in that country, not only of a truce of friendship, but when it is accepted, the other side sets up three poles or boughs, which is a signal that they accept the truce, too. But then this is a known condition of a truce: that you are not to pass beyond their three poles toward them, nor they to come past your three poles, or boughs, toward you; so that you are perfectly secure within the three poles, and all the space between your poles and theirs is allowed like a market for free converse, traffic, and commerce. When you go there you must not carry your weapons with you. And if they come into that space, they stick up their javelins and lances all at the first poles and come on, unarmed. But if any violence is offered them, and the truce thereby broken, away they run to the poles and lay hold of their weapons, and the truce is at an end.

Another Adventure

It happened one evening, when we went on shore, that a greater number of their people came down than usual, but all were very friendly and civil. They brought several kinds of provisions, for which we satisfied them with such toys as we had. The women also brought us milk and roots and several things very acceptable to us. All was quiet, and we made us a little tent or hut of some boughs of trees and lay on shore all night.

I know not what was the occasion, but I was not so well satisfied to lie on shore as the rest. The boat was riding at anchor at about a stone's cast from the land, with two men in her to take care of her. I made one of them come on shore, and getting some boughs of trees to cover us also in the boat, I spread the sail on the bottom of the boat and lay under the cover of the branches of the trees all night in the boat.

About two o'clock in the morning, we heard one of our men make a terrible noise on the shore, calling out for God's sake to bring the boat in and come and help them, for they were all like to be murdered. At the same time, I heard the fire of five muskets, which was the number of guns they had, and that three times over; for, it seems, the natives here were not so easily frightened with guns as the savages were in America, where I had to do with them. All this while I knew not what was the matter, but rousing immediately from sleep with the noise, I caused the boat to be thrust in, and I resolved, with three fusils we had on board, to land and assist our men.

We got the boat soon to the shore, but our men were in too much haste; for being come to the shore, they plunged into the water to get to the boat with all the expedition they could, being pursued by between three and four hundred men. Our men were but nine in all, and only five of them had fusils with them; the rest had pistols and swords, indeed, but they were of small use to them.

We took up seven of our men, and with difficulty enough, too—three of them being very badly wounded. That which was still worse was that while we stood in the boat to take our men in, we were in as much danger as they were in on shore; for they poured their arrows in upon us so thick that we were glad to barricade the side of the boat up with the benches and two or three loose boards, which, to our great satisfaction, we had by mere accident in the boat. And yet, had it been daylight, they are, it seems, such exact marksmen that if they could have seen but the least part of any of us, they would have been sure of us. We had, by the light of the moon, a little sight of them as they stood pelting us from the shore with darts and arrows. Having got ready our firearms, we gave them a volley that we could hear, by the cries of some of them, had wounded several. However, they stood thus in battle array on the shore till break of day, which we suppose was that they might see the better to take their aim at us.

In this condition, we lay and could not tell how to weigh our anchor or set up our sail, because we must needs stand up in the boat, and they were as sure to hit us as we were to hit a bird in a tree with small shot. We made signals of distress to the ship, and though she rode a league off, yet my nephew, the captain, hearing our firing and by glasses perceiving the posture

We gave them a volley

we lay in and that we fired toward the shore, pretty well understood us; and weighing anchor with all speed, he stood as near the shore as he dared with the ship and then sent another boat, with ten hands in her, to assist us. But we called to them not to come too near, telling them what condition we were in. However, they stood in near to us, and one of the men—taking the end of the tow line in his hand and keeping one boat between him and the enemy, so that they could not clearly see him—swam on board us and made fast the line to the boat; upon which we slipped out a little cable, and leaving our anchor behind, they towed us out of reach of the arrows; we all the while lying close behind the barricade we had made.

As soon as we were got from between the ship and the shore, so that we could lay her side to the shore, she ran along just by them and poured in a broadside among them, loaded with pieces of iron and lead, small bullets, and such stuff, besides the great shot, which made a terrible havoc among them.

When we were got on board and out of danger, we had time to examine into the occasion of this fray; and, indeed, our supercargo, who had been often in those parts, explained it. He said he was sure the inhabitants would not have touched us after we had made a truce, if we had not done something to provoke them to it. At length, it came out that an old woman had come to sell us some milk and had brought it within our poles; a young woman came with her, bringing some roots or herbs. While the old woman (whether she was mother to the young woman or no they could not tell) was selling us the milk, one of our men made advances to the wench who was with her, at which the old woman made a great noise. However, the seaman would not quit his prize but carried her out of the old woman's sight into the trees, it being almost dark. The old woman then went away without her and, as we may suppose, made an outcry among the people she came from; who, upon notice, raised this great army upon us in three or four hours, and it was great odds but we had all been destroyed.

One of our men was killed with a lance thrown at him, just at the beginning of the attack, as he sallied out of the tent they had made; the rest made it back safely—all but the fellow who was the occasion of all the mischief, who paid dearly enough for his black mistress, for we could not hear what became of him for a great while. We lay upon the shore two days after, though the wind was favorable, and made signals for him and made our boat sail up shore and down shore several leagues, but in vain. We finally were obliged to give him over, and if he alone had suffered for it, the loss had been less.

I could not satisfy myself, however, without venturing on shore once more, to see if I could learn anything of him or them. It was the third night after the action that I had a great mind to learn, if I could by any means, what mischief we had done and how the game stood on the Indians' side. I was careful to do it in the dark, lest we should be attacked again. But I ought, indeed, to have been sure that the men I went with had been under my command before I engaged in a thing so hazardous and mischievous as I was brought into by it, without design.

To the Rescue

We took twenty (as stout fellows with us as any on the ship), besides the supercargo and myself, and we landed two hours before midnight, at the same place where the Indians stood drawn up on the evening before. I landed here, because my design, as I have said, was chiefly to see if they had quitted the field and to find out if they had left any marks behind them of the mischief we had done them. I thought that if we could surprise one or two of them, perhaps we might get our man again by way of exchange.

We landed without any noise and divided our men into two bodies, whereof the boatswain commanded one, and I the other. We neither saw nor heard anybody stir when we landed. We marched up, one body at a distance from the other, to the place, but at first could see nothing, it being very dark, till by and by our boatswain, who led the first party, stumbled and fell over a dead body. This made them halt awhile, for knowing by the circumstances that they were at the place where the Indians had stood, they waited for my coming up there. We concluded to halt till the moon began to rise, which we knew would be in less than an hour, when we could easily discern the havoc we had made among them. We found thirty-two bodies upon the ground, whereof two were not quite dead; some had an arm and some a leg shot off, and one his head. Those that were wounded, we suppose, they had carried away.

When we had made, as I thought, a full discovery of all we could come to the knowledge of, I resolved on going on board; but the boatswain and his party sent me word that they were resolved to make a visit to the Indian town, where these dogs, as they called them, dwelt, and they asked me to go along with them. If they could find them, as they still fancied they should, they did not doubt of getting a good booty; and it might be they might find Tom Jeffry there (that was the name of the man we had lost).

Had they sent to ask my leave to go, I knew well enough what answer to have given them; for I should have commanded them instantly to return on board, knowing it was not a hazard fit for us to run, who had a ship and shiploading in our charge and a voyage to make that depended very much upon the lives of the men. But as they sent me word they were resolved to go, and only asked me and my company to go along with them, I positively refused and rose up, for I was sitting on the ground, in order to go to the boat. One or two of the men began to importune me to go; and when I refused, they began to grumble and say they were not under my command, and they would go anyway.

"Come, Jack," said one of the men, "will you go with me? I'll go for one."

Jack said he would—and then another—and, in a word, they all left me but one, whom I persuaded to stay, and a boy left in the boat. So the supercargo and I, with the third man, went back to the boat, where we told them we would stay for them and take in as many of them as should be left, for I told them it was a mad thing they were going about and supposed most of them would have the fate of Tom Jeffry.

They told me, like seamen, they would without fail make it back, and they would take care, etc.; so away they went. I entreated them to consider the ship and the voyage, that their lives were not their own, and that they were entrusted with the voyage in some measure; that if they miscarried, the ship might be lost for want of their help and that they could not answer for it to God or man. But I might as well have talked to the mainmast of the ship: They were so determined upon their journey that they only gave me good words and begged me not to be angry. They did not doubt but they would be back again in about an hour at most, for the Indian town, they said, was not more than half a mile off, though they found it more than two miles before they got to it.

Well, they all went away, and though the attempt was desperate, and such as none but madmen would have gone about, yet, to give them their due, they went about it warily and boldly. They were gallantly armed, for they had every man a fusil or musket, a bayonet, and a pistol; some of them had broad cutlasses, some of them had sabers, and the boatswain and two more had poleaxes; besides all which, they had among them thirteen hand grenadoes.[2] Bolder fellows, and better provided, never went about any wicked work in the world.

When they went out, their chief design was plunder, and they were in mighty hopes of finding gold there; but a circumstance that none of them was aware of set them on fire with revenge and made devils of them all.

Revenge

When they came to the few Indian houses that they thought had been the town, which was not above half a mile off, they were under a great disappointment, for there were not more than twelve or thirteen houses; and where the town was, or how big, they knew not. They consulted, therefore, what to do and were some time before they could resolve; for if they fell upon these, they must cut all their throats; and it was ten to one but some of them might escape, it being in the night, though the moon was up; and if one escaped, he would run and raise all the town, so they should have a whole army upon them. On the other hand, if they went away and left those untouched, for the people were all asleep, they could not tell which way to look for the town. However, the last was the best advice, so they resolved to leave them and look for the town as well as they could. They went on a little way and found a cow tied to a tree. This, they presently concluded, would be a good guide to them; for, they said, the cow certainly belonged to the town before them or the town behind them, and if they untied her, they should see which way she went: If she went back, they'd let her go, but if she went forward, they would follow her. So they cut the cord, which was made

---

2. Grenades.

of twisted flags, and the cow went on before them, directly to the town; which, as they reported, consisted of more than two hundred houses or huts, and in some of these they found several families living together.

Here they found all in silence, as profoundly secure as sleep could make them. First, they called another council, to consider what they had to do; and, in a word, they resolved to divide themselves into three bodies and so set three houses on fire in three parts of the town. Then, as the men came out, they would seize them and bind them (if any resisted, they need not be asked what to do then), and so search the rest of the houses for plunder. But they resolved to march silently first through the town and see what dimensions it was of, and if they might venture upon it or not.

They did so and desperately resolved that they would venture upon them. But while they were encouraging one another to the work, three of them who were a little before the rest called out aloud to them and told them that they had found Tom Jeffry. They all ran up to the place, where they had found the poor fellow hanging up naked by one arm, and his throat cut. There was an Indian house just by the tree, where they found sixteen or seventeen of the principal Indians

The cow went on before them

who had been concerned in the fray with us before, and two or three of them wounded with our shot. Our men found they were awake and talking one to another in that house, but knew not their number.

The sight of the poor mangled comrade so enraged them, as before, that they swore to one another they would be revenged and that not an Indian that came into their hands should have any quarter. To work they went immediately and yet not so madly as might be expected from the rage and fury they were in. Their first care was to get something that would soon take fire; but after a little search, they found that would be to no purpose, for most of the houses were low and thatched with flags and rushes, of which the country is full. So they presently made some wildfire, as we call it, by wetting a little powder in the palm of their hands, and in a quarter of an hour they set the town on fire in four or five places, and particularly that house where the Indians were not gone to bed.

As soon as the fire began to blaze, the poor frightened creatures began to rush out to save their lives, but met with their fate in the attempt—especially at the door, where our men drove them back, the boatswain himself killing one or two with his poleax. The house being large, and many in it, he did not care to go in but called for a hand grenado and threw it among them, which at first frightened them, but when it burst, made such havoc among them that they cried out in a hideous manner. In short, most of the Indians who were in the open part of the house were killed or hurt with the grenado, except two or three more who pressed to the door, which the boatswain and two more kept, with their bayonets on the muzzles of their pieces, and dispatched all that came in their way. But there was another apartment in the house, where the prince or king, or whatever he was, and several others were; and these were kept in till the house, which was by this time all in a light flame, fell in upon them, and they were smothered together.

All this while they fired not a gun, because they would not waken the people faster than they could master them. But the fire began to waken them fast enough, and our fellows were glad to keep a little together in bodies, for the fire grew so raging, all the houses being made of light combustible stuff, that they could hardly bear the street between them; and their business was to follow the fire, for the surer execution. As fast as the fire either forced the people out of those houses that were burning, or frightened them out of others, our people were ready at their doors to knock them on the head, still calling and halloing one to another to remember Tom Jeffry.

While this was doing, I must confess I was very uneasy—especially when I saw the flames of the town, which, it being night, seemed to be close by. My nephew, the captain, who was roused by his men, seeing such a fire, was very uneasy, not knowing what the matter was or what danger I was in, especially hearing the guns, too, for by this time they began to use their firearms. A thousand thoughts oppressed his mind concerning me and the supercargo. What would become of us? At last, though he could ill spare any more men, yet not knowing what exigence we might be in, he took another boat and, with thirteen men and himself, came ashore to me.

He was surprised to see me and the supercargo in the boat with no more than two men; and though he was glad that we were well, yet he was in the same impatience with us to know what was doing, for the noise continued and the flames increased. In short, it was next to an impossibility for any men in the world to restrain their curiosity to know what had happened, or their concern for the safety of the men. In a word, the captain told me he would go and help his men, let what would come. I argued with him, as I did before with the men, the safety of the ship, the danger of the voyage, the interest of the owners and merchants, etc., and told him I and the two men would go and see if we could at a distance learn what was likely to be the situation and come back and tell him. It was as vain to talk to my nephew as it was to talk to the rest before: He would go, he said, and he only wished he had left but ten men in the ship, for he could not think of having his men lost for want of help—he had rather lose the ship, the voyage, and his life, and all—and away he went.

I was no more able to stay behind now than I was to persuade them not to go. So, in short, the captain ordered two men to row back the pinnace and fetch twelve men more, leaving the longboat at an anchor; and when they came back, six men should keep the two boats and six more come after us. He left only sixteen men on the ship, for the whole ship's company consisted of sixty-five men, whereof two were lost in the late quarrel that brought this mischief on.

On the March

Being now on the march, you may be sure we felt little of the ground we trod on; and being guided by the fire, we kept no path but went directly to the place of the flame. If the noise of the guns was surprising to us before, the cries of the poor people were now quite of another nature and filled us with horror. I must confess I was never at the sacking of a city or at the taking of a town by storm. I had heard of Oliver Cromwell taking Drogheda,[3] in Ireland, and killing man, woman, and child; and I had read of Count Tilly sacking the city of Magdeburg and cutting the throats of twenty-two thousand, of all sexes; but I never had an idea of the thing itself before, nor is it possible to describe it or the horror that was upon our minds at hearing it. However, we went on, and at length came to the town, though there was no entering the streets of it for the fire. The first object we met with was the ruins of a hut or house, or rather the ashes of it, for the house was consumed; and just before it, plainly now to be seen by the light of the fire, lay four men and three women killed, and, as we thought, one or two more lay in the heap among the fire. In short, there were such instances of rage altogether barbarous, and of a fury something beyond what was human, that we thought it impossible our men could be guilty of it; or, if they were the authors of it, we thought they ought to be every one of them put to the worst of deaths. But this was not all: We saw the fire increased ahead, and the cry went on just as the fire went on, so that we were in the utmost confusion. We advanced a little way farther, and behold, to our astonishment, three naked women, crying in the most dreadful manner, came flying as if they had wings, and after them sixteen or seventeen men, natives, in the same terror and consternation, with three of our English butchers in the rear, who, when they could not overtake them, fired in among them. One who was killed by their shot fell down in our sight. When the rest saw us, believing us to be

---

3. Crusoe is here acting as a spokesman for those who were appalled at atrocities committed in the name of religion. First Crusoe refers to the Catholic town of Drogheda (about 31 miles from Dublin, Ireland), which became a byword because when Oliver Cromwell's Protestant armies captured it in 1649, the inhabitants were brutally massacred. But even that paled in comparison with the infamous sack of Protestant Magdeburg, the capital of Saxony, in 1631. Count Tilly's Catholic armies were determined to crush the city; consequently, when the city at last surrendered, the sack and destruction were so terrible, "Magdeburg" continues to be a by-word even today for senseless slaughter. Will and Ariel Durant, in their monumental *The Story of Civilization,* note that "on May 20, after holding out for six months, the city was taken; the victorious troops ran riot in four days of pillage; in the greatest shambles of the war, 20,000 persons were slain—not only the garrison of 3,000 men, but 17,000 of the 36,000 inhabitants, and all of the city burned to the ground. A contemporary writer described the scene: 'Then there was naught but beating and burning, plundering, torture, and murder. . . . In this frenzied rage the great and splendid city that had stood like a fair princess in the land was now . . . given over to the flames, and thousands of innocent men, women, and children, in the midst of a horrible din of heart-rending shrieks and cries, were tortured and put to death in so cruel and shameful a manner that no words would suffice to describe, nor tears to bewail it.' " (Will and Ariel Durant, *The Age of Reason Begins,* vol. 7 of *The Story of Civilization* (New York: Simon and Schuster, 1961), pp. 562–63).

their enemies and that we would murder them as well as those that pursued them, they set up a most dreadful shriek, especially the women; and two of them fell down, as if already dead, with the fright.

My very soul shrunk within me and my blood ran chill in my veins when I saw this; and I believe, had the three English sailors that pursued them come on, I would have made our men kill them all. However, we took some means to let the poor flying creatures know that we would not hurt them; and immediately they came up to us, and kneeling down, with their hands lifted up, they made piteous lamentation to us to save them, which we let them know we would; whereupon they crept together in a huddle close behind us, as for protection. I left my men drawn up together, charging them to hurt nobody but, if possible, to get at some of our people and see what devil it was possessed them and what they intended to do, and to command them off, assuring them that if they stayed till daylight they would have a hundred thousand men about their ears. I left them and went among those flying people, taking only two of our men with me; and there was, indeed, a piteous spectacle among them. Some of them had their feet terribly burned with trampling and running through the fire; others their hands burned; one of the women had fallen down in the fire and was very much burned before she could get out again; and two or three of the men had cuts on their backs and thighs from our men pursuing them; and another was shot through the body and died while I was there.

I would fain have learned what the occasion of all this was, but I could not understand one word they said; though, by signs, I perceived some of them knew not what was the occasion themselves. I was so terrified in my thoughts at this outrageous attack that I could not stay there, but went back to my own men and resolved to go into the middle of the town, through the fire or whatever might be in the way, and put an end to it, cost what it would. Accordingly, I came back to my men, told them my resolution, and commanded them to follow me. At that very moment, four of our men came, with the boatswain at their head, roving over heaps of bodies they had killed, all covered with blood and dust, as if they wanted more people to massacre. Our men hallooed to them as loud as they could hallo. With much ado one of them made them hear, so that they knew who we were and came up to us.

As soon as the boatswain saw us, he set up a hallo like a shout of triumph, for having, as he thought, more help come. Without waiting to hear me, he said, "Captain, noble captain! I am glad you are come; we have not done half yet. Villainous, hellhound dogs! I'll kill as many of them as poor Tom has hairs upon his head. We have sworn to spare none of them; we'll root out the very nation of them from the earth." And thus he ran on, out of breath, too, with action, and would not give us leave to speak a word.

At last, raising my voice that I might silence him a little, I said, "Barbarous dog! What are you doing? I won't have one creature touched more, upon pain of death. I charge you, upon your life, to stop your hands and stand still here, or you are a dead man this minute."

"Why, sir," said he, "do you know what you do, or what they have done? If you want a reason for what we have done, come hither." And with that he showed me the poor fellow hanging, with his throat cut.

I confess I was urged then myself, and at another time would have been as violent as they. But I thought they had carried their rage too far, and I remembered Jacob's words to his sons Simeon and Levi: "Cursed be their anger, for it was fierce; and their wrath, for it was cruel." But I had now a new task upon my hands; for when the men I led saw the sight, as I had done, I had as much to do to restrain them as I should have had with the others. Nay, my nephew himself fell in with them and told me, in their hearing, that he was only concerned for fear of the men being overpowered. As to the people, he thought not one of them ought to live, for they had all glutted themselves with the murder of the poor man and they ought to be used like murderers. Upon these words, away ran eight of my men, with the boatswain and his crew, to complete their bloody work. Seeing it quite out of my power to restrain them, I came away pensive and sad, for I could not bear the sight, much less the horrible noise and cries of the poor wretches that fell into their hands.

Return to the Boat

I got nobody to come back with me but the supercargo and two men, and with these I walked back to the boat. It was a very great piece of folly in me, I confess, to venture back as it were alone; for as it began now to be almost day, and the alarm had run over the country, there stood about forty men armed with lances and bows, at the little place where the twelve or thirteen houses stood, mentioned before. But by accident I missed the place and came directly to the seaside; and by the time I got to the seaside, it was broad day. Immediately, I took the pinnace and went on board and sent her back to assist the men in what might happen.

I observed, about the time that I came to the boat, that the fire was pretty well out and the noise abated. But in about half an hour after I got on board, I heard a volley of our men's firearms and saw a great smoke. This, as I understood afterward, was our men falling upon the men who, as I said, stood at the few houses on the way, of whom they killed sixteen or seventeen and set all the houses on fire, but did not meddle with the women or children.

By the time the sailors got to shore again with the pinnace, our men began to appear. They came dropping in, not in two bodies as they went, but straggling here and there in such a manner that a small force of resolute men might have cut them all off. But the dread of them was upon the whole country; and the natives were surprised and so frightened that I believe a hundred of them would have fled at the sight of but five of our men. Nor in all this terrible action was there a man that made any considerable defense. They were so surprised, between the terror of the fire and the sudden attack of our men in the dark, that they knew not which way to turn themselves, for if they fled one way, they were met by one party; if back again, by another—so that they were everywhere knocked down. Nor did any of our men receive the least hurt, except one that sprained his foot, and another that had one of his hands burned.

I was very angry with my nephew, the captain, and indeed with all the men, in my mind, but with him in particular, as well for his acting so out of his duty as commander of the ship and having the charge of the voyage upon him, as in his prompting, rather than cooling, the rage of his men in so bloody and cruel an enterprise. My nephew answered me very respectfully but told me that when he saw the body of the poor seaman whom they had murdered in so cruel and barbarous a manner, he was not master of himself; neither could he govern his passion. He owned he should not have done so, as he was commander of the ship; but as he was a man, and nature moved him, he could not bear it. As for the rest of the men, they were not subject to me at all, and they knew it well enough; so they took no notice of my feelings.

The next day we set sail, so we never heard any more of it. Our men differed in the account of the number they had killed; but according to the best of their accounts put all together, they killed or destroyed about one hundred and fifty people—men, women, and children—and left not a house standing in the town. As for the poor fellow Tom Jeffry, as he was quite dead . . . , it would do him no service to bring him away; so they only took him down from the tree where he was hanging by one hand.

However, just as our men thought this action, I was against them in it, and

I always after that time told them God would blast the voyage, for I looked upon all the blood they shed that night to be murder in them. For though it is true that they had killed Tom Jeffry, yet Jeffry was the aggressor, had broken the truce, and had violated a young woman of theirs, who came down to them innocently, on the faith of the public capitulation.

The boatswain defended this quarrel when we were afterward on board. He said it was true that we seemed to break the truce, but we really had not; and that the war was begun the night before by the natives themselves, who had shot at us and killed one of our men without any just provocation; so that as we were in a capacity to fight them now, we might also be in a capacity to do ourselves justice upon them in an extraordinary manner; that although the poor man had taken a little liberty with the wench, he ought not to have been murdered, and in such a villainous manner; and that they did nothing but what was just and what the laws of God allowed to be done to murderers.

One would think this should have been enough to have warned us against going on shore among heathens and barbarians; but it is impossible to make mankind wise but at their own expense. Their experience seems to be always of most use to them when it is dearest bought.

We were now bound to the Gulf of Persia, and from thence to the coast of Coromandel, only to touch at Surat; but the chief of the supercargo's design lay at the Bay of Bengal, where, if he missed his business outward-bound, he was to go up to China and return to the coast as he came home.

In the Gulf of Persia

The first disaster that befell us was in the Gulf of Persia, where five of our men, venturing on shore on the Arabian side of the gulf, were surrounded by the Arabians and either all killed or carried away into slavery. The rest of the boat's crew were not able to rescue them and had but just time to get off their boat. I began to upbraid them with the just retribution of Heaven in this case, but the boatswain very warmly told me that he thought I went further in my censures than I could show any warrant for in Scripture, and he referred to Luke 13:4, where our Savior intimates that those men on whom the Tower of Siloam fell were not sinners above all the Galileans. But that which put me to silence in the case was that not one of these five men who were now lost were of those who went on shore to the massacre of Madagascar—so I always called it, though our men could not bear to hear the word *massacre* with any patience.

But my frequent preaching to them on this subject had worse consequences than I expected. The boatswain, who had been the head of the attempt, came up boldly to me one time and told me he found that I brought that affair continually upon the stage; that I made unjust reflections upon it and had used the men very ill on that account, and himself in particular; that as I was but a passenger and had no command on the ship or concern in the voyage, they were not obliged to bear it; that they did not know but I might have some ill design in my head and perhaps to call them to an account for it when they came to England; and that, therefore, unless I would resolve to have done with it and also not to concern myself any further with him or any of his affairs, he would leave the ship, for he did not think it safe to sail with me among them.

I heard him patiently enough till he had done, and then I told him that I confessed I had all along opposed the massacre of Madagascar and that I had, on all occasions, spoken my mind freely about it, though not more upon him than any of the rest; that as to having no command on the ship, that was true; nor did I exercise any authority, only took the liberty of speaking my mind in things that publicly concerned us all; and what concern I had in the voyage was none of his business; but that I was a considerable owner in the ship. In that claim, I conceived I had a right to speak even further than I had done and would not be accountable to him or anyone else, and I began to be a little warm with him. He made but little reply to me at that time, and I thought the affair had been over. We were at this time in the road at Bengal; and being willing to see the place, I went on shore with the supercargo, in the ship's boat, to divert myself. Toward evening, as I was preparing to go on board, one of the men came to me and told me he would not have me trouble myself to come down to the boat, for they had orders not to carry me on board anymore. Anyone may guess what a surprise I was in at so insolent a message; and I asked about the man who bade him deliver that message to me. He told me the coxswain. I said no more to the fellow but bade him let them know that he had delivered his message and that I had given him no answer to it.

I immediately went and found the supercargo and told him the story, adding, what I presently foresaw, that there would be a mutiny on the ship. I entreated him to go immediately on board the ship in an Indian boat and acquaint the captain of it. But I might have spared this intelligence, for before I had spoken to him on shore, the matter was effected on board. The boatswain, the gunner, the carpenter, and all the inferior officers, as soon as

I was gone off in the boat, came up and desired to speak with the captain; and there the boatswain, making a long harangue, repeated all he had said to me. He told the captain in a few words that as I was now gone peaceably on shore, they were loath to use any violence with me, which, if I had not gone on shore, they would otherwise have done, to oblige me to have gone. They therefore thought fit to tell him that as they shipped themselves to serve on the ship under his command, they would perform it well and faithfully; but if I would not quit the ship, or the captain oblige me to quit it, they would all leave the ship and sail no farther with him. At the word *all*, he turned his face toward the mainmast, which was, it seems, the signal agreed on between them, at which, the seamen, being got together there, cried as one, "One and all! One and all!"

Anger of the Men

My nephew, the captain, was a man of spirit and of great presence of mind; and though he was surprised, you may be sure, at the thing, yet he told them calmly that he would consider the matter, but that he could do nothing about it till he had spoken to me. He used some arguments with them to show them the unreasonableness and injustice of the thing, but it was all in vain. They swore, shaking hands around before his face, that they would all go on shore, unless he would promise them he would not permit me to come anymore on board the ship.

This was very hard on him, who knew his obligation to me and did not know how I might take it; so he began to talk warmly to them, telling them that I was a very considerable owner of the ship and that, in justice, he could not put me out of my own house; that this was next door to serving me as the famous pirate Kidd had done, who made a mutiny on the ship, set the captain on shore on an uninhabited island, and ran away with the ship; that, let them go onto what ship they would, if ever they came to England again, it would cost them very dear; that the ship was mine and that he could not put me out of it; and that he would rather lose the ship, and the voyage, too, than disoblige me so much—so they might do as they pleased. However, he would go on shore and talk with me. He invited the boatswain to go with him; perhaps they might accommodate the matter with me. But they all rejected the proposal and said they would have nothing to do with me anymore; and if I came on board, they would all go ashore.

"Well," said the captain, "if you are all of this mind, let me go on shore and talk with him."

So away he came to me with this account, a little after the message had been brought to me from the coxswain.

I was very glad to see my nephew, I must confess; for I was not without apprehensions that they would confine him by violence, set sail, and run away with the ship. Then I would be stripped naked in a remote country, having nothing to help myself; in short, I would be in a worse case than when I was alone on the island. But they did not come to that length, it seems, to my satisfaction. When my nephew told me what they had said to him, and how they had sworn and shaken hands that they would, one and all, leave the ship if I was suffered to come on board, I told him he should not be concerned at it at all, for I would stay on shore. I only desired he would take care and send me all my necessary things on shore and leave me a sufficient sum of money, and I would find my way to England as well as I could.

This was a heavy piece of news to my nephew, but there was no way to help it but to comply; so, in short, he went on board the ship again and satisfied the men that his uncle had yielded to their importunity and had sent for his goods from on board the ship. So the matter was over in a few hours, the men returned to their duty, and I began to consider what course I should steer.

I was now alone in the most remote part of the world, as I think I may call it, for I was nearly three thousand leagues by sea farther off from England than I was at my island; only, it is true, I might travel here by land over the Great Mogul's country to Surat, might go from thence to Bassora by sea, up the Gulf of Persia, and take the way of the caravans over the desert of Arabia, to Aleppo and Scanderoon; from thence by sea again to Italy, and so overland into France. This, put together, might at least be a full diameter of the globe or more.

I had another way before me, which was to wait for some English ships, which were coming to Bengal from Achin, on the island of Sumatra, and get passage on board them for England. But as I came hither without any concern with the East India Company, so it would be difficult to go from hence without their license, unless with great favor of the captains of the ships or the company's factors; and to both I was an utter stranger.

Here I had the mortification to see the ship set sail without me—a treatment I think a man in my circumstances scarcely ever met with, except from pirates running away with a ship and setting those that would not agree with their villainy on shore. Indeed, this was next door to it both ways. However, my nephew left me two servants, or rather, one companion and one servant; the first was clerk to the purser, whom he engaged to go with me, and the other was his own servant. I took me also a good lodging in the house of an Englishwoman, where several merchants lodged, some Frenchmen, two Italians, or rather Jews, and one Englishman. Here I was handsomely enough housed; and that I might not be said to run-rashly upon anything, I stayed here more than nine months, considering what course to take and how to manage myself. I had some English goods with me of value and a considerable sum of money; my nephew had furnished me with a thousand pieces of eight and a letter of credit for more, if I had occasion, that I might not be straitened, whatever might happen.

I quickly disposed of my goods to advantage; and, as I originally intended, I bought here some very good diamonds, which, of all other things, were the most proper for me in my present circumstances, because I could always carry my whole estate about me.

After a long stay here, and many proposals made for my return to England but none falling out to my satisfaction, the English merchant who lodged with me, and with whom I had become well acquainted, came to me one morning.

"Countryman," said he, "I have a project to communicate to you, which, as it suits with my thoughts, may, for aught I know, suit with yours also when you shall have thoroughly considered it. Here we are posted—you by accident, and I by my own choice—in a part of the world very remote from our own country; but it is in a country where, by us who understand trade and business, a great deal of money is to be got. If you will put one thousand pounds to my one thousand pounds, we will hire a ship here, the first we can get to our minds; you shall be captain, I'll be merchant, and we'll go on a trading voyage to China. For what should we stand still for? The whole world is in motion, rolling around and around; all the creatures of God, heavenly bodies and earthly, are busy and diligent: Why should we be idle? There are no drones in the world but men: Why should we be of that number?"

I liked this proposal very well, the more so because it seemed to be expressed with so much goodwill and in so friendly a manner. I will not say but that I might, by my loose, unhinged circumstances, be the fitter to embrace a proposal for trade or, indeed, anything else; otherwise, trade was none of my element. However, I might perhaps say with some truth that if trade was not my element, rambling was; and no proposal for seeing any part of the world that I had never seen before could possibly come amiss to me.

It was, however, some time before we could get a ship to our satisfaction, and when we had got a vessel, it was not easy to get English sailors—that is to say, so many as were necessary to make the voyage and manage the sailors that we should pick up there. After some time we signed on a mate, a boatswain, and a gunner, all English; a Dutch carpenter, and three foremast men. With these we found we could do well enough, having Indian seamen, such as they were, to make up the rest of the crew.

Chapter 12

LIVING IN FEAR

There are so many travelers who have written a history of their voyages and travels this way that it would be very little diversion to anybody to give a long account of the places we went and the people who live there; these things I leave to others and refer the reader to those journals and travels of Englishmen, of which I find many are published and more promised every day. It is enough for me to tell you that we made this voyage to Achin, on the island of Sumatra, and from thence to Siam, where we exchanged some of our wares for opium and some arrack[1]—the first a commodity that bears a great price among the Chinese, and which, at that time, was much wanted there. In a word, we went up to Suskan, made a very great voyage, were eight months out, and returned to Bengal; and I was very well satisfied with my adventure. I observe that our people in England often admire how officers, whom the company sent into India, and the merchants who generally stay there get such very great estates as they do and sometimes come home worth sixty or seventy thousand pounds at a time. But it is no wonder, or at least we shall see so much further into it, when we consider the innumerable ports and places where they have a free commerce, that it will be done; and much less it will be so when we consider that at those places and ports where the English ships come, there are such great and constant demands for the growth of all other countries that there is a certain outlet for the returns, as well as a market abroad for the goods carried out.

In short, we made a very good voyage, and I got so much money by my first adventure, and such an insight into the method of getting more, that had I been twenty years younger, I should have been tempted to have stayed here and sought no further for making my fortune. But what was all this to

---

1. For several centuries, Western nations traded opium and arrack liquor to the Chinese; sadly, this infamous trade did much to destroy the very fiber of the Chinese people (as a case in point, read Pearl Buck's *The Good Earth*).

a man upward of threescore, who was already rich enough and who came abroad more in obedience to a restless desire of seeing the world than a covetous desire of gaining by it? And, indeed, I think it was with great justice that I now call it restless desire, for it was so. When I was at home, I was restless to go abroad; and when I was abroad, I was restless to be at home. I say, what was this gain to me? I was rich enough already, nor had I any uneasy desires about getting more money; and therefore the profit of the voyage to me was of no great force for prompting me forward to further undertakings. Hence, I thought that by this voyage I had made no progress at all, because I was come back, as I might call it, to the place from whence I came, as to a home—whereas, my eye, like that which Solomon speaks of, was never satisfied with seeing. I was come into a part of the world that I was never in before, and that part, in particular, which I had never heard much of, and I was resolved to see as much of it as I could. Then I thought I might say I had seen all the world that was worth seeing.

But my fellow traveler and I had different notions. I do not say this to insist on my own, for I acknowledge his were the most just and the more suited to the end of a merchant's life: who, when he is abroad upon adventures, is wise to stick to that as the best thing for him which he is likely to get the most money by. My new friend kept himself to the nature of the thing and would have been content to have gone like a carrier's[2] horse, always to the same inn, backward and forward, provided he could, as he called it, find his account in it. On the other hand, mine was the motion of a mad, rambling boy who never cares to see a thing twice. But this was not all: I had a kind of impatience upon me to be nearer home and yet the most unsettled resolution imaginable which way to go. In the interval of these consultations, my friend, who was always upon the search for business, proposed another voyage to me among the Spice Islands and to bring home a loading of cloves from the Manillas,[3] or thereabouts—places, indeed, where the Dutch trade, but where the islands belong partly to the Spaniards; though we went not so far, but to some other where they have not complete power, as they have at Batavia, Ceylon, etc.

We were not long in preparing for this voyage; the chief difficulty was in bringing me to come into it. However, at last, nothing else offering, and finding that really stirring about and trading—the profit being so great and, as I may say, certain—had more pleasure in it, and had more satisfaction to my

---

2. One who delivers goods and parcels for hire.

3. The islands then dominated by Manilla, today the capital of the Philippines.

mind, than sitting still, which, to me especially, was the unhappiest part of life, I resolved on this voyage, too. We made it very successfully, touching at Borneo and several islands whose names I do not remember, and coming home in about five months. We sold our spice, which was chiefly cloves and nutmegs, to the Persian merchants, who carried them away to the Gulf; and making near five to one, we really got a great deal of money.

My friend, when we made up this account, smiled at me: "Well, now," said he, with a sort of agreeable insult upon my indolent temper, "is not this better than walking about here, like a man with nothing to do, and spending our time in staring at the nonsense and ignorance of the pagans?"

"Why, truly," said I, "my friend, I think it is, and I begin to be a convert to the principles of merchandising. But I must tell you," said I, "by the way, you do not know what I am doing; for if I once conquer my backwardness and embark heartily, as old as I am, I shall harass you up and down the world till I tire you; for I shall pursue it so eagerly I shall never let you lie still."

But, to be short with my speculations, a little while after this there came in a Dutch ship from Batavia; she was a coaster, not a European trader, of about two hundred tons' burden. The men, as they pretended, having been so sickly that the captain had not hands enough to go to sea with, he lay by at Bengal; and having, it seems, got money enough or being willing for other reasons to go for Europe, he gave public notice he would sell his ship. This came to my ears before my new partner heard of it, and I had a great mind to buy it; so I went to him and I told him of it.

He considered awhile, for he was no rash man either; but musing some time, he replied, "She is a little too big. However, we will have her."

Accordingly, we bought the ship, and agreeing with the master, we paid for her and took possession. When we had done so, we resolved to engage the men, if we could, to join with those we had, for pursuing our business; but, suddenly, they having received not their wages but their share of the money, as we afterward learned, not one of them was to be found. We inquired much about them and at length were told that they were all gone together by land to Agra, the great city of the Mogul's residence, from thence to travel to Surat and go by the sea to the Gulf of Persia.

A Fortunate Disappointment

Nothing had so much troubled me in a good while as that I should miss the opportunity of going with them. Such a ramble, I thought, and in such company as would both have guarded and diverted me, would have suited mightily with my great design; and I should have both seen the world and gone homeward, too. But I was much better satisfied a few days after, when I came to know what sort of fellows they were. In short, their history was that this man they called "Captain" was the gunner only, not the commander; that they had been on a trading voyage in which they had been attacked on shore by some of the Malays, who had killed the captain and three of his men; and that, after the captain was killed, these men, eleven in number, had resolved to run away with the ship, which they did, and brought her to Bengal, leaving the mate and five men more on shore.

Well, let them get the ship how they would, we came honestly by her, as we thought, though we did not, I confess, examine into things so exactly as we ought; for we never inquired anything of the seamen, who would certainly have faltered in their account, contradicted one another, and perhaps contradicted themselves. Somehow or other we should have had reason to have suspected them. But the man showed us a bill of sale for the ship, to one Emanuel Clostershoven (or some such name, for I suppose it was all a forgery) and called himself by that name, and we could not contradict him. Withal, having no suspicion of the thing, we went through with our bargain.

We picked up some more English sailors here after this, and some Dutch; and now we resolved on a second voyage to the southeast for cloves, etc.— that is to say, among the Philippine and Moluccas isles. In short, not to fill up this part of my story with trifles when what is to come is so remarkable, I spent, from first to last, six years in this country, trading from port to port, backward and forward, and with very good success, and was now entering the last year with my new partner, going on the ship above mentioned on a voyage to China but planning first to go to Siam to buy rice.

On this voyage, being by contrary winds obliged to beat up and down a great while in the Straits of Malacca and among the islands, we were no sooner clear of those difficult seas than we found our ship had sprung a leak, and we were not able, by all our industry, to find out where it was. This forced us to make some port. My partner, who knew the country better than I did, directed the captain to put into the river of Cambodia; for I had made the English mate, one Mr. Thompson, captain, not being willing to take the charge of the ship upon myself. This river lies on the north side of the great bay or gulf that goes up to Siam. While we were here and going often on shore for refreshment, there came to me one day an Englishman, and he was,

There came to me an Englishman

it seems, a gunner's mate on board an English East India ship that rode on the same river at or near the city of Cambodia.

What brought him hither, we knew not; but he came to me, and speaking English, he said, "Sir, you are a stranger to me, and I to you; but I have something to tell you that very nearly concerns you."

In Danger

I looked steadfastly at him a good while and thought at first I had known him; but I did not.

"If it very nearly concerns me," said I, "and not yourself, what moves you to tell it to me?"

"I am moved," said he, "by the imminent danger you are in, and, for aught I see, you have no knowledge of it."

"I know no danger I am in," said I, "but that my ship is leaky, and I cannot find the source. But I intend to lay her aground tomorrow to see if I can find it."

"But, sir," said he, "leaky or not leaky, find it or not find it, you will be wiser than to lay your ship on shore tomorrow when you hear what I have to say to you. Do you know, sir," said he, "the town of Cambodia lies about fifteen leagues up this river, and there are two large English ships about five leagues on this side, and three Dutch?"

"Well," said I, "and what is that to me?"

"Why, sir," said he, "is it for a man that is upon such adventures as you are to come into a port and not examine first what ships there are there and whether he is able to deal with them? I suppose you think you are a match for them?"

I was amused very much at his discourse, but not amazed at it, for I could not conceive what he meant. I turned short upon him and said: "Sir, I wish you would explain yourself. I cannot imagine what reason I have to be afraid of any of the company's ships, or Dutch ships. I am no interloper. What can they have to say to me?"

He looked like a man half angry and half pleased, and pausing awhile but smiling, he said, "Well, sir, if you think yourself secure, you must take your chance. I am sorry your fate should blind you against good advice; but assure yourself, if you do not put to sea immediately, you will the very next tide be attacked by five longboats full of men, and perhaps, if you are taken, you will be hanged for a pirate, and the particulars be examined afterward. I thought, sir," added he, "I should have met with a better reception than this for doing you a piece of service of such importance."

"I can never be ungrateful," said I, "for any service or to any man that offers me any kindness; but it is past my comprehension that they should have such a design upon me. However, since you say there is no time to be lost, and that there is some villainous design on hand against me, I will go on board this minute and put to sea immediately, if my men can stop the leak, or if we can continue without stopping it. But, sir," said I, "shall I go away ignorant of the cause of all this? Can you give me no further light into it?"

"I can tell you but part of the story, sir," said he. "But I have a Dutch seaman here with me, and I believe I could persuade him to tell you the rest, though there is scarcely time for it. The short of the story is this—the first part of which I suppose you know well enough—that you were with this ship at Sumatra; that there your captain was murdered by the Malays, with three of his men; and that you, or some of those that were on board with you, ran away with the ship and are since turned pirates. This is the sum of the story, and you will all be seized as pirates, I can assure you, and executed with very little ceremony; for you know merchant ships show but little law to pirates, if they get them into their power."

"Now you speak plain English," said I, "and I thank you; and though I know nothing that we have done like what you speak of, for I am sure we came honestly and fairly by the ship, yet seeing such an attack is brewing, as you say, and that you seem to mean honestly, I will be upon my guard."

"Nay, sir," said he, "do not talk of being upon your guard; the best defense is to be out of the danger. If you have any regard for your life, and the lives of all your men, put to sea without fail at high water. As you have a whole tide before you, you will be gone too far out before they can come down; for they will come away at high water, and as they have twenty miles to come, you will get nearly two hours of them by the difference of the tide, not reckoning the length of the way. Besides, as they are only boats and not ships, they will not venture to follow you far out to sea, especially if it blows."

"Well," said I, "you have been very kind in this. What shall I do for you to make you amends?"

"Sir," said he, "you may not be willing to make me any amends, because you may not be convinced of the truth of it. But I will make an offer to you: I have nineteen months' pay due to me on board the ship ———, which I came out of England on; and the Dutchman that is with me has seven months' pay due to him. If you will make good our pay to us, we will go along with you. If you find nothing more in it, we will desire no more; but if we do convince you that we have saved your lives, and the ship, and the lives of all the men on her, we will leave the rest to you."

I consented to this readily and went immediately on board, and the two men with me.

As soon as I came to the ship's side, my partner, who was on board, came out on the quarterdeck and called to me with a great deal of joy: "Oh, ho! Oh, ho! We have stopped the leak! We have stopped the leak!"

"Say you so?" said I. "Thank God! But weigh anchor, then, immediately."

"Weigh!" said he. "What do you mean by that? What is the matter?"

"Ask no questions," said I, "but all hands to work, and weigh without losing a minute."

He was surprised, but he called the captain and immediately ordered the anchor to be pulled up, and though the tide was not quite down, yet a little land breeze blowing, we stood out to sea. Then I called him into the cabin and told him the story; and we called in the men, and they told us the rest of it. As it took up a great deal of time, before we had done, a seaman came to the cabin door and called out to us that the captain bade him tell us we were being chased.

"Chased!" said I. "By what?"

"By five sloops, or boats," said the fellow, "full of men."

"Very well," said I. "Then it is apparent there is something in it."

In the next place, I ordered all our men to be called up and told them that there was a design to seize the ship and to take us for pirates, and I asked them if they would stand by us and by one another. The men answered cheerfully, one and all, that they would live or die with us. Then I asked the captain what way he thought best for us to manage a fight with them; for resist them I was resolved we would, and that to the last drop. He said readily that the way was to keep them off with our great shot as long as we could and then to fire at them with our small arms to keep them from boarding us. But when neither of these would do any longer, we would retire to our close quarter;[4] perhaps they had not materials to break open our bulkheads or get in upon us.

Flight

The gunner had, in the meantime, orders to bring two guns to bear fore and aft, out of the steerage, to clear the deck, and to load them with musket bullets and small pieces of old iron and what came next to hand; and thus we made ready to fight. But all this while we kept out to sea, with wind enough, and could see the boats at a distance, being five large longboats, following us with all the sail they could make.

Two of these boats (which by our glasses we could see were English) had outsailed the rest, were nearly two leagues ahead of them, and gained upon us considerably, so that we found they would come up with us. We fired a gun without ball to intimate that they should bring to, and we put out a flag of truce as a signal for parley. But they came crowding after us, till they came within shot. Notwithstanding this, they came on till they were near enough to call to them with a speaking trumpet that we had on board; so we called to them and bade them keep off at their peril.

It was to no avail: They crowded after us and endeavored to come under our stern so as to board us on our quarter. Seeing they were determined for mischief and depended upon the strength that followed them, I ordered to

---

4. Draw close enough to grapple or board.

bring the ship to, so that they lay upon our broadside. Immediately, we fired five guns at them, one of which had been leveled so true as to carry away the stern of the hindermost boat and bring them to the necessity of taking down their sail and running all to the head of the boat to keep her from sinking; so she lay by and had enough of it. But seeing the foremost boat crowd on after us, we made ready to fire at her in particular. While this was doing, one of the three boats that was behind, being forwarder than the other two, made up to the boat that we had disabled, to relieve her, and we could see her take out the men. We called again to the foremost boat and offered a truce, to parley again and to know what her business was with us; but they had no answer, only she crowded closely under our stern. Upon this, our gunner, who was a very dexterous fellow, ran

We could see the boats at a distance

out his two chase-guns and fired again at her. But the shot missing, the men in the boat shouted, waved their caps, and came on. The gunner, getting quickly ready again, fired among them a second time, one shot of which, though it missed the boat itself, yet fell in among the men, and we could easily see had done a great deal of mischief among them. But we took no notice of that, tacked the ship again, and brought our quarter to bear upon them. Firing three guns more, we found the boat was almost split to pieces; in particular, her rudder and a piece of her stern were shot quite away, so they hauled her sail immediately and were in great disorder. But to complete their misfortune, our gunner let fly two guns at them again; where he hit them we could not tell, but we found the boat was sinking and some of the men already in the water. Upon this, I immediately manned out our pinnace, which we had kept close by our side, with orders to pick up some of the men, if they could, and save them from drowning, and immediately to come on board ship with them, because we saw the rest of the boats coming up. Our men in the pinnace followed their orders and took up three men, one of whom was just drowning, and it was a good while before we could recover him. As soon as they were on board, we crowded all the sail we could make and stood farther out to sea. We found that when the other three boats came up to the first two, they gave up their chase.

Being thus delivered from a danger that, though I knew not the reason of it, yet seemed to be much greater than I apprehended, I resolved that we should change our course and not let anyone know whither we were going. So we stood out to sea eastward, quite out of the course of all European

They hauled her sail immediately

ships, whether they were bound to China or anywhere else within the commerce of the European nations.

Deliberation as to Future Movements

When we were at sea, we began to consult with the two seamen and inquire what the meaning of all this should be. The Dutchman let us into the secret at once, telling us that the fellow who sold us the ship, as we said, was no more than a thief that had run away with her. Then he told us that the captain, whose name too he mentioned, though I do not remember it now, was treacherously murdered by the natives on the coast of Malacca, with three of his men—and that he, this Dutchman, and four more got into the woods, where they wandered about a great while, till at length he, in particular, in a miraculous manner, made his escape and swam off to a Dutch ship that, sailing near the shore on its way from China, had sent their boat on shore for fresh water; that he dared not come to that part of the shore where the boat was, but made shift in the night to take to the water farther off. He swam a great while, until at last the ship's boat took him up.

He then told us that he went to Batavia, where two of the seamen belonging to the ship had arrived, having deserted the rest in their travels, and gave an account that the fellow who had run away with the ship sold her at Bengal to a set of pirates, who were gone a-cruising in her, and that they had already taken an English ship and two Dutch ships very richly laden.

This latter part we found to concern us directly, though we knew it to be false. Yet, as my partner said very justly, if we had fallen into their hands, and they had had such a prepossession against us beforehand, it had been in vain for us to have defended ourselves, or to hope for any good quarter at their hands—especially considering that our accusers had been our judges and that we could have expected nothing from them but what rage would have dictated and an ungoverned passion have executed. Therefore, it was his opinion we should go directly back to Bengal, from whence we came, without putting in at any port whatever; because there we could give a good account of ourselves, could prove where we were when the ship put in, of whom we bought her, and the like; and, what was more than all the rest, if we were put upon the necessity of bringing it before the proper judges, we should be sure to have some justice and not be hanged first and judged afterward.

I was some time of my partner's opinion; but after a little more serious thinking, I told him I thought it was a very great hazard for us to attempt returning to Bengal, for that we were on the wrong side of the Straits of

Malacca, and if the alarm was given, we should be sure to be waylaid on every side, as well by the Dutch at Batavia as the English elsewhere; that if we should be taken as it were running away, we should even condemn ourselves, and there would lack no more evidence to destroy us. I also asked the English sailor's opinion, who said he was of my mind and that we should certainly be taken. This danger a little startled my partner and all the ship's company, and we immediately resolved to go away to the coast of Tonquin and on to the coast of China and, pursuing the first design as to trade, find some way or other to dispose of the ship and come back in some of the vessels of the country, such as we could get. This was approved as the best method for our security; and accordingly we steered away north-northeast, keeping about fifty leagues off from the usual course to the eastward. This, however, put us to some inconvenience; for, first, the winds, when we came that distance from the shore, seemed to be more steadily against us, blowing almost trade, as we call it, from the east and east-northeast, so that we were a long while upon our voyage, and we were but ill provided with victuals for so long a run. What was still worse, there was some danger that those English and Dutch ships, whose boats pursued us, whereof some were bound that way, might have got in before us, and if not, some other ship bound to China might have information of us from them and pursue us with the same vigor.

I must confess I was now very uneasy and thought myself, including the late escape from the longboats, to have been in the most dangerous condition that ever I was in through all my past life; for whatever ill circumstances I had been in, I was never pursued for a thief before; nor had I ever done anything that merited the name of dishonest or fraudulent, much less thievish. I had chiefly been my own enemy, or, as I may rightly say, I had been nobody's enemy but my own. But now I was embarrassed in the worst condition imaginable, for though I was perfectly innocent, I was in no condition to prove that innocence easily, and if I had been taken, it had been under a supposed guilt of the worst kind—at least, a crime esteemed so among the people I had to do with. This made me very anxious to make an escape; though which way to do it, I knew not, or what port or place we should go to. My partner seeing me thus dejected, though he was the most concerned at first, began to encourage me. Describing to me the several ports of that coast, he told me he would put in on the coast of Cochin China, or the Bay of Tonquin, intending afterward to go to Macao, a town once in possession of the Portuguese and where still a great many European families resided—

particularly, the missionary priests usually went thither in order to proceed from there on to China.

Hither, then, we resolved to go. Accordingly, though after a tedious and irregular course, and being very much straitened for provisions, we came within sight of the coast very early in the morning. Upon reflection on the past circumstances we were in and the danger if we had not escaped, we resolved to put into a small river—which, however, had depth enough of water for us—and see if we could, either overland or by the ship's pinnace, come to know what ships were in any port thereabouts. This happy step was, indeed, our deliverance; for though we did not immediately see any European ships in the Bay of Tonquin, yet the next morning there came into the bay two Dutch ships. A third, without any colors spread out but that we believed to be a Dutchman, passed by at about two leagues' distance, steering for the coast of China; and in the afternoon went by two English ships steering the same course. Thus we thought we saw ourselves beset with enemies both one way and the other.

The place we were in was wild and barbarous, and the people were thieves, even by occupation or profession. Though, it is true, we had not much to seek of them and, except getting a few provisions, cared not how little we had to do with them, yet it was with much difficulty that we kept ourselves from being insulted by them several ways. We were on a small river of this country, within a few leagues of its utmost limits northward; and by our boat we coasted northeast, to the point of land that opens the great Bay of Tonquin. It was in this beating up along the shore that we discovered we were surrounded by enemies. The people we were among were the most barbarous of all the inhabitants of the coast, having no correspondence with any other nation and dealing only in fish and oil and such gross commodities. It may be particularly seen that they are the most barbarous of any of the inhabitants. Among other customs, they have this one: that if any vessel has the misfortune to be shipwrecked upon their coast, they presently make the men all prisoners or slaves. It was not long before we found a piece of their kindness this way, on the occasion following.

Our Ship Springs a Leak

I have observed above that our ship had sprung a leak at sea and that we could not find it; and it happened that, as I have said, it was stopped unexpectedly, in the happy minute of our being about to be seized by the Dutch and English ships near the Bay of Siam. Yet, as we did not find the ship so perfectly tight or sound as we desired, we resolved while we were at this place to lay her on shore and take out what heavy things we had on board and clean her bottom, if possible, to find out where the leaks were. Accordingly, having lightened the ship and brought all our guns and other movables to one side, we tried to bring her down that we might come at her bottom. But, on second thoughts, we did not care to lay her on dry ground; neither could we find out a proper place for it.

The inhabitants, who had never been acquainted with such a sight, came, wondering, down the shore to look at us. Seeing the ship down on one side in such a manner and heeling in toward the shore, and not seeing our men, who were at work on her bottom with stages and with their boats on the offside, they presently concluded that the ship was cast away and lay fast on the ground. On this supposition, they all came about us in two or three hours' time, with ten or twelve large boats, having some of them eight, some ten men in a boat, intending, no doubt, to have come on board and plundered the ship, and if they found us there, to have carried us away for slaves to their king, or whatever they call him, for we knew nothing of their governor.

When they came up to the ship and began to row around her, they discovered us all hard at work on the outside of the ship's bottom and side, washing, and graving, and stopping, as every seafaring man knows how. They stood for a while gazing at us, and we, who were a little surprised, could not imagine what their design was. But being willing to be sure, we took this opportunity to get some of us into the ship, and others to hand down arms and ammunition to those who were at work to defend themselves with, if there should be occasion. It was no more than need—for in less than a quarter of an hour's consultation, they agreed, it seems, that the ship was really a wreck and that we were all at work endeavoring to save her, or to save our lives by the help of our boats; and when we handed our arms into the boat, they concluded, by that motion, that we were endeavoring to save some of our goods. Upon this, they took it for granted we all belonged to them, and away they came directly upon our men, as if it had been in a line of battle.

Our men, seeing so many of them, began to be frightened, for we lay but in an ill posture to fight; and they cried out to us to know what they should do. I immediately called to the men that worked upon the stages to slip them down and get up the side onto the ship, and I bade those in the boat to row around and come on board. The few who were on board worked with all the strength and hands we had to bring the ship to rights. However, neither the men upon the stages nor those in the boats could do as they were ordered before the Cochin Chinese were upon them. Two of their boats boarded our longboat and began to lay hold of the men as their prisoners.

The first man they laid hold of was an English seaman, a stout, strong fellow who, having a musket in his hand, never offered to fire it but laid it down in the boat, like a fool, as I thought. But he understood his business better than I could teach him, for he grappled the pagan and dragged him by main force out of their boat into ours, where . . . the fellow died in his hands. In the meantime, a Dutchman who stood next took up the musket and with the butt end of it so laid about him that he knocked down five of them who attempted to enter the boat. But this was doing little toward resisting thirty or forty men who, fearless because ignorant of their danger, began to throw themselves into the longboat, where we had but five men in all to defend it. However, the following accident, which caused our laughter, gave our men a complete victory.

A Novel Mode of Warfare

Our carpenter being prepared to grave the outside of the ship, as well as to pay the seams where he had caulked her to stop the leaks, had got two kettles just let down into the boat, one filled with boiling pitch and the other with resin, tallow, oil, and such stuff as the shipwrights use for that work; and the man that attended the carpenter had a great iron ladle in his hand, with which he supplied the men that were at work with the hot stuff. Two of the enemy's men entered the boat just where this fellow stood, being in the fore-sheets; he immediately saluted them with a ladleful of the stuff, boiling hot, which so burned and scalded them, being half-naked, that they roared out like bulls and, enraged by the fire, leaped both into the sea.

The carpenter saw it and cried out, "Well done, Jack! Give them some more of it."

Stepping forward himself, he took one of the mops, and dipping it in the pitch pot, he and his man threw it among the enemy so plentifully that, in short, of all the men in the three boats, there was not one that escaped being scalded and burned with it, in a most frightful, pitiful manner, and made such a howling and crying that I never heard a worse noise: for it is worth observing that, though pain naturally makes all people cry out, yet every nation has a particular way of exclamation and makes a noise as different one from another as their speech. I cannot give the noise these creatures made a better name than howling, nor a name more proper to the tone of it; for I never heard anything more like the noise of the wolves that, as I have said, I heard howl in the forest on the frontiers of Languedoc.

"Well done, Jack! Give them some more of it!"

I was never better pleased with a victory in my life—not only as it was a perfect surprise to me and that our danger was imminent before, but as we got this victory without any bloodshed, except of that man the fellow killed with his naked hands, and which I was very much concerned at; for I was sick of killing such poor savage wretches, even though it was in my own defense, knowing they came on errands that they thought just and knew no better; and that though it may be a just thing, because necessary (for there is no necessary wickedness in nature), yet I thought it was a sad life, when we must be always obliged to be killing our fellow creatures to preserve ourselves. Indeed, I think so still, and I would even now suffer a great deal, rather than I would take away the life even of the worst person injuring me. I believe all considering people, who know the value of life, would be of my opinion, if they entered seriously into the consideration of it.

But to return to my story: All the while this was doing, my partner and I, who managed the rest of the men on board, had with great dexterity brought the ship almost to rights, and having got the guns into their places again, the gunner called to me to bid our boat get out of the way, for he would let fly among them. I called back again to him and bid him not offer to fire, for the carpenter would do the work without him; I bid him heat another pitch kettle, which our cook, who was on board, took care of. The enemy was so terrified with what they had met with in their first attack that they would not come on again; and some of them who were farthest off, seeing the ship swim, as it were, upright, began, as we suppose, to see their mistake and gave over the enterprise, finding it was not as they expected.

Thus we got clear of this merry fight; and having got some rice and some roots and bread, with about sixteen hogs, on board two days before, we resolved to stay here no longer but go forward, whatever came of it; for we made no doubt but we should be surrounded the next day with rogues enough, perhaps more than our pitch kettle would dispose of for us. We therefore got all our things on board the same evening, and the next morning we were ready to sail. In the meantime, lying at anchor at some distance from the shore, we were not so much concerned, being now in a fighting posture, as well as in a sailing posture, if any enemy had presented.

The next day, having finished our work within board and finding our ship was perfectly healed of all her leaks, we set sail. We would have gone into the Bay of Tonquin, for we wanted to inform ourselves of what was to be known concerning the Dutch ships that had been there. But we dared not stand in there, because we had seen several ships go in, as we supposed, but a little before. So we kept on northeast, toward the island of Formosa, as much afraid of being seen by a Dutch or English merchant ship, as a Dutch or English merchant ship in the Mediterranean is of an Algerine man-of-war.

When we were thus got to sea, we kept on northeast, as if we would go to the Manillas or the Philippine Islands; and this we did that we might not fall into the way of any of the European ships. Then we steered north, till we came to the latitude of 22 degrees 20 minutes, by which means we made the island of Formosa directly, where we came to an anchor, in order to get water and fresh provisions. The people there, who are very courteous and civil in their manners, supplied us willingly and dealt very fairly and punctually with us in all their agreements and bargains, which is what we did not find among other peoples. This may be owing to the remains of Christianity that was once planted here by a Dutch missionary of Protestants and is a testimony of what I have often observed, namely, that the Christian religion always civilizes the people and reforms their manners, where it is received, whether it works saving effects upon them or not.

From thence we sailed still north, keeping the coast of China at an equal distance, till we knew we were beyond all the ports of China where our European ships usually came—being resolved, if possible, not to fall into any of their hands, especially in this country, where, as our circumstances were, we could not fail of being entirely ruined.

Being now come to the latitude of 30 degrees, we resolved to put into the first trading port we should come at. Standing in for the shore, a boat came off two leagues to us with an old Portuguese pilot on board, who, knowing us to be a European ship, came to offer his service, which, indeed, we were glad of. We took him on board, upon which, without asking whither we would go, he dismissed the boat he came in and sent it back.

A boat came off two leagues to us

Chapter 13

PEKIN

I thought it was now so much in our power to have the old man carry us whither we would that I began to talk to him about carrying us to the Gulf of Nanquin, which is the most northern part of the coast of China. The old man said he knew the Gulf of Nanquin very well; but, smiling, he asked us what we would do there. I told him we would sell our cargo and purchase chinaware, calicoes, raw silks, tea, wrought silks, etc., and so would return by the same course we came. He told us our best port would have been to put in at Macao, where we could not have failed of a market for our opium to our satisfaction and might for our money have purchased all sorts of China goods as cheaply as we could at Nanquin.

Not being able to put the old man out of his talk, of which he was very opinionated or conceited, I told him we were gentlemen as well as merchants and that we had a mind to see the great city of Pekin and the famous court of the monarch of China.

"Why, then," said the old man, "you should go to Ningpo, where, by the river that runs into the sea there, you may go within five leagues of the great canal. This canal is a navigable stream that goes through the heart of that vast empire of China, crosses all the rivers, passes some considerable hills by the help of sluices and gates, and goes up to the city of Pekin, being in length nearly two hundred and seventy leagues."

"Well," said I, "Seignior Portuguese, but that is not our business now. The great question is, if you can carry us up to the city of Nanquin, can we travel from there to Pekin afterward?"

He said we could do so very well and that there was a great Dutch ship gone up that way just before. This gave me a little shock, for a Dutch ship was now our terror, and we had much rather have met the devil, at least if he had not come in too frightful a figure. We depended upon it that a Dutch

ship would be our destruction, for we were in no condition to fight them—
all the ships they trade with in those parts being of great burden and of much
greater force than we were.

The old man found me a little confused and under some concern when he
named a Dutch ship, and he said to me, "Sir, you need be under no apprehensions of the Dutch. I suppose they are not now at war with your nation?"

"No," said I, "that's true. But I know not what liberties men may take
when they are out of the reach of the laws of their own country."

"Why," said he, "you are no pirates; what need you fear? They will not
meddle with peaceable merchants, sure."

If I had any blood in my body that did not fly up into my face at that
word, it was hindered by some stop in the vessels appointed by nature to
circulate it, for it put me into the greatest disorder and confusion imaginable;
nor was it possible for me to conceal it, but the old man easily perceived it.

"Sir," said he, "I find you are in some disorder in your thoughts at my talk.
Pray be pleased to go which way you think fit, and depend upon it, I'll do
you all the service I can."

"Why, seignior," said I, "it is true I am a little unsettled in my resolution,
at this time, whither to go in particular; and I am something more so for
what you said about pirates. I hope there are no pirates on these seas. We are
but in an ill condition to meet with them, for you see we have but a small
force and are but very weakly manned."

"Oh, sir," said he, "don't be concerned. I do not know that there have been
any pirates on these seas these fifteen years, except one, which was seen, as
I hear, in the Bay of Siam about a month since. But you may be assured she
is gone to the southward; nor was she a ship of any great force or fit for the
work. She was not built for a privateer but was run away with by a reprobate
crew that was on board after the captain and some of his men had been
murdered by the Malayans at or near the island of Sumatra."

"What?" said I, seeming to know nothing of the matter. "Did they murder
the captain?"

"No," said he, "I don't know that they murdered him; but as they afterward ran away with the ship, it is generally believed that they betrayed him
into the hands of the Malayans, who did murder him, and perhaps they
procured them to do it."

"Why, then," said I, "they deserve death as much as if they had done it
themselves."

"Nay," said the old man, "they do deserve it, and they will certainly have it, if they light upon any English or Dutch ship; for they have all agreed together that if they meet that rogue, they'll give him no quarter."

"But," said I to him, "you say the pirate is gone out of these seas. How can they meet with him, then?"

"Why, that's true," said he, "they do say so. But he was, as I tell you, in the Bay of Siam, on the river Cambodia, and was discovered there by some Dutchmen who belonged to the ship and who were left on shore when they ran away with her; and some English and Dutch traders being on the river, they were within a little of taking him. Nay," said he, "if the foremost boats had been well seconded by the rest, they had certainly taken him. But he, finding only two boats within reach of him, tacked about and fired at those two and disabled them before the others came up, and then standing off to sea, the others were not able to follow, and so he got away. But they have all so exact a description of the ship that they will be sure to know her; and wherever they find her, they have vowed to give no quarter either to the captain or seamen, but to hang them all up at the yardarm."

"What?" said I. "Will they execute them, right or wrong? Hang them first and judge them afterward?"

"Oh, sir," said the old pilot, "there is no need to make a formal business of it with such rogues as those. Let them tie them back to back and set them a-diving—'tis no more than they rightly deserve."

I knew I had my old man fast on board and that he could do no harm, so I turned short upon him. "Well, now, seignior," said I, "this is the very reason why I would have you carry us up to Nanquin and not put back to Macao, or to any other part of the country where the English or Dutch ships come; for be it known to you, seignior, those captains of the English and Dutch ships are a parcel of rash, proud, insolent fellows that neither know what belongs to justice, nor how to behave themselves as the laws of God and nature direct. But being proud of their offices and not understanding their power, they would act the murderers to punish robbers and would take upon themselves to insult men falsely accused and determine them guilty without due inquiry. Perhaps I may live to bring some of them to account for it, when they may be taught how justice is to be executed and that no man ought to be treated as a criminal till some evidence may be had of the crime and that he is the man."

With this I told him that this was the very ship they attacked, and I gave him a full account of the skirmish we had with their boats and how foolishly and cowardly they behaved. I told him all the story of our buying the ship, and how the Dutchmen served us. I told him the reasons I had to believe the story of killing the master by the Malayans was true, as also the running away with the ship; but it was all a fiction of their own to suggest that the men had turned pirates, and they ought to have been sure it was so before they ventured to attack us by surprise and oblige us to resist them; adding that they would have the blood of those men whom we killed there in just defense to answer for.

The old man was amazed at this account and told us we were very much in the right to go away to the north; and that, if he might advise us, it should be to sell the ship in China, which we might very well do, and buy or build another in the country. "And," said he, "though you will not get so good a ship, yet you may get one able enough to carry you and all your goods back again to Bengal or anywhere else."

I told him I would take his advice when I came to any port where I could find a ship for my turn or get any customer to buy this. He replied that I should meet with customers enough for the ship at Nanquin, that a Chinese junk would serve me very well to go back again, and that he would procure me people both to buy one and sell the other.

"Well, but, seignior," said I, "as you say they know the ship so well, I may, perhaps, if I follow your measures, be instrumental to bring some honest, innocent men into a terrible broil and perhaps to be murdered in cold blood; for wherever they find the ship they will prove the guilt upon the men by proving this was the ship; and so innocent men may probably be overpowered and murdered."

"Why," said the old man, "I'll find out a way to prevent that also; for as I know all those commanders you speak of very well, and shall see them all as they pass by, I will be sure to set them to rights in the thing and let them know that they had been so much in the wrong; that though the people who were on board at first might run away with the ship, yet it was not true that they had turned pirates; and that, in particular, these were not the men who first went off with the ship, but innocently bought her for their trade. I am persuaded they will so far believe me as at least to act more cautiously for the time to come."

While these things were passing between us by way of discourse, we went forward directly for Nanquin and, in about thirteen days' sail, came to an anchor at the southwest point of the great Gulf of Nanquin; where, by the way, I came by accident to understand that two Dutch ships were gone the length before me and that I should certainly fall into their hands. I consulted my partner again in this exigence, and he was as much at a loss as I was and would very gladly have been safely on shore almost anywhere. Then I asked the old pilot if there was no creek or harbor that I might put into and pursue my business with the Chinese privately and be in no danger of the enemy. He told me that if I would sail to the southward about forty-two leagues, there was a little port called Quinchang, where the fathers of the mission usually landed from Macao on their way to teach the Christian religion to the Chinese, and where no European ships ever put in; and if I thought to put in there, I might consider what further course to take when I was on shore. He confessed, he said, it was not a place for merchants, except that at some certain times they had a kind of a fair there, when the merchants from Japan came over thither to buy Chinese merchandise.

We all agreed to go back to this place. The name of the port as he called it I may perhaps spell wrong, for I do not particularly remember it, having lost this, together with the names of many other places set down in a little pocketbook that was spoiled by water in an accident, which I shall relate later. But this I remember: that the Chinese or Japanese merchants we corresponded with called it by a different name from that which our Portuguese pilot gave it and pronounced it as above, Quinchang.

Bound for Quinchang

As we were unanimous in our resolution to go to this place, we weighed anchor the next day, having only gone twice on shore where we were to get fresh water; on both occasions, the people of the country were very civil to us and brought an abundance of things to sell to us; I mean of provisions, plants, roots, tea, rice, and some fowls—but nothing without money.

We did not come to the other port (the wind being contrary) for five days; but it was very much to our satisfaction. I was joyful, and I may say thankful, when I set my foot on shore, resolving, and my partner, too, that if it was possible to dispose of ourselves and our effects any other way, though not every way to our satisfaction, we would never set one foot on board that unhappy vessel again. Indeed, I must acknowledge that of all the circumstances of life that ever I had any experience of, nothing makes mankind so completely miserable as that of being in constant fear. Well does the Scripture say, "The fear of man bringeth a snare." It is a life of death, and the mind is so entirely oppressed by it that it is capable of no relief, and all the vigor of nature that usually supports men under other afflictions, and is present with them in the greatest exigencies, fails them here.

Nor did it fail of its usual operations upon the mind by heightening every danger, representing the English and Dutch captains to be men incapable of hearing reason, or of distinguishing between honest men and rogues or between a story calculated for our own turn, made out of nothing, on purpose to deceive, and a true genuine account of our whole voyage, progress, and design. For we might in many ways have convinced any reasonable creature that we were not pirates: the goods we had on board, the course we steered, our frankly showing ourselves and entering into such and such ports, even our very manner, the force we had, the number of men, the few

The people brought an abundance of things to sell to us

arms, the little ammunition, short provisions—all these would have served to convince any men that we were no pirates. The opium and other goods we had on board would make it appear the ship had been at Bengal. The Dutchmen, who, it was said, had the names of all the men that were on the ship, might easily see that we were a mixture of English, Portuguese, and Indians, and but two Dutchmen on board. These, and many other particular circumstances, might have made it evident to the understanding of any commander, whose hands we might fall into, that we were no pirates.

But fear, that blind, useless passion, worked another way and threw us into the vapors; it bewildered our understandings and set the imagination at work to form a thousand terrible things that perhaps might never happen. We first supposed, as indeed everybody had related to us, that the seamen on board the English and Dutch ships, but especially the Dutch, were so enraged at the name of a pirate, and especially at our beating off their boats and escaping, that they would not give themselves leave to inquire whether we were pirates or not, but would execute us offhand, without giving us any room for a defense. We reflected that there really was so much apparent evidence before them that they would scarcely inquire after any more; as, first, that the ship was certainly the same and that some of the seamen among them knew her and had been on board her; and, secondly, that when we had intelligence at the river of Cambodia that they were coming down to examine us, we fought their boats and fled; so that we made no doubt but they were as fully satisfied of our being pirates as we were satisfied of the contrary. And as I often said, I know not but I should have been apt to have taken those circumstances for evidence, if the tables were turned and my case was theirs, and have made no scruple of cutting all the crew to pieces, without believing, or perhaps considering, what they might have to offer in their defense.

But be that as it may, these were our apprehensions; and both my partner and I scarcely slept a night without dreaming of halters and yardarms, that is to say, gibbets; of fighting and being taken; of killing and being killed. One night I was in such a fury in my dream, fancying the Dutchmen had boarded us, and I was knocking one of their seamen down, that I struck my doubled fist against the side of the cabin I lay in with such a force as wounded my hand grievously, broke my knuckles, and cut and bruised the flesh, so that it awakened me out of my sleep.

Another apprehension I had was the cruel usage we might meet with from them if we fell into their hands. Then the story of Amboyna[1] came into my head, and how the Dutch might perhaps torture us as they did our countrymen there, and make some of our men, by extremity of torture, confess those crimes they never were guilty of, or own themselves and all of us to be pirates. So they would put us to death with a formal appearance of justice, and they might be tempted to do this for the gain of our ship and cargo, which was worth four or five thousand pounds altogether.

---

1. An island in the Moluccas that the Dutch then controlled.

Anxious Meditations

These things tormented me, and my partner, too, night and day; nor did we consider that the captains of ships had no authority to act thus; and if we had surrendered prisoners to them, they could not answer their destroying us or torturing us, but would be accountable for it when they came to their country. This, I say, gave me no satisfaction; for if they were to act thus with us, what advantage would it be to us that they should be called to an account for it? Or, if we were first to be murdered, what satisfaction would it be to us to have them punished when they came home?

I cannot refrain taking notice here of what reflections I now had upon the vast variety of my particular circumstances—how hard I thought it was that I, who had spent forty years in a life of continual difficulties and was at last come, as it were, to the port or haven that all men drive at, namely, to have rest and plenty, should be a volunteer in new sorrows by my own unhappy choice; and that I, who had escaped so many dangers in my youth, should now come to be hanged in my old age, and in so remote a place, for a crime that I was not in the least inclined to, much less guilty of.

After these thoughts, something of religion would come in; and I would be considering that this seemed to me to be a disposition of immediate Providence, and I ought to look upon it and submit to it as such; that although I was innocent as to men, I was far from being innocent as to my Maker; and I ought to look in and examine what other crimes in my life were most obvious to me and for which Providence might justly inflict this punishment as a retribution; and that I ought to submit to this just as I would to a shipwreck, if it had pleased God to have brought such a disaster upon me.

In its turn, natural courage would sometimes take its place, and then I would be talking myself up to vigorous resolutions: I would not be taken to be barbarously used by a parcel of merciless wretches in cold blood; it were much better to have fallen into the hands of the savages, though I was sure they would feast upon me when they had taken me, than those who would perhaps glut their rage upon me by inhuman tortures and barbarities. In the case of the savages, I always resolved to die fighting to the last gasp, and why should I not do so now, seeing it was much more dreadful, to me at least, to think of falling into these men's hands than ever it was to think of being eaten by men? For the savages, give them their due, would not eat a man till he was killed and dead, but these men had many arts beyond the cruelty of death. Whenever these thoughts prevailed, I was sure to put myself into a kind of fever with the agitation of a supposed fight: My blood would boil and my eyes sparkle, as if I was engaged, and I always resolved to take no quarter at their hands; but even, at last, if I could resist no longer, I would blow up the ship and all that was on her and leave them but little booty to boast of.

The greater weight the anxieties and perplexities of these things were to our thoughts while we were at sea, the greater was our satisfaction when we saw ourselves on shore. My partner told me he dreamed that he had a very heavy load upon his back that he was to carry up a hill, and he found that he was not able to stand longer under it. But the Portuguese pilot came and took it off his back, and the hill disappeared, the ground before him appearing all smooth and plain. Truly it was so: They were all like men who had a load taken off their backs. For my part, I had a weight taken off my heart that it was not able any longer to bear; and as I said above, we resolved to go no more to sea in that ship.

When we came on shore, the old pilot, who was now our friend, got us a lodging and a warehouse for our goods, which, by the way, was much the same: It was a little house, or hut, with a larger house adjoining to it, all built with canes and palisaded around with large canes to keep out pilfering thieves, of which, it seems, there were not a few in that country. However, the magistrates allowed us a little guard, and we had a soldier with a kind of halberd, or half-pike, who stood sentinel at our door and to whom we allowed a pint of rice and a little piece of money, about the value of three-pence, per day, so that our goods were kept very safe.

The fair, or mart, usually kept at this place, had been over for some time. However, we found that there were three or four junks on the river, and two Japanners (I mean ships from Japan), with goods that they had bought in China, that were not yet gone away, having some Japanese merchants still on shore.

Father Simon

The first thing our old Portuguese pilot did for us was to get us acquainted with three missionary Romish priests who were in the town and who had been there some time converting the people to Christianity. We thought they made but poor work of it and made them but sorry Christians when they had done; however, that was none of our business. One of these was a Frenchman, whom they called Father Simon; another was a Portuguese; and a third a Genoese. Father Simon was courteous, easy in his manner, and very agreeable company; the other two were more reserved, seemed rigid and austere, and applied seriously to the work they came about, namely, to talk with and insinuate themselves among the inhabitants whenever they had opportunity. We often ate and drank with those men; and though, I must confess, the conversion, as they call it, of the Chinese to Christianity is so far from the true conversion required to bring heathen people to the faith of Christ that it seems to amount to little more than letting them know the name of Christ, say some prayers to the Virgin Mary and her Son in a tongue that they understand not, and to cross themselves and the like; yet it must be confessed that the religionists, whom we call missionaries, have a firm belief that these people will be saved and that they are the instruments of it. On this account, they undergo not only the fatigue of the voyage and the hazards of living in such places, but oftentimes death itself and the most violent tortures, for the sake of this work.

But to return to my story: This French priest, Father Simon, was appointed, it seems, by order of the chief of the mission, to go up to Pekin, the royal seat of the Chinese emperor. He waited only for another priest, who was ordered to come to him from Macao, to go along with him. We scarcely ever met together but he was inviting me to go on that journey, telling me how he would show me all the glorious things of that mighty empire and, among the rest, the greatest city in the world—"a city," said he, "that your London and our Paris put together cannot be equal to." This was the city of Pekin, which, I confess, is very great and infinitely full of people. But as I looked on those things with different eyes from those of other men, so I shall give my opinion of them in a few words, when I come in the course of my travels to speak more particularly of them.

But first, I come to my friar or missionary. Dining with him one day and being very merry together, I showed some little inclination to go with him; and he pressed me and my partner very hard, and with a great many persuasions, to consent.

"Why, Father Simon," said my partner, "should you desire our company so much? You know we are heretics, and you do not love us, nor cannot keep us company with any pleasure."

"Oh," said he, "you may perhaps be good Catholics in time. My business here is to convert heathens, and who knows but I may convert you, too?"

"Very well, Father," said I, "so you will preach to us all the way?"

"I will not be troublesome to you," said he. "Our religion does not divest us of good manners. Besides, we are here like countrymen—and so we are, compared with the place we are in—and if you are Huguenots and I a Catholic, we may all be Christians at last. At least we are all gentlemen and we may converse so, without being uncomfortable with one another."

I liked this part of his discourse very well, and it reminded me of my priest that I had left in the Brazils; but this Father Simon did not come up to his character by a great deal; for though Father Simon had no appearance of criminal levity in him, yet he had not that fund of Christian zeal, strict piety, and sincere affection to religion that my other good ecclesiastic had.

But to leave him a little—although he never left us, nor ceased soliciting us to go with him—we had something else before us first. We had all this while our ship and our merchandise to dispose of, and we began to be very doubtful what we should do, for we were now in a place of very little business. And once I was about to venture to sail for the river of Kilam and the city of Nanquin, but Providence seemed now more visibly, as I thought, than ever to concern itself in our affairs. I was encouraged, from this very time, to think I should, one way or other, get out of this entangled circumstance and be brought home to my own country again, though I had not the least view of the manner.

Providence, I say, began here to clear up our way a little; and the first thing that offered was, our old Portuguese pilot brought a Japanese merchant to us, who inquired what goods we had. He ended up by buying all our opium— and gave us a very good price for it, paying us in gold by weight, some small pieces of our own coin, and some in small wedges of about ten or twelve ounces each.

While we were dealing with him for our opium, it came to me that he might perhaps deal for the ship, too, and I asked the interpreter to propose it to him. He shrunk up his shoulders at it when it was first proposed to him; but a few days after, he came to me, with one of the missionary priests for his interpreter, and told me he had a proposal to make to me, which was this: He had bought a great quantity of goods of us, when he had no thoughts of proposals made to him of buying the ship; therefore, he had no money to pay for the ship. But if I would let the same men who were on the ship navigate her, he would hire the ship to go to Japan and would send them from thence to the Philippine Islands with another loading, which he would pay the freight of before they left Japan; and at their return he would buy the ship. I began to listen to this proposal, and so eager was I to continue

rambling that I could not but begin to entertain a notion of going myself
with him and so to set sail from the Philippine Islands away to the South
Seas. Accordingly, I asked the Japanese merchant if he would not hire us to
go to the Philippine Islands and discharge us there. He said no, he could not
do that, for then he could not have the return of his cargo; but he would
discharge us in Japan at the ship's return. Well, I was still
for taking him at that proposal and going

He came to me with one of the missionary priests

myself; but my partner, wiser than I, persuaded me not to, representing the
dangers, as well of the seas as of the Japanese, who are a false, cruel, and
treacherous people; likewise those of the Spaniards at the Philippines, more
false, cruel, and treacherous even than they.

But to bring this long turn of our affairs to a conclusion: The first thing
we had to do was to consult with the captain of the ship, and with his men,
and find out if they were willing to go to Japan. While I was doing this, the

young man whom my nephew had left with me as my companion for my travels came to me and told me that he thought that voyage promised very fair and that there was a great prospect of advantage, and he would be very glad if I undertook it; but that if I would not, and would give him leave, he would go as a merchant, or as I pleased to order him; and that if ever he came to England, and I was there and alive, he would render me a faithful account of his success, which should be as much mine as I pleased. I was really loath to part with him; but considering the prospect of advantage, which really was considerable, and that he was a young fellow as likely to do well in it as any I knew, I inclined to let him go; but I told him I would consult my partner and give him an answer the next day.

My partner and I discussed it, and my partner made a most generous offer: "You know it has been an unlucky ship," said he, "and we both resolved not to go to sea in it again. If your steward" (so he called my man) "will venture on the voyage, I will leave my share of the vessel to him and let him make the best of it. And if we live to meet in England, and he meets with success abroad, he shall account for one half of the profits of the ship's freight to us, and the other shall be his own."

If my partner, who was no way concerned with my young man, made him such an offer, I could do no less than offer him the same. All the ship's company being willing to go with him, we made over half the ship to him in property and took a writing from him, obliging him to account for the other, and away he went to Japan. The Japan merchant proved a very punctual, honest man to him; protected him in Japan and got him a license to come on shore, which the Europeans in general have not lately obtained; paid him his freight very punctually; sent him to the Philippines, loaded with Japanese and Chinese wares, and a supercargo of their own, who, trafficking with the Spaniards, brought back European goods again, and a great quantity of cloves and other spices. There he was not only paid his freight punctually and at a very good price, but not being willing to sell the ship then, the merchant furnished him goods on his own account. With some money and some spices of his own that he brought with him, he went back to the Manillas to the Spaniards, where he sold his cargo very well. Here, having got a good acquaintance at Manilla, he got his ship made a free ship, and the governor of Manilla hired him to go to Acapulco in America, on the coast of Mexico. He gave him a license to land there, travel to Mexico, and pass on any Spanish ship to Europe with all his men. He made the voyage to Acapulco very happily, and there he sold his ship. Having there also obtained allowance to travel by land to Portobello, he found means, somehow or other, to get to Jamaica with all his treasure. About eight years after, he came to England, exceedingly rich; of which I shall take notice in its place. In the meantime I return to our particular affairs.

Being now to part with the ship and ship's company, it came before us, of course, to consider what recompense we should give to the two men who gave us such timely notice of the design against us on the river Cambodia. The truth was, they had done us a very considerable service and deserved well at our hands—though, by the way, they were a couple of rogues, too; for, as they believed the story of our being pirates, and that we had really run away with the ship, they came down to us, not only to betray the design that was formed against us, but to go to sea with us as pirates. One of them confessed afterward that nothing else but the hopes of going a-roguing brought him to do it. However, the service they did us was not the less, and therefore, as I had promised to be grateful to them, I first ordered the money to be paid them that they said was due to them on board their respective ships; over and above that, I gave each of them a small sum of money in gold, which contented them very well. Then I made the Englishman the gunner on the ship, the gunner being now made second mate and purser; the Dutchman I made boatswain. So they were both very well pleased and proved very serviceable, being both able seamen and very stout fellows.

In China

We were now on shore in China. If I thought myself banished and remote from my own country at Bengal, where I had many ways to get home for my money, what could I think of myself now, when I had gone about a thousand leagues farther off from home and perfectly destitute of all manner of prospect of return? All we had for it was this: that in about four months' time there was to be another fair at the place where we were, and then we might be able to purchase all sorts of the manufactures of the country and withal might possibly find some Chinese junks or vessels from Tonquin that were be to be sold and that would carry us and our goods whither we pleased. This I liked very well and resolved to wait; besides, as our particular persons were not offensive, if any English or Dutch ships came thither, perhaps we might have an opportunity to load our goods and get passage to some other place in India nearer home. Upon these hopes, we resolved to continue here; but to divert ourselves, we took two or three journeys into the country.

First, we went ten days' journey to the city of Nanquin, a city well worth seeing, indeed. They say it has a million people in it. It is regularly built, the streets all exactly straight and crossing one another in direct lines, which gives the figure of it great advantage. But when I come to compare the miserable people of these countries with ours—their fabrics, their manner of living, their government, their religion, their wealth, and their glory, as some call it— I must confess that I scarcely think it worth my while to mention them here.

It is very observable that we wonder at the grandeur, the riches, the pomp, the ceremonies, the government, the manufactures, the commerce, and the conduct of these people; not that it is to be wondered at, or, indeed, in the least to be regarded, but because, having a true notion of the barbarity of those countries, and the rudeness and ignorance that prevail there, we do not expect to find any such thing so far off. Otherwise, what are their buildings to the palaces and royal buildings of Europe? What is their trade to the universal commerce of England, Holland, France, and Spain? What are their cities to ours for wealth, strength, gaiety of apparel, rich furniture, and infinite variety? What are their ports, supplied with a few junks and barks, to our navigation, our merchant fleets, our large and powerful navies? Our city of London has more trade than half their mighty empire; one English, Dutch, or French man-of-war of eighty guns would be able to fight almost all the shipping belonging to China. But the greatness of their wealth and trade, the power of their government, and the strength of their armies may be a little surprising to us, because, as I have said, considering them as a barbarous nation of pagans, little better than savages, we did not expect such things among them. This, indeed, is the advantage with which all their greatness and power is represented to us; otherwise, it is in itself nothing at all, for what I have said of their ships may be said of their armies and troops: All the forces of their empire, though they were to bring two million men into the field together, would be able to do nothing but ruin the country and starve themselves, if they were to besiege a strong town in Flanders, or to fight a disciplined army. One good line of German cuirassiers or of French cavalry might withstand all the horse[2] of China; a million of their foot[3] would not stand before one embattled body of our infantry, posted so as not to be surrounded, though they were not to be one to twenty in number. Nay, I do not boast if I say that thirty thousand German or English foot and ten thousand horse, well managed, could defeat all the forces of China. And so of our fortified towns and of the art of our engineers in assaulting and defending towns. There is not a fortified town in China that could hold out one month

---

2. Cavalry.
3. Foot soldiers.

against the batteries and attacks of a European army; and, at the same time, all the armies of China could never take such a town as Dunkirk, provided it was not starved—no, not in ten years' siege. They had firearms, it is true, but they are awkward and uncertain in their going off; and their powder has but little strength.

Their armies are badly disciplined and lack skill to attack or discipline in retreat. Therefore, I must confess, it seemed strange to me, when I came home and heard our people say such fine things of the power, glory, magnificence, and trade of the Chinese; because, as far as I saw, they appeared to be a contemptible herd or crowd of ignorant, sordid slaves, subjected to a government qualified only to rule such a people. And were not its distance inconceivably great from Muscovy, and the Muscovite empire in a manner as rude, impotent, and ill-governed as they, the czar of Muscovy might with ease drive them all out of their country and conquer them in one campaign. Had the czar (who is now a growing prince) fallen this way, instead of attacking the warlike Swedes, and equally improved himself in the art of war, as they say he has done, and if none of the powers of Europe had envied or interrupted him, he might by this time have been emperor of China, instead of being beaten by the king of Sweden at Narva, when the latter was not one to six in number.

As their strength and their grandeur, so their navigation, commerce, and husbandry are very imperfect, compared with the same things in Europe. Also, in their knowledge, in their learning, and in their skill in the sciences, they are either very awkward or defective, though they have globes or spheres and a smattering of the mathematics and think they know more than all the world besides. But they know little of the motions of the heavenly bodies; and so grossly and absurdly ignorant are their common people that when the sun is eclipsed, they think a great dragon has assaulted it and is going to run away with it; and they fall a-clattering with all the drums and kettles in the country to frighten the monster away, just as we do to hive a swarm of bees.

As this is the only excursion of the kind that I have made in all the accounts I have given of my travels, so I shall make no more such. It is none of my business, nor any part of my design, but to give an account of my own adventures through a life of inimitable wanderings and a long variety of changes, which, perhaps, few that come after me will have heard the like of. I shall therefore say very little of all the mighty places, desert countries, and numerous people I have yet to pass through, more than relates to my own story, and which my concern among them makes necessary.

We Set Out for Pekin

I was now, as near as I can compute, in the heart of China, about 30 degrees north of the line, for we were returned to Nanquin. I had, indeed, a mind to see the city of Pekin, which I had heard so much of, and Father Simon importuned me daily to do it. At length, his time of going away being set and the other missionary who was to go with him being arrived from Macao, it was necessary that we should resolve either to go or not; so I referred it wholly to my partner and left it wholly to his choice, who at length resolved it in the affirmative, and we prepared for our journey. We set out with very good advantage, as to finding the way; for we got leave to travel in the retinue of one of their mandarins, a kind of viceroy or principal magistrate in the province where they reside and who take great state upon them, traveling with great attendance and great homage from the people, who are sometimes greatly impoverished by them, being obliged to furnish provisions for them and all their attendants on their journeys. That which I particularly observed in our traveling with his baggage was this: that though we received sufficient provisions both for ourselves and our horses from the country, as belonging to the mandarin, yet we were obliged to pay for everything we had, after the market price of the country, and the mandarin's steward collected it duly from us; so that our traveling in the retinue of the mandarin, though it was a very great kindness to us, was not such a mighty favor from him, but was a great advantage to him, considering there were more than thirty other people who traveled in the same manner besides us, under the protection of his retinue; for the country furnished all the provisions for nothing to him, and yet he took our money for them.

On the Way to Pekin

We were twenty-five days traveling to Pekin through a country infinitely populous but, I think, badly cultivated. The husbandry, the economy, and the way of living were miserable, though they boast so much of the industry of the people. I say miserable, if compared with our own, but not so to these poor wretches, who know no other. The pride of the people is infinitely great and exceeded by nothing but their poverty in some parts, which adds to that which I call their misery. I must needs think the native savages of America live much more happily than the poorer sort of these, because as they have nothing, so they desire nothing; whereas, these are proud and insolent and in the main are in many parts mere beggars and drudges. Their ostentation is inexpressible, and if they can, they love to keep multitudes of servants or slaves, which is to the last degree ridiculous, as well as the contempt of all the world but themselves.

I must confess I traveled more pleasantly afterward in the deserts and vast wildernesses of Grand Tartary than here, and yet the roads here are well paved and well kept and very convenient for travelers. But nothing was more awkward to me than to see such a haughty, imperious, insolent people in the midst of the grossest simplicity and ignorance. My friend Father Simon and I used to be very merry upon these occasions, to see the beggarly pride of these people. For example, coming by the house of a country gentleman, as Father Simon called him, about ten leagues off the city of Nanquin, we had first of all the honor to ride with the master of the house about two miles. The state he rode in was a perfect Don Quixotism, being a mixture of pomp and poverty. His habit was very proper for a scaramouch,[4] or merry-andrew, being a dirty calico, with hanging sleeves, tassels, and cuts and slashes almost on every side. It covered a taffeta vest, as greasy as a butcher's, and which testified that his honor must be a most exquisite sloven. His horse was but a poor, starved, hobbling creature, and he had two slaves following him on foot to drive the poor creature along; he had a whip in his hand, and he belabored the beast as fast about the head as his slaves did about the tail. Thus he rode by us, with about ten or twelve servants, going from the city to his countryseat about half a league before us. We traveled on gently, but this figure of a gentleman rode away before us; and as we stopped at a village about an hour to refresh us, when we came by the countryseat of this great man, we saw him in a little place before his door, eating a repast. It was a kind of garden, but he was easy to be seen; and we were given to understand that the more we looked at him, the better he would be pleased. He sat under a tree, something like the palmetto, which effectually shaded him over the head and on the south side; but under the tree was placed a large umbrella, which made that part look well enough. He sat lolling back in a great elbow-chair,[5] being a heavy, corpulent man, and had his meat brought him by two women slaves. He had two more, one of whom fed the squire with a spoon, and the other held the dish with one hand and scraped off what he let fall upon his worship's beard and taffeta vest.

Thus leaving the poor wretch to please himself with our looking at him, as if we admired his pomp, though we really pitied and ridiculed him, we pursued our journey. Only Father Simon had the curiosity to stay and inform

---

4. Clown or actor.
5. A massive armchair.

himself what dainties the country justice had to feed on in all his state, which he had the honor to taste of, and which was, I think, a mess of boiled rice, with a great piece of garlic in it, and a little bag filled with green pepper and another plant that they have there, something like our ginger, but smelling like musk and tasting like mustard; all this was put together, and a small piece of lean mutton boiled in it, and this was his worship's repast. Four or five servants more attended at a distance, who we supposed were to eat of the same after their master.

As for our mandarin with whom we traveled, he was respected as a king, surrounded always with his gentlemen and attended in all his appearances with such pomp that I saw little of him but at a distance. But this I observed: that there was not a horse in his retinue but that our carriers' packhorses in England seemed to me to look much better—though it was hard to judge rightly, for they were so covered with equipage, mantles, trappings, etc., that we could scarcely see anything but their feet and their heads as they went along.

I was now lighthearted. All my trouble and perplexity that I have given an account of being over, I had no anxious thoughts about me, which made this journey the pleasanter to me. Nor had I any ill accident attending me—only in passing or fording a small river, my horse fell and made me free of the country, as they call it—that is to say, threw me in. The place was not deep, but it wetted me all over. I mention it because it spoiled my pocketbook, wherein I had set down the names of several people and places that I had occasion to remember, and which not taking due care of, the leaves rotted and the words were never after to be read, to my great loss, as to the names of some of the places I touched at on this journey.

At length we arrived at Pekin. I had nobody with me but the youth whom my nephew the captain had given me to attend me as a servant, and who proved very trusty and diligent; and my partner had nobody with him but one servant, who was a kinsman. As for the Portuguese pilot, he being desirous to see the court, we bore his charges for his company and to use him as an interpreter, for he understood the language of the country and spoke good French and a little English. Indeed, this old man was a most useful implement to us everywhere, for we had not been above a week at Pekin when he came to us, laughing.

"Ah, Seignior Inglese," said he, "I have something to tell that will make your heart glad."

"My heart glad?" said I. "What can that be? I don't know anything in this country that can either give me joy or grief to any great degree."

"Yes, yes," said the old man in broken English, "make you glad, me sorry."

"Why," said I, "will it make you sorry?"

"Because," said he, "you have brought me here twenty-five days' journey and will leave me to go back alone. And which way shall I get to my port afterward, without a ship, without a horse, without *pecune?*"—so he called money, being his broken Latin, of which he had abundance to make us merry with.

In short, he told us that there was a great caravan of Muscovite and Polish merchants in the city, preparing to set out on their journey by land to Muscovy, within four or five weeks; and he was sure we would take the opportunity to go with them and leave him behind to go back alone.

I confess I was greatly surprised with this good news and had scarcely power to speak to him for some time; but at last I turned to him.

"How do you know this?" said I. "Are you sure it is true?"

"Yes," said he. "I met this morning in the street an old acquaintance of mine, an Armenian, who is among them. He came last from Astracan[6] and was designing to go to Tonquin, where I formerly knew him, but he has altered his mind and is now resolved to go with the caravan to Moscow, and so down the river Wolga[7] to Astracan."

"Well, seignior," said I, "do not be uneasy about being left to go back alone. If this be a method for my return to England, it shall be your fault if you go back to Macao at all."

We then went to consult together what was to be done; and I asked my partner what he thought of the pilot's news and whether it would suit with his affairs. He told me he would do just as I would; for he had settled all his affairs at Bengal and left his effects in such good hands that as we had made a good voyage here, if he could invest it in China silks, wrought and raw, such as might be worth the carriage, he would be content to go to England and then make his voyage back to Bengal by the company's ships.

---

6. Astrakhan.

7. Volga.

Chapter 14

THE GREAT CARAVAN

Having resolved upon this, we agreed that if our Portuguese pilot would go with us, we would bear his charges to Moscow, or to England, if he pleased. Nor, indeed, were we to be esteemed overly generous in that either, if we had not rewarded him further, the service he had done us being really worth more than that; for he had not only been a pilot to us at sea, but he had been like a broker for us on shore; and his procuring for us the Japanese merchant was some hundreds of pounds in our pockets. So we consulted together about it, and being willing to gratify him (which was but doing him justice) and very willing also to have him with us besides (for he was a most necessary man on all occasions), we agreed to give him a quantity of coined gold—which, as I compute it, came to about one hundred and seventy pounds sterling between us—and to bear all his charges, both for himself and his horse, except only a horse to carry his goods. Having settled this between ourselves, we called him to let him know what we had resolved. I told him he had complained of our being willing to let him go back alone, and I was now about to tell him we were resolved he should not go back at all; that as we had resolved to go Europe with the caravan, we resolved also he should go with us and that we called him to know his mind. He shook his head and said it was a long journey and that he had no *pecune* to carry him thither or to subsist himself when he came there. We told him we believed it was so, and therefore we had resolved to do something for him that should let him see how sensible we were of the service he had done us, and also how agreeable he was to us. Then I told him what we had resolved to give him here, which he might lay out as we would do our own; and as for his charges, if he would go with us we would set him safely on shore (life and casualties excepted) either in Muscovy or England, whichever he preferred, at our own charge, excepting only the carriage of his goods.

He received the proposal like a man transported and told us he would go with us over the whole world; and so we all prepared for our journey. However, as it was with us so it was with the other merchants. They had many things to do, and instead of being ready in five weeks, it was four months and some days before all things were got together.

It was the beginning of February, our calendar, when we set out from Pekin. My partner and the old pilot had gone expressly back to the port where we had first put in, to dispose of some goods that we had left there; and I, with a Chinese merchant whom I had some knowledge of at Nanquin, and who came to Pekin on his own affairs, went to Nanquin, where I bought ninety pieces of fine damasks, with about two hundred pieces of other very fine silks of several sorts, some mixed with gold, and had all these brought to Pekin before my partner's return. Besides this, we bought a very large quantity of raw silk and some other goods, our cargo amounting, in these goods only, to about three thousand five hundred pounds sterling; which, together with tea and some fine calicoes and three camels' loads of nutmegs and cloves, all loaded on eighteen camels for our share, besides those we rode upon. With two or three spare horses and two horses loaded with provisions, there were, in short, twenty-six horses and camels in our retinue.

The company was very great and, as far as I can remember, made between three and four hundred horses and upward of one hundred and twenty men, very well armed and provided for all events; for as the Eastern caravans are subject to be attacked by the Arabs, so are these by the Tartars—but they are not altogether so dangerous as the Arabs, nor so barbarous when they prevail.

The company consisted of people of several nations; but there were about sixty of them merchants or inhabitants of Moscow, though of them some were Livonians; and to our particular satisfaction, five of them were Scots, who appeared also to be men of great experience in business and of very good substance.

When we had traveled one day's journey, the guides, who were five in number, called all the gentlemen and merchants—that is to say, all the passengers except the servants—to a great council, as they called it. At this council, everyone deposited a certain quantity of money to a common stock for the necessary expense of buying forage on the way, where it was not otherwise to be had, and for satisfying the guides, getting horses, and the like; and here they constituted the journey, as they call it: They named captains and officers to draw us all up, gave the word of command in case of an attack, and gave everyone their turn of command; nor was this forming us into order any more than what we found needful on the way, as shall be observed.

A House of Chinaware

The road all on this side of the country was very populous and was full of potters and earth-makers—that is to say, people that temper the earth for the chinaware. As I was coming along, our Portugal pilot, who had always something or other to say to make us merry, came hurrying to me and told me he would show me the greatest rarity in all the country, and that I should have this to say of China, after all the ill-humored things that I had said of it, that I had seen one thing that was not to be seen in all the world beside. I was very importunate to know what it was; at last he told me it was a gentleman's house built with chinaware.

"Well," said I, "are not the materials of their buildings the product of their own country? And so it is all chinaware, is it not?"

"No, no," said he, "I mean it is a house *all* made of chinaware, such as you call it in England, or as it is called in our country, porcelain."

"Well," said I, "such a thing may be. How big is it? Can we carry it in a box upon a camel? If we can, we will buy it."

"Upon a camel!" said the old pilot, holding up both his hands. "Why, there is a family of thirty people lives in it."

I was then curious, indeed, to see it; but when I came to it, it was nothing but this: It was a timber house, or a house built, as we call it in England, with lath and plaster; but all this plastering was really chinaware—that is to say, it was plastered with the earth that makes chinaware. The outside, which the sun shone hot upon, was glazed and looked very well, perfectly white and painted with blue figures, as the large chinaware in England is painted, and hard as if it had been burned. As to the inside, all the walls, instead of wainscot, were lined with hardened and painted tiles, like the little square tiles we call galley tiles in England, all made of the finest china, and the figures exceedingly fine indeed, with extraordinary variety of colors, mixed with gold, many tiles making but one figure, but joined so artificially, the mortar being made of the same earth, that it was very hard to see where the tiles met. The floors of the rooms were of the same composition and as hard as the earthen floors we have in use in several parts of England; as hard as stone and smooth, but not burned and painted, except some smaller rooms, like closets, which were all, as it were, paved with the same tile; the ceiling and all the plastering work in the whole house were of the same earth; and, after all, the roof was covered with tiles of the same, but of a deep shining black. This was a chinaware house indeed, truly and literally to be called so, and had I not been upon the journey, I could have stayed some days to see and examine the particulars of it. They told me there were fountains and fish ponds in the garden, all paved on the bottom and sides with the same; and fine statues set up in rows on the walks, entirely formed of the porcelain earth and burned whole.

As this is one of the singularities of China, so they may be allowed to excel in it; but I am very sure they excel in their accounts of it; for they told me such incredible things of their performance in crockery ware, for such it is, that I care not to relate, as knowing it could not be true. They told me, in particular, of one workman that made a ship, with all its tackle, and masts, and sails in earthenware, big enough to carry fifty men. If they had told me he launched it and made a voyage to Japan in it, I might have said something to it indeed; but as it was, I knew the whole of the story, which was, in short, asking pardon for the word, that the fellow lied; so I smiled and said nothing to it.

This odd sight kept me two hours behind the caravan, for which the leader of it for the day fined me about the value of three shillings and told me if it had been three days' journey outside the wall, as it was three days within, he must have fined me four times as much and made me ask pardon the next council day. I promised to be more dutiful; and, indeed, I found afterward the orders made for keeping all together were absolutely necessary for our common safety.

In two days more we passed the great China wall, made for a fortification against the Tartars. A very great work it is, going over hills and mountains in a needless track, where the rocks are impassable and the precipices such as no enemy could possibly enter, or indeed climb up, or where, if they did, no wall could hinder them. They tell us its length is near a thousand English miles,[1] but that the country is five hundred in a straight measured line, which the wall bounds, without measuring the windings and turnings it takes; it is about four fathoms high, and as many thick in some places.

I stood still an hour or thereabouts without trespassing our orders (for so long the caravan was in passing the gate), to look at it on every side, near and far off (I mean what was within my view); and the guide of our caravan, who had been extolling it for the wonder of the world, was mighty eager to hear my opinion of it. I told him it was a most excellent thing to keep out the

---

1. Actually, it is more than 2,000 miles long.

Tartars, which he happened not to understand as I meant it and so took it for a compliment.

But the old pilot laughed. "Oh, Seignior Inglese," said he, "you speak in colors."

"In colors!" said I. "What do you mean by that?"

"Why, you speak what looks white this way, and black that way—colorful one way, and dull another. You tell him it is a good wall to keep out Tartars; you tell me it is good for nothing but to keep out Tartars. I understand you, Seignior Inglese, I understand you; but Seignior Chinese understood you his own way."

"Well," said I, "seignior, do you think it would stand off an army of our country people, with a good train of artillery? Or our engineers, with two companies of miners? Would not they batter it down in ten days, that an army might enter in battalia²? Or blow it up in the air, foundation and all, that there should be no sign of it left?"

"Aye, aye," said he. "I know that."

The Chinese wanted mightily to know what I said, and I gave him leave to tell him a few days after, for we were then almost out of their country, and he was to leave us a little time after this. But when he knew what I said, he was silent all the rest of the way, and we heard no more of his fine story of the Chinese power and greatness while he stayed.

After we passed this mighty nothing called a wall (something like the Picts' wall—so famous in Northumberland—built by the Romans), we began to find the country thinly inhabited and the people rather confined to live in fortified towns or cities, as being subject to the inroads and depredations of the Tartars, who rob in great armies and therefore are not to be resisted by the unprotected inhabitants of an open country. And here I began to find the necessity of keeping together in a caravan as we traveled, for we saw several troops of Tartars roving about. But when I came to see them distinctly, I wondered more that the Chinese empire could be conquered by such contemptible fellows; for they are a mere horde of wild fellows, keeping no order and understanding no discipline or manner of fight. Their horses are poor lean creatures, taught nothing and fit for nothing; and this we found the first day we saw them, which was after we entered the wilder part of the country. Our leader for the day gave leave for about sixteen of us to go a-hunting, as they call it; and what was this but hunting of sheep! However,

---

2. Battle formation.

it may be called hunting, too, for the creatures are the wildest and swiftest of foot that ever I saw of their kind. Only they will not run a great way, and you are sure of sport when you begin the chase, for they appear generally thirty or forty in a flock and, like true sheep, always keep together when they fly.

An Encounter with Tartars

In pursuit of this odd sort of game, it was our hap[3] to meet with about forty Tartars. Whether they were hunting mutton, as we were, or whether they looked for another kind of prey, we knew not; but as soon as they saw us, one of them blew a kind of horn very loud, but with a barbarous sound that I had never heard before and, by the way, never care to hear again. We all supposed this was to call their friends about them, and so it was; for, in less than ten minutes, a troop of forty or fifty more appeared at about a mile's distance; but our work was over first, as it happened.

One of the Scots merchants of Moscow happened to be among us, and as soon as he heard the horn, he told us that we had nothing to do but to charge them immediately, without loss of time; and drawing us up in a line, he asked if we were resolved. We told him we were ready to follow him, so he rode directly toward them. They stood gazing at us like a mere crowd, drawn up in no order, nor showing the face of any order at all; but as soon as they saw us advance, they let fly their arrows, which, however, missed us, very happily. It seems they mistook not their aim but their distance; for their arrows all fell a little short of us, but with so true an aim that had we been about twenty yards nearer, we must have had several men wounded, if not killed.

Immediately, we halted, and though it was at a great distance, we fired and sent them leaden bullets for wooden arrows, following our shot full gallop, to fall in among them sword in hand—for so our bold Scot that led us directed. He was, indeed, but a merchant, but he behaved with such vigor and bravery on this occasion, and yet with such cool courage, too, that I never saw any man in action fitter for command. As soon as we came up to them, we fired our pistols in their faces and then drew; but they fled in the greatest confusion imaginable. The only stand any of them made was on our right, where three of them stood and, by signs, called the rest to come back to them, having a kind of scimitar in their hands and their bows hanging to their backs. Our brave commander, without asking anybody to follow him, galloped up close to them and, with his fusil, knocked one of them off his horse and killed the second with his pistol; the third ran away, and thus

---

3. Luck.

As soon as they saw us, one of them blew a kind of horn

ended our fight. But we had this misfortune attending it: that all our mutton we had in chase got away. We had not a man killed or hurt; but as for the Tartars, there were about five of them killed. How many were wounded we knew not; but this we knew: that the other party were so frightened with the noise of our guns that they made off and never made any attempt upon us.

We were all this while in the Chinese dominions, and therefore the Tartars were not so bold as afterward. But in about five days we entered a vast, great, wild desert that held us three days' and nights' march. We were obliged to carry our water with us, in great leathern bottles, and to encamp all night, just as I have heard they do in the desert of Arabia.

I asked our guides whose dominion this was in, and they told me this was a kind of border that might be called no man's land, being a part of Great Karakathy, or Grand Tartary. However, it was all reckoned as belonging to China, but there was

Our commander killed the second with his pistol

no care taken here to preserve it from the inroads of thieves, and therefore it was reckoned the worst desert in the whole march, though we were to go over some much larger.

In passing this wilderness, which was at first very frightful to me, we saw, two or three times, little parties of the Tartars, but they seemed to be upon their own affairs and to have no design upon us. So, like the man who met the devil, if they had nothing to say to us, we had nothing to say to them: We let them go. Once, however, a party of them came so near as to stand and gaze at us. Whether it was to consider if they should attack us or not, we knew not; but when we had passed at some distance by them, we made a rear guard of forty men and stood ready for them, letting the caravan pass half a mile or thereabouts before us. But after a while they marched off; only we found they saluted us with five arrows at their parting, which wounded a horse so that it disabled him, and we left him the next day, poor creature, in great need of a good farrier. They might shoot more arrows, which might fall short of us; but we saw no more arrows or Tartars that time.

We traveled nearly a month after this, the ways not being so good as at first, though still in the dominions of the emperor of China. We lay for the most part in the villages, some of which were fortified, because of the incursions of the Tartars. When we were come to one of these towns (it was about two and a half days' journey before we came to the city of Naum), I wanted to buy a camel, of which there are plenty to be sold all the way upon that road, and horses also, such as they are, because, so many caravans coming that way, they are often wanted. The person that I spoke to, to get me a camel, would have gone and fetched one for me, but I, like a fool, must be officious and go myself along with him. The place was about two miles out of the village, where, it seems, they kept the camels and horses feeding under a guard.

A Second Encounter

I walked it on foot, with my old pilot and a Chinese, being very desirous of a little variety. When we came to the place, it was a low, marshy ground, walled around with a stone wall, piled up dry, without mortar or earth among it, like a park, with a little guard of Chinese soldiers at the door. Having bought a camel and agreed for the price, I came away, and the Chinese man that went with me led the camel when suddenly up came five Tartars on horseback. Two of them seized the fellow and took the camel from him, while the other three stepped up to me and my old pilot, seeing us, as it were, unarmed, for I had no weapon about me but my sword, which could but ill defend me against three horsemen. The first that came up stopped short upon my drawing my sword, for they are arrant cowards. But a second, coming upon my left, gave me a blow on the head, which I never felt till afterward and wondered, when I came to myself, what was the matter and where I was, for he laid me flat on the ground. But my never-failing old pilot, the Portuguese (so Providence, unlooked for, directs deliverances from

Two of them seized the fellow and took the camel

dangers that to us are unforeseen), had a pistol in his pocket, which I knew nothing of, nor the Tartars either. If they had, I suppose they would not have attacked us, but cowards are always boldest when there is no danger. The old man seeing me down, with a bold heart stepped up to the fellow who had struck me, and laying hold of his arm with one hand and pulling him down by main force a little toward him with the other, he shot him . . . and laid him dead upon the spot. He then immediately stepped up to him who had stopped us, as I said, and before he could come forward again, he made a blow at him with a scimitar, which he always wore. But missing the man, he struck his horse on the side of his head. . . . The poor beast, enraged with the wound, was no more to be governed by his rider, though the fellow sat well enough, too, but away he flew and carried him quite out of the pilot's reach. At some distance, rising upon his hind legs, the horse threw down the Tartar and fell upon him.

In this interval, the poor Chinese came in who had lost the camel, but he had no weapon. However, seeing the Tartar down and his horse fallen upon him, away he ran to him, and seizing upon an ugly, ill-favored weapon he had by his side (something like a poleax but not a poleax either), he wrenched it from him and made shift to knock his Tartarian brains out with it. But my old man had the third Tartar to deal with still. Seeing that he did not fly as he expected, nor come on to fight him as he apprehended, but merely stood stock still, the old man stood still, too, and fell to work with his tackle to charge his pistol again. But as soon as the Tartar saw the pistol, away he scoured and left my pilot, my champion I called him afterward, a complete victory.

By this time, I was a little recovered; for I thought, when I first began to wake, that I had been in a sweet sleep; but, as I said above, I wondered where I was, how I came upon the ground, and what was the matter. But a few moments after, as sense returned, I felt pain, though I did not know where; so I clapped my hand to my head and took it away bloody. Then I felt my head ache; and then in a moment memory returned, and everything was clear to me again. I jumped upon my feet instantly and got hold of my sword, but no enemies were in view. I found a Tartar lying dead, and his horse standing very quietly by him; and, looking farther, I saw my champion and deliverer, who had been to see what the Chinese had done, coming back with his saber in his hand. The old man, seeing me on my feet, came running to me and embraced me with a great deal of joy, being afraid before that I had been killed. Seeing me bloody, he would see how I was hurt; but it was not much—only what we call a broken head. Neither did I afterward find any great inconvenience from the blow, for it was well again in two or three days.

We made no great gain, however, by this victory, for we lost a camel and gained a horse. But that which was remarkable, when we came back to the village, the man demanded to be paid for the camel. I disputed it, and it was brought to a hearing before the Chinese judge of the place. To give him his due, he acted with a great deal of prudence and impartiality; and having heard both sides, he gravely asked the Chinese man that went with me to buy the camel, whose servant he was?

"I am no servant," said he, "but went with the stranger."

"At whose request?" said the justice.

"At the stranger's request," said he.

"Why, then," said the justice, "you were the stranger's servant for the time; and the camel being delivered to his servant, it was delivered to him, and he must pay for it."

I confess the thing was so clear that I had not a word to say; but admiring to see such just reasoning upon the consequence and an accurate stating of the case, I paid willingly for the camel and sent for another; but, you may observe, I did not go to fetch it myself anymore, for I had had enough of that.

The city of Naum is a frontier of the Chinese empire. They call it forti-fied, and so it is, as fortifications go there; for this I will venture to affirm: that all the Tartars in Karakathy, which, I believe, are some millions, could not batter down the walls with their bows and arrows. But to call it strong, if it were attacked with cannon, would be to make those who understand it laugh at you.

Another Alarm

We lacked, as I have said, above two days' journey of this city when messengers were sent expressly to every part of the road to tell all travelers and caravans to halt till they had a guard sent for them; for an unusual body of Tartars, making ten thousand in all, had appeared on the way about thirty miles beyond the city.

This was very bad news to travelers; however, it was carefully done of the governor, and we were very glad to hear we should have a guard. Accordingly, two days after, we had two hundred soldiers sent us from a garrison of the Chinese on our left, and three hundred more from the city of Naum, and with these we advanced boldly. The three hundred soldiers from Naum marched in our front, the two hundred in our rear, and our men on each side of our camels, with our baggage, and the whole caravan in the center. In this order, and well prepared for battle, we thought ourselves a match for the whole ten thousand Mogul Tartars, if they had appeared. But the next day, when they did appear, it was quite another thing.

It was early in the morning when, marching from a well-situated little town called Changu, we had a river to pass, which we were obliged to ferry. Had the Tartars had any intelligence,[4] then had been the time to have attacked us, when the caravan being over, the rear guard was behind; but they did not appear there. About three hours after, when we were entered upon a desert of about fifteen or sixteen miles over, behold, by a cloud of dust they raised, we saw an enemy was at hand. And they were at hand, indeed, for they came on upon the spur.[5]

The Chinese, our guard in the front, who had talked so big the day before, began to stagger; and the soldiers frequently looked behind them, which is a certain sign in a soldier that he is just ready to run away. My old pilot was of my mind, and being near me, he called out.

"Seignior Inglese," said he, "those fellows must be encouraged, or they will ruin us all; for if the Tartars come on, they will never stand it."

---

4. Espionage system.
5. At a fast pace.

"I am of your mind," said I. "But what must be done?"

"Done?" said he. "Let fifty of our men advance and flank them on each wing and encourage them, and they will fight like brave fellows in brave company. But without this, they will every man turn his back."

Immediately, I rode up to our leader and told him, who was exactly of our mind. Accordingly, fifty of us marched to the right wing, and fifty to the left, and the rest made a line of rescue. And so we marched, leaving the last two hundred men to make a body by themselves and to guard the camels; only that, if need were, they should send a hundred men to assist the last fifty.

In a word, the Tartars came on, and an innumerable company they were. How many we could not tell, but ten thousand, we thought, was the least. A party of them came on first and viewed our posture, traversing the ground in the front of our line. As we found them within gunshot, our leader ordered the two wings to advance swiftly and give them a salvo on each wing with their shot, which was done. They went off—I suppose back to give an account of the reception they were likely to meet with; and, indeed, that salute cloyed their stomachs, for they immediately halted, stood awhile to consider it, and wheeling off to the left, they gave over their design and said no more to us for that time; which was very agreeable to our circumstances, which were but very indifferent for a battle with such a number.

Two days after, we came to the city of Naum. We thanked the governor for his care of us and collected to the value of a hundred crowns, or thereabouts, which we gave to the soldiers sent to guard us; and here we rested one day. This is a garrison indeed, and there were nine hundred soldiers kept here. But the reason of it was that formerly the Muscovite frontiers lay nearer to them than they do now, the Muscovites having abandoned that part of the country, which lies from this city west for about two hundred miles, as desolate and unfit for use and more especially as being very remote and difficult to send troops thither for its defense; for we were yet about two thousand miles from Muscovy, properly so called.

After this, we passed several great rivers and two dreadful deserts, one of which we were sixteen days passing over, and which, as I said, was to be called no man's land. On the 13th of April, we came to the frontiers of the Muscovite dominions. I think the first town or fortress, whichever it may be called, that belonged to the czar of Muscovy was called Arguna, being on the west side of the river Arguna.

Chapter 15

THE IDOL

I could not but discover an infinite satisfaction that I was so soon arrived in, as I called it, a Christian country—or at least, in a country governed by Christians, for though the Muscovites do, in my opinion, but barely deserve the name of Christians, yet such they pretend to be and are very devout in their way. It would certainly occur to any man who travels the world as I have done, and who had any power of reflection, what a blessing it is to be brought into the world where the name of God and a Redeemer is known, adored, and worshiped; and not where the people, given up by Heaven to strong delusions, worship the devil and prostrate themselves to stocks and stones; worship monsters, elements, horrid-shaped animals, and statues or images of monsters. Not a town or city we passed through but had their pagodas, their idols, and their temples and ignorant people worshiping even the works of their own hands. Now we came where, at least, a face of the Christian worship appeared; where the knee was bowed to Jesus; and whether ignorantly or not, yet the Christian religion was owned and the name of the true God was called upon and adored. It made my soul rejoice to see it.

I saluted the brave Scots merchant I mentioned above with my first acknowledgment of this; and taking him by the hand, I said to him, "Blessed be God, we are once again among Christians."

He smiled and answered, "Do not rejoice too soon, countryman. These Muscovites are but an odd sort of Christians; and but for the name of it, you may see very little of the substance for some months further of our journey."

"Well," said I, "but still it is better than paganism and worshiping of devils."

"Why, I will tell you," said he, "except the Russian soldiers in the garrison, and a few of the inhabitants of the cities upon the road, all the rest of this country, for more than a thousand miles farther, is inhabited by the worst and most ignorant of pagans."

And so, indeed, we found it.

We were now launched into the greatest piece of solid earth, if I understand anything of the surface of the globe, that is to be found in any part of the world. We had, at least, twelve thousand miles to the sea, eastward; two thousand to the bottom of the Baltic Sea, westward; and above three thousand, if we left that sea and went on west, to the British and French channels. We had fully five thousand miles to the Indian or Persian Sea, south; and about eight hundred to the Frozen Sea, north. If some people may be believed, there might be no sea northeast till we come around the Pole and consequently into the northwest, and so have a continent of land into America,[1] the Lord knows where; though I could give some reasons why I believe that to be a mistake.

As we entered into the Muscovite dominions a good while before we came to any considerable towns, we had nothing to observe there but this: first, that all the rivers ran to the east. As I understood by the charts that some in our caravan had with them, it was plain that all those rivers ran into the great river Yamour, or Gamour; which river, by the natural course of it, must run into the East Sea, or Chinese Ocean. The story they tell us, that the mouth of this river is choked up with bulrushes of a monstrous growth—namely, three feet about, and twenty or thirty feet high—I must be allowed to say, I believe nothing of it. But as its navigation is of no use, because there is no trade that way—the Tartars, to whom it alone belongs, dealing in nothing but cattle—nobody that ever I heard of has been curious enough either to go down to the mouth of it in boats, or come up from the mouth of it in ships, as far as I can find. But this is certain, that this river running east, in the latitude of about 50 degrees, carries a vast concourse of rivers along with it and finds an ocean to empty itself in at that latitude; so we are sure of sea there.

Some leagues to the north of this river, there are several considerable rivers, whose streams run as due north as the Yamour runs east. These are all found to join their waters with the great river Tartarus, named so from the northernmost nations of the Mogul Tartars; who, as the Chinese say, were the first Tartars in the world; and who, as our geographers allege, are the Gog and Magog mentioned in sacred history. These rivers running all northward, as well as all the other rivers I am yet to speak of, make it evident that the

---

1. The far north was still not explored much at this time.

Northern Ocean bounds the lands also on that side; so that it does not seem rational in the least to think that the land can extend itself to join with America on that side, or that there is not a communication between the Northern and Eastern Oceans. But of this I shall say no more. It was my observation at that time, and therefore I take notice of it in this place.

We now advanced from the river Arguna by easy and moderate journeys and were very visibly obliged to the care the czar of Muscovy had taken to have cities and towns built in as many places as it was possible to place them, where his soldiers kept garrisons—something like the stationary soldiers placed by the Romans in the remotest countries of their empire; some of which I had read of were placed in Britain, for the security of commerce and for the lodging of travelers. And thus it was here; for wherever we came, though at these towns and stations the garrisons and governors were Russians and professed Christians, yet the inhabitants were mere pagans—sacrificing to idols and worshiping the sun, moon, and stars, or all the host of heaven; and not only so, but were, of all the heathens and pagans that ever I met with, the most barbarous, except only that they did not eat men's flesh, as our savages of America did.

An Idol

Some instances of this we met with in the country between Arguna, where we entered the Muscovite dominions, and a city of Tartars and Russians together, called Nortziousky, in which was a continued desert or forest, which cost us twenty days to travel over. In a village near the last of these places, I had the curiosity to go and see their way of living, which was most brutish and insufferable. They had, I suppose, a great sacrifice that day; for there stood out, upon an old stump of a tree, an idol made of wood, frightful as the devil—at least, as anything we can think of to represent the devil can be made. It had a head not resembling any creature that the world ever saw: ears as big as goats' horns, and as high; eyes as big as a crown piece; a nose like a crooked ram's horn, and a mouth extended four-cornered, like that of a lion, with horrible teeth hooked like a parrot's underbill. It was dressed up in the filthiest manner that you could suppose: Its upper garment was of sheepskins, with the wool outward; a great Tartar bonnet was on the head, with two horns growing through it; it was about eight feet high, yet had no feet or legs, nor any other proportion of parts.

This scarecrow was set up at the outer side of the village; and when I came near to it, there were sixteen or seventeen creatures—whether men or women

I could not tell, for they made no distinction by their habits—all lying flat upon the ground around this formidable block of shapeless wood. I saw no motion among them, any more than if they had all been logs of wood, like the idol, and at first I really thought they had been so. But when I came a little nearer, they started up upon their feet and raised a howling cry, as if they had been so many deep-mouthed hounds, and walked away, as if they were displeased at our disturbing them. A little way off from the idol, and at the door of a tent or hut made all of sheepskins and cow skins dried, stood three butchers—I thought they were such when I came nearer to them, for I found they had long knives in their hands; and in the middle of the tent appeared three sheep killed, and one young bullock, or steer. These, it seems, were sacrifices to that senseless log of an idol; the three men were priests belonging to it, and the seventeen prostrated wretches were the people who brought the offering and were making their prayers to that stock.

I confess I was more moved at their stupidity and brutish worship of a hobgoblin than ever I was at anything in my life—to see God's most glorious and best creature, to whom He had granted so many advantages, even by creation, above the rest of the works of His hands, vested with a reasonable soul, and that soul adorned with faculties and capacities adapted both to honor his Maker and to be honored by Him, sunk and degenerated to a degree so very stupid as to prostrate itself to a frightful nothing, a mere imaginary object dressed up by themselves and made terrible to themselves by their own contrivance, adorned only with clouts and rags—and that this should be the effect of mere ignorance, wrought up into hellish devotion by the devil himself, who, envying his Maker the homage and adoration of His creatures, had deluded them into such sordid and brutish things as one would think would shock nature itself!

But what signified all the astonishment and reflection of thoughts? And thus it was, and I saw it before my eyes, and there was no room to wonder at it or think it impossible. All my admiration turned to rage, and I rode up to the image or monster—call it what you will—and with my sword made a stroke at the bonnet that was on its head and cut it in two. One of our men who was with me took hold of the sheepskin that covered it and pulled at it, when, behold, a most hideous outcry and howling ran through the village, and two or three hundred people came about my ears, so that I was glad to scour for it, for we saw some had some bows and arrows. But I resolved from that moment to visit them again.

A Plot Against the Idol

Our caravan rested three nights at the town, which was about four miles off, in order to provide some horses that they wanted, several of the horses having been lamed and jaded with the badness of the way and long march over the last desert; so we had some leisure here to put my design in execution. I had communicated it to the Scots merchant of Moscow, of whose courage I had sufficient testimony. I told him what I had seen and with what indignation I had since thought that human nature could be so degenerate. I told him that if I could get but four or five men well armed to go with me, I was resolved to go and destroy that vile, abominable idol and let them see that it had no power to help itself and consequently could not be an object of worship, or be prayed to, much less help them that offered sacrifices to it.

He laughed at me and said, "Your zeal may be good, but what do you propose to gain by it?"

"Propose?" said I. "To vindicate the honor of God, which is insulted by this devil worship."

"But how will it vindicate the honor of God," said he, "when the people will not be able to know what you mean by it, unless you could speak to them and tell them so? And then they will fight you and beat you, too, I assure you; for they are desperate fellows, especially in defense of their idolatry."

"Can we not," said I, "do it in the night and then leave them the reasons and the causes in writing in their own language?"

"Writing?" said he. "Why, there is not a man in five nations of them that knows anything of a letter or how to read a word anyway."

"Wretched ignorance!" said I to him. "However, I have a great mind to do it. Perhaps nature may draw inferences from it to them, to let them see how brutish they are to worship such horrid things."

"Look you, sir," said he, "if your zeal prompts you to it so warmly, you must do it. But in the next place, I would have you consider these wild nations of people are subjected by force to the czar of Muscovy's dominion; and if you do this, it is ten to one but they will come by thousands to the governor of Nertzinskay[2] and demand satisfaction. And if he cannot give them satisfaction, it is ten to one but they revolt, and it will occasion a new war with all the Tartars in the country."

This, I confess, put new thoughts into my head for a while. But I harped

---

2. Evidently, this is the same city as Nortziousky.

upon the same string still; and all that day I was uneasy to put my project
into execution. Toward the evening, the Scots merchant met me by accident
in our walk about the town and desired to speak with me.

"I believe," said he, "I have put you off your good design. I have been a
·little concerned about it since, for I abhor idolatry as much as you do."

"Truly," said I, "you have put off a little the execution of it; but you have
not put it out of my thoughts. I believe I shall do it before I quit this place,
though I were to be delivered up to them for satisfaction."

"No, no," said he. "God forbid they should deliver you up to such a crew
of monsters! They shall not do that either; that would be murdering you,
indeed."

"Why," said I, "how would they use me?"

"Use you?" said he. "I'll tell you how they served a poor Russian who
affronted them in their worship just as you did, and whom they took prisoner after they had lamed him with an arrow so that he could not run away.
They took him, and stripped him . . . , and set him upon the top of the idol-
monster, and stood all around him, and shot . . . arrows into him. . . . And
then they burned him . . . as a sacrifice to the idol."

"And was this the same idol?" said I.

"Yes," said he, "the very same."

"Well," said I, "I will tell you a story."

So I related the story of our men at Madagascar, and how they burned and
sacked the village there and killed man, woman, and child for their murdering one of our men, just as it is related before; and I added that I thought we
ought to do so to this village.

He listened very attentively to the story; but when I talked of doing so to
that village, said he, "You mistake very much. It was not this village—it was
almost a hundred miles from this place; but it was the same idol, for they
carry him about in procession all over the country."

"Well," said I, "then that idol ought to be punished for it; and it shall,"
said I, "if I live this night out."

In a word, finding me resolute, he liked the design and told me I should
not go alone, but he would go with me. But he would go first and bring a
stout fellow, one of his countrymen, to go also with us—"and one," said he,
"as famous for his zeal as you can desire anyone to be against such devilish
things as these." In a word, he brought me his comrade, a Scotsman whom
he called Captain Richardson. I gave him a full account of what I had seen
and also what I intended; and he told me readily he would go with me if it

cost him his life. So we agreed to go—only we three. I had, indeed, proposed it to my partner, but he declined it. He said he was ready to assist me to the utmost, and upon all occasions, for my defense; but this was an adventure quite out of his way. So, I say, we resolved upon our work, only we three and my manservant, and to put it in execution that night about midnight, with all the secrecy imaginable.

However, upon second thoughts, we were willing to delay it till the next night, because the caravan being to set forward in the morning, we supposed the governor could not pretend to give them any satisfaction upon us when we were out of his power. The Scots merchant, as steady in his resolution for the enterprise as bold in executing, brought me a Tartar's robe or gown of sheepskins, and a bonnet, with a bow and arrows, and provided the same for himself and his countryman, so that the people, if they saw us, should not determine who we were.

The first night we spent in mixing up some combustible matter, with aqua vitae, gunpowder, and such other materials as we could get; and having a good quantity of tar in a little pot, about an hour after night we set out upon our expedition.

We came to the place about eleven o'clock at night and found that the people had not the least thought of danger attending their idol. The night was cloudy; yet the moon gave us light enough to see that the idol stood just in the same posture and place that it did before. The people seemed to be all at their rest. Only in the great hut or tent, as we called it, where we saw the three priests, whom we mistook for butchers, we saw a light, and going up close to the door, we heard people talking as if there were five or six of them. We concluded, therefore, that if we set wildfire to the idol, these men would come out immediately and run up to the place to rescue it from the destruction that we intended for it; and what we intended to do with them we knew not. Once we thought of carrying it away and setting fire to it at a distance; but when we came to handle it, we found it too bulky for our carriage; so we were at a loss again. The second Scotsman was for setting fire to the tent or hut and knocking the creatures that were there on the head when they came out. But I could not join with that. I was against killing them, if it were possible to avoid it.

"Well, then," said the Scots merchant, "I will tell you what we will do: We will try to make them prisoners, tie their hands, and make them stand and see their idol destroyed."

As it happened, we had twine or packthread enough about us, which we used to tie our firelocks together with; so we resolved to attack these people first and with as little noise as we could. The first thing we did is, we knocked at the door. When one of the priests came to it, we immediately seized upon him, stopped his mouth, tied his hands behind him, and led him to the idol, where we gagged him that he might not make a noise, tied his feet also together, and left him on the ground.

Two of us then waited at the door, expecting that another would come out to see what the matter was; but we waited so long till the third man came back to us; and then nobody coming out, we knocked again gently, and immediately came two more, and we served them just in the same manner, but were obliged to go all with them and lay them down by the idol some distance from one another. When going back, we found two more were come out to the door, and a third stood behind them within the door. We seized the two and immediately tied them, when the third, stepping back and crying out, my Scots merchant went in after them, and taking out a composition we had made that would only smoke and stink, he set fire to it and threw it in among them. By that time the other Scotsman and my man, taking charge of the two men already bound and tied together also by the arm, led them away to the idol and left them there, to see if their idol would relieve them, making haste back to us.

When the furze we had thrown in had filled the hut with so much smoke that they were almost suffocated, we then threw in a small leather bag of another kind, which flamed like a candle, and following it in, we found there were but four people who, as we supposed, had been about some of their diabolical sacrifices. They appeared, in short, frightened to death—at least so as to sit trembling and stupid and not able to speak either for the smoke.

In a word, we took them and bound them as we had done the others, all without any noise. I should have said we brought them out of the house or hut first; for indeed we were not able to bear the smoke any more than they were. When we had done this, we carried them all together to the idol. When we came there, we fell to work with him. First we daubed him all over, and his robes also, with tar and such other stuff as we had, which was tallow mixed with brimstone; then we stopped his eyes, ears, and mouth full of gunpowder; then we wrapped up a great piece of wildfire in his bonnet; and then sticking all the combustibles we had brought with us upon him, we looked about us to see if we could find anything else to help to burn him. Then my Scotsman remembered that by the tent or hut, where the men were, there lay a heap of dry forage, whether straw or rushes I do not remember. Away he and the other Scotsman ran and fetched their arms full of that. When we had done this, we took all our prisoners and brought them, having untied their feet and ungagged their mouths, and made them stand up, and set them before their monstrous idol, and then set fire to the whole.

The Idol Is Blown Up

We stayed by it a quarter of an hour, or thereabouts, till the powder in the eyes, mouth, and ears of the idol blew up and, as we could perceive, had split and deformed the shape of it—in a word, till we saw it burned into a mere block or log of wood. Setting dry forage to it, we found it would be soon quite consumed, so we began to think of going away.

But the Scotsman said, "No, we must not go, for these poor, deluded wretches will all throw themselves into the fire and burn themselves with the idol."

So we resolved to stay till the forage was burned down, too, and then came away and left them.

After the feat was performed, we appeared in the morning among our fellow travelers, exceedingly busy in getting ready for our journey; nor could any man suggest that we had been anywhere but in our beds, as travelers might be supposed to be, to fit themselves for the fatigues of the day's journey.

But the affair did not end so. The next day came a great number of the country people to the town gates, and in a most outrageous manner they demanded satisfaction of the Russian governor for the insulting of their priests and burning of their great Cham Chi-Thaungu. The people of Nertzinskay were at first in a great consternation, for they said the Tartars were already no less than thirty thousand strong. The Russian governor sent out messengers to appease them and gave them all the good words possible, assuring them that he knew nothing of it and that there had not a soul in his garrison been abroad, so that it could not be from anybody there; but if they could let him know who did it, they should be exemplarily punished. They returned haughtily that all the country reverenced the great Cham Chi-Thaungu, who dwelt in the sun, and no mortal would have dared to offer violence to his image but some Christian miscreant; and they therefore resolved to declare war against him and all the Russians, who, they said, were miscreants and Christians.

The governor, still patient and unwilling to make a breach, or to have any cause of war alleged to be given by him—the czar having strictly charged him to treat the conquered country with gentleness and civility—gave them still all the good words he could. At last he told them there was a caravan gone toward Russia that morning, and perhaps it was some of them who had done them this injury; and that if they would be satisfied with that, he would send after them to inquire into it. This seemed to appease them a little. Accordingly, the governor sent after us and gave us a particular account how the thing was, intimating withal that if any in our caravan had done it, they should make their escape; but that whether we had done it or not, we should make all the haste forward that was possible and that, in the meantime, he would keep them in play as long as he could.

This was very friendly in the governor. However, when it came to the caravan, there was nobody knew anything of the matter; and as for us that were guilty, we were least of all suspected. However, the captain of the caravan for the time took the hint that the governor gave us, and we traveled two days and two nights without any considerable stop, and then we lay at a village called Plothus; nor did we make any long stop here, but hastened on toward Jarawena, another of the czar of Muscovy's colonies, where we expected we should be safe. But upon the second day's march from Plothus, by the clouds of dust behind us at a great distance, some of our people began to be sensible we were being pursued. We had entered a great desert and had passed by a great lake called Schaks Oser, when we perceived a very great body of horse appear on the other side of the lake, to the north; we traveling west. We observed they went away west, as we did, but had supposed we would have taken that side of the lake, whereas we very happily took the south side. In two days more they disappeared again, for they, believing we were still before them, pushed on till they came to the river Uda, a very great river when it passes farther north, but when we came to it, we found it narrow and fordable.

The third day they had either found their mistake or had intelligence of us and came pouring in upon us toward the dusk of the evening. We had, to our great satisfaction, just pitched upon a place for our camp, which was very convenient for the night; for as we were upon a desert (though but at the beginning of it) that was above five hundred miles over, we had no towns to lodge at and, indeed, expected none but the city Jarawena, which we had yet two days' march to. The desert, however, had some few woods in it on this side, and little rivers, which ran all into the great river Udda. It was in a narrow strait, between little but very thick woods, that we pitched our little camp for that night, expecting to be attacked before morning.

Nobody knew but ourselves what we were pursued for; but as it was usual for the Mogul Tartars to go about in troops in that desert, so the caravans always fortify themselves every night against them, as against armies of robbers. It was, therefore, no new thing to be pursued.

But we had this night, of all the nights of our travels, a most advantageous camp; for we lay between two woods, with a little rivulet running just before our front, so that we could not be surrounded or attacked any way but in our front or rear. We took care also to make our front as strong as we could by placing our packs, with our camels and horses all in a line, on the inside of the river and felling some trees in our rear.

In this posture we encamped for the night; but the enemy was upon us before we had finished. They did not come on us like thieves, as we expected, but sent three messengers to us to demand the men to be delivered to them that had abused their priests and burned their god Cham Chi-Thaungu with fire, so that they might burn them with fire. Upon this, they said, they would go away and do us no further harm; otherwise they would destroy us all. Our men looked very blank at this message and began to stare at one another to see who looked with the most guilt on their faces; but "nobody" was the word—nobody did it. The leader of the caravan sent word he was well assured that it was not done by any of our camp; that we were peaceful merchants traveling on our business; that we had done no harm to them or to anyone else; and that, therefore, they must look further for their enemies who had injured them, for we were not the people. So he desired them not to disturb us, for if they did we should defend ourselves.

They sent three messengers to us

They were far from being satisfied with this for an answer, and a great crowd of them came running down in the morning, by break of day, to our camp. But seeing us in such an unaccountable situation, they dared come no farther than the brook in our front, where they stood and showed us such a number that indeed terrified us very much; for those that estimated lowest spoke of ten thousand. Here they stood and looked at us awhile, and then setting up a great howl, they let fly a great number of arrows among us; but we were well enough fortified for that, for we sheltered under our baggage, and I do not remember that one of us was hurt.

Sometime after this we saw them move a little to our right and expected them on the rear, when a cunning fellow, a Cossack of Jarawena, in the pay of the Muscovites, calling to the leader of the caravan, said to him, "I'll go send all these people away to Sibeilka." This was a city four or five days' journey at least to the right and rather behind us. So he took his bow and arrows, and getting on horseback, he rode away from our rear directly, as it were, back to Nertzinskay. After this he took a great circuit about and came directly on the army of the Tartars, as if he had been sent expressly to tell them a long story that the people who had burned the Cham Chi-Thaungu were gone to Sibeilka, with a caravan of miscreants, as he called them—that is to say, Christians—and that they had resolved to burn the god Schal-Isar, belonging to the Tongueses.

As this fellow was himself a Tartar and perfectly spoke their language, he counterfeited so well that they all believed him, and away they drove in a most violent hurry to Sibeilka, which, it seems, was five days' journey to the north; and in less than three hours they were entirely out of our sight, and we never heard any more of them, nor whether they went to Sibeilka or no. So we passed away safely on to Jarawena, where there was a garrison of Muscovites, and there we rested five days, the caravan being exceedingly fatigued with the last day's hard march and with want of rest in the night.

March Through a Desert

From this city we had a frightful desert, which held us twenty-three days' march. We furnished ourselves with some tents here, for the better accommodating ourselves in the night; and the leader of the caravan procured sixteen carriages, or wagons of the country, for carrying our water or provisions. These carriages were our defense every night around our little camp, so that had the Tartars appeared, unless they had been numerous indeed, they would not have been able to hurt us.

We may well be supposed to have wanted rest again after this long journey; for in this desert we neither saw house nor tree, and scarcely a bush; though we saw abundance of the sable hunters, who are all Tartars of the Mogul Tartary, of which this country is a part. They frequently attack small caravans, but we saw no numbers of them together.

After we had passed this desert, we came into a country pretty inhabited—that is to say, we found towns and castles, settled by the czar of Muscovy, with garrisons of stationary soldiers to protect the caravans and defend the country against the Tartars, who would otherwise make it very dangerous traveling. His czarist majesty had given such strict orders for the well guarding of the caravans and merchants that, if there were any Tartars heard of in the country, detachments of the garrison were always sent to see the travelers safely from station to station. And thus the governor of Adinskoy, whom I had an opportunity to make a visit to by means of the Scots merchant, who was acquainted with him, offered us a guard of fifty men, if we thought there was any danger, to the next station.

I thought, long before this, that as we came nearer to Europe we should find the country better inhabited and the people more civilized. But I found myself mistaken in both, for we had yet the nation of the Tongueses to pass through, where we saw the same tokens of paganism and barbarity as before; only, as they were conquered by the Muscovites, they were not so dangerous. But for rudeness of manners and idolatry, no people in the world ever went beyond them. They were clothed all in skins of beasts, and their houses were built of the same. You knew not a man from a woman, neither by the ruggedness of their countenances nor their clothes; and in the winter, when the ground was covered with snow, they lived underground in vaults, which had cavities going from one to another.

If the Tartars had their Cham Chi-Thaungu for a whole village or country, these had idols in every hut and every cave. Besides, they worshiped the stars, the sun, the water, the snow, and, in a word, everything they did not understand, and they understood but very little; so that every element, every uncommon thing, set them sacrificing. I met with nothing peculiar myself in all this country, which I reckon was, from the desert I spoke of last, at least four hundred miles, half of it being another desert, which took us up to twelve days' severe traveling, without house or tree; and we were obliged again to carry our own provisions, as well water as bread. After we were out of this desert and had traveled two days, we came to Janezay, a Muscovite city, or station, on the great river Janezay, which, they told us there, parted Europe from Asia.

Here I observed ignorance and paganism still prevailed, except in the Muscovite garrisons. All the country between the river Oby and the river Janezay was as entirely pagan, and the people as barbarous, as the remotest of the Tartars—nay, as any nation, for aught I know, in Asia or America. I also found, which I observed to the Muscovite governors whom I had an opportunity to converse with, that the poor pagans were not much wiser, or nearer Christianity, for being under the Muscovite government, which they acknowledged was true enough. But that, as they said, was none of their business. If the Czar expected to convert his Siberian, Tonguese, or Tartar subjects, it should be done by sending clergymen among them, not soldiers; and, they added (with more sincerity than I expected), they found it was not so much the concern of their monarch to make the people Christians as it was to make them subjects.

From this river to the great river Oby, we crossed a wild, uncultivated country, barren of people and good management. Otherwise, it was in itself a most pleasant, fruitful, and agreeable country. What inhabitants we found in it were all pagans, except such as were sent among them from Russia; for this was the country—I mean on both sides of the river Oby—whither the Muscovite criminals that were not put to death were banished, and from whence it was next to impossible they should ever get away.

Chapter 16

NEARING HOME

I have nothing material to say of my particular affairs till I came to Tobolski, the capital city of Siberia, where I continued some time on the following account.

We had now been almost seven months on our journey, and winter began to come on apace; whereupon my partner and I called a council about our particular affairs, in which we found it proper, as we were bound for England and not for Moscow, to consider how to dispose of ourselves. They told us of sledges and reindeer to carry us over the snow in the wintertime; and, indeed, they have such things that it would be incredible to relate the particulars of, by which means the Russians travel more in winter than they can in summer, as in these sledges they are able to run night and day. The snow, being frozen, is one universal covering to nature, by which the hills, vales, rivers, and lakes are all smooth and hard as a stone, and they run upon the surface, without any regard to what is underneath.

But I had no occasion to urge a winter journey of this kind: I was bound to England, not to Moscow, and my route lay one of two ways: Either I must go on as the caravan went, till I came to Jaroslaw, and then go off west for Narva and the Gulf of Finland and so on the Dantzic, where I might possibly sell my Chinese cargo to good advantage; or I must leave the caravan at a little town on the Dwina, from whence I had but six days by water to Archangel, and from thence might be sure of shipping either to England, Holland, or Hamburg.

Now, to go on any of these journeys in the winter would have been preposterous; for as to Dantzic, the Baltic would have been frozen up, and I could not get passage; and to go by land in those countries was far less safe than among the Mogul Tartars. Likewise, to go to Archangel in October, all the ships would be gone from thence, and even the merchants who dwell there in summer retire south to Moscow in the winter, when the ships are gone. So I could have nothing but extremity of cold to encounter, with a scarcity of provisions, and must lie in an empty town all the winter. Upon the whole, I thought it much my better way to let the caravan go and make provision to winter where I was, at Tobolski, in Siberia, in the latitude of about 60 degrees, where I was sure of three things to wear out a cold winter with—namely, plenty of provisions, such as the country afforded, a warm house, with fuel enough, and excellent company.

I was now in quite a different climate from my beloved island, where I never felt cold, except when I had my ague. On the contrary, I had much to do to bear any clothes on my back and never made any fire but without doors, which was necessary for dressing my food, etc. Now I had three good vests, with large robes or gowns over them, to hang down to the feet and button close to the wrists; and all these lined with furs, to make them sufficiently warm.

As to a warm house, I must confess I greatly disliked our way in England of making fires in every room in the house in open chimneys, which, when the fire was out, always kept the air in the room cold as the climate. But taking an apartment in a good house in the town, I ordered a chimney to be built like a furnace, in the center of six several rooms, like a stove; the funnel to carry the smoke went up one way, the door to come at the fire went in another, and all the rooms were kept equally warm, but no fire seen, just as they heat the bagnios[1] in England. By this means we had always the same climate in all the rooms, and an equal heat was preserved; and how cold soever it was without, it was always warm within; and yet we saw no fire nor were ever incommoded with smoke.

The most wonderful thing of all was that it should be possible to meet with good company here, in a country so barbarous as that of the most northerly parts of Europe, near the Frozen Ocean, within but a very few degrees of Nova Zembla.[2] But this being the country where the state criminals of Muscovy, as I observed before, were all banished, this city was full of noblemen, gentlemen, soldiers, and courtiers of Muscovy. Here was the famous Prince Galitzin, the old General Robostiski, and several other persons of note, and some ladies. By means of my Scots merchant, whom, nevertheless, I parted with here, I made an acquaintance with several of these gentlemen; and from these, in the long winter nights in which I stayed here, I received several very agreeable visits.

---

1. Bathing house or Turkish bath.
2. A group of islands in the Arctic Ocean, north of Archangel.

I was talking one night with Prince ——, one of the banished ministers of state belonging to the czar of Muscovy, that the discourse of my particular case began. He had been telling me abundance of fine things of the greatness, the magnificence, the dominions, and the absolute power of the emperor of the Russians. I interrupted him and told him I was a greater and more powerful prince than even the czar of Muscovy was, though my dominions were not so large or my people so many. The Russian grandee looked a little surprised and, fixing his eyes steadily upon me, began to wonder what I meant. I told him his wonder would cease when I had explained myself. First, I told him I had absolute disposal of the lives and fortunes of all my subjects; that notwithstanding my absolute power, I had not one person disaffected to my government, or to my person, in all my dominions. He shook his head at that and said that there, indeed, I outdid the czar of Muscovy. I told him that all the lands in my kingdom were my own, and all my subjects were not only my tenants, but tenants at will; that they would all fight for me to the last drop; and that never tyrant, for such I acknowledged myself to be, was ever so universally beloved, and yet so horribly feared, by his subjects.

After amusing him with these riddles in government for a while, I opened the case and told him the story at large of my living on the island, and how I managed both myself and the people that were under me, just as I have since written it down. They were exceedingly taken with the story, and especially the prince, who told me, with a sigh, that the true greatness of life was to be masters of ourselves; that he would not have exchanged such a state of life as mine to be czar of Muscovy; and that he found more felicity in the retirement he seemed to be banished to here than ever he found in the highest authority he enjoyed in the court of his master the czar; that the height of human wisdom was to bring our dispositions down to our circumstances and to make a calm within, under the weight of the greatest storms without. When he came first hither, he said, he used to tear the hair from his head and the clothes from his back, as others had done before him. But a little time and consideration had made him look into himself, as well as around him, to things without; he found that the mind of man, if it was but once brought to reflect upon the state of universal life and how little this world was concerned in its true felicity, was perfectly capable of making a felicity for itself, fully satisfying to itself and suitable to its own best ends and desires, with but very little assistance from the world. Air to breathe in, food to sustain life, clothes for warmth, and liberty for exercise, in order to health, completed, in his opinion, all that the world could do for us. And though the greatness, the authority, the riches, and the pleasures that some enjoyed in the world had much in them that was agreeable to us, yet all those things chiefly gratified the coarsest of our affections, such as our ambition, our particular pride, avarice, vanity, and sensuality—all which, being the mere products of the worst part of man, were in themselves crimes and had in them the seeds of all manner of crimes; but neither were related to, nor concerned with, any of those virtues that constituted us wise men, nor of those graces that distinguished us as Christians. That being now deprived of all the fancied felicity which he enjoyed in the full exercise of all those vices, he said he was at leisure to look upon the dark side of them, where he found all manner of deformity, and was not convinced that virtue only makes a man truly wise, rich, and great, and preserves him in the way to a superior happiness in a future state. In this, he said, they were more happy in their banishment than all their enemies were, who had the full possession of all the wealth and power they had left behind them.

"Nor, sir," said he, "do I bring my mind to this politically, from the necessity of my circumstances, which some call miserable. But if I know anything of myself, I would not now go back, though the czar my master should call me and reinstate me in all my former grandeur. I say I would no more go back to it than I believe my soul, when it shall be delivered from this prison of the body and has had a taste of the glorious state beyond life, would come back to the jail of flesh and blood it is now enclosed in and leave heaven, to trail in the dirt and crime of human affairs."

He spoke this with so much warmth in his temper, so much earnestness and motion of his spirits, that it was evident it was the true sense of his soul: there was no room to doubt his sincerity. I told him I once thought myself a kind of monarch in my old station, of which I had given him an account; but that I thought he was not only a monarch but a great conqueror, for he had got a victory over his own exorbitant desires and the absolute dominion over himself—for he whose reason entirely governs his will is certainly greater than he that conquers a city.

"But, my lord," said I, "shall I take the liberty to ask you a question?"

"With all my heart," said he.

"If the door of your liberty was opened," said I, "would you not take hold of it to deliver yourself from this exile?"

"Hold," said he. "Your question is subtle and requires some serious, just distinctions to give it a sincere answer; and I will give it to you from the bottom of my heart. Nothing that I know of in the world would move me to deliver myself from this state of banishment, except these two: first, the enjoyment of my relations; and, secondly, a little warmer climate. But I protest to you that to go back to the pomp of the court, the glory, the power, the hurry of a minister of state; the wealth, the gaiety, and the pleasures of a courtier; if my master should send me word this moment that he restores me to all he banished me from, I protest, if I know myself at all, I would not leave this wilderness, these deserts, and these frozen lakes for the palace at Moscow."

"But, my lord," said I, "perhaps you not only are banished from the pleasures of the court and from the power, authority, and wealth you enjoyed before, but you may be absent, too, from some of the conveniences of life: your estate, perhaps, confiscated, and your effects plundered; and the supplies left you here may not be suitable to the ordinary demands of life."

"Aye," said he, "that is as you suppose me to be a lord, or a prince, etc.; so, indeed, I am. But you are now to consider me only as a man, a human creature, not at all distinguished from another; and so I can suffer no want, unless I should be visited with sickness and distempers. However, to put the question out of dispute, you see our way of life: We are, in this place, five persons of rank; we live perfectly retired, as suited to a state of banishment; we have something rescued from the shipwreck of our fortunes, which keeps us from the mere necessity of hunting for our food. But the poor soldiers, who are here without that help, live in as much plenty as we, who go in the woods and catch sables and foxes. The labor of a month will maintain them a year. And as the way of living is not expensive, so it is not hard to get sufficient for ourselves. So that objection is out."

I have not room to give a full account of the most agreeable conversation I had with this truly great man; in all which he showed that his mind was so inspired with a superior knowledge of things, so supported by religion, as well as by a vast share of wisdom, that his contempt of the world was really as much as he had expressed and that he was always the same to the last, as will appear in the story I am going to tell.

I had been here eight months, and a dark, dreadful winter I thought it. The cold was so intense that I could not so much as look abroad without being wrapped in furs and a mask of fur before my face—or rather a hood, with only a hole for breath and two for sight. The little daylight we had was, as we reckoned, for three months not above five hours a day, and six at most; only that the snow lying on the ground continually, and the weather being clear, it was never quite dark. Our horses were kept, or rather starved, underground; and as for our servants, whom we hired here to look after ourselves and our horses, we had, every now and then, their fingers and toes to thaw and take care of, lest they should mortify and fall off.

It is true, within doors we were warm, the houses being close, the walls thick, the lights small, and the glass all double. Our food was chiefly the flesh of deer, dried and cured in the season; bread good enough, but baked as biscuits; dried fish of several sorts, and some flesh of mutton and of buffaloes, which is pretty good meat. All the stores of provisions for the winter are laid up in the summer, and well cured. Our drink was water, mixed with aqua vitae instead of brandy; and for a treat, mead instead of wine, which, however, they have very good. The hunters, who venture abroad in all weathers, frequently brought us in fine venison and sometimes bear's flesh, but we did not much care for the latter. We had a good stock of tea, with which we treated our friends, and we lived very cheerfully and well, all things considered.

The hunters brought us in fine venison

It was now March, the days grown considerably longer, and the weather at least tolerable; so the other travelers began to prepare sledges to carry them over the snow and to get things ready to be going. But my measures being fixed, as I have said, for Archangel, and not for Muscovy or the Baltic, I made no motion, knowing very well that the ships from the south do not set out for that part of the world till May or June; and that if I was there by the beginning of August, it would be as soon as any ships would be ready to go away. Therefore I made no haste to be gone, as others did. In a word, I saw a great many people, nay, all the travelers, go away before me. It seems every year they go from thence to Muscovy for trade, to carry furs, and to buy necessaries, which they bring back with them to furnish their shops. Also, others went on the same errand to Archangel; but then they, all having to come back again more than eight hundred miles, went out before me.

Preparations for Departure

In the month of May, I began to make all ready to pack up; and as I was doing this, it occurred to me that, seeing all these people were banished by the czar of Muscovy to Siberia and yet, when they came there, were left at liberty to go whither they would, why they did not then go away to any part of the world, wherever they thought fit. I began to examine what should hinder them from making such an attempt. But my wonder was over when I entered upon that subject with the person I have mentioned, who answered me thus:

"Consider, first, sir," said he, "the place where we are; and, secondly, the condition we are in—especially the generality of the people who are banished hither. We are surrounded with stronger things than bars or bolts: on the north side, an unnavigable ocean, where ship never sailed and boat never swam; every other way we have above a thousand miles to pass through the czar's own dominions, and by ways utterly impassable except by the roads made by the government and through the towns garrisoned by his troops; so that we could neither pass undiscovered by the road, nor subsist any other way; so that it is in vain to attempt it."

I was silenced, indeed, at once and found that they were in a prison every jot as secure as if they had been locked up in the castle at Moscow. However, it came into my thoughts that I might certainly be made an instrument to procure the escape of this excellent person and that, whatever hazard I ran, I would certainly try if I could carry him off. Upon this, I took an occasion, one evening, to tell him my thoughts. I represented to him that it was very easy for me to carry him away, there being no guard over him in the country; and as I was not going to Moscow but to Archangel, and that I went in the retinue of a caravan, by which I was not obliged to lie in the stationary towns in the desert, but could encamp every night where I would, we might easily pass uninterrupted to Archangel, where I would immediately secure him on board an English ship and carry him safely along with me. As to his subsistence and other particulars, it should be my care till he could better supply himself.

He heard me very attentively and looked earnestly on me all the while I spoke. Nay, I could see in his very face that what I said put his spirits into an exceeding ferment: His color frequently changed, his eyes looked red, and his heart fluttered, till it might be even perceived in his countenance. Nor could he immediately answer me when I had done and, as it were, hesitated to hear what he would say to it.

But after he had paused a little, he embraced me and said, "How unhappy we are, unguarded creatures as we are, that even our greatest acts of friendship are made snares unto us, and we are made tempters of one another! My dear friend," said he, "your offer is so sincere, has such kindness in it, is so disinterested in itself, and is so calculated for my advantage that I must have very little knowledge of the world if I did not both wonder at it and acknowledge the obligation I have upon me to you for it. But did you believe I was sincere in what I have often said to you of my contempt of the world? Did you believe I spoke my very soul to you, and that I had really obtained that degree of felicity here that had placed me above all that the world could give me? Did you believe I was sincere when I told you I would not go back, if I was recalled even to be all that I once was in the court, with the favor of the czar my master? Did you believe me, my friend, to be an honest man? Or did you believe me to be a boasting hypocrite?"

Here he stopped, as if he would hear what I would say; but, indeed, I soon after perceived that he stopped because his spirits were in motion, his great heart was full of struggles, and he could not go on.

I was, I confess, astonished at the thing as well as at the man, and I used some arguments with him to urge him to set himself free; that he ought to look upon this as a door opened by Heaven for his deliverance and a summons by Providence, who has the care and disposition of all events, to do himself good and to render himself useful in the world.

He had by this time recovered himself. "How do you know, sir," said he warmly, "but that, instead of a summons from Heaven, it may be a feint of another instrument; representing in alluring colors to me the show of felicity as a deliverance, which may in itself be my snare and tend directly to my ruin? Here I am free from the temptation of returning to my former miserable greatness; there I am not sure but that all the seeds of pride, ambition, avarice, and luxury, which I know remain in nature, may revive and take root and, in a word, again overwhelm me; and then the happy prisoner, whom you see now master of his soul's liberty, shall be the miserable slave of his own senses, in the full enjoyment of all personal liberty. Dear sir, let me remain in this blessed confinement, banished from the crimes of life, rather than purchase a show of freedom at the expense of the liberty of my reason, and at the future happiness that I now have in my view but shall then, I fear, quickly lose sight of; for I am but flesh—a man, a mere man. I have passions and affections as likely to possess and overthrow me as any man. Oh, be not my friend and tempter both together!"

If I was surprised before, I was quite dumb now and stood silent, looking at him and, indeed, admiring what I saw. The struggle in his soul was so great that, though the weather was extremely cold, it put him into a most violent sweat, and I found he wanted to give vent to his mind. So I said a word or two that I would leave him to consider of it and wait on him again, and then I withdrew to my own apartment.

About two hours after, I heard somebody at or near the door of my room, and I was going to open the door, but he had opened it and come in.

"My dear friend," said he, "you had almost overset me, but I am recovered. Do not take it ill that I do not accept your offer. I assure you it is not for want of sense of the kindness of it in you. I came to make the most sincere acknowledgment of it to you, but I hope I have got the victory over myself."

"My lord," said I, "I hope you are fully satisfied that you do not resist the call of Heaven."

"Sir," said he, "if it had been from Heaven, the same power would have influenced me to have accepted it. But I hope, and am fully satisfied, that it is from Heaven that I decline it, and I have infinite satisfaction in the parting that you shall leave me an honest man still, though not a free man."

I had nothing to do but to acquiesce and make professions to him of my having no end in it but a sincere desire to serve him. He embraced me with deep feeling and assured me he was sensible of that and should always acknowledge it; and with that he offered me a very fine present of sables—too much, indeed, for me to accept from a man in his circumstances, and I would have avoided them, but he would not be refused.

The next morning I sent my servant to his lordship with a small present of tea, two pieces of Chinese damask, and four little wedges of Japanese gold, which did not all together weigh above six ounces or thereabouts, but were far short of the value of his sables, which, when I came to England, I found worth nearly two hundred pounds. He accepted the tea, one piece of the damask, and one of the pieces of gold, which had a fine stamp upon it, of the Japanese coinage, which I found he took for the rarity of it. But he would not take any more, and he sent word by my servant that he desired to speak with me.

When I came to him, he told me I knew what had passed between us and hoped I would not move him any more in that affair; but since I made such a generous offer to him, he asked me if I had kindness enough to offer the same to another person that he could name to me, in whom he had a great share of concern. I told him that I could not say I was inclined to do so much for any but himself, whom I valued highly and should have been glad to have been the instrument of his deliverance. However, if he would please to name the person to me, I would give him my answer. He told me it was his only son, who, though I had not seen him yet, was in the same condition with himself and more than two hundred miles from him, on the other side of the Oby; but if I consented, he would send for him.

I made no hesitation but told him I would do it. I made some ceremony in letting him understand that it was wholly on his account, and that seeing I could not prevail on him, I would show my respect to him by my concern for his son; but these things are too tedious to repeat here. He sent the next day for his son. In about twenty days he came back with the messenger, bringing six or seven horses loaded with very rich furs that, in the whole, amounted to a very great value. His servants brought the horses into the town, but left the young lord at a distance till night, when he came incognito into our apartment. His father presented him to me, and, in short, we concerted the manner of our traveling and everything proper for the journey.

I had bought a considerable quantity of sables, black fox skins, fine ermines, and such other furs as are very rich in that city, in exchange for some of the goods I had brought from China—in particular, for the cloves and nutmegs, of which I sold the greatest part here and the rest afterward at Archangel, for a much better price than I could have got at London. My partner, who was sensible of the profit, and whose business, more particularly than mine, was merchandise, was mightily pleased with our stay, on account of the transactions we made here.

Departure

It was the beginning of June when I left this remote place—a city, I believe, little heard of in the world. Indeed, it is so far out of the road of commerce that I know not how it should be much talked of. We were now reduced to a very small caravan, having only thirty-two horses and camels in all, and all of them passed for mine, though my new guest was proprietor of eleven of them. It was most natural, also, that I should take more servants with me than I had before; and the young lord passed for my steward. What great man I passed for myself, I know not; neither did it concern me to inquire. We had here the worst and the largest desert to pass over that we met with on our whole journey. I call it the worst because the way was very deep in some places and very uneven in others. The best we had to say for it was that we thought we had no troops of Tartars or robbers to fear and that they never came on this side of the river Oby, or at least very seldom; but we found it otherwise.

My young lord had a faithful Siberian servant who was perfectly acquainted with the country and led us by private roads, so that we avoided coming into the principal towns and cities upon the great road, such as Tumen, Soloy Kamskoi, and several others; because the Muscovite garrisons that are kept there are very curious and strict in their observation upon travelers and searching lest any of the banished persons of note should make their escape that way into Muscovy. But by this means, as we were kept out of the cities, so our whole journey was a desert, and we were obliged to encamp and lie in our tents, when we might have had very good accommodation in the cities on the way. This young lord was so sensible of this that he would not allow us to lie abroad when we came to several cities on the way, but lay abroad himself, with his servant, in the woods and met us always at the appointed places.

We had just entered Europe, having passed the river Kama, which in these parts is the boundary between Europe and Asia. The first city on the European side was called Soloy Kamskoi, which is as much as to say, the great city on the river Kama. Here we thought to see some evident alteration in the people, but we were mistaken, for as we had a vast desert to pass, which was nearly seven hundred miles long in some places, but not above two hundred miles over where we passed it, so till we came past that horrible place, we found very little difference between that country and the Mogul Tartary. The people were mostly pagans and little better than the savages of America. Their houses and towns were full of idols, and their way of living wholly barbarous, except in the cities and the villages near them, where they are Christians, as they call themselves, of the Greek Church, but have their religion mingled with so many relics of superstition that it is scarcely to be known in some places from mere sorcery and witchcraft.

One More Adventure

In passing this forest, I thought, indeed, we must (after all our dangers were, to our imagination, escaped) have been plundered and robbed and perhaps murdered by a troop of thieves. Of what country they were, I am yet at a loss to know; but they were all on horseback, carried bows and arrows, and were at first about forty-five in number. They came so near to us as to be within two musket shots and, asking no questions, surrounded us with their horses and looked very earnestly upon us twice. At length, they placed themselves just in our way; upon which we drew up in a little line before our camels, being not above sixteen men in all. Being drawn up thus, we halted and sent out the Siberian servant, who attended his lord, to see who they were. His master was the more willing to let him go because he was not a little apprehensive that they were a Siberian troop sent out after him. The man came up nearer them with a flag of truce and called to them; but though he spoke several of their languages, or dialects of languages rather, he could not understand a word they said. However, after some signs to him not to come near them at his peril, the fellow came back no wiser than he went; only that by their dress, he said he believed them to be some Tartars of Kalmuck, or of the Circassian hordes, and that there must be more of them upon the great desert, though he never heard that any of them were seen so far north before.

About an hour after, they again made motion to attack us and rode around our little wood to see where they might break in. But finding us always ready to face them, they went off again; and we resolved not to stir for that night.

This was small comfort to us; however, we had no remedy. There was, on our left hand, at about a quarter of a mile distant, a little grove very near the road. I immediately resolved we should advance to those trees and fortify ourselves as well as we could there; for, first I considered that the trees would in a great measure cover us from their arrows, and in the next place, they could not come to charge us in a body. It was, indeed, my old Portuguese pilot who proposed it, and who had this excellency attending him: that he was always readiest and most apt to direct and encourage us in cases of the most danger. We advanced immediately, with what speed we could, and gained that little wood. The Tartars, or thieves, for we knew not what to call them, kept their stand and did not attempt to hinder us. When we came thither, we found, to our great satisfaction, that it was a swampy piece of ground. On the one side was a very great spring of water, which, running out in a little brook, was a little farther joined by another of the like size and was, in short, the source of a considerable river, called afterward the Wirtska. The trees that grew about this spring were not more than two hundred, but they were very large and stood pretty thick, so that as soon as we got in, we saw ourselves perfectly safe from the enemy unless they attacked us on foot.

While we stayed here waiting the motion of the enemy some hours, without perceiving that they made any movement, our Portuguese, with some help, cut several arms of trees half off and laid them hanging across from one tree to another and, in a manner, fenced us in. About two hours before night, they came down directly upon us; and though we had not perceived it, we found they had been joined by some more, so that they were near fourscore horse; whereof, however, we fancied some were women. They came on till they were within half-shot[3] of our little wood, when we fired one musket without ball and called to them in the Russian tongue to know what they wanted and bade them keep off. But they came on with a double fury up to the wood side, not imagining we were so barricaded that they could not easily break in. Our old pilot was our captain, as well as our engineer, and desired us not to fire upon them till they came within pistol shot, that we might be sure to kill and that when we did fire we should be sure to take good aim. We bade him give the word of command, which he delayed so long that they were some of them within two pikes' length of us when we let fly. We aimed so true that we killed fourteen of them and wounded several others, as also several of their horses; for we had all of us loaded our pieces with two or three bullets at least.

They were terribly surprised with our fire and retreated immediately about one hundred rods[4] from us, in which time we loaded our pieces again. Seeing them keep that distance, we sallied out and caught four or five of their horses, whose riders we supposed were killed. Coming up to the dead, we judged they were Tartars, but knew not how they came to make an excursion of such an unusual length.

We slept little, you may be sure, but spent the most part of the night in strengthening our situation, barricading the entrances into the wood, and keeping a strict watch. We waited for daylight, and when it came, it gave us a very unwelcome discovery indeed; for the enemy, who we thought were discouraged with the reception they met with, were now greatly increased and had set up eleven or twelve huts or tents, as if they were resolved to besiege us. This little camp they had pitched upon the open plain, about three-quarters of a mile from us. We were indeed surprised at this discovery; and now, I confess, I gave myself over for lost, and all that I had. The loss of my effects did not lie so near me, though very considerable, as the thoughts of falling into the hands of such barbarians at the latter end of my journey, after so

---

3. Half the distance a gunshot could reach.
4. About 1,650 feet.

many difficulties and hazards as I had gone through, and even in sight of our port, where we expected safety and deliverance. As to my partner, he was raging and declared that to lose his goods would be his ruin and that he would rather die than be starved, and he was fighting to the last drop.

The young lord, a gallant youth, was for fighting to the last also; and my old pilot was of opinion that we were able to resist them all in the situation we were then in. Thus we spent the day in debates of what we should do. Toward the evening we found that the number of our enemies still increased, so I began to inquire of those people we had brought from Tobolski, if there were no private ways by which we might avoid them in the night and perhaps retreat to some town or get help to guard us over the desert. The Siberian who was servant to the young lord told us, if we decided to avoid them and not fight, he would engage to carry us off in the night to a way that went north, toward the river Petrou, by which he made no question but we might get away and the Tartars never discover it. But he said his lord had told him he would not retreat but would rather choose to fight. I told him he mistook his lord; for that he was too wise a man to love fighting for the sake of it; that I knew his lord was brave enough by what he had showed already; but that his lord knew better than to desire seventeen or eighteen men to fight five hundred, unless an unavoidable necessity forced them to do it; and that if he thought it possible for us to escape in the night, we had nothing else to do but to attempt it. He answered that if his lordship gave him such orders, he would lose his life if he did not perform it. We soon brought his lord to give that order, though privately, and we immediately prepared for putting it in practice.

And first, as soon as it began to be dark, we kindled a fire in our little camp, which we kept burning and prepared so as to make it burn all night, that the Tartars might conclude we were still there. But as soon as it was dark, and we could see the stars (for our guide would not stir before), having all our horses and camels ready loaded, we followed our new guide, who I soon found steered himself by the north star.

After we had traveled two hours very hard, it began to be lighter still; not that it was dark all night, but the moon began to rise, so that, in short, it was rather lighter than we wished it to be. But by six o'clock the next morning, we had got above thirty miles, having almost ruined our horses. Here we found a Russian village, named Kermazinskoy, where we rested and heard nothing of the Kalmuck Tartars that day. About two hours before night we set out again and traveled till eight the next morning, though not quite so hard as before. About seven o'clock we passed a little river called Kirtza and came to a good, large town inhabited by Russians, called Ozomoys. There we heard that several troops of Kalmucks had been abroad upon the desert, but that we were now completely out of danger of them, which was to our great satisfaction. Here we were obliged to get some fresh horses, and having need enough of rest, we stayed five days; and my partner and I agreed to give the honest Siberian who brought us thither the value of ten pistoles.

Nearing Home

In five days more, we came to Veuslima upon the river Wirtzogda, and running into the Dwina. We were, very happily, near the end of our travels by land, that river being navigable, in seven days' passage, to Archangel. From hence, we came to Lawrenskoy, the 3rd of July. Providing ourselves with two luggage boats and a barge for our own convenience, we embarked the 7th, and arrived all safe at Archangel the 18th, having been a year, five months, and three days on the journey, including our stay of eight months at Tobolski. We were obliged to stay at this place six weeks for the arrival of the ships and must have tarried longer had not a Hamburger come in about a month sooner than any of the English ships. When, after some consideration that the city of Hamburg might happen to be as good a market for our goods as London, we all took freight with him. Having put our goods on board, it was most natural for me to put my steward on board to take care of them; by which means my young lord had a sufficient opportunity to conceal himself, never coming on shore again all the time we stayed there. This he did that he might not be seen in the city, where some of the Moscow merchants would certainly have seen and discovered him.

We then set sail from Archangel the 20th of August that same year, and after no extraordinarily bad voyage, we arrived safely in the Elbe the 18th of September. Here my partner and I found a very good sale for our goods, as well those of China as the sables, etc., of Siberia; and dividing the produce, my share amounted to £3475 17s. 3d., including about six hundred pounds' worth of diamonds, which I purchased at Bengal.

Here the young lord took his leave of us and went up the Elbe, in order to go to the court of Vienna, where he resolved to seek protection and could correspond with those of his father's friends who were left alive. He did not part without testimonies of gratitude for the service I had done him and for my kindness to the prince, his father.

To conclude: Having stayed nearly four months in Hamburg, I came from thence by land to The Hague, where I embarked in the packet and arrived in London the 10th of January 1705, having been absent from England ten years and nine months. And here I resolved to prepare for a longer journey than all these, having lived a life of infinite variety seventy-two years and learned sufficiently to know the value of retirement and the blessing of ending our days in peace.

THE END

DISCUSSION WITH PROFESSOR WHEELER

(For Formal School, Home School, and Book Club Discussions)

First of all, permit me to define my perception of the role of the teacher. I believe that the ideal teaching relationship involves the teacher and the student, both looking in the same direction, and both having a sense of wonder. A teacher is *not* an important person dishing out rote learning to an unimportant person. I furthermore do not believe that a Ph.D. automatically brings with it omniscience, despite the way some of us act. In discussions, I tell my students beforehand that my opinions and conclusions are no more valid than theirs, for each of us sees reality from a different perspective.

Now that my role is clear, let's continue. The purpose of the discussion sections of the series is to encourage debate, to dig deeper into the books than would be true without these sections, and to spawn other questions that may build on the ones I begin with here. If you take advantage of these sections, you will be gaining just as good an understanding of a book as you would were you actually sitting in one of my classroom circles.

Be sure to keep a journal as you read, because if you don't, most of your insights will be lost forever. Whatever you do, don't merely regurgitate the plot; rather, use each sentence, each paragraph, as a springboard to a fuller understanding of what life is all about. For example, if you are reading about a person, who does that character remind you of in real life? In previous readings? On television or cinema? Why? Draw parallels and spell out differences.

Each of us ought to daily hone our writing skills, our ability to express ourselves with clarity, verve, and power. Here are a number of things you can do to accelerate your progress as a writer:

1. Keep a dictionary at your side at all times; the starting minimum would be a full-sized, hardback collegiate. For those who wish to develop into

wordsmiths, invest in an Oxford Unabridged and use it whenever more limited dictionaries fail to fully explain, or even list, an older word. Make it a practice to keep 3x5 cards at your side at all times. When you come across an unfamiliar word, don't take the easy way out and pass over it, but stop, look it up, copy it down on one side of a card, and on the other side write down the definition(s) and, if possible, use the word in a sentence. Study these cards every day, and only when the definition and sentence use spring immediately to mind should you move the card into your inactive file; periodically refresh your memory by going through that stack as well. As you consistently try to add new words to your vocabulary every day, you will be amazed at how much richer life will become.

2. At the back of your journal, reserve a section for vivid metaphors and similes. Each time you find one that jumps out at you, write it down, along with the source and page. Over time, you will develop an appreciation for fresh imagery and avoid hackneyed, cliché-saturated speech.

3. Also keep a place in the back of the journal for writing down insightful lines that don't incorporate metaphors—lines that are aphoristic, that successfully express great truths, living embodiments of Pope's "What oft was thought / But ne'er so well expressed" (*An Essay in Criticism,* 1711).

4. Make it a habit to write down memorable first and last lines and paragraphs in books, chapters, stories, articles, and essays. Have a "Best List" and a "Worst List." Which beginning lines pull you into a story? How do they do that? Unfortunately, too many would-be writers don't pay enough attention to make-or-break lines, not realizing that if the first line/paragraph fails to hook the browsing reader, that person will never stay around long enough to read the rest of what they have spent so much time writing.

    The concluding line/paragraph is second only in impact to the beginning one, for it represents the adieu, the distillation, the tug-at-the-heart, that builds on all that has gone before. As with the beginning line, finding just the right way of saying it, getting the right ring or the right tone, is likely to take a lot of effort and frequently a lot of time. The definitive starting point for your list ought to be the beginning and ending paragraphs of Dickens's *Tale of Two Cities.*

5. Pay particular attention (in another section of your journal) to character portraits. Why and how are some characters made so real that it seems

you have known them always? Bringing a character to life in print is really the ultimate Pygmalion act. It takes some writers a full book to accomplish it; others can pull it off in mere paragraphs or a page or two.

6. Pay particular attention to dialogue, because when it is done well, it carries the story along. The most effective type of writing—and the most difficult to do—is dialogue that reveals character, thus letting the reader arrive at his or her own conclusions rather than having the writer tell the reader what kind of person the character is.

7. Finally, watch for vivid examples of personification (making inanimate things seem human).

As you do all of these things, and continue to write yourself, your own personal style will deepen, broaden, and become more self-assured and professional.

Don't Begin the Next Section Until the Introduction Has Been Read.

— — —

QUESTIONS TO DEEPEN YOUR UNDERSTANDING

Chapter 1. Wanderlust

1. Evidently, the tribute to Crusoe's wife was almost a tribute to Defoe's: "She was, in a few words, the stay of all my affairs, the center of all my enterprises, the engine that, by her Prudence, reduced me to the happy compass I was in, from the most extravagant and ruinous projects that filled my head; and did more to guide my rambling genius than a mother's tears, a father's instructions, a friend's counsel, or all my reasoning powers could do. I was happy in listening to her and in being moved by her entreaties; and to the last degree desolate and dislocated in the world by the loss of her."

However, note that nothing was said about *her* dreams and *her* goals. This shows graphic evidence of Crusoe's (and Defoe's) priorities. Neither was there much worry about the children he had sired in old age, when the wanderlust swept him back out to sea. But here, too, this was consistent with Defoe's own lifestyle.

Clearly, Crusoe deserted his children after his wife died, leaving them to grow up without a father or mother. Looking at contemporary society, are children still abandoned by parents today in cases of widowhood, divorce, separation? Compare. Is modern absentee parenthood really much different from what Defoe did? Discuss.

2.   Note the items Crusoe takes back home to his island. Imagine yourself in his shoes today. What items would you have placed on board your ship for sustaining settlers on such an island? Compare what you would have chosen with those Crusoe chose. How many of your items are the result of 300 years of technological progress?

3.   There is also much in this book about idleness. Defoe can hardly have been idle a moment of his life and was always restless in any lull. To him, idleness was a gross misuse of God's greatest gift to us: our time.

What do you think Defoe's reactions would be to the 35 to 40 hours a week the average American dedicates to watching television? What counsel do you think he would give us? What would he say about the content of what we watch? About the messages the commercials bring us?

Chapter 2. Disaster at Sea
4.   There are two incredible survival stories in this chapter. We may be confident that they are based on real happenings, and in all probability, on personal interviews of the survivors. Defoe always had to know things firsthand, if at all possible.

Defoe's handling of the woman's account of her survival has much to say about his response to overwhelming disaster. Defoe respects emotion and is willing to let it run its course before he intrudes. This is in sharp contrast to the often abysmally poor taste of modern media interviewers, who show no hesitation in walking up to someone, microphone in hand, who has just lost a child in a car accident, whose husband has been murdered, etc., and asking the most crass and insensitive questions imaginable. How should we differentiate between the public's right to know and the victim's right to privacy and personal space? What can we learn from the fire-at-sea story?

5. In those far-off days, there was no radio, no wireless, no possible source of electronic communication whatsoever; thus when faced with disaster at sea, they had no way of attracting the attention of those who might come to their rescue. They were totally at the mercy of the elements. With such daunting odds, would you have risked your life on the high seas? Why or why not?

6. Defoe drew upon contemporary accounts of rescues at sea for his portrayal of the rescued in these two stories, especially the psychological aspects. Given the fact that both shiploads had given up their lives for lost, with virtually no hope that anyone could possibly rescue them, place yourself vicariously on each of those ships and describe how you might have responded to the miracle of being saved.

Chapter 3. Back Home

7. Thomas Wolfe said in *Look Homeward, Angel* that "you can't go home again." It is never the same. That is true here, too, as Crusoe returns to his island. He has outgrown it and is ready to go on. He is perfectly willing to play St. Nicholas and distribute gifts—in almost a regal manner. In fact, he sees himself as a king and glories in the power this gives him—but not enough, it turns out, to persuade him to stay there!

In our own lives, how does this truth come into play? Is it generally wise to go back to where we have accomplished much and then do it again? What are the dangers? What would it mean in terms of our personal growth, or lack of it?

Chapter 4. Civil War on the Island

8. There are some interesting similarities in this chapter to Nordhoff and Hall's Bounty Trilogy (*Mutiny on the Bounty, Men Against the Sea,* and *Pitcairn's Island*), only, for some unexplainable reason, no two men on Crusoe's island apparently desire the same woman.

There are similarities in terms of excess leisure time as well. Most contemporary writers (including W. Somerset Maugham, Zane Grey, and James Michener) who have roved the South Pacific agree that the idleness inherent in tropical paradises is incredibly destructive and tends to bring out the worst in people.

Is it possible that there is no such thing as a real-life Shangri-la? Is happiness likely in a hothouse environment devoid of stress or trauma? If all this is true, what are the ramifications in terms of our personal priorities in life? What lessons about life can we learn from this chapter?

9. The Spanish governor finds himself unable to sleep: Something—he knows not what—is wrong. Have you ever experienced this mysterious sixth sense that telegraphs a message you have no way of verifying at the time? Discuss this unexplainable phenomenon. Could it be a Higher Power stepping in on our behalf, or is it pure chance? Defoe labels it "Providence." What would you label it?

10. Defoe paints a vivid picture of two distinct camps: one of sloth, and one of industry. Studying these pictures, to what philosophical conclusions do you arrive?

Chapter 5. A Dangerous Expedition

11. Fascinating indeed is Defoe's treatment of the Spanish gentlemen. This was not a time known for tolerance. And there was most certainly no monopoly of kindness or cruelty on either the Catholic or the Protestant side. One of the saddest lessons of history has to do with our inability to learn how to treat others kindly as a result of our own mistreatment. The Inquisition was a terrible thing, and Protestants like Defoe were always throwing it in the faces of Catholics; yet Protestants did little better when the roles were reversed—even John Calvin, in his Geneva city of refuge, burned at the stake those who disagreed with him theologically.

Hence the stunning impact of Defoe—living as he did in a Europe divided between Catholic armies and Protestant armies and responsible for blood beyond belief—when he praised the Spaniards, especially their governor. In fact, the Spanish governor is probably the most idealized person in the entire saga. What can we learn from all this?

Chapter 6. War with the Savages

12. What terrible forces are set in motion when the three English reprobates decide to look for slaves (so they won't have to work)?

13. In an interesting discussion with a certain savage, the subject of grief was

introduced. What is the significance of the resulting proverb?: "In trouble to be troubled, / Is to have your trouble doubled."

14. The governor plays Santa Claus to his islanders. Why is it that giving—giving without getting gifts in return—is one of life's greatest joys? Why shouldn't receiving represent the greater joy? Discuss.

Chapter 7. The Governor Brings Gifts
15. In this chapter, Crusoe brings to the island all the things he longed for when he was stranded there years ago. Interestingly enough, we discover that this bounty failed to ensure "utopia." Again, evidence that mere *things* do not ensure happiness.

Today, in our personal gift-giving, more and more families are returning to simple gifts that are handcrafted, rather than costly store-bought gifts. What can we learn from this chapter in terms of our own giving? Do *things* bring us happiness? Discuss.

Chapter 8. The French Priest
16. Building on Chapter 5, Defoe now takes from France (England's other most hated enemy besides Spain) and from the Catholic clergy (another despised foe) and comes up with an idealized Christian missionary. In this respect, the book was far ahead of its time. Note that the very qualities Defoe admires most in the priest would have almost certainly cost him his life had Inquisition leaders discovered them. What are the qualities Defoe admires most in the priest?

What about the priest's missionary zeal? Do we still have it in this pure sense today? Why, or why not?

17. Note the uncertainties of travel back then—for instance, the French priest failed five times in reaching his planned destinations. If that happened to you in your travels, how would you react or respond?

18. What did the priest mean (both scripturally and in island application) by pointing out the possibility of there being an Achan in the camp? Furthermore, do you agree with the premise that living at variance with divine law results in certain trauma, trouble, and tragedy? Discuss.

19. Do you agree with the priest's contention that a sexual relationship unsanctified by marriage vows cannot be blessed by God or even be successful? Discuss.

Furthermore, do you agree that society and its governing body has the right to expect compliance to the divine law of marriage?

20. The priest declared that a marriage between one who believes in a God and one who does not would be totally unacceptable. This contention remains an issue even in our day. Discuss—especially where the children of such a union would be concerned.

Chapter 9. Will Atkins Finds God

21. This is my favorite chapter in the book. Amazing indeed that Defoe was capable of writing one of the most moving stories of conversion that our literature knows. The ultimate sinner, Will Atkins, finds his Lord. And even more incredible, thanks to the agape love of the French priest, a slave mistress finds self-respect in marriage and her husband's rejected God!

The dialogue between Atkins and his longtime chattel/now partner is very moving. This one chapter is worthy of a great deal of thought and reflection. There are so many aspects of Judeo-Christian life and thought addressed here. See how many you can find—then discuss them.

22. Interesting, Atkins's contention that wounding one's parents has an impact on those who do the wounding with proportionate pain and trauma. Do you agree? Why or why not?

23. Note Atkins's contention that without strong marriage laws, "order and justice could not be maintained, and men would run from their wives and abandon their children, mix confusedly with one another, and neither families be kept entire nor inheritances be settled by legal descent." Today in America, with one out of every two marriages ending in divorce, with one-third of all children born outside of the marriage bond, with the attendant anguish caused by all this, just how prophetic are Atkins's words? Discuss.

24. Defoe (through Crusoe) points out that in this life we must remember that appearances may be misleading. One may be the greatest reprobate

of all time, but all is not lost so long as that person still lives and breathes. What implications are there here, in terms of our daily interactions with people, some of whom are almost impossible to deal with without rage?

25. In Defoe's society, book ownership was rare and readers few. Such Bibles as existed were thus highly valued. Today Bibles are everywhere, hence they are often taken for granted. Is there a relationship between scarcity and perceived value? Discuss.

Chapter 10. The Last of the Island

26. This is the chapter that brings to a close the island saga and completes the starvation story begun in Chapter 2. That story of maternal devotion—in which a mother gives her life for her son and for her maid—is one of the most powerful such stories I have ever heard in my lifetime. What it reveals is that once one reaches the point at which the body is starving to death, only with superhuman will and the enlisting of a Higher Power can one hold off that usurper from within: the body battling for life itself. Only with such reinforcements can one avoid losing all self-control and degenerating into bestiality.

Compare this two-part story with other true stories of disaster and/or survival—such as the story of the Donner party—and study the similarities and differences. Then discuss how you might have reacted in such a situation.

Chapter 11. Massacre

27. A most disturbing chapter! Even more so when one takes into consideration how typical it was of Western treatment of natives in other parts of the world during that part of human history (and reflected by our own treatment of Native Americans and transplanted Africans in American history). The mob frenzy in this chapter is akin to the behavior of lynch mobs in our own heritage. The perception, for centuries, appeared to be this: A culture different from the dominant one is more beast than human; thus its members do not have to be treated as if they were human beings. There is much more discussion potential in this numbing chapter.

28. What have we learned in this respect since the Civil War? What impact do books such as Harriet Beecher Stowe's *Uncle Tom's Cabin* and Harper Lee's *To Kill a Mockingbird* have on our social awareness and treatment of others?

29. As we learned earlier, Defoe presents this lynch scene in the larger context of two true accounts of wanton destruction of human life: one Protestant at Drogheda, Ireland, 70 years before this book was published; and one Catholic, in Magdeburg, Saxony, 88 years before (Defoe played no favorites). What lessons do you think he hoped we would learn from all this? What do we learn about mob psychology? Note, too, that Defoe's fictional crew-turned-mob terribly avenged their comrade's death without considering at all the crime *he* had committed. Are we guilty of similar behavior today? Discuss.

30. A moral force—it is never easy to represent one, and often most unpopular. In fact, it can be life-threatening, as Crusoe discovers after the terrible massacre on Madagascar. Are such spokespersons treated differently today? Discuss.

31. Have you ever, like Crusoe, been accused of something you didn't do? If all the circumstantial evidence is against you, how can you possibly prove your innocence? What alternatives are there in such a case?

Chapter 12. Living in Fear

32. Another powerful chapter! If you ever wanted to find a piece of writing that synthesized raw fear and its effects on the body and thinking processes, this would be it—especially the aspect of irrational fear that is its outgrowth. Discuss such fears in your own experience or in the lives of those you have known.

33. When something (perhaps a price, a deal, etc.) seems too good to be true, ought we to be wary? Ought we to question why, for what reason, this is so?

34. What did you learn in this section about life and trade in a Far East dominated by European powers—powers that were almost continually at war with each other? Compare the qualities, positive as well as

negative, of each colonizing race (as articulated by Crusoe). Do you sense bias? Where? Discuss.

Chapter 13. Pekin

35. To me, this chapter was exciting, for the long trek out of imperial China into the no man's land of the Tartars brought me into a world different from any I had known.

The Portuguese pilot is a marvelous creation. He is a study in selflessness and in faithfulness. What qualities do you feel the pilot brings out? What can we learn from him?

What about the proud country gentleman from near Nanquin (today, Nanking)? What lessons or insights about life do you think Defoe expected us to gain from his brief appearance in the book?

A picaresque novel is one in which the protagonist learns and grows as the result of moving around or travel. In this respect, how does Crusoe grow, and what causes these changes? How about the reader—is there parallel growth there?

Chapter 14. The Great Caravan

36. Such a journey as Crusoe took in this chapter will never be experienced again; neither can the wild nomadic world portrayed here be seen today as it was then (when Western weaponry so totally stacked the odds against more primitive cultures). Though, in principle, the same technological gap between East and West may still exist in some places today, our experiences with Japan, Korea, and Vietnam ought to have taught us a few hard-earned lessons in that respect. Of Vietnam and Laos it was said by war spokespersons that we had to bomb them in order to save them. How can a civilization be saved by having it destroyed? What about life itself—ought we to be able to live more at peace with ourselves if we kill or destroy as a group rather than doing it one on one? In this respect, read the literature written during or after the Civil War, World War I, World War II, the Korean War, and the Vietnam War, and pay particular attention to the returning veterans. How did they deal with this issue? How did they subsequently achieve inner peace? Or did they?

Today, death can be rained down by missiles launched hundreds of miles away—does such distance lessen accountability for the results? Why or why not?

37. Our media is saturated with gratuitous violence and death. Do those who are responsible for such cinematographic maiming and slaughter express remorse for these acts? What are the effects of all these R-rated films on the psyche of those who watch them? Discuss.

38. What is the role of property in our lives? If we all owned property in common, how would society change? Would it be for the better or for the worse? Why?

39. Compare travel then to travel today. What are the most significant differences or changes? What is still the same?

40. Pay particular attention to Defoe's perception of the world's geography. Look for errors—a lot of geographical discoveries have been made since 1719. List them. When were these discoveries made?

Chapter 15. The Idol

41. What I found sadly amusing here was that the same righteous person who roundly condemned the mariners for the massacre in Chapter 11, after they at least had *some* provocation, was willing (even eager) to do the same thing here *without* any provocation. In fact, at no time in the long saga of Crusoe does he appear less admirable than he does in this section—not only by the gratuitous insult to the people and clergy of the area, but also by his subsequent lying and subterfuge, needlessly placing the lives of thousands of people at risk. This chapter does not reveal the same level of tolerance for the beliefs of others we read about earlier. What might Defoe be saying about mankind's consistency (or lack thereof)?

42. Serious students of religion recognize one great reality, which seems to have escaped Defoe: One's religion is often an accident of birth. In other words, were I born in Iran, most likely I'd be a Moslem; were I born in India, most likely I'd be a Hindu; were I born in Tibet, most likely I'd believe in the divinity of the Dalai Lama; were I born in Burma, the odds are I'd believe in Buddhism; were I born in a Brazilian jungle, my religion would most likely be a primitive form of pantheism. Defoe's generation had little respect for non-Christian religions. Today much of that has changed as nationalism has swept the globe and the era of mission-

aries has ebbed. We still have missionaries, but now they tend to have more respect for the cultures of those they seek to convert than was true in centuries past. The same is true with travelers.

Does God have ways of reaching His children wherever they might be and however they might perceive or conceptualize Him? Or do you feel that God arbitrarily speaks only to certain groups, as so many have maintained for so long? Discuss.

43. Crusoe put down the great Chinese civilization in Chapters 13 and 14 simply because it was no match for the more technological West in terms of weaponry. This bias is evident as well in Defoe's cutting the length of the Great Wall of China in half and reminds me of Mark Twain's similar chip-on-the-shoulderish attitude to all things not American in *Innocents Abroad*. Are we still guilty of such putdowns of other cultures today? If so, how should we change that attitude?

Compare everyday life in China with its counterpart in Russia at that time. Similarities? Differences?

44. At the time that Defoe wrote, little of the earth's topography had been accurately mapped; much remained unexplored. Distances in less-civilized areas remained guesstimates. Keep that in mind as Crusoe tosses off geographic commentary. In some cases, he's off by thousands of miles. Might this not be a good incentive for you to do some geographic research of your own so as to arrive at accurate figures?

One of the saddest realities of our times is revealed to us by tests: Most of us major in minors. While most Americans score well on media, pop culture, and sports questions, when it come to questions dealing with such things as history or geography, ignorance rivaling that of Defoe's day is graphically evident. Each of us makes choices as to what to fill our minds with. How clear are your understanding and knowledge of the peoples and places on this incredible planet we live on?

Chapter 16. Nearing Home

45. This chapter contains quite a few insights into the impact of Siberia on the Russian psyche—especially in terms of Crusoe's dialogue with the Russian prince. Siberia has always been the place Russia's rulers have sent those who either disagreed with them or who displeased them. Compare

what is experienced or discussed here regarding Siberia with other reading you may have done (perhaps you have read some of the great novels by Tolstoy, Dostoyevsky, or Solzhenitsyn that explore the impact of Siberia on the Russian people). A key question to ask after such a study is this: Is freedom internal or external? Apply this same question to Crusoe on the island.

46. There is a fascinating statement made in this section to the effect that "the true greatness of life was to be masters of ourselves." Do you agree? Why or why not? What lessons about life and perceived success had the Russian prince learned in Siberia (lessons that would have probably remained unlearned in the palace of the czar)?

47. There is much in this account dealing with vast Russian deserts. Most of us perceive Siberia as being a perpetually frozen wasteland. How do these accounts change your perception of Russia?

48. Compare Crusoe's "going home" (literal, not spiritual) with Defoe's real life "going home." What does "home" mean to you?

CODA

Reactions, responses, and suggestions are very important to us. Also, if a particular book—especially an older one—has been loved by you or your family, and you would like to see us incorporate it into this series, drop us a line, with any details about its earliest publisher, printing date, and so on, and send it to

Joe Wheeler, Ph.D.
c/o Focus on the Family
Colorado Springs, CO 80920

ABOUT THE EDITOR

Joseph Leininger Wheeler's earliest memories have to do with books and stories—more specifically, of listening to his mother read aloud both in public and to him at home. Wheeler recalls that, as soon as he was able to read, he followed his mother around the house, relentlessly reading his storybooks to her.

Shortly after Wheeler turned eight, his parents moved from California to Latin America as missionaries. From the third through the tenth grade, he was home-schooled by his mother. Of those years, he says today, "I was incredibly lucky and blessed. My mother, a trained teacher and elocutionist, was a voracious reader of books worth reading and had memorized thousands of pages of readings, poetry, and stories. All of that she poured into me. Wherever we went, she encouraged me to devour entire libraries."

At 16, Wheeler returned to California to complete his high school years at Monterey Bay Academy near Santa Cruz. Because of his inherited love of the printed word, Wheeler majored in history at Pacific Union College in the Napa Valley, completing both bachelor's and master's degrees there. After completing a master's in English at California State University in Sacramento, Wheeler attended Vanderbilt University, where he obtained a Ph.D. in English.

Today, after 34 years of teaching at the adult education, college, high school, and junior high levels, Wheeler is Professor Emeritus at Columbia Union College in Takoma Park, Maryland. The world's foremost authority on frontier writer Zane Grey, Wheeler is also the founder and executive director of Zane Grey's West Society and Senior Fellow for Cultural Studies at the Center for the New West in Denver, Colorado. He is editor/compiler of the popular *Christmas in My Heart* series (Review & Herald; Doubleday, Dell, Bantam); editor/compiler of the story anthologies *Dad in My Heart* and *Mom in My Heart* (Tyndale House); and editor/compiler of Focus on the Family's *Great Stories Remembered* and *Great Stories* series (Tyndale House). Along the way, Wheeler has established nine libraries in schools and colleges, as well as building up his own collection (as large as some college libraries).

Joe Wheeler and his wife, Connie, are the parents of two grown children, Greg and Michelle, and now make their home in Conifer, Colorado.

Focus on the Family®

Welcome to the Family!

Whether you received this book as a gift, borrowed it from
a friend, or purchased it yourself, we're glad you read it! It's just
one of the many helpful, insightful, and encouraging
resources produced by Focus on the Family.

In fact, that's what Focus on the Family is all about—providing inspiration, information, and biblically based advice to people in all stages of life.

It began in 1977 with the vision of one man, Dr. James Dobson, a licensed
psychologist and author of 16 best-selling books on marriage, parenting,
and family. Alarmed by the societal, political, and economic pressures
that were threatening the existence of the American family, Dr. Dobson
founded Focus on the Family with one employee—an assistant—
and a once-a-week radio broadcast, aired on only 36 stations.

Now an international organization, Focus on the Family is dedicated
to preserving Judeo-Christian values and strengthening the family
through more than 70 different ministries, including eight separate
daily radio broadcasts; television public service announcements;
11 publications; and a steady series of award-winning books and
films and videos for people of all ages and interests.

Recognizing the needs of, as well as the sacrifices and important
contribution made by, such diverse groups as educators, physicians,
attorneys, crisis pregnancy center staff, and single parents,
Focus on the Family offers specific outreaches to uphold and
minister to these individuals, too. And it's all done for one purpose,
and one purpose only: to encourage and strengthen individuals
and families through the life-changing message of Jesus Christ.

• • •

For more information about the ministry, or if we can be of help to your
family, simply write to Focus on the Family, Colorado Springs, CO 80995
or call 1-800-A-FAMILY (1-800-232-6459). Friends in Canada may write
Focus on the Family, P.O. Box 9800, Stn. Terminal, Vancouver, B.C. V6B 4G3
or call 1-800-661-9800. Visit our Web site—www.family.org—
to learn more about the ministry or to find out if there is a
Focus on the Family office in your country.

We'd love to hear from you!